T0304505

NIGHT OWLS

NIGHT OWLS

A. R. VISHNY

HARPER
An Imprint of HarperCollinsPublishers

To Savta Edith, the Reader, and Saba Meir, the Writer

In the village there lived a great woman.

Not like the brazen giants of Greek fame, nor that mighty woman and her torch of copper. This Daughter of Exiles was fashioned with clay, sacred words, a breath of life, and a promise of truth. She was a magnificent theater, an imposing creation, a muse and protector both, a home for the stories of her makers.

This Grand Dame was a stage fashioned in the style of her people. And in her embrace, the tempest-tost lived and died to the mighty roar of applause. When they told a story in their familiar tongue, they would be heard.

And when her audience dwindled and died, her wallpaper peeled and her bricks crumbled, many believed she, too, had perished. Who, they wondered, would fill the theater? Who would care to hear an old story in a language they could not speak? Surely, the Grand Dame had spent her last breath and had nothing more to say.

But she had not. For she still stood on the avenue, unwilling to fade into memory. For she was more than a building, more than a vessel for someone else's dreams. She *was* the dream, born out of such longing and stubborn desire to live and breathe free that she could not die.

It was then that her sisters found her, Daughters of Exiles themselves, who could still hear her heartbeat in the walls and knew she had not yet told her final tale. When they breathed life back into her, she glowed again, a place for memories to be cast in silver, for breathless whispers and longing gazes, for stories to come alive and live endlessly.

And so this Grand Dame lived and lived well, bright and hungry and never more alive.

1

CLARA

It was seven in the evening, and Clara Sender was already considering murder.

On the one hand, murder was . . . less than ideal. Perhaps a bit extreme. It had been a long time since Clara murdered anyone. She didn't like to do it. Even though it came easily to her, naturally, she was not an animal, whatever the Sages had to say about it. She had a gift, a purpose, and *a calling*. The point of her gift was not to chase her cravings; it was to finish the work that she had started, to build a great and resilient theater on the avenue where she had made her home against all odds.

Which was precisely the problem, and exactly why Clara probably needed to murder Boaz Harari. Clara loved her life and her work, and she was not about to let him destroy everything she had built with his apologies and excuses and his sweatiness and that look he'd get on his face, no matter how angry she was with him. Like he was enjoying himself. Like he found her amusing.

She'd show him *amusing*.

Standing in the doorway of her office, Boaz appeared to have taken a brief detour to hell on the way to the theater. His dark brown curls sat messy, sweat shone on his forehead, and he'd clearly run the entire way to the Grand Dame Cinema, because he was still breathing heavily, and she could see his pulse in his neck.

"Look, I *know* I'm late," he said quickly at her appraisal, needlessly adjusting the collar of his shirt and making a futile attempt at raking his hair back into place. "But there was a track fire, and the N was jammed up for ages. Look, it's on the MTA website and everything."

He thrust out his phone toward Clara. She was unmoved.

"An hour late," she said. "An *hour*." After the little episode last week, Clara swore she would fire Boaz if he showed up five minutes late. He'd missed his shift entirely, and her sister, Molly, had to cover for him in the box office. It had been nothing short of a disaster. Molly had many virtues, and none of them involved giving out the proper change, or unjamming the paper in the ticket machine, or ensuring that parents with small children didn't confuse the latest animated feature with the slasher film banned in several countries.

"The N wasn't running!" repeated Boaz, as if she hadn't heard him the first time. "Please? I tried—it's not my fault the subway sucks."

As comanager of the Grand Dame Cinema, Clara did not abide lateness. In this life and her first, she despised it and frankly didn't think she was asking for all that much. But showing up reliably on time was clearly too much for Boaz, who had worn her patience down to the bone since the day he started six months ago, with his perpetual tardiness and parade of excuses. There was the cat. Then the old lady. Then the funeral. And another funeral. And another.

One or two incidents of lateness she could excuse. But how many funerals could possibly be in that boy's calendar? He was eighteen, *actually* eighteen. She only looked the part of an eighteen-year-old. Yet somehow, he managed to have more old ladies in his life than Clara ever had.

"Then you should have left earlier."

"I could have left at dawn and been late," he practically shouted. "The track was *literally on fire*, I swear."

"I told you after the last time," she said. "If you are going to be late, don't bother coming back."

"And yet here I am," he said.

"Because you cannot follow basic instructions," she said, her voice icy. He probably thought he could charm and lie his way into a reprieve, the way he had done a dozen other times. She could see all the tells as clear as day. She would have been able to see them even without her powers: his quickening pulse, the way he avoided her gaze, the way he was rubbing the back of his neck in a reflex that seemed specifically designed to remind her how satisfying it would be to sink her teeth into him. "I have had enough of your excuses, and I *know* you're lying to me."

"How?" he blurted. His eyes widened a moment later, realizing too late his mistake.

She had caught him.

Clara pressed the tips of her fingers together. "I. Always. Know."

"Oh, really?" he said, at last meeting her eyes with his warm brown ones. And there was that infuriating glint. "Always?"

Boaz had been a mistake, the worst idea she'd had since she and Molly took over the theater in 1952. Clara ordinarily had a rule when it came to hiring: bubbes, sweet little grandmothers who thought everything she and her sister did was simply wonderful. She loved the local East Village bubbes best of all, with their lavender-dyed hair and heavy-rimmed glasses and their stories about how the Village had been so much better when there was a chance of running into Lou Reed or David Bowie on a morning bagel run. And East Village bubbes loved her. They loved her Yiddish and her sensible clothes, and they faithfully bought passes to her film festivals season after season.

Best of all, they loved sending her Nice Jewish Boys. After all, to the ordinary eye, Clara and Molly were the young and talented stewards of one of the great landmarks of the neighborhood, an independent cinema that honored its roots as a Yiddish stage. Who wouldn't want them for granddaughters? Those East Village bubbes were single-mindedly determined to see to it that she and Molly would at last find their basherts, their soulmates, and be happily wed. The patronage of East Village bubbes kept the theater lights on.

Even better, their well-meaning attempts at matchmaking kept the Sender sisters very well fed.

Their last box office attendant, a long-time bubbe, had retired to Boca Raton, and the Senders had a problem. The local print newspapers where they used to run their ads were online-only if they still existed at all, and while Clara was content to simply source the community centers, Molly insisted they ought to try posting online. *Even the bubbes have computers these days*, she said. And when they were flooded with responses from people who were most definitely not bubbes: *Maybe we should try talking to some of them. Maybe some fresh blood would be a good thing. What's the harm?*

Which was how Clara made the mistake of giving Boaz a call.

On paper, he had credentials: an acceptable GPA from a fancy prep school, some brief customer service experience working at a wedding catering company, and a passion for film and independent cinemas demonstrated by a very extended and slightly desperate cover letter. He had shown up to his interview with his encyclopedic knowledge of film history and his easy Hebrew. He told her all about the big project he'd done for a media studies class he'd just finished, where he'd seen every single mummy movie he could get his hands on to make some conclusion about colonialism and monster films. He told her about his obsession with that ridiculous one with Brendan Fraser, about how he had dressed as a different character from the movie for every Purim since eighth grade.

The interview had gone on for well over an hour. The time flew when they spoke, and at one point, he made her laugh so hard she had forgotten to pretend to breathe. And for a brief, foolish moment, Clara forgot her rules. She thought maybe Molly had a point. Maybe change was good for their business.

So Clara made him the job offer, a choice she had regretted every day since.

Her sister always said that he was Clara's type. That Clara could die a thousand times and would still keep dreaming of a handsome nerd who could make Shabbos all kinds of holy. *You can take the girl out of the shtetl, but not the shtetl out of the girl.* It was Molly's favorite refrain, not least because the only village *she'd* ever called home was below Fourteenth Street. Molly was wrong, of course. Clara did not want her handsome nerd. She didn't want anyone at all. That would be a violation of her first rule, the most important, the one that kept them alive: *No romance.*

And even if Clara did want a handsome nerd—which she

didn't—it wouldn't be Boaz. Nope. Boaz was about the last person she could ever possibly want in a romantic way. For starters, she could not fall in love with someone who always showed up late. And secondly . . .

She'd come up with a secondly later.

Clara sighed, putting her head in her hands. She'd done her hair too tight today, two French braids that joined in a carefully pinned knot at the base of her neck. They were making her head throb. Or maybe it was Boaz giving her the headache.

She glanced at him, his stubbornly messy hair, that pleading expression on his face. There was a small scar below his lip she'd never noticed before. He probably had run into a wall once. *That* was the type of person he was, the type to be so incredibly careless that he couldn't be bothered to look properly at the things right in front of him.

The headache was definitely Boaz.

"If you're late again," she said at last, "you'll wish I'd fired you today."

It clearly took Boaz a moment to realize that she *wasn't* firing him. There was a long pause. "What is that supposed to mean?" he said, laughing uneasily.

"Do you really want to know?" said Clara, keeping her voice light. Her eyes darted down his face, his lips, his *neck*. She could hardly let him know what she could potentially do to him, but it would be just too fun. Boaz was the type to blush. She wanted to make him blush.

But she couldn't. If she didn't follow her own rules, then where would they be?

"Right, yeah," said Boaz. "Well, should I take a fresh cash

box? Or do you want me to take it over from Molly and Anat . . . Actually, now that I think about it, could I start with a fresh one? I want my count to be accurate."

"Who is Anat?"

Boaz furrowed his brow, as if she, Clara, was the one who was talking nonsense. "What do you mean, 'Who is Anat?'"

"I mean, there is no one working at this cinema named Anat."

"Well, I figured she wasn't working here," said Boaz. "Just . . . you know . . . Anat? Molly's girlfriend?"

Now it was Clara's turn to laugh uneasily. "Molly doesn't have a girlfriend."

"Really?"

"I think I would know if my own sister was dating someone," said Clara.

Boaz bit his lip. "Well . . . okay, then," he said at last. "I'll just . . . um . . . go downstairs to the box office. You know where to find me." He backed out of the doorway before darting down the hall.

The moment he disappeared, Clara wondered if she ought to have followed him. What did he mean? He didn't seriously think . . . He couldn't possibly . . . Molly wasn't dating anyone. That was the first rule. *The* rule. The one that mattered, frankly, more than any other. There were only two rules. *No romance. Only feed on Jews.* The second rule wasn't even to protect them so much as it was to protect the Jews they lived among. False accusations that Jews drained young Christians of their blood for wine or matzahs or whatever else had haunted Jewish communities for hundreds of years. A single blood libel could turn a disappearance or unsolved murder into a catastrophe for the community, leaving trails of torture and the execution of innocents in their wake. And while they could not stop a conspiracy theory, they would not enable one.

Clara looked down at her accounting books, but she suddenly couldn't make sense of the numbers. Her brain was filled with Boaz, his voice ringing in her ears, his smell—coffee and something sweet—still lingering. The walls of her office, a deep shade of burgundy and filled with old cast pictures from the theater's glory days, felt like they were closing in around her.

It wasn't just the question. *Boaz*, the handsome nerd who could not show up on time if his life depended on it, knew something she did not, in *her* cinema.

The third time she lost track of a row in the grid, Clara huffed and stormed out of her office and down the narrow corridor toward the stairs. She strode past the old framed posters for her favorite plays, *Mirele Efros: The Jewish Queen Lear* and *Shulamis*, and Molly's beloved *Got Fun Nekome (God of Vengeance)*. In another age, this hall had been dressing rooms and rehearsal spaces for the Yiddish theater troupes who made their home on Second Avenue. Her footsteps were swallowed up by the thick carpet as she emerged into the dim lobby, where fake gas lamps flickered in sconces against the wall.

In its original life, the Grand Dame had been built to resemble a palace straight from Andalusian Spain, a temple to theater. She had been among the finest on the Yiddish Rialto, a stretch of playhouses along Second Avenue in downtown Manhattan that had been the center of American Yiddish theater in the first decades of the twentieth century. Clara and her sister had saved the theater from an ignoble death at the hands of time and developers . . . with a bit of help. They had restored the great chandelier, the gilt columns, the finely patterned wallpapers, installing screens where there had been stages. And in that they had given the Grand Dame a second life, just as surely as they had been given theirs.

As Clara strode down the revitalized halls, the doors of auditorium one opened, and people poured out in a steady stream, seeking the bathrooms and a trash bin for their empty bags of popcorn. Clara easily wove between them as she made her way to the box office at the front, reminding herself to walk at a mortal human pace lest any of the bleary-eyed moviegoers notice, to where Boaz had already settled onto the teetering stool in front of the register, squeezed between filing cabinets and boxes with the remains of promotional flyers for events long past.

"What was that supposed to mean?" she asked irritably. He turned to look at her, unbothered, completely unsurprised by the fact that she had followed him down there. Had she been that obvious? "Where's Molly?"

Boaz shrugged. "They wandered off; I don't know."

"They *left*?" Clara didn't know a thing about this girl Anat, but Molly knew very well she wasn't supposed to leave the theater on a Thursday night. They were busy. There was work to be done. Clara needed her to help with the concessions or else to mind the projection rooms. She *did not* have permission to just run off. With a girl. That she was dating.

"You know, there's no need to be so weird about Molly seeing a girl," said Boaz. "It's hardly surprising. Honestly, I think it'd be more surprising if she were with a guy. Have you met your sister?"

"I don't care what gender Molly prefers; it's all the same to me." More specifically, Clara had known for a hundred years that Molly preferred women. She'd long, *long* ago gotten over her surprise. And Molly was welcome to entertain as many women as she wanted. She could have a whole theater full of them, if that was her desire.

She just wasn't allowed to *date*. Flirtations were how they fed, how they survived. But dating? Dating left a trail, secrets and whispers and grudges. Dating meant broken hearts and bad tempers and vengeful dreams. Dating meant desire. And there was nothing more dangerous than desire. Desire had caused both of their first deaths.

And so help her, Clara would not let it kill them again.

2

MOLLY

Molly and Anat crept into auditorium one after the credits finished and the last stragglers finally rose from their red-cushioned seats. After a slight disaster last week with an industrial-size bag of coffee beans, Molly had suggested they instead make out in the storage closet where they kept posters and décor for their events and festivals, which had been mostly a success, though it meant quite a great deal of direct eye contact with multiple life-size cutouts of Winona Ryder.

"Did they really need to stay and read every. Single. Credit?" groaned Anat, racing down the aisle toward the screen and narrow remainder of the old stage, trying to keep her dry-cleaning bag from dragging along the floor, her Doc Martens clomping and squeaking as she went. She took one look at the time on her phone and grimaced. "Can we make this quick? I have work I need to finish for my immersive theater project."

"This is immersive theater," said Molly, lingering behind a moment to turn off the projector and adjust the auditorium lights.

"Well, I'm waiting for you to convince my professor. Otherwise, I've still got to work on our original adaptation of Ginsberg's 'Kaddish,'" said Anat. "You're going to come, though, right? We're running a few performances at the end of the month."

"Yes, of course, and keep your voice down!" said Molly, glancing back at the door of the projection room, half expecting her sister to burst through. She was certain that Clara didn't know *yet*—she was far too absorbed in trying to pretend she was above human crushes to care—but it was only a matter of time, and she'd rather Anat not be here when it happened. The whole point of having a living girlfriend was that she stay that way.

Auditorium one remained the clearest evidence that the Grand Dame had once been a Yiddish theater, one of the largest along Second Avenue. The details in the lobby—the old posters and preserved light fixtures that had been the fruits of countless salvage trips and digging through neighboring theater basements—were one thing. But this, the original stage, the dress circle, the giant chandelier set with a Star of David and made to resemble the sky at twilight . . . there was nothing like it.

"When are you going to tell your sister?" said Anat, laying the bag across the seats in the front row. "Like, she has to suspect something by now?"

"On a day when I feel like losing a limb," Molly muttered. She pulled out her phone, checking to see if the light would be okay for the shot. "Could you stand up there? We can do it like we did last time, get a shot of you like this and one in the costume."

"Before that . . ." Anat rummaged through the giant shopping bag she had with her until at last she pulled out a small paper bag and handed it to Molly. "I hope you like egg bagels. It was either that or some majorly suspect rainbow ones."

"You buy me rainbow bagels, and it's over for us. . . . Oh, you even got a salt packet!" said Molly gratefully. She *was* a little hungry, and bread with salt, while far less satisfying, was the only thing that Clara and she could eat that didn't turn to ash in their mouths.

Well, the only *food* thing. But she was not going to accept the alternative from Anat. She had considered going after one of the stragglers, except that would have been against Clara's rules. *No romance. Only feed on Jews.* As if a single bite out of an unsuspecting non-Jew would be enough to get the Cossacks to descend with the pitchforks. But America, for all its many faults, was still America, and Molly had long been firmly of the opinion that in di goldene medine she should be free to bite whoever she wanted, whenever she wanted. Molly spilled the salt packet into the bottom of the bag and dipped a hunk of bagel into it before popping it into her mouth. When she pulled out her phone again, she saw a new set of notifications. "Oh, it looks like the Museum at Eldridge Street, Hey Alma, and *Forverts* shared your last video."

"Great! I'm famous exclusively to the Jewish press, just like my savta always wanted," said Anat, rolling her eyes. "You know that stopped being exciting after the tenth time they did that?"

"Oh, I love Hey Alma, and I would have *killed* to be this regularly covered by *Forverts*," said Molly defensively. She would never forget the first time she saw her name in print. She'd been sixteen and convinced she had more or less achieved true stardom, despite her name being last in a long list of cast members.

"But even then, you would have been more excited by coverage in an English newspaper."

"*Forverts* is in English now."

"Not the point!" Anat sighed. "Come on, get the shots so that I can change. Before your sister murders us both."

Molly set aside her bagel and—trying to ignore the creeping hunger that no bagel could ever satisfy—began to record on her phone. Anat was a natural, grinning and laughing and tucking her short, wavy dark hair behind her ears as she tried some of the poses and expressions they'd practiced the previous week, from an old acting guide that broke down a list of the thirty-six essential expressions a truly talented actor should be able to make. Watching her, Molly felt something squeeze in her chest and refuse to let go.

After a bunch of different poses, Molly let her descend from the stage and grab the dry-cleaning bag. Anat shouted at her to watch the door.

"No one's going to come in," said Molly, dutifully pretending to watch the door and not Anat.

"Except for your sister," she said. "Though if we're getting murdered tonight, I suppose there are worse things to be wearing."

At last, Anat announced she had finished, and Molly gasped.

She'd known what costume she was planning on wearing. They'd agreed on it. Molly was the one who had gone through all the trouble of digging it out from one of the storage rooms and mending the moth holes. She had spent weeks preparing herself to do this with Anat, to film *this* specific costume, the last one Molly ever wore onstage.

And still her first impulse was to tell Anat to take it off, to put it away, to film another costume another night. Molly swallowed hard as she tried to come up with a way to say she had changed her mind, that some things were best left forgotten.

But Anat seemed so pleased and utterly oblivious to Molly's

hesitation. "Isn't it great?" said Anat, twirling. The costume had been for *Di Shturem: The Yiddish Tempest*, when Molly had played the villain, the vengeful sheyd, Chenya, her frankly inspired take on Shakespeare's Caliban. It was a long green silk dress, with a purposely uneven hem and a rather daring neckline for the age, and a deeper emerald coat that moved across the floor like water, with tattered lace along the hem, the perfect outfit for a demon forever trying to seduce the rebbe's daughter. It had been her favorite costume, the best she'd ever worn, and Anat was objectively beautiful in it, the kind of beautiful that made Molly want to rip the dress off her for reasons that had nothing to do with its past and everything to do with *now*. Molly didn't think she could ever bring herself to put it on again, but things could be different. No, things *were* different. It was a different century, and Molly was still here, and if she had been rescued from the dustbin of history, then why not that dress?

"You look . . ." Molly searched for the word, but was suddenly struggling to grasp it, even though she expected—

"Like a bagel?"

Molly startled. "*A bagel?*"

"Well, you're looking at me the way you looked at those salt bagels I got you last week from Kossar's," said Anat, laughing. If Molly could, she would have blushed. That wasn't what she thought, exactly.

She'd never bitten Anat, and she wasn't going to, if she could help it. Instead, she took another bite of salted bagel to dull the hunger. She could help it. She wouldn't.

"Could you do the makeup? I forgot to bring a mirror, and I'm not risking a run to the bathroom."

Molly waved her over, taking the palette of face paint from her.

Anat sat in one of the seats in the first row, and Molly crouched in front of her, hesitating for just a second. Standing close to her was like stepping up to a radiator after coming in from the cold. Just being near her made Molly warm. "I was going to say that you look the part."

"Yeah, eh . . . about that?" said Anat. "I was looking over the script, and I'm not sure I . . . get the part, exactly?"

"What's there not to get?" said Molly. She used water from Anat's bottle to wet the blending sponge and began to attempt re-creating the green-gray she'd once worn onstage. "You're a sheyd, a demon, who has lived forever in this village that is between worlds, neither living nor dead, where an esteemed rebbe has been trapped for over ten years. To get out, the rebbe must make sure his daughter marries the handsome student that has lost himself here in the midst of a great blizzard, but you, Chenya, have other plans."

"Yes, yes, I get that," said Anat. "I just . . . thought you said this was *The Tempest*."

"It is!" Molly blended the paint into the hollows of Anat's cheeks, one hand holding back her hair. Molly smiled as she let herself take her time.

"Shakespeare's *The Tempest*."

"Shakespeare's *The Tempest* in Yiddish," said Molly. "I thought you figured it out after the *Mirele Efros* episode we did—that the best Yiddish plays did not simply translate dialogue. They translated the whole show," said Molly. "Speaking of the script, would you hate me if I asked you to rerecord? You were pronouncing your Yiddish like Hebrew again. It's supposed to be KHA-vertes; front-load the emphasis . . ."

"I already did that one, like, ten times!" She sighed. "And I thought that was just 'inspired by' *King Lear*," said Anat. "But this is . . . not *The Tempest*."

"Hold still!" said Molly. Anat had shifted closer to Molly, so close they might as well have just started making out again. "It's Yiddish theater. Yiddish theater was about being relevant to its audience." She took a black crayon and set to work lining Anat's eyes. Her hazel eyes looked green in that dress.

"So *are* all the shows set in a shtetl?" Anat closed her eyes, and Molly was close enough to her girlfriend's face to hear her pulse, to smell her tea tree shampoo and something else that Molly could never quite pinpoint, even though they had been dating for months. "Is the Yiddish Hamlet some yeshiva student?"

"Not all of them. Sometimes the shows are set on the Lower East Side?" she said. "Or Vilna or Warsaw . . ." Anat snorted, almost smudging the makeup as Molly worked. "What, and next are you going to complain that *Rent* was set in the Village when it should have been set in nineteenth-century Paris to be a proper adaptation of *La Bohème*? Or that *West Side Story* doesn't have anything to do with Shakespeare because it's not in Verona? We are the reason that Broadway cares about speaking directly to its audience while the West End is all about glam-rock megamusicals and dancing cats."

Anat laughed. "Eh, I think there is a *little* more to modern British theater than *Cats*?"

"No, it is *all* dancing cats."

"That came out in the eighties! They do other things now!"

Molly snapped shut the face paint palette. "British theater has given us nothing of value since Shakespeare, which I think we can all agree is far improved in the Yiddish."

Anat opened her eyes, and despite Molly's best attempts at

keeping her face unreadable, she knew from her girlfriend's smile that she had failed. "I really should have bought you that second bagel."

Molly's mouth had gone dry, her words abandoning her.

"Though I suppose if you want to change me, that would be totally fine. I mean, the whole immortal monster in the shape of an incredibly hot woman who can shift into an owl would be an adjustment for sure, but I think I'd be able to cope—"

"I am not going to bite you!" said Molly. "And I'm not turning you. That's not how being an Estrie works."

"I *know*, you've told me a hundred times, I need to be dying first. . . ."

But clearly Anat didn't get it or she would stop asking. Molly *had* told her a hundred times, and she still fielded the questions on a biweekly basis. Being an Estrie wasn't the sort of thing a girl wanted to be or chose to be when there was another way. It was the very last resort. They were not willing monsters. "You are not a bagel."

"Of course, you would rather bite some random dude you find off the street? Which, for the record, is unsanitary. Like if I picked up a random bottle of Coke I saw lying out on the sidewalk and took a sip, you'd be, like, *Ew, Anat, that's gross*, and then probably dump me."

"I would not dump you; I would take you to the hospital to get your stomach pumped. Now get up onstage and give me your best 'seducing the rebbe's daughter' face so you can go work on your project."

"Which one of the thirty-six expressions is that?" Anat giggled. "For the life of me, I don't know how anyone thought you were straight," she added, doing what was a *very* compelling "seducing the rebbe's daughter" face, in Molly's expert opinion. They took short clips doing her best attempt at Chenya's lines, trying to keep the accent straight, until Molly was satisfied that she'd gotten a shot she could use. Later, she could stitch it all together and post it online. Together they had done over a dozen so far with the costumes, along with others where they just used Anat's voice over photos and pictures Molly had found in their basement. Molly had even expressed interest in finally getting around to digitizing their film collection as a pretext to learning how to edit video content for the internet, an interest that Clara had thankfully not questioned.

The videos had been Molly's idea. Clara had finally relented and let Molly get social media a couple of years ago, with the caveat that it was *exclusively* professional accounts for the theater. Updates, photos of the theater, promotional material only. Nothing with their faces, of course. Otherwise, any ordinary patron could find them out, could see easily with a quick scroll that they had been eighteen for far too long.

At first, that had been enough. She liked taking glamor shots of the latte art she managed at the concession stand, and posting film trivia had been fun, and she'd gotten a bit of engagement.

But then she decided that lattes weren't the most interesting thing she could do. She was an actress. Molly Sender lived on the Yiddish stage, and basically died on it, too.

Clara knew how to run a theater, but she could be such a bubbe when it came to the internet. No matter how many times Molly tried to convince Clara that it was possible to create content without exposing all their secrets, she couldn't get her sister to budge. So she decided she would do it without her sister's help.

Molly had been brainstorming potential content on an off day at the concession stand. She had all the pieces together, scripts, a title, a mission statement, to bring Second Avenue's Yiddish theater history back to life. All she needed was someone who wasn't her to appear on camera.

And then Anat had stepped into the theater and bought a cappuccino, and when she pulled her wallet out of her canvas bag, Molly noticed the quote on the front. *We are such stuff as dreams are made on.*

"You like *The Tempest*?" Molly had asked.

"I love it," she said, her accent curling around the words. When they locked eyes, Molly felt as though she were being seen, *properly* seen. It caught her off guard. In her first life and second, she had become so accustomed to people looking at her without really seeing her, their gaze never cutting through all her smoke and mirrors, the protections that being an actress, and then an Estrie, provided. That look from Anat made her knees weak. "It's my favorite. My school took a field trip to see it done in Hebrew at Habima, and it made me want to be an actress. My first week in the city I got this quote as a tattoo. My parents can never find out—they'd be furious—but they won't. They're back in Ra'anana."

"Where's the tattoo?" Because there suddenly was nothing more important than knowing who this girl was, who was quite literally *such stuff as dreams are made on* . . .

Anat smirked and said, without missing a beat, "Wouldn't you like to know."

And that was that.

Molly turned at the sound of the garment bag being zipped. Anat was back in the jeans and chunky sweater she'd been wearing, but she still had on the face paint, slightly smudged along the collar of her sweater. Only then Molly realized the face that she'd given

22

Anat. It wasn't unlike what she'd worn onstage, the mottled gray complexion, the veins of green, the deep set of her eyes, but what it *really* looked like was Molly. Her real face—what looked back at her from the mirror when she let her hair down.

She hadn't meant to do it, and there was no way Anat could know. Anat knew plenty: they'd been dating since August, and once Molly decided to tell her what she was, there were few secrets left between them. Anat knew Molly's real age, her diet, even how she died.

But Anat had not seen Molly's real face, the monster that emerged from her features the moment she let her hair loose, the face she wore to feed or to fly. And she never would. Anat might believe them to be such stuff as dreams were made on but that face was the stuff of nightmares.

3

BOAZ

The moment Boaz Harari stepped out of the Grand Dame, his shoulders eased.

It was only by sheer luck that he had not been burned worse than the tracks of the N train, which, for the record, had really been on fire. He had not lied about that. The fire just wasn't the main reason for his late arrival. He wasn't about to tell Clara the real reason. She already thought he was a hot mess. She didn't need to know just how hot the mess was.

Boaz kept the hood of his deep green sweatshirt up, even as he stood on the NQR platform. A group of guys about his age were shouting on one end, passing a brown-bag-wrapped bottle between them.

On the other side of the platform, he saw her.

She had always been there, for as long as he'd been taking the N between Union Square and his home in Gravesend, Brooklyn. The first time he saw her, he hadn't realized what he was looking at. That was always the problem. If he wasn't paying close enough attention, he couldn't quite tell the difference between the living and the dead.

Boaz had missed the signs and thought he could help. He had tried pulling her back from the yellow line, just as the train began rumbling down the tunnel, when he had realized what exactly she was planning to do. But when he reached and grasped for her, his hand passed straight through her chest. There was no grabbing hold of a ghost. She leapt out onto the tracks, and the train screeched into the station.

She did this just about every time Boaz took the subway home. Waiting and leaping. He had tried a few times to talk to her. He had even poked around online to see if he could find an obituary, so he could get a full name and maybe some hint about how she could be helped. But she was stubborn. Despite his best efforts, he couldn't get her to move on.

The N train at last rumbled in, and Boaz carefully averted his eyes.

He had barely settled into his seat when he felt his phone buzz, and a WhatsApp notification warned him it was Daniel.

Daniel: Hey, wanna come over? I'm in Brooklyn tonight

Boaz: Why are you in Brooklyn?? Go back uptown, hang out with your cool YU friends . . .

Daniel: Cool? Srsly? Who are you and what did you do with Boaz?

Boaz: Oh that was autocorrect. I meant boring

Daniel: Phew. You coming?

It was tempting. Daniel was about the only person from high school Boaz actually considered a friend, and he'd barely seen him since he started at Yeshiva University in the fall. NYU might have been manageable for their friendship, but Washington Heights was basically Canada, as far as Boaz was concerned. There was never a time that going up there was convenient, so the only reason he'd seen Daniel at all the last few months was for the High Holidays.

But he couldn't. Not tonight.

Boaz: Can't. I got a thing with Hila
Daniel: Oh no is it a dead people thing? Don't tell me it's a dead people thing
Boaz: . . .
Daniel: What do I need to do to see you? Die?
Boaz: I mean . . .
Daniel: BOAZ
Boaz: Sorry bad joke

It was November, and Brooklyn was finally beginning to feel like it. Gravesend had been swallowed by a heavy, chilled night, the kind that could have foreshadowed snow. Boaz shivered when he stepped out of the station, yanking up the zipper of his hoodie and jamming his hands into the pockets of his jeans, wishing he'd thought to bring his jacket.

He kept his head down the entire walk from the station. A preservation technique. The usual dead would try anyway to get his attention: Mrs. Abulafia, who refused to move on because she liked to watch the pigeons and keep tabs on her grandchildren, or Anthony Janszoon van Salee, the early Gravesend settler, who Boaz had made the mistake of interviewing for a history project and who now accosted him at every available opportunity to regale him with more stories and gossip that had gone stale four hundred years ago. Boaz could feign interest during his waking hours, but at one in the morning he did not need to hear about the treachery of the Dutch West India Company or how Anthony would never have done something so dishonorable as pay his debts with a dead goat, that if a perfectly healthy goat simply expired on the spot after taking one whiff of the unwashed scoundrel, then that was *hardly* his fault.

"Harari, my dear boy! Just the man I wanted to see." Boaz could hear him call, his voice loud enough that it made Boaz startle, a near impossible feat nowadays. A lifetime of small talk with the dead had made him hard to spook.

"Can't talk, Anthony!" he said, glancing back just long enough to see Anthony flicker in and out of view, less than six inches from his face. "I need to go home—"

"But I think I've finally cracked it," he persisted as Boaz crossed the street, narrowly avoiding being taken out by a late-night cyclist as he tried to put distance between himself and the seventeenth-century gentleman. "Proof, you see, that my claims in Manhattan and Brooklyn still hold."

"Even if that were true, what would you do with Wall Street?" said Boaz, quickening his pace. "We've been over this! One, no one will give you *Wall Street*. Two, what would you do with it?"

"By all rights, it is mine to do with as I please!" said the ghost of Anthony, still keeping pace. "And it's not just Wall Street. It's that lovely stretch of land by the sea that has since been desecrated by that horrid carnival."

"They're not giving you Coney Island, either!"

"If you would only send a missive through the proper channels . . .

I'd be happy to dictate the letters to you, if we could maybe begin this evening."

Boaz had at last reached the front door of his apartment building, and he began to fumble for his keys, praying that Anthony would not try to follow him up the stairs. "*Good night*, Anthony."

Most of the lights in the apartment were off, save for some dim lamplight in the living room, where his aunt Hila was watching a movie on her iPad, her dark, pin-straight hair pulled into a low ponytail. From the look of it, one of her favorite Israeli melodramas. She didn't look up when he entered and abandoned his sneakers at the door. He crept in and, leaning against the back of the worn black leather sofa, at last said, "Oh, is this one of the musical ones?"

But, like all Hararis, she had too much experience with ghosts to be easily startled. So she did not jump when he spoke, but when she looked up, her eyes widened, just enough for Boaz to notice. She yanked her earbuds out and whacked the hand that was gripping the back of the sofa.

"Ma zeh, Boazi?" *What's this?* She continued in rapid Hebrew, keeping her voice low. "I see how you've been setting your mother off. You look more like Eli every day."

At this, Boaz grimaced. He knew it was not entirely untrue. They both had the same dark hair and more or less the same nose, and what he always thought was a bit too much eyebrow.

But he was nothing like his father. He would not just disappear on his wife and newborn. He wouldn't go over seventeen years without so much as a phone call, and if he died, he'd have the decency to do it somewhere where he could be found. But it was no use arguing with her on that one, so instead, he asked his aunt, "So did you try? Have any luck this time? Did she finally want to talk about Dad?"

28

He hoped today his mother would have at least tried talking about his dad, especially after that morning. He had been halfway out the door to work, arguing with his mom about his hours and why he would *not* consider taking a full-time job at his grandparents' wedding catering company, and in the middle of their yelling, his mother had called him by his father's name.

She almost never said his father's name. She almost never spoke of him. Boaz could, and he did. When he was little, it was out of curiosity, a desire for answers. When he did, mostly his mother would turn away from that, complain of a headache, or tell Boaz to stop asking foolish questions, as if he were asking about the possibility of getting a pet unicorn for Chanukah, and not about his father. Boaz thought his mother just didn't like to talk about it, but every so often she would . . . and at some point, his aunt Hila had asked him to tell her every time his mother mentioned him, every time something slipped through.

"No, no, I didn't," she said. "She forgot him as soon as you left for work, didn't say another word. But she offered me tea, we had a wonderful chat about how I could convince you to give college a try, and she went to bed." Hila unfolded her legs. "And because we were not in a rush, I thought we could try together."

Boaz's heart skipped a beat. He hadn't even bothered to ask if he could be the one to try this month. Because the answer was always a resounding no. "We?"

"Oh, don't look so excited. You can assist."

"With the ring?"

"With getting the mirrors," she said evenly. "One thing at a time, yes?"

Like Boaz, Aunt Hila had the Harari curse: she saw the dead, like all born Hararis for over two hundred years. Unlike most Hararis, though, she was not a trainwreck who wasted all her energy trying to look normal and avoiding direct eye contact with the ghosts who liked bothering her in public.

Hila had made the dead her career, turned it into a whole big Bravo show that had just wrapped its fourth season. When she put their old family ring on, Hila could reach just about anyone. It was like she had a direct line to the World to Come. The dead almost always answered her calls.

Except his father.

When Hila tried to call his father, she could never reach him. Boaz had watched her try too many times to count, reaching out into the dark and finding nothing.

If his dad was dead, his mom would have mourned him. She would have told Boaz stories about him. She would at least look interested when he brought him up, instead of glazing over like she did when he spouted off facts about obscure silent films. But apart from the occasional slip, she never seemed to care. She didn't mourn, and she didn't talk about him, not even to curse him for leaving them behind.

Hila pulled a candle from the leather handbag resting on the couch beside her, followed by a black drawstring pouch, dumping the ring onto her hand. "Get the mirror from your mother's room and cover the ones in your room and the bathroom."

"I know," he said, tiptoeing into his mother's room, where she was already sleeping soundly. He must have seen Hila call ghosts a thousand times. The onyx ring emblazoned with a simple Star of David and nothing else was an old family heirloom. It definitely went back at least as far as Damascus, but before that was anyone's guess. Hila claimed it went back to King Solomon, but he always thought that seemed a bit far-fetched, if only because from everything he knew about his family, he sincerely doubted their ability to keep hold of anything for that long.

Boaz dragged out the standing mirror as silently as he could, shutting the door behind him. The mirror in his bedroom was a cheap one that hung over the door, and a few prior attempts with Hila had taught him enough to know the easiest way to cover that one was to unhook it and lay it face down on the floor.

The toughest one was the one in the bathroom, the sliding door of their medicine cabinet. He grabbed one of the towels hanging on the rack and did his best to drape it over the top, but after a few attempts he gave up and settled for it covering only about half and looking ready to slide off altogether. Nothing ever came when Hila tried to call his dad anyway; this time wasn't going to be any different.

Hila was still rummaging through her bag when he emerged. "Do you have a lighter?" she said. "Mine's empty."

Boaz did, a habit Hila had taught him. It was a safety precaution. A flame, no matter how small, could at once draw a ghost while also keeping them from crossing the boundaries they ought not to cross. He dug it out of his pocket and tossed it to Hila. She lit the candle and set it on the coffee table, across from the mirror, before perching on it herself, sitting cross-legged and sliding on the ring.

Boaz watched her closely, even though by now he knew exactly what she would do. She stared into the mirror until her eyes slid just slightly out of focus, as if she were staring at something through the glass. "Boazi, move, you're in the reflection."

Boaz shuffled, still craning his neck to see. Hila raised her hands as if she were a Kohen about to give the priestly blessing, her fingers tight around the ring and splayed in the familiar V shape. Long ago, he'd learned the easiest way to annoy Hila was to call them Star Trek hands. His senior year Talmud teacher insisted it was witchcraft, and worse still, avodah zara, idol worship. If Hila hadn't intervened and reminded the dean whose avodah zara had paid for the new media lab, then he probably wouldn't have graduated on time.

She was still staring into the mirror, her eyes trained on it, concentrating so intently that Boaz would not have been surprised if she burned a hole right through the glass with her gaze. Her mouth moved, her voice barely more than a whisper as she recited his father's name. Her fingers folded, as if she were clutching invisible curtains, before yanking with all her strength.

Boaz kept his eyes trained away from the mirror, despite every temptation to do otherwise. He was supposed to let Hila focus. According to her, terrible things could happen if she lost it. The hungriest of spirits or worse could slip through. People could become possessed. His only job now was to make sure the flame did not go out and that he did not stare directly into the mirror. Hila was still facing forward, but her eyes had rolled back so that only the whites were visible. The candle wavered, and Boaz wondered what she was seeing and whether she was any closer to finding his father than the countless other times she had tried.

Tap tap tap.

Boaz froze. That was new. Usually, these attempts were over quickly and were never more than this, Hila in front of a mirror, reaching and coming back empty. When they went looking for his father, nothing answered. But this . . .

32

Was probably the faucet. That faucet was very temperamental, had been for years, and no amount of pleading with the super had gotten him to come and fix it. Yes, that was probably what it was.

Tap tap tap.

All right, it was a bit louder than the faucet ever managed, and heavier. But . . .

Tap tap tap . . . thud.

No, that was definitely more than a leaky faucet.

He opened his mouth to say something, to see if Hila heard it, but he wasn't sure what would happen if he broke her concentration now. Now, when she was maybe closer than ever to finding his father, seemed particularly foolish.

He crept toward the bathroom, alternating between watching the door and watching Hila. But she hadn't moved, and the candle in front of her burned as bright as ever; it was only the tapping that got louder and more urgent. Heart pounding, he turned the knob and pushed, noticing the fallen towel on the floor even before he flicked on the lights.

For a moment, he saw nothing. Just the crumpled towel and his own reflection staring back at him from the mirror.

Until he realized that it was absolutely *not* his reflection staring back at him.

No, the face in the mirror was older than his and just enough unlike it. It was longer, fuller, the lines along his brow deeper. His dark hair was carefully combed back, and his nose was just off center, as if he'd broken it in a fight. Photos of his father were impossible to come by; Boaz had to rely on Hila's descriptions of him, but he had committed every single detail she told him to memory.

Boaz looked at his father's reflection, watched as it gave a small wave, as if him showing up in the mirror of their bathroom, after nearly eighteen years of nothing, was entirely normal.

"Hila!" Boaz shouted. He knew it would wake up his mother, that it would startle Hila out of her trance. But he didn't care. She needed to come here, she needed to see—

Only the shape was gone as quickly as it appeared, vanishing the moment Boaz approached the glass, and by the time Hila came rushing up behind him, the only face staring back at him in the mirror was his own.

There was once a girl who dreamed of flight.

The details varied, but the substance remained the same. In her dreams, she would marry a handsome scholar, so esteemed that they would travel far and wide. He would be invited to teach in Paris, in Berlin, in New York City. He would speak in halls filled with eager and attentive students by day, and by night he'd return to her. By lamplight he would read her poetry and ask her opinion on everything, more often than not deciding that she was right.

Sometimes she dreamed she would marry a clever and talented merchant with a ship of his own. They would circumnavigate the world in it, never remaining in any one port more than a week at a time. She dreamed of what tropical islands and the Ivory Coast and Goa would look like from the deck of a grand sailing vessel.

When she was not busy with her chores, coaxing eggs from chickens who would not lay them, or begging the old and half-starved cow for a bit more milk, she was staring up at the sky. She'd climb trees, the tallest she could find, so that she might look out past her shtetl, her village, down the road and past the horizon. Up there alone, a cool autumn breeze cradling the small of her back and catching in the sleeves of her dress, she dreamed they were wings, that at any moment the winds would lift her into the air, and she would soar.

That was the dream. She would marry, and her husband would give her wings. Together they would fly from this place, where there was never enough of anything and each day was the same as the last. Never mind that she could not afford shoes and that she was always hungry. For what she lacked in money, she possessed in ambition and faith. She was diligent and obedient and believed with all her heart that one day her prayers would be answered. Even if her scholar was not quite so handsome, or her merchant not quite so clever, at least the winds would still turn her way.

But there would be no handsome scholar or clever merchant to whisk her away, to give her wings and a place to land.

Instead, there was the butcher's son.

It was a good match, her parents said. The best that a girl with all dreams and no shoes could hope to have. Her father could not believe his luck. They were penniless, so deep in debt that they were all but buried alive by it, only for the butcher to offer a hand, and a house, and food enough for them all.

But the village was small, and people talked, and anyone with eyes could see that from birth the boy had been cursed with a streak of terrible cruelty. The girl knew the stories: the kittens he killed for sport, the way he had begged to take up his father's knife and learn the butcher trade at an age when most boys still cried at the thought of a gentle animal being brought to slaughter.

Four days before her wedding, after she had immersed herself for the first time in the mikveh, the butcher and his wife invited the girl and her family for dinner, to discuss the final arrangements for the wedding party. But try as she might to care about the elaborate feast they had planned in her honor, she could not shake the desperate desire to be anywhere else. When the girl could take no more talk of fish and cake and the rabbi's poor health, she excused herself, and slipped outside into the descending twilight. She wandered away from the stifling house to the cowshed, where the butcher's cows had already been led for the night. Ignoring the smell, she found one cow who came closer to her as she entered.

Even in the rapidly fading light, the girl could tell the cow was not well. For all the abundant grain in the shed, the cow was thin, her eyes glassy and so impossibly sad when she craned her neck out and nuzzled the girl's hand.

"You like her?" said the butcher's son. The girl had not heard him enter, but there he stood, close enough that she could smell his sweat. "She looks like you. The same eyes, same dull face."

The girl did not know what to say to that, so she said nothing, continuing instead to let the cow nuzzle her hand. She wished she could take the cow home with her, that the two of them could flee to some other village, somewhere far away from butchers.

"She is good for nothing," he said. "We had been promised a healthy cow, but within a month of her purchase, her milk went sour, and her calves were born dead. She won't leave her stall unless she is dragged. We can't even eat her, because my father thinks she's sick." He stepped closer to her, until he was standing just behind her. "I disagree. I think she is just insolent. I think that she has some funny ideas in her head, and has forgotten what she is and why we bought her."

"If she is sick or unhappy, then maybe you should help her." The back of her throat burned with bile. She turned away from him, refusing to meet his eyes out of fear for what she might see. "Don't you see she is unhappy?"

"Oh, I'll help her," he said. "I'll help her remember that she is nothing more than a useless cow."

The girl who dreamed of wings, she had believed. She believed that she earned her miracle. She did not need the Red Sea to part, or for ten plagues to descend upon them. One would have been enough.

Why, a few frogs surely would be enough to stop a wedding. For all the terrible things that had befallen them in other seasons that they had endured, this was hardly such a great ask.

But as the day drew nearer, her prayers went unanswered. There would be no handsome scholar to charm her father, no clever merchant who could make her family's debts disappear. There would be no changing her fate.

So, the night before the wedding, the girl had crept out of bed carefully, holding her breath as she crossed the creaking floorboards. She slept in the narrow loft space of her parents' house, and ordinarily it was too drafty and cold, but tonight she could scarcely breathe. It was as though she were being smothered by dread of the terrible promise of what the new day would bring. She needed air.

She forced open the window, throwing back the shutters. It was the month of Kislev, when the nights were long and no amount of Chanukah light could chase them away. A cool gust of air swept through her thin nightdress and caressed her face, an exquisite relief from the stale and heavy air of the house. She stuck her head out the window and breathed, and for a moment she was the happiest she had been in weeks. Cold, sweet air and heavy blue night. She wanted to wrap herself in it, to wear it from head to toe. She wanted to slide into it and never come back.

Which was when she realized she could. She could take to the air. Maybe the wretched man that was to be her husband had given her wings after all, and she simply needed the nerve to use them.

She pushed the window open farther and then stepped out onto the sill and leaned forward, holding fast to the frame. Why did she ever think that flying would be so hard? On the contrary, it was easy. She had been waiting for a sign, when really all she had needed was enough nerve.

The girl stood for a moment there at the window, her nightdress billowing about her, poised to take flight, when her eyes met eyes.

There, on a tree just beyond the window, sat an owl in the branches. At first, she thought it to be of an ordinary variety. It had thick gray feathers that reflected the moonlight back. It was, perhaps, larger than any owl she had seen, and with eyes that seemed particularly clever, though in truth all owls had that look about them.

Until the owl spoke.

"You want to fly?" asked the owl, opening its beak. The owl spoke in the voice of a woman, low and calm and almost curious.

The girl, so close to the edge and so eager for the dark, did not think to question why an owl could speak to her in a voice that she understood. "Yes," said the girl, her voice hoarse and desperate. "Yes, please."

"But you cannot fly like that," said the owl. "You have no feathers, no wings."

"Please," the girl whispered, more urgently. Her eyes began to burn with tears as she clutched the edge of the window, eyeing the drop into the dark. "Please, I need to fly."

The owl stared at her long and hard before at last opening its wings and, with an impatient flutter, landing beside her on the sill.

"Let me give you wings, then," said the owl.

And the girl, who had wanted nothing more in all her life than for someone, anyone, to say such a thing to her, nodded, stepping back down onto the creaking floor. She did not care who or what would give them to her, just so long as she might fly at last.

"Yes, please," said the girl. "Please, I want wings."

"Then you shall have them," said the owl. And in the pale moonlight, the owl became not a woman, but something more. A woman with hands like claws, mottled and dangerous, with wide eyes blank and filled with moonlight, and teeth sharper than even the sharpest of her soon-to-be-husband's knives. The word that came to mind was *sheydim*, the demons that old yentas in the village feared and blamed for all their ordinary woes, the things that new mothers feared most of all when birth was done. Still, she was not afraid.

"Please," she said again, thinking she might be swallowed up in the woman's eyes, the moonlight. She was certain that she had never seen anything so beautiful in all her days.

The woman took the girl in her arms, embraced her as a daughter, and the girl could not remember a time she was so loved. True and deep and without condition. And when the woman's teeth sank deep into her neck, she finally felt like she could breathe.

4

CLARA

It was Clara's turn to pay rent.

She had dreaded it the entire afternoon, spending far too long dithering over the sun-faded magazines in the newsstands before she settled on a copy of *Vanity Fair* featuring the latest it boy actor, a young Brit with dark curls, an olive complexion, and a dimpled smirk. She didn't recognize his name, but she decided to bring the entire magazine with her just in case. The Prince of Demons wouldn't accept the same face twice.

The last time she had paid, she had been so angry at Boaz for showing up late with some ridiculous excuse about a man in his neighborhood who claimed to own Wall Street that she'd paid with Boaz's face. Maybe he'd let her advance her rent this time and save herself the trouble.

The entrance to Gehinnom was along the Bowery. Tucked between a derelict bodega and a restaurant supply store, the door would, to most, appear only as vacant space. The more discerning would see an entrance to the best nightclub in New York City, the premiere gathering place for anyone without a heartbeat.

Clara glanced over her shoulder before trying the door. The moment her hand touched the surface, bright silver lines emerged in the dark, weaving and curling around each other until they formed the outline of a doorknob, inches from where her hand rested.

Inside it might very well have been night. The same thick darkness of the door swallowed her for a moment before pinpricks of light like stars appeared, as if she were adrift in space. The Prince of Demons, for all his many faults, loved to impress.

Clara stepped confidently toward the silvery outline of a staircase. Like stepping out into open air. To an untrained guest, it might have been unnerving, but she did not fear falling. The open air was freedom, and this was nothing more than a trick of light.

At this hour, the club was quiet and almost empty. Onstage, the band playing was invisible even to her own eyes, a trumpet and violin floating several feet above the ground, and a drum set tapping out its own beat. The shiny black marble floor was pristine and looked freshly mopped, the spindly silver tables and chairs along the wall neatly lined up. Along the stretch of bar, there were only two shadowy figures perched, both with the large, birdlike talons in place of feet that marked them as sheydim. One glanced over as Clara swept past them to get the attention of the bartender, and she wondered whether she ought to let her hair down. She'd kept it pinned in the same neat chignon she wore in the theater. Here, no one would so much as flinch at the sight of her face, but her habits kept her safe. The greatest danger to them and their way of life was not a single, great error, after all, but rather a dozen tiny slip-ups that, combined, would invite a danger they would not be able to overcome. Devorah had taught her that.

"Excuse me?" She waved down the bartender, who was half asleep. When he turned to face her, his eyes were blank, whites without irises, the same as hers when she let her hair down. "Is he in? Can I speak with him?"

The bartender yawned, waving his hand lazily toward the door just past the end of the bar, and she took it as an invitation to try for the office.

Beyond the nondescript door was a long, winding hallway, impossibly long and entirely useless. Clara never understood the point, save that Ashmodai loved an illusion more than any being in this world or the World to Come.

At last she came to a set of double doors marked with silver. She knocked, but in lieu of answer, the door swung open.

"Why, hello, little bird."

Clara stepped inside, grimacing. Ashmodai's frankly excessive preference for black, highly polished marble continued here. She could see hints of her own reflection in the dark tile, looking back at her from a hundred different angles, watching her from all sides in the cavernous, sparsely furnished space. The only interruptions in the walls were a bright fireplace glowing on one end and a long bookcase filled with identical leather-bound volumes, which she suspected were an illusion, too.

Ashmodai, the Prince of Demons and manager of Gehinnom, was the only bit of color in the dark. For all the faces that he could possibly take—and he could take many—he always wore the same for her, a young man with bright red hair and startling green eyes, his features too perfect, too symmetrical.

"You don't usually come this early," he said. "I did not think you could fly by day."

"I walked," she said stiffly.

"Well, then you should take a seat," he said as something cold touched the back of Clara's legs. Behind her, a white marble chair had appeared where there previously had been none.

Clara stayed standing. The first time she'd met Ashmodai, Devorah had been with her. She'd thought that they would find life easier in Manhattan if the Prince of Demons liked them, or at the very least, did not despise them. It did not do for a monster to make an enemy out of the shadows, not when the shadows were their home: vacant hotel rooms and apartments, charming suitors and whoever else it took to secure a place to land. It had been work, exhilarating but exhausting all the same, constantly having to befuddle building supers and bellhops and nosy neighbors just for a place to sleep. With Devorah, that life had been exciting. It had made her feel creative and invincible.

But they weren't. Devorah had taught them that, too.

And once she was gone, Clara and Molly had wanted a home. They disagreed on many things, but on this they never had. Whatever thrill came from wandering, they needed a proper nest. But they could not risk leaving a trail of papers and documents and paychecks. There was simply no way they could find anything approaching a long-term home among the rules and public ordinances of the living.

So they had paid a visit to Ashmodai. He had informed them of a property that would serve their purposes perfectly, a recently abandoned Yiddish stage that he could make home for them, for the price of their loyalty, and no less than one face a month, to be paid in the method of their choosing. For that, they could have the space with his protection, a space where they could live among and apart from the living, in plain sight and yet unrecognized for what they truly were.

It was, all in all, not unreasonable, certainly not with what rents in the Village were like. And he had never tried to increase it, not even when photography was so easy and cheap. From what Clara could tell, he liked to wear fresh faces, required variety, and, given that he could not leave the confines of Gehinnom, needed them delivered.

His only, infuriating request was that they always be delivered in person.

Clara tore off the cover of the magazine and handed it to him, her arms stiff. "This shouldn't take long."

"Now, that is no way to do business," he said, clicking his tongue. He reached over to take the cover from her. He eyed the boy on the front. "Oh, this will do nicely," he said, before his face began to shift. In an instant, he became the cover model. "I daresay, I am beginning to think you have something of a type. This one isn't so different than the one you brought last month."

"He does not look anything like Boaz," huffed Clara. He did look quite a lot like Boaz, but it was entirely a coincidence and nothing more. "Is it settled, then?"

Ashmodai stared at her through his stolen face, cocking an eyebrow. "Is something troubling you, my little bird?"

"What difference does it make to you?" she said stiffly, glancing at her watch. The sooner she was out of here and back at the Grand Dame, the happier she'd be. After all, she apparently couldn't leave for more than five minutes without Molly breaking rules and making a mess of things, or Boaz flirting with disaster. Really, herding cats would have been easier.

"Ah, the well-being and happiness of my tenants is always a

concern of mine," he said. "Come, you cannot keep secrets from me. I will find out."

"It's nothing," she said. "Molly is seeing someone."

"And?" said Ashmodai. "Forgive me, but from the long look on your face, I thought you had discovered a leviathan in the plumbing."

"We don't fall in love," said Clara shortly. "That's the rule."

"Whose rule? Where is it written?" Ashmodai sighed. "Forgive me, but I think that you live your life in fear of a ghost."

"I . . . I don't know what you're talking about." Clara's monster rippled beneath the surface of her skin, and she turned, intending to leave.

But the door was gone, replaced by a solid wall of marble, reflecting her own face back at her. Her real face. It was not a reflection of the one she wore into the club, with her hair pinned up and her features plain and ordinary. The face staring back at her had hair wild and matted hanging to her waist, her eyes bright white and blank, her teeth razor sharp.

"You are afraid of her," he said.

"Of who?" Clara forced herself to look away from her reflection. No, she was not afraid of *her*. That reflection, the monster that she became, had been her great salvation, the thing that had saved her from falling into the dark, plummeting off that sill when all she wanted to do was fly. Nor was she afraid of Devorah, who had made her that monster, had given her wings and teeth and then taught her to use both.

"Take it from someone who knows this world much better than you do: Birds should not remain in their nests forever. Were you truly given wings for that?"

"I like my nest," she said tersely. "And unlike you, I can leave whenever I wish."

That new, attractive face of his split in a dangerous smirk. "Do what you will, little bird, but consider that your gifts are meant for more than hiding in your little theater, afraid of your appetites."

"I *am not* afraid," sputtered Clara. No. *No.* She was not going to fall for it. That was never going to be a conversation she had with Ashmodai. She glared at him. "Put the door back. I need to get to work."

"What do you mean? It's been there the whole time," he said. Indeed, when Clara turned around again, the door had returned soundlessly, as if it had never been gone in the first place.

Clara stopped, her hands tightening into fists. But when she turned to retort, he was gone. Ashmodai had vanished, leaving nothing but his empty desk and a fire crackling away in the hearth. He could not leave the club, but she had better things to do than chase him down, and she hated to be here a second longer than necessary. When she forced the door open, she expected to find herself back at the end of the maze of hallways. But instead, the door opened up right beside the dance floor. She stepped out just as the ghostly band struck up their next song.

5

MOLLY

Anat: I'm outside. You coming or not?

It was two minutes after nine. She needed to keep this promise to Anat, because Anat had been right: it wasn't fair that she had to keep lying to her friends. Anat wasn't Molly. Lying wasn't a necessary part of her survival in the city. Clara had come back from Ashmodai looking stricken and insisted they needed to talk, which was enough to tell her that she ought to stay clear of her sister. This was either about the social media account or Anat, and she wasn't giving either of those up.

Anat was waiting for her just beyond the doors of the theater wearing a crop top and the vintage pencil skirt that Molly had given her because she couldn't fit into it. On Anat's taller, leaner frame, it was just tight enough to make Molly want to tear it off. When she saw Molly, she waved. "What do you think? It's great, isn't it?"

"Of course it's great; I picked it out!" Molly glanced up once, to make sure Clara's head wasn't poking out from one of the windows, before running to embrace her. Even in the bitter cold, her girlfriend was deliciously warm. Molly didn't want to let go, and even after she did, she kept one arm woven around Anat's as they set off back down Twelfth Street. They walked several blocks, past the used book carts outside the Strand bookstore and at least two cafés Molly swore had not been there the last time she had walked this way. They kept going and were halfway down University Place when Molly at last asked, "So where's this party, anyway?"

"Friend of a friend's. Her dad's a producer or something, so she's got a place on Minetta Lane . . . like, *owns* it, owns it. Can you imagine? Or I guess you could; you probably remember a time when you could buy a brownstone down here for ten dollars and a few pounds of herring."

"I have *never* paid for anything with herring," began Molly. But then Anat kept going down University Place, and Molly froze. "Wait, we're crossing through Washington Square Park?"

"Um, yeah?" said Anat, tugging on Molly's hand. "That's how you get to Minetta Lane."

"It doesn't have to be. We could cross over to the west side and then go down . . ."

Anat tugged Molly's hand again, but Molly would not budge. "Come on, my shoes aren't comfortable enough to walk an extra twenty minutes. . . ."

"Well, who told you to wear uncomfortable shoes?"

"Oh my god, seriously?" said Anat. "Don't tell me you're afraid of the park at night. It's not even late. It's still busy, perfectly well lit, also you're basically a vampire—"

"It's . . ." Molly struggled for the words. She *never* crossed Washington Square Park if she could avoid it. And she almost always could. She always flew the long way when she needed to go

49

to the West Village, which hardly made a difference with her wings. But she wasn't sure how to explain it in a way that didn't make her sound like some superstitious old yenta. "I don't . . . like Washington Square Park. Bad memories."

Anat's brow furrowed. "Bad memories?"

"Ghosts," said Molly, evasively. That day still had a way of sneaking up on her. She and Clara almost never spoke of it, but every so often, she'd smell burning or hear screaming out on the street, and even if it was something completely innocent, she'd remember that day, how it felt to watch something burn, to watch desperate girls try to fly—how it felt to be able to do nothing but watch.

Anat squeezed Molly's hand. "Come on, I'll stay close."

"Anat, I . . ."

But Anat wove her arm through Molly's, and with her so warm and near, Molly decided she couldn't say no to her. Not even for this. She probably was just being a superstitious old yenta.

They made their way past couples and clusters of students, and Molly took care not to breathe. She didn't *need* to breathe, but it was a habit she saw no point in breaking, and it helped Clara and her pass, made the act more natural. But now Molly just needed to focus on keeping herself calm. It was just a November night.

When they reached the outskirts of the park, Molly made a point not to look at the buildings that bordered the park, instead staring resolutely at the neat trees and the path leading down to the fountain. She *could* do this, she reasoned, as long as she didn't look back. She would *not* look back.

Anat pulled her toward the gates, and she followed, quickening her own pace. The faster they crossed the park and made it to Mac-Dougal, the faster she could put it all behind her. She could tuck it all back away and not think about it, she could . . .

They passed the fountain and had just made it to one of the paths spidering out from the center when Anat stopped. Still clutching Molly's hand, she looked up at her, her eyes shining in the dark. "Are you okay?"

Molly nodded, and then added, her voice too high-pitched, "I'm okay."

"You can breathe, you know," said Anat. "It's fine. You're *fine*, see? It'll be fine."

Molly tried breathing, but now that she wasn't, it suddenly seemed an entirely impossible thing to do. Her whole chest hitched strangely, and about the only thing she could do was look at Anat desperately, watching *her* chest rise and fall, trying to figure out how she could do the same, how she ought to match her girlfriend's breathing, how she ought to know better, how to find air . . .

But before she could, Anat leaned forward, pulling Molly into a tight, earnest kiss. Anat's free hand traveled up Molly's neck, resting for a moment just at the nape. Molly returned the favor, almost desperately. With Anat pressed up against her, and so close, she could hear her heartbeat clearly. It was all she could hear, her heart and her breathing, and for a wild instant she thought she might be able to match it, like her heart, too, might start beating. She felt dizzy and desperate and, for a moment, almost alive.

At last Anat pulled away, smiling. "Better?"

The most Molly could do was nod. She was past the point of actual speech.

Anat hardly spoke the rest of the walk over, which was fine by Molly. She didn't need to talk, and it let them cut through the park faster. Cold seemed to have descended. The November chill was little more than a light inconvenience for Molly, but it clearly was running straight through Anat. Her hands were icy by the time they reached Minetta Lane, and her teeth wouldn't stop chattering.

"You want my jacket?" said Molly as they waited to buzz up. Anat said nothing, so she pulled it off anyway and put it across her shoulders. Anat looked up at Molly, still shivering, but shifted a bit closer to her. Molly turned and kissed her cheek lightly, unsettled by how cold she still was.

Whoever lived here had to be loaded. It was a beautifully maintained version of the kind of building that playwright Eugene O'Neill probably got drunk in, where the sense of ghosts was thick, but nothing went noticed among the revelry of the future finance bros and trust-funded artists of America. The apartment itself was packed. It was big for the Village, with nice high ceilings and gleaming parquet floors . . . or floors that probably did gleam, when they weren't sticky with spilled alcohol. It was like being caught in a glue trap, as Molly picked her way between sweaty, shouty students.

"So, where are your friends?" said Molly, craning her neck. "That's why we're here, right? To prove to your friends that I . . ."

She didn't need to finish the thought, because at once a couple of girls beelined straight toward her. Molly was sure she'd seen them before, in Anat's Instagram posts, though for the life of her, she couldn't remember their names.

"Oh my god, you're here!" said the first girl, who was willowy and towered over both her and Anat. The statement, she realized belatedly, was not directed at Anat. "You're Molly, right? I can't believe you made it!"

"I know, I can't believe it, either!" said Molly. Anat was still shivering and practically glued to Molly's side. For all of Anat's talk about how important it was that Molly meet her friends, she seemed entirely uninterested in talking to any of them. Instead, her girlfriend kept a cold hand on Molly's arm, not uttering a single word as girls kept introducing themselves to Molly, trying to make themselves heard over the blaring music. Was Anat always like this at parties? If so, this was the last time Molly would agree to go to one. She could decipher about half of what these alleged friends said to her, and Molly realized too late she had smiled and nodded her way into disaster.

"Oh, excellent," said the other girl, whose thick curls rivaled Molly's own. She took one of Anat's hands and began to pull her. "Anat is *great* at karaoke. You should have seen her last week when we managed to sneak into Marie's Crisis."

"Wait, what?"

"It wasn't *hard*. Half the time they don't even check IDs."

"No, I mean . . ." Molly looked to Anat, who hadn't said two words since her friends arrived. "What did I just agree to?"

The curly-haired girl giggled. "Karaoke. Come on! Anat said that you've done professional theater? She talks so much about you."

The two girls pulled them both toward the corner of the living room, where someone had set up a cheap karaoke machine that, from the look of it, no one was using anyway, save for the microphone. *Damn theater kids.* She should have expected as much when Anat had hyped up this party as one that was in fact *her people*. Anat's people were Molly's people, too, and if there was one thing that had not changed in the slightest between centuries, it was just how fond their people were of spontaneously bursting into song.

"Yeah, last time is how we learned that Anat only knows the Hebrew lyrics to 'I'll Make a Man Out of You,'" said the tall girl.

"We'll sing together," said Anat suddenly. Molly almost missed what she said. "Right? Can we sing together?"

"The lady speaks!" her curly-haired friend practically cheered, pushing the both of them toward the microphone. "Go on!"

"I can't." Molly at last dug in her heels. There was absolutely no way she could risk it. Half the audience had their phones out, and the other half could just as easily whip them out. Clara was already going to murder her for having a girlfriend. If a video of her wound up online? "Anat, you know I can't."

"No, you can," she said earnestly. "I know you can."

"*No*," said Molly. "*You* can. Go ahead! I will keep proving to your friends that I exist."

Anat let go of Molly's arm, but it seemed only reluctantly, while Molly hung back, muttering half-formed excuses to her friends about her vocal nodes, which they mostly couldn't hear anyway over the sounds of the party. Anat nudged her way to the front, spent half a second choosing a song, and claimed the microphone.

Anat's eyes met Molly's, her smile so serene that for a brief moment Molly was at ease again. She must have warmed up, and she had to be pleased, didn't she? Molly was here, proof that she existed. She had done her part.

The song began, and it took Molly exactly three notes to recognize it: "Some of These Days." It was an old song, a Shelton Brooks jazz standard, but it was one of Molly's favorites. Before her first death, she had seen Sophie Tucker sing it live. The record was one of the first she'd ever bought, when at last Clara and she had moved into the Grand Dame and got a record player of their own. *Some of these days, you'll miss your honey. Some of these days, you'll feel so lonely . . .*

But when Anat began to sing, it was neither the familiar English lyrics that came out of Anat's mouth nor even the Hebrew Molly knew she could do, but perfect Yiddish.

Molly's jaw dropped. It wasn't the singing: She knew Anat could sing. It was that, apart from the Yiddish that fused its way into English or Hebrew, Anat didn't speak it. *Really* didn't speak it. Doing even a few lines for *The Second Avenue Spiel* videos took practice. And even then, Molly always thought it sounded a bit odd, a bit off; she could practically hear the effort that came with it.

But what came out of her mouth now was *perfect*. The accent, the cadence, the theatricality . . . She didn't sing like she'd practiced for hours in her dorm room. She was singing like a native speaker, as though she'd emerged from the cradle speaking Yiddish.

But if anyone else in the room thought it was strange, they didn't show it. The vast majority of the crowd clearly did not recognize the tune, but no one seemed to think it was strange, at least not from Anat, for whom bilingual karaoke was apparently a regular party trick.

When Anat finished, the room burst into applause. The girl in charge of the karaoke machine reached over to take the microphone from Anat and hand it over to the next singer, but Anat just stood there, clutching the microphone and staring unblinkingly through the crowd, straight at Molly. Molly thought she saw something almost strained about the way she was smiling.

When the girl lost her patience, she plucked the microphone from Anat's grip, and Anat shuddered, her whole body convulsing. It was enough that Molly saw it, clear as anything, but over so quickly that she could not say whether anyone else did.

"How did you do that?" asked Molly, just as Anat's curly-haired friend rushed forward to take the microphone. "I've never heard Yiddish that good from you."

"I don't know," said Anat, the same fixed smile on her face, and Molly saw in it alarm even worse than her own.

6

BOAZ

Boaz rolled his shoulders to fight the strain. Aunt Hila just *had* to live on the top floor of her walk-up, even though she had enough money to move into Manhattan, or at least into a building with an elevator.

And of course Aunt Hila just had to refuse to use Instacart after they once thought pitted black olives were a suitable substitute for Kalamata, preferring instead to send Boaz out to buy groceries for her. Boaz didn't mind that, mostly. Aunt Hila gave him far more cash than necessary to get the things off her list on purpose, and always let him keep the change. And frankly, no number of trips to NetCost would pay off everything he owed Aunt Hila.

At least this time it was a perfect cover for what he actually needed to do.

Boaz gasped a sigh of relief when he reached the landing of the top floor and saw Hila's door, the usual cluster of hamsas hanging just below the apartment number and the dusty pink mezuzah fixed to the doorframe. When he put the bags down to get to the doorbell, one of them clanked ominously.

"Boazi?" called Hila through the door. Followed by her rapid Hebrew. "Those better not be my eggs you're breaking."

"Four cans of tomatoes, Doda Hila? Really?" called Boaz in Hebrew, wiping sweat from his forehead. The deadbolt clicked. "What do you need with four cans of tomatoes—"

The door swung open. At once he was met with the familiar waft of her very floral perfume.

"Pfft, your accent gets worse by the day. You sound like an American," she said, taking a couple of the bags over the threshold and pulling him into a quick hug. "What are we going to do with you?"

"What am I supposed to sound like, a Swede?" he said before stepping inside and taking the bags toward the kitchen.

Aunt Hila laughed. "Don't know where you got your sense of humor. There's nothing funny in our family."

"No, actually, I had something I wanted to ask you." The apartment was spacious for a one-bedroom but was nevertheless cramped, evidence of his aunt Hila's preference for maximalism. Her heavy furniture was all slightly too big for the space. She'd added things as Boaz had grown up, but nothing that went into the house ever left. On the floor was an ornate carpet in various shades of pink, and sprawled out on it was Hila's cat, Mishmish, who gave Boaz a withering scowl before racing past him and sprawling out along the couch cushions, as if trying to block Boaz from sitting. Boaz had been on Mishmish's bad side for years, and there would be severe consequences for him if he even entertained the thought that they were friends. He had several scars along his forearms to prove it.

Hila used to talk about getting a house in Gravesend, something large enough that Boaz and his mother could just move in with her. It *would* have made sense for all of them, would have solved all the late-night calls. His mother liked Hila. Even his mom's parents liked the idea, and they had only barely warmed to Hila because she helped his mom with rent and paid the astronomical tuition at Arbel Academy after his brief educational career at a local yeshiva ended when the resident restroom ghost decided to humiliate Boaz with the help of the school's delicate plumbing. Hila had been more of a parent than the missing father they couldn't bear to speak about. If their daughter refused to move back in with them, then with Hila was the next best thing.

But whenever they talked about it, it would set his mother off. She'd remember his father, would start talking about how he was still in the walls of the apartment, that they couldn't possibly leave him behind. And that usually ended the conversation.

Mishmish hissed at Boaz, and Boaz tried to carefully ignore him by pretending to be deeply invested in the posters along the wall from Aunt Hila's previous tours—*Hila Harari: Live in London*, *Hila Harari and the Ghosts of the West*, and her greatest pride, *Hila Harari: Undead at Radio City Music Hall*—from his vantage point on the couch. Hila's giant leather tote, her favorite purse, was sitting on the floor, just by the side table. Boaz made a point not to look at it, even when Aunt Hila barked out, "Well, what is it? What did you want to talk about?"

"Last night," said Boaz. "I've been thinking . . ." He trailed off as Aunt Hila disappeared around the corner into the kitchen.

Aunt Hila entered the living room minutes later carrying a teetering tray on which were balanced two small coffee cups and a bowl of dates. At the sight of it, Boaz shook his head. "Oh no, absolutely not."

"You drink your coffee like a good boy," she said, taking the patterned cup and saucer from the tray and physically putting it into Boaz's hands. "Come on, I made it the way you like it, too much sugar."

"I was just thinking," said Boaz, taking a small, reluctant sip. "I mean, I know what I saw in the mirror—"

"You shouldn't have seen anything," said Hila evenly, taking her perch on the sofa opposite. At once, Mishmish leapt up from his seat to join her, and to have a better vantage point from which to glare at Boaz. "Because you should have covered it properly, instead of leaving it like that—like a doggy door for the dead. If you want to start using the ring, you need to show me that you can follow instructions. You are lucky that that was all that happened."

Boaz huffed. "But wouldn't it be a good thing? To try something different? I mean, I saw him. Maybe that's the secret, maybe we've been doing it wrong. . . ."

He realized too late that it was the absolute wrong thing to say.

Hila's eyes narrowed. "Boazi, how old am I?"

"Um, this isn't a trick question, is it?"

She raised a threatening eyebrow at him. "How. Old. Am. I?"

"Well, you don't look a day over twenty-five—"

"Forty," she said. "You remember the party I threw, that lovely dinner we had over in Williamsburg. That was a big party, yes?"

It had been. Mostly with Hila's fancy friends, but his mother's parents had even gone, and she had even earned a grunt of approval from his grandfather, which was very high praise. "I hate parties. I do not like birthdays. But do you know why I threw it?"

"To show off to Mom's parents?" he suggested.

"Because no one in our family who sees the dead makes it to forty," she said. "*No one.* Not my father. Not his father, not his sister. Remember when I tried to do that family tree? Not a single one of us has since *at least* 1840, and I bet before that. The ones who carry the ring are lucky if they make it to thirty."

Boaz swallowed hard. He knew this, objectively. Hila had started the family tree after he made the mistake of asking her for help on a family history project for school. She'd forced him into a six-month-long joint research effort that far exceeded the scope of the two-page paper the homework assignment had called for. He'd sat there while she conducted seemingly endless depressing interviews with several different Harari ghosts through mirrors with the ring. It was the last time that Boaz had ever asked Hila for help with homework. The scattered Hararis still in Israel were Hararis by marriage, cousins, and embittered widows. He only remembered meeting his grandmother once before she died, on a trip he'd taken with his mom and Hila, and most of the visit involved Hila yelling at her mother about his father, his grandmother yelling at Hila, his mother crying, and Boaz dutifully drinking the tea he was offered and wishing he were just about anywhere else.

Now that he thought about it, he spent a lot of time dutifully drinking hot beverages he hadn't asked for. He took the tiniest possible sip. Maybe if he stretched the cup out long enough, Hila would forget. "I know."

"You know, you know, you know," she said, her voice rising. "You know why I've made it this long? Because I don't wear the ring whenever I feel like it. The ring isn't a smart phone. When I wear it, I see into Olam Ha-Ba. It is a dangerous thing to do. I don't use it to chase every whim and regret, no matter how much it hurts."

"But this isn't a whim, it's *Dad*," he said. He was so irritated he hadn't realized he'd made it to the bottom of his coffee cup; when he took another sip, he got a small mouthful of grounds.

"Hararis always die at the hands of their own ghosts," she said. "*Always*. Even when there is a body to bury." She finished her own cup of coffee and set it down before picking up a date. "That is the curse. They do not leave us alone. So we are going to be very careful, so that we both grow nice and old, yes?" Hila gave him a tight smile, before reaching out her hand. "Give me your cup."

He handed her the cup and focused on trying to rip the pit out of a new date. There was little use in arguing with Aunt Hila when it came to reading coffee grounds, or when it came to the ring. This wasn't the first time he'd heard some version of this, so he didn't say the thing he wanted to more than anything else: that sometimes it seemed like she didn't even want to find Dad, that she wasn't really trying.

Boaz didn't remember his dad, who had vanished when he was barely six months old. But he knew that if Hila had disappeared, or his mom, or any of the people he cared about, and he had a ring that would let him see and speak into the World to Come, he wouldn't stop until he had answers. And, sure, Hila had tried. But only in her own small ways. Nothing *real*. She wouldn't do anything that broke one of her own rules.

And maybe that was the problem. She wouldn't even consider that maybe, if they wanted to find his father, or to at least get an answer about where he had gone, they'd need to break some rules.

Hila swirled the grounds at the base of the cup before tipping it out onto her own saucer. She waited a beat and then turned it back over, and Boaz seized his chance, reaching for another date and swinging his hand just slightly too wide, to send Hila's cup flying.

"Boaz!" she yelped. He'd been a little too enthusiastic, sending most of the coffee dregs flying at her. "I just got these dry cleaned. . . ."

"Sorry, sorry," he mumbled. "Do you want . . ."

"No, no, you stay. . . ." she said, putting down his cup and heading to the bathroom to assess the damage. "You are worse than Mishmish, I swear. . . ."

Boaz knew he'd only have seconds. Just as the water began to run, he reached into Hila's bag. He had seen it so many times, the tiny velvet pouch, the pouch that only came out when she was going to do a reading, that he had seen her carefully stow away before leaving last night with a warning to him that he should get some sleep and not trust his eyes.

For a moment, he wondered whether she had locked it away, whether this had been another poorly thought through scheme, and that he'd have to figure out how to find and break into a safe in order to get ahold of the ring, when his fingers brushed a soft bit of fabric.

He snatched it, quickly shoving the surprisingly heavy pouch into his pocket and nudging her bag back into place just as she emerged from the bathroom. "Boaz, it would have been nice to have done something besides just sitting there. . . ."

"I know, I know, I'm sorry," he said quickly, grabbing paper towels from the kitchen and busying himself trying to blot the bits of coffee out of the carpet. The ring was a noticeable weight in his pocket, and he was convinced that Hila knew he had taken it, even as he looked up and saw that she wasn't looking at him at all, but instead at his coffee cup.

"Matok sheli, I don't like this," she said, squinting into the cup. She shook her head. "No, I don't like that at all."

Boaz stood up. If he was there much longer, Hila would absolutely figure it out, and then she'd take the ring back and he'd never, ever get to try it. Forget growing old together; she might even murder him. "I need to get going anyway. I promised Daniel we'd FaceTime tonight—"

"Oh, no, you're not," she said. "Not until we figure out why your grounds look like this."

Boaz was halfway to the door, and Mishmish was on his trail, hissing at him indignantly as he went. "I *need* to get going, Doda Hila, sorry."

He zipped up his hoodie, but before he made it to the door, she caught him by the shoulder. The back of his neck prickled. He didn't like the look she gave him. She said she always worried about him, but this was more than worry; it was alarm. "Whatever you're doing, I suggest you stop."

"What? I'm not doing anything," said Boaz, shrugging away from her. "I swear, it's all business as usual."

But this clearly didn't satisfy Aunt Hila, who put her hand on the doorknob to keep him from leaving. "Promise me that whatever it is, you'll stop it," she said.

Boaz glanced at his watch, ignoring the heavy feeling in his pocket, so heavy he felt like he might tip sideways. "Fine. I'll be careful."

"You'll *stop*."

"I'll stop it," he said, without an ounce of conviction. "I promise."

7

CLARA

Clara didn't think it was possible to be this hungry. She had already devoured the slightly stale loaf Molly had left in the kitchenette on the top floor of the cinema, their apartments, with a fistful of salt. She had rummaged through their cabinets of perfunctory china, all the dainty, decorative plates Molly had hoarded over the years but that they scarcely used, combing through the cabinets for any more bread, even though she knew it was of little use. It did nothing but whet her appetite, setting her senses roaring, her thoughts consumed with the need for something that could satisfy her.

Clara knew she shouldn't have gone this long. She could go three days, *maybe* four without drinking from a man. Clara had never known anything other than hunger in her first life, so she figured she could tolerate it perfectly well in this one. She knew how to manage her limits, knew how to make her cravings productive, and how to ration her opportunities so as not to draw suspicion. . . .

Boaz.

It had been all his fault. If he had shown up when he was

supposed to the other night, then she would have had time to find a proper meal. Instead, she had let herself get past the point of reasonable. Between that and the afternoon she'd wasted paying rent to Ashmodai, there had been no time to hunt, and now she was deeply regretting not draining Boaz dry when she had the chance.

Clara let out a long sigh and made her way to the door, grabbing her notebook off the table so she'd have something to do with her hands. The sun was just beginning to set, and night made for easy hunting. With a bit of luck, she wouldn't even need to leave the theater.

Clara made her way back down to the lobby, trying to avoid breathing. With the lobby buzzing with people, the tables and the few strategically placed sofas all occupied, the smells were enough to send her head spinning. She wouldn't be able to cling to her composure for very long.

Ordinarily, she preferred hunting outside the theater, perhaps finding an evening minyan she could join or a wedding to crash. She was always on the lookout for free events, lectures, and screenings at synagogues and community centers and any Jewish-adjacent museum, which provided the best opportunities to painlessly accost a fellow Jew who could spare her a few moments of time—and his neck. She had it down to a science, and it was the main reason she and Molly had lived for as long as they had in one city.

But that took strategy and planning, and right now she was far past the point for any of that.

She strode over to the box office counter, cursing when she remembered Boaz was still on shift. *He* was the problem, the distraction that had driven her to this. Maybe, she thought, as she drew closer, she should just make things cleaner and send him home early, tell him he could have the night off.

Yes, she would send him home, take over the box office, and then find a more suitable dinner.

"Hey there. . . ." The moment Clara spoke, she realized how strange and stiff her voice sounded. She tried to loosen her shoulders and unclench her jaw, and even forced a smile. She had no idea whether it made her look relaxed or even more murderous. "How is it going? Not too busy, I hope."

Boaz turned briefly from the register to look her way, and he looked distinctly . . . charmed.

Shit.

Clara recognized all the signs. His eyes were just a touch unfocused. He was struggling to suppress a smile, and there was a very light flush creeping up his neck.

But she could not bite Boaz *now*.

At least, not in the box office.

"Well, we're nearly sold out on the Monthly Miyazaki screening," he said. "Turns out people love an excuse to watch *Spirited Away* in costume? Just a heads-up, like, there are at least five No-Faces in there, and one of them is pretty terrifying. And that French surrealist romance is doing well—I think because the *Times* gave it a glowing review yesterday. Still not convinced it makes any sense, though, between you and me, but the people like what they like."

"So not that busy?" said Clara, sliding ever so slightly closer to Boaz. Did he really find this charming? This wasn't supposed to be charming.

"I mean, probably the busiest night we've had all week, but sure?" Boaz handed the receipt to the customer and turned back to her, his gaze still lingering on her ever so slightly too long. Was

68

he being weirder than usual? It sure seemed like it. His hand kept drifting toward his pocket, like he was checking to make sure something was still there, and he kept shifting uncomfortably in his seat.

She had thought about biting him. Of course she had thought of it. He was there, and convenient, and remarkably lacking in common sense for someone who had lived all his eighteen years in New York City. She knew that she could have probably had him whenever she wanted, that he'd forget before her lips left his neck, just like all the rest.

But that wasn't how she did things. She didn't like to talk to her meals beyond what it took to get them alone. She didn't want to have to *see them* every day, even if she knew they wouldn't remember. Still . . .

"Fine. Well, if it's so busy, I'll just . . . join you here." She sat on the stool beside him, turning on the cash register and pounding her pin number into the screen, trying not to look too irritated. Maybe this was a better plan. She didn't need to send him home. She could find a suitable meal, and Boaz could keep selling tickets, because she wasn't going to bite him. She wasn't.

"Are you okay?"

"Fine!" she said loudly. "Fine, totally fine!"

"Are you sure?" Another couple came up to the window, and judging by the baffling all-white face makeup one of them was wearing, they were probably there for the *Spirited Away* screening. Boaz turned away from her and started the sale. "You're looking, er . . . um, paler than normal."

"Excuse me?" Why did he have to be so devoted to his work all of a sudden? She needed him to leave so that she could take over the ticketing and find herself a suitable meal, which, if he didn't leave soon, would absolutely end up being Boaz. The whole box office was thick with his scent, and his neck was just *there*, close enough to touch.

"Sorry, sorry. You look great, actually. Fantastic, really. Um . . ."

He spun a bit in the chair, his knee just brushing hers. It was just a second, and he shot her an awkward smile, before turning back to the small line that had developed on the sidewalk beyond the box office window. The touch was enough to make her stomach ache, and her fists tightened as she tried to think of something else that wasn't what her mouth on his neck might feel like.

She chanced a breath to relax and immediately regretted it. The box office was tight, barely a few square feet, and with both of them tucked into it, there was nowhere for her to go without moving closer to him. She shifted a bit, their knees knocking again. When he glanced over curiously, his eyes wide and neck stretched toward her, she had to physically bite down on her lip, so hard it hurt. She wasn't sure how much longer she'd be able to go before she'd snap and do something reckless.

Thankfully, she did not need to wait long.

Her rescue came in the form of light brown curls and a pug nose and friendly blue eyes. All fine enough, but the details made little difference to her. It wasn't his looks that made him her much-needed dinner; it was his T-shirt, a classic from the Columbia University Hillel with the university's name spelled out phonetically in Hebrew. It was like someone had delivered her a gift wrapped up neatly with a bow.

Clara braced herself and forced a smile. She would still need to charm him, which was hard enough without the thick glass between them. "Hi! How can I help you?"

"Oh, just one for that French one," he said, already sliding his credit card under the gap in the glass. "Sorry, I can't pronounce the name, but did you see the *Times* review of it? It sounds totally wild."

Boaz leaned over. "If you like wild, you're going to *love it*," he said, without missing a beat, making Columbia Hillel Boy chuckle, and it took all of Clara's efforts not to snap. How was *Boaz* better at flirting with her dinner than she was?

"*I* liked it," muttered Clara, louder than she intended.

"Clara loves wild. I think that's why she hired me," he said, flashing a grin.

Of course. Of course he was better at this than she was. Because Boaz's sole reason for existence was to annoy her to the point of violence.

Focus, now. If she got too mad, she'd lose her chance. Even puppy-faced boys could sense when they ought to keep their distance from her . . . except when it came to Boaz.

Clara turned her back to Boaz and attempted an eye flutter and a slightly too late laugh. She thought it got the boy's attention, but he could just have been studying the showtimes displayed behind her. It was so easy for Molly, who could have charmed anyone without even having to try. Molly's meals were known, on occasion, to propose marriage to her in the brief interval between when she set eyes on them and when she took a first bite. Usually, Clara's charmed men were befuddled more than anything else, and only with effort. Except for Boaz, apparently, though he was probably just permanently befuddled.

Clara pretended to swipe the credit card, to give herself some time. She needed him hooked, needed his eyes to unfocus and for him to accept everything she said as truth. And that would only happen if he met her gaze for long enough, and with just enough interest. "So what brings you all the way down from Morningside Heights?" she tried, making a show of manually entering the card number into the register.

"The . . . movie?" he said. "You guys are the only theater in the city screening it."

"Oh, right." She laughed again, forcing it to sound light and airy. She hated the way it sounded on her, like she was all bubbles where her brain ought to be. But boys seemed to like it; the thought that she didn't have much going on up there put them at ease. "Of course . . ."

She pretended to wait for the transaction to go through. Boaz, at least, was busy trying to tell a bunch of middle schoolers off for attempting to see an R-rated movie without their parents. She stared up at the boy, forcing herself to make eye contact, to hold it even though a part of her was cringing deeply with embarrassment. . . .

And *there* it was. His blue eyes glazed, his focus shifted. It was a subtle change across his face, but she'd seen enough of those to know it meant she had his attention, and her dinner. "Ah, well. I'm glad you made it down here," she said, at last sliding back the credit card. He barely seemed to register that it was there, and she saw how clumsy his hands looked as he belatedly reached for it, while not letting his gaze leave Clara's. "It's theater four, on the left," she said, staring meaningfully at Columbia Hillel as she slid him his ticket. "Do you need help finding it?"

Columbia Hillel nodded a bit unsteadily.

"Yeah," he said, and cleared his throat. "Uh, yeah, where is theater four?"

Boaz turned, his brows knit together. But he only opened and closed his mouth as Clara slid down from the stool, trying not to appear too eager. She forced herself not to so much as glance at Boaz as she swept past him.

"It's right down here," Clara said when the boy approached her, turning down the hallway leading toward the bathrooms first, stopping only when she reached the very end of the dimly lit hallway, right by the supply closet that she and Molly both preferred for dining in.

"Down here?" He ambled toward her, still wearing the glazed expression she'd left him with at the box office. *Excellent, dinner.*

Columbia Hillel had at least six inches on her, and something about the lumbering way he moved almost made her regret choosing him. Boys like this reminded her of the man who had once been her betrothed, the man who had driven her straight into the arms of Devorah. Though she did suppose that it should have made things easier. Drinking that monster dry had been the first meal of her second life, and to this day, it was the best.

She allowed him to approach her and got down to business. He was too tall, even when she dutifully let him lean down to kiss her once, returning the favor as she began removing the bobby pins one by one from her hair. This one, though, was a little too eager, and even as she pulled back to better brace herself against the wall, he leaned forward, trying to push himself against her.

"Whoa, there," she said as he stopped only a couple of inches from her face. He was eager enough to listen, eager to do whatever she said, and still it was too much. "There's no need for all of that, now."

She reached for another bobby pin, but he caught one of her hands, and again she had to push him back, even as he moaned, "Let me, please? Let me——"

"Stop that!" Clara sighed, annoyed. She'd have to take things into the closet now, the moment she got her hair down and her teeth out, it would be easy enough——

"Hey, asshole!"

Clara recognized the voice a second before the punch was thrown.

Boaz.

In an instant, everything came apart, all of the work she'd put in for the meal undone. Boaz's punch landed on Columbia Hillel's shoulder, not enough to do much except startle him. He didn't move, though, strong as Clara's pull on him was, so Boaz practically threw himself at the boy to shove him aside.

"Boaz, it's——"

But her attempt to call off Boaz was lost as he shouted at Columbia Hillel, "What do you think you're doing? She said to stop."

The push was enough to momentarily break the charm. Clara watched as Columbia Hillel shook his head, dazed by the interruption. She was so *hungry*, and she needed him to come back and give her his neck and needed Boaz to go away.

Columbia Hillel, stuck between the lingering pull toward Clara and Boaz, who was still shouting at him and threatening to call the police, decided that the only logical course of action was to return fire and launch himself at Boaz, knocking him to the ground.

"Enough! Both of you!" Clara shouted, trying to pull Boaz off the floor and away from her dinner, stopping Columbia Hillel's fist before he landed a proper punch. She locked eyes once again and watched the pug-nosed boy's expression glaze once more. "*Go.*"

Whatever lingering influence she had on him was enough. He scrambled to his feet, eyeing the both of them with a mix of confusion and alarm before hurrying away.

"Damn it, Clara, you should have let me finish him off," said Boaz, his voice slightly hoarse. "I knew there was something weird about that guy. I didn't like the way he was looking at you at all. . . ."

But Clara didn't hear half of what Boaz was saying. She was still holding on to him, and they were both on the floor, and all she noticed was the fact that in the tussle, Boaz's lip had split open and was now bleeding. Not a lot, but enough for her to at last abandon all reason, and logic, and good sense. . . .

She pulled him closer and pressed her lips to his.

The taste of his blood mixed into the kiss, igniting her and burning down her self-control. Her senses all electrified, the hungriest parts of her roaring with satisfaction. It would have been better, cleaner, if she'd finished letting down her hair so she could get a proper bite. Her hand drifted back to her hair and then changed course, landing in his curls instead.

Strangest of all, he was kissing her back, his lips soft against hers, for a split second even pulling himself closer.

That shift of his own body nearer to her, that he came even though she hadn't even charmed him, that he was kissing *her*, the real her, of his own volition—that was enough to break the spell.

She pulled back, jumping to her feet. It was as though someone had doused her in ice water. "Um, thank you . . . for that."

And before he could say anything, before he could notice that she had licked her lips in spite of herself, hoping for one last taste of him, she bolted.

8

MOLLY

Molly had the afternoon off, which was ideal.

Her sister had gone past the point of hangry, and she didn't need to be there when at last Clara lost it. It served her right. Clara always criticized *her* for not waiting until she was murderous before finding a neck. And while Molly knew it was jealousy more than anything else, that Clara wished she had as easy a time drawing men as she did, it was still annoying. It wasn't her fault that she was good at taking care of herself and her hungers.

She and Anat had spent a lovely afternoon on something of a bread crawl. Anat had found at least four different bakeries stretching all the way down to the Lower East Side that they had yet to try, a couple of Chinese bakeries with delicate steamed buns and milk bread, a new Jewish bakery that specialized in pletzels, giant bread wheels that frankly made Molly *almost* as weak in the knees as Anat did, and the wild card, a punk-themed bakery on St. Marks, Punk-pernickle, where every roll, cookie, and loaf shared a name with a noted band in the genre. And though she had her doubts, Molly had to admit that the Ramones Marbled Rye was frankly one of the best she'd ever had.

Anat had been talking about this outing for over a week, but today she spoke little. She stayed close to Molly, walking arm in arm with her the way she ordinarily liked for at least half the bread crawl, leaning on her when they scanned menus or stopped to eat, but something was off. Molly had chalked it up to maybe a rough night before or a long rehearsal for school, but that didn't explain how confused she'd been in the Chinese bakery, why she kept asking what exactly milk bread *was* when *she* was the one who had introduced Molly to it in the first place. Nor did it explain why she suddenly didn't get *any* of the puns in Punkpernickle. Sure, they were mostly about bands from before her time, from a time when St. Marks was actually punk, but *not a single one* . . .

Now, as they tottered back to the Grand Dame under the weight of several heavy bags of loaves and pletzels, an unusual silence fell. Ordinarily, Anat was all chatter, and the rare silences that fell between them were normally not this . . . odd.

The light always had a way of making Molly's brain sluggish. She blamed it on her condition, though in truth she was pretty sure the day had had that effect on her even before her first death. She had always preferred stage lights to the real thing.

They had reached the scaffolding by the Chase Bank, a few blocks down, when Anat stared down at the pavement.

Molly had shown her this on one of their earliest proper dates. Anat might have never noticed them if she hadn't. Most people didn't. The stars in front of the Chase Bank were the last remnants of the Yiddish Walk of Fame, a project by the long gone Second Avenue Deli in an optimistic effort to memorialize the decades when the most exciting work being done on any American stage was happening not up on Forty-Second Street, but *here*. She had been right in the center of the storm. She could have been the lightning.

A moment that had passed, like all storms eventually do. And she was still here. "There you are!" said Anat, pointing down at Molly's name, her stage name, not far from the door of the bank. *Molly Lewis*. Molly had come up with it not long after she started auditioning. It had seemed a logical choice at the time. Minka Levinsky was a girl who worked in a sweatshop to help her ailing mother make their meager rent. Minka Levinsky was a poor girl with a habit of attracting gossip. Minka Levinsky would never have a future beyond the Yiddish stage, two different directors had told her as much. But Molly Lewis could be someone, anyone . . .

Or no one.

Because now all that remained of Molly Lewis was this star, so worn down from foot traffic it was difficult to read even in broad daylight. Molly let that name die with her. She had become a Sender the moment Devorah turned her, and she'd never looked back.

"Remember when we met her?" Anat asked suddenly, pointing to one of the stars on the pavement. Molly looked down, confused. The name was worn to almost nothing, but she knew the layout of the stars well enough to know whose it was. "Bessie Thomashefsky?"

"You took me, remember?" Anat murmured, almost dreamily. "That was the best night."

"Um . . . no," said Molly. "Bessie Thomashefsky died in 1962. What are you talking about?" Molly racked her brain. They'd gone to an event last month, a presentation from Folksbiene at the Museum of Jewish Heritage. Was that what she was talking about? Or maybe a documentary. Molly herself had seen Bessie live, met her on a number of occasions before her first death, but Anat . . .

"Then you took me to that restaurant in Chinatown. I'd never been somewhere so fancy," she said. "Oh, vos iz geven der nomen . . ." *Oh, what was the name . . .*

"Anat!" shouted Molly. She didn't like this at all. A chill ran down her spine that had nothing to do with the November weather. "Is this some kind of bit?" Molly's voice shook. She didn't want to look unnerved, but Anat had gone too far. Fine, she wanted to learn enough Yiddish to surprise Molly at karaoke. But that didn't explain how she could know about that date.

Anat looked up suddenly, her brow furrowed. "What?"

"You tell me!" said Molly. "Why do you even know about that night?"

"What night?" she asked. She rubbed a temple, wincing. "Wow, I just got hit with the worst migraine."

But a migraine didn't explain how Anat could possibly know anything about the last date she'd gone on with a beating heart. Because Molly remembered vividly the night she had seen Bessie Thomashefsky at the Grand, and then followed it with a memorable dinner at Mon Lay Won, the fanciest restaurant she could afford in Chinatown. The opening night for *Di Shturem* had been a week away, and she'd made a point to go all out, knowing she'd be too busy the next few weeks for a proper date as they prepared. She'd never forget that night, because it had been perfect. And because it was the last proper date she'd ever had with Lena. "What, did you find that online?"

"Find what?" Anat asked. "I swear, I don't know what you're talking about, and my head is pounding."

"This isn't something for, like, a method acting class, is it?"

"Ew, no." Anat laughed uneasily. "Why would I take method acting? I'm not *that* insufferable." Anat looked down at her phone. "Shit, shit, shit . . . Where has all the time gone? I was supposed to be at rehearsal half an hour ago. Why didn't you say something to me?"

"How am I supposed to know your schedule if you don't—"

Anat pulled her into a tight hug and kissed her lightly, and the only thing Molly noticed was how cold she was to the touch. She tried to write it off to the freezing, sharp wind that had followed them all through the Village, but Molly couldn't shake the worry as she watched Anat dart off that something was very, *very* wrong with her girlfriend.

9

BOAZ

Boaz didn't know how long it would take Hila to notice the ring was missing. She wasn't due to film a new season until January, though. And she said it herself: she didn't use the ring unless she had a reason. She wouldn't have put it on the other night if Boaz hadn't asked.

Still, he couldn't stop checking his phone, dreading the moment she'd notice. The only greater distraction than the fear of Hila finding out was the ring itself. He swore he could hear the ring buzzing in his ears, that it seemed to add another ten pounds to his pocket and weighed just as much when he slipped it on a chain and tried wearing it around his neck, even though it wasn't that big.

He couldn't work up the nerve to try it on in the night and instead spent the whole evening staring at it, turning it over in his palm. He'd gotten as far as digging out an extra Shabbat candle and lighting it, but at the last minute lost his nerve.

He had seen Hila do it plenty, knew all the steps for her preferred readings, but beyond that, the ring was a giant unknown. Hila had never even let him touch the thing, convinced that even with it just sitting in his palm, he'd somehow manage to unleash an army of the undead on Manhattan or something. His aunt could call the long-lost relatives of anyone with enough money to pay, or with enough television-worthy tragedy to earn an appearance on her show.

But he never saw the mirror, never saw what she was seeing, this glimpse into Olam Ha-Ba that was supposed to be so dangerous. Hila always warned him not to look, told him she'd make him regret it if he did. A film crew or an audience would see only Hila, talking with her reflection. He had tried, on a few occasions, only for Hila to shut the whole thing down before he caught a glimpse of anything at all.

So he didn't sleep, which meant he felt as dead as the group of old ghosts on his early subway ride into Manhattan, and it also meant he arrived in the Village two hours before his Sunday morning shift. Which was just as well. At least Clara couldn't complain about him being late.

For most of his life, Boaz had been looking. Since he first learned what he could do, that the people he sometimes saw at school, on the street, on the subway, weren't visible to anyone else. After spending a whole week in third grade having to listen to the dads of other kids come in and talk about being professors and real estate brokers and lawyers, he looked harder than he ever had. What was the point of being able to talk to the dead if he couldn't *find* the one person he was interested in talking to?

When Boaz arrived in the East Village, there was nothing open except bagel shops, bodegas, and grocery stores. The supers were still spraying down the pavement, and the ground was littered with the mush of damp fallen leaves and the last bits of refuse from the previous night. Boaz clutched his cup of coffee, swallowing a yawn. He couldn't go to the theater. The Grand Dame wasn't even open yet, and though there was a chance that Clara might let him in if she knew he was already there, then what? They'd talk about whatever *that* was yesterday, which sounded about as bad as telling Hila he'd taken the ring. His stomach jumped even at the idea. In fact, he was much more prepared to court ghosts.

When he'd met Clara, Boaz was struck first by how pretty she was. No, more than pretty. Unusual. She had these wide eyes that he swore could see straight through someone, and they lit up when she laughed. She was shorter than him, and slight, but gave off the distinct impression that she could face down a train and win.

He had not meant to give up the anecdote about his obsession with *The Mummy* in his interview. He was not in the habit of admitting to strangers that he'd dressed as every single character from that movie for Purim (including Evelyn Carnahan, on a dare). But once he started talking, he couldn't stop. And it had been worth making a bit of a fool out of himself just to see her laugh.

Plus, she was brilliant. She knew everything about classic cinema. He'd never met anyone who could claim to have seen more of Boris Karloff's filmography than he had. She even claimed to have seen his debut, *The Lightning Raider*, the full 1919 version, the one that was supposed to be lost. She said she had a copy. He'd only stopped trying to press her for details about it when she'd told him that he looked a bit like a young Boris Karloff, which was either a very flattering compliment or a dig at his eyebrows.

Of course, they would never happen. His mother and grandparents might forgive the fact that she wasn't Syrian on a good day, but frankly it wouldn't matter what they thought, because he and

Clara were never going to get there. Kiss aside, he still wasn't convinced she even *liked* him. Any goodwill he'd earned from her from his interview had long since evaporated, and she was way, *way* out of his league. She managed the best independent theater in the East Village, one of the best in Manhattan, even though she was only . . . eighteen? Nineteen? Boaz worked part-time in the box office while assuring Hila he did in fact have a plan for the future (he did not), and in his off hours, he watched old movies and tried, unsuccessfully, to tune out the dead.

After about three laps around the block, he gave up and grabbed a bench at St. Mark's Church in-the-Bowery. Apart from a couple of enterprising pigeons picking at the discarded half of a shawarma, it was quiet, just far enough from the theater that there was no chance Clara would see him lurking outside like someone with something to hide. Or someone so afraid of being late again that he arrived ridiculously early.

Boaz scrolled through his WhatsApp. There was a new message from Aunt Hila, another highly detailed grocery list. So she still hadn't noticed the ring was missing. A few texts from Daniel, some not-so-subtle attempts to get him to spend next Shabbat with him in Washington Heights, an effort to convince Boaz that he, too, would find joy and purpose and opportunity in the fishbowl of Yeshiva University, surrounded by a not insignificant number of his high school classmates.

He pulled the ring out from beneath his shirt. By the light of day, it was somewhat less intimidating. Maybe even a little lighter. Or maybe it was just him. And there were no mirrors here, or candles. It couldn't hurt, he decided, to put it on for a moment, to see the way it felt on his hand.

Boaz took a deep breath and slid it onto his ring finger. He was half expecting it to be too small, because he knew it fit Hila perfectly. But he slipped it on without trouble, though it was no less heavy than it had been around his neck.

He held his hands up to the light, wondering whether he was supposed to be feeling anything. Nothing seemed that different, though maybe he needed the mirror and candle.

"You gonna eat that?"

Boaz looked up. Sitting next to him on the bench was a young man bundled up in a coat more appropriate for an Arctic expedition than a mild November morning in New York City. That he had appeared so suddenly, so quietly, was enough for Boaz to suspect that he was dead, a fact confirmed when the man flickered in and out of sight, vanishing when Boaz turned his head one way, only to reappear a moment later.

The sudden appearance of a dead man beside him when he was just trying to mind his own business and kill time should have freaked him out. It was the sort of unwelcome interruption that had driven other Hararis to drink. But other Hararis had not been born and raised in a city as vast as this. The dead could surprise him. "Go for it, man," he muttered. He didn't even get off the bench.

The man looked down at the moldering half shawarma. "You sure?"

"Mm-hmm," said Boaz, still examining the ring, even holding his hands out and attempting the splayed fingers. He was only half listening. "All yours."

"You sure?"

The man clearly wasn't going to be able to eat the shawarma, and Boaz promising it to him wasn't going to get him to disappear.

He knew he should get up and go. "*Yes*," said Boaz impatiently.

"Really?"

"No, I was lying," said Boaz. He'd meant it sarcastically. He was tired, and the coffee had not done enough to drive away his headache, and what he really wanted was for this ghost to leave him alone and let him figure out the ring.

He realized his mistake at once. Most ghosts didn't do sarcasm.

The dead who lingered were always hungry. They wanted *something*, whether it was a word with their beloved, a missing limb, or a shawarma. No desire was inconsequential to the dead.

The ring on his finger began to burn cold. The man's formerly calm, curious face twisted. Boaz jumped up from the bench as the man doubled in height. The ghost's pale face turned bright red with rage, and the whites of his eyes disappeared, instead going entirely black.

"What did you say?" he bellowed. "What did you say?"

Boaz glanced around. The early morning joggers and the half-asleep students clutching bags of bagels to their chests didn't so much as give him or the towering, enraged ghost slowly making his way to Boaz a passing glance.

"Sorry, I didn't mean—"

"What did you do that for?"

Boaz turned. A woman in a suit with shoulder pads like a line-backer's, a young man in a line cook's apron, and a man in a fedora and long trench coat were racing toward him. All were flickering in and out of his vision, there and not there and there again. In seconds, he was surrounded by other souls none too happy with him. They shouted at him, demanding to know why he had been so cruel as to deny a discarded shawarma to a dead man.

He was ridiculously outnumbered, and if he tried to run, he risked possession. It had never happened to him before, but he'd heard stories. If a ghost wanted it bad enough, or they were angry enough, they might just try it.

And there were about fifteen ghosts around him who looked particularly eager to try.

There was nothing to do but try and deescalate, and fast. "You can have the shawarma!" he shouted over the ghostly din. "I'm sorry! You can have it! It's right there. I promise you it's all yours!"

He turned and saw, past the wall of ghosts, a police officer standing a few feet from him, arms folded with a familiar expression. The look of someone who, upon looking at him, saw nothing but a skinny, distressed Middle Eastern guy shouting at the air.

"Is everything all right here?" he said, his voice sharp.

"Oh, me?" said Boaz quickly. "Was just . . . practicing a monologue for a class. I'm fine."

Boaz grasped for the ring, trying to take it off as it grew colder and colder still. Surely it would burn off one of his fingers. He slid it off, unsure of what he was supposed to do with it. The hungry ghost froze.

"It was a mistake!" said Boaz quickly, making an effort to give a bit of theater kid, which made him sound a complete fool, but was enough to get the officer to at last turn away from him and continue down the block. "Of course you can have it. I would never . . . and I really got to get going to the theater. Seriously. So enjoy!"

For a moment, the ghost just stared at him. Then he crouched down and picked up the shawarma. Then it was Boaz's turn to freeze.

Because *that* never happened.

Ghost shawarma wasn't a thing. Food, inanimate objects? Strictly of this world. The only thing of this world a ghost could interact with was *him*, or perhaps a vulnerable body they might manage to possess. But that wasn't what had happened. It *definitely* wasn't what had happened, because a moment later, after taking one satisfied bite of the shawarma, the ghost settled back on the bench and then vanished entirely.

When Boaz turned back around, he found the other ghosts had all fallen silent and were staring at him. "Now you all can go, too, unless you have something to say."

None of them moved.

"I said, *go*," said Boaz irritably, glancing at the time on his phone. He slid the ring back on, now that it didn't burn cold, if only because he didn't know what to do with it otherwise, and remembering the way the shawarma ghost had looked at it, figured they might actually listen if he wore it. "Go!" he said again.

At last, the ghosts seemed to understand, and they all dispersed.

All but one, the man with the fedora, who beckoned Boaz over.

"Arbet ir in teater?" he said once, and then again when Boaz stared at him blankly. Boaz could speak Hebrew without a problem, a smidge of Arabic, and his high school French. Whatever this ghost spoke, it was none of these things.

"I'm sorry, I don't understand."

"Nu?" The man gestured wildly, and Boaz had a hunch on the language.

"Oh, are you speaking Yiddish? Sorry, not really my thing. . . ."

The man let out a long, disappointed sigh and continued. "Di meydlekh in teater zeynen shlekht."

"Again, really not following."

"Shlekht, zeynen shlekht!" The man repeated himself again and again to an uncomprehending Boaz.

"I need to go, sir. Sorry," he said, glancing at his watch. He couldn't linger here much longer unless he wanted to risk being late *again*. And something about this ghost made him uneasy. Boaz turned away and practically ran toward the Grand Dame. When he'd put a full block between himself and the police officer, he quickly pulled up Google Translate, and after a few tries, keyed in the best approximation of what he'd heard the man say.

Di meydlekh in teater zeynen shlekht.

The girls in the theater are evil.

10

CLARA

Boaz had gotten here an hour early. She had watched him from the window, circling the neighborhood and clearly trying to avoid coming by, but also clearly enough afraid of her to show up in the Village obscenely early.

That meant one of two things. Either he was being his usual, ridiculous self. Or he hadn't forgotten yesterday's kiss.

Shit.

She should have let down her hair. *Then* he would have forgotten. The whole incident would have slipped from his mind like water. Men never remembered her teeth, her real face, the monster that emerged when she let down her hair. Over time, they forgot her face entirely, the details becoming so fuzzy that the fact that she had stayed in place, that she had not aged, did not register to the people who came and went from the theater.

But there had been no teeth. Her hair had stayed up. She had just kissed him, a foolish thing that he might in time forget, but not half as fast as she would have liked.

Clara had certainly wished the whole thing would slip from *her* mind. She wasn't sure how she was supposed to face him now. The very thought of it made her hot with embarrassment all over again. She still couldn't say what exactly had possessed her, how she had let herself get so hungry. The moment Boaz had left the theater, she'd tracked down Columbia Hillel over in Union Square to finally get a proper bite; the whole thing had been a mess.

It wouldn't happen again. It couldn't.

She made her way downstairs fifteen minutes before opening to unlock the doors of the lobby. Something was splattered across the glass doors—letters, from the look of it. She fumbled anxiously for her keys, forcing the door open roughly and stepping out into the early morning glare to get a better look.

די גראַנד דאַמע מוזן ברענען

The Grand Dame must burn.

The words were painted across the glass doors in gleaming red. They'd been inked with a careful, expert hand. She stared at the letters, unable to understand why someone would do that, why they would threaten them in perfect Yiddish.

"Good . . . morning." Boaz, though still early, was somehow still panting like he'd run there. Why was that boy always running? He kept glancing behind him, so that even Clara craned her neck to see what he'd been running from. Nothing. "What . . . happened? What does that even . . ."

"Di Grand Dame muzn brenen," muttered Clara. "The Grand Dame must burn."

Boaz stared at the graffiti, his brow furrowed and his jaw tight. He shook his head. "Well, that's dark. Do you have, I don't know, Yiddish-speaking enemies? Did you beef with a klezmer band?

Or some really angry Hasidim?" Clara glared at Boaz. "Sorry. I shouldn't joke about this. Do you have security cameras? Maybe that will give you an idea. . . ."

"They aren't working." More specifically, they had never worked. Clara did not need video evidence of her and her sister's comings and goings and transformations saved anywhere. Besides, they were up all night anyway and lived over the theater. She always figured that if there was any kind of trouble, any kind of break-in, either she or Molly would catch it. How had they missed this?

"And why would they write it in Yiddish?" Clara wondered aloud. "It can't be an antisemitic thing. Antisemites don't usually go through the trouble of translating out a threat. . . ."

"Well, that's what Google Translate is for."

"What?"

"Google Translate?" said Boaz. "You know, when you put one language into Google, and they . . . Don't tell me you've never used Google Translate."

"Why would I need to?" she said irritably. "I already speak six languages."

"There's more than six . . . You know what?" Boaz shook his head. "Doesn't matter. But you should figure out who is either so fluent in Yiddish that they could threaten you in it or who is technologically competent enough to do a Google search."

And knows enough to know that the Yiddish would mean something to us.

Clara folded her arms. It had been years since they had a problem with this. Mostly because few recognized the theater anymore for what it used to be. There were always the awful emails that came with any announcement of their Jewish Film Festival, but those were easy to ignore, especially once she figured out how to train her email filters. But Molly and she took great care not to make themselves the story, to leave as little trace behind as possible.

"Hey, I can take care of it. I'm sure that you have better things to do than clean up this shit." He stepped closer, their arms brushing.

Clara flinched away. "You don't mind?" Clara needed air, desperately. She needed to clear her head. Because even if Boaz couldn't see it, she certainly understood the threat, and everything that it meant. Someone was after them who knew they spoke Yiddish, who *knew* their secret. If it weren't the start of the shift and a bright, cloudless day, she'd have gone for a fly. Even as she briefly abandoned Boaz to gallantly scrub at the graffiti, her mind came up blank. Molly and she did not make enemies. Even Devorah . . . Well, she hadn't made enemies either. Had she? Not the sort who would have known her fate, surely. Not ones who would have gone so long before trying to come for them.

When Boaz had gotten the words down to little more than a few stubborn, pinkish streaks, Clara emerged from the theater and told him to stop. "It looks great, Boaz. I'll get the window guys to take care of the rest."

Boaz met her gaze, still clutching the sponge. Clara tried not to watch the little river of suds, now stained pink, run down his wrists. She'd never thought of biting anyone *there*, but it was suddenly *very* tempting. She could see his little pulse and everything. "Listen," he began, after a moment. "About last night . . ."

No. They were not going to talk about it. Clara would actually probably die a second time from pure embarrassment if she spoke of it, and her Estrie powers wouldn't even be enough to save her.

But she was rescued from the discussion by Molly, who finally decided to grace them with her presence. Her hair was piled on top of her head in her usual messy bun, and she carried a full-size baguette tucked under her arm. She tore off a large chunk. "What, is there a party going on here? Why wasn't I invited?"

"Did you hear anything weird last night?" asked Clara, turning suddenly toward her sister. "Or see anything? Seeing as you got back so late?"

She shook her head and took another bite of baguette. "See what?"

"Someone graffitiing the door in Yiddish," said Clara, before explaining to Molly what they had found. "You wouldn't know anyone who would do something like that? Or someone who knows . . ." She didn't want to say it aloud, not in front of Boaz. But when Molly didn't seem to follow, she simply switched to Yiddish. "About us? About what happened? Why would they mention fire if not . . ."

Molly bit her lip before at last saying, "Anat knows. But she would never do something like that. Let me talk to her. Maybe she can tell me."

Molly turned to leave, but before she could, Clara caught her by the arm. "First, you're going to tell me all about this *Anat*."

MOLLY

"She's none of your business."

They'd gotten as far as Clara's office before Molly said anything. This argument was inevitable. She'd known it the moment she had first put Anat's number in her phone, the first time she called it. And yet, standing opposite her sister, she could think of nothing to say that would stop her sister from exploding.

"So you do have a girlfriend, then?" said Clara. Her sister's hair was still up in its usual prissy bun, but Molly could see the monster, just beneath that thin mask of humanity they both wore.

"Did you forget our rules? Or need I remind you—"

"*Your* rules," said Molly, her voice rising. *The rules, the rules.* She'd had it with the rules. If she heard another word about them, she might actually lose it. "They're *your rules*, so by all means, go ahead and make *yourself* miserable with them."

"You can't keep seeing her. I won't allow it," said Clara, folding her arms. "And they're not mine. They were Devorah's—"

"And you're not Devorah," said Molly. "And you're nothing

like her, so stop pretending and *leave me alone*."

"Excuse me?" Clara's voice rose, and Molly knew this was going to be bad. The last time they'd shouted at each other, it was over Molly's failed attempts to catch and kill the Son of Sam, and that had been in the '70s. "I'm not pretending to be anyone—"

"*Yes, you are! Don't lie to me!*" Molly needed to hit something, and before she could think better of it, she punched the firmly shut door; her hand went straight through.

And that was what it took to make Clara snap.

"*You're impossible!*" She was shrieking now, her hand for a moment twitching toward her hair, as if to let it down. Instead, she caught herself, balling her hands into fists. "I can't allow this. You're going to get us both killed."

"What are you going to do? Throw me out?"

"Maybe I will!"

Molly had caught Clara in a lie, of course. Clara could scream all she wanted, but she wouldn't throw Molly out. Who else would work the theater? And Clara needed *her*. There were few enough like them, rare birds among a small people. Literally. They were sisters, or even closer. They'd known each other well over a hundred years, and the kind of bond they'd forged was deeper than blood. They'd survived death. They could survive this.

So she fled the Grand Dame to Anat.

Anat lived in one of the big freshman buildings at NYU. Molly remembered the building from when it was new and had still been a hotel and speakeasy. She'd gone to a handful of parties there not long after her first death, when she was always ravenous and East Tenth Street was "uptown." Even as a dorm room, the vibe had changed little. The air still felt tense with enthusiasm and excess and about the same amount of squirreled-away alcohol.

When she arrived in front of the narrow high-rise, she texted Anat, expecting her to come down and sign her in. But after a moment of waiting, she instead got a message.

Anat: Not feeling well. Can you come up?
Molly: Fine. What floor are you on again? And leave
the window open
Anat: Sixth

Molly backed away from the building, looking up at the windows. She went as far as the opposite end of the street, ducking behind a couple of parked cars, before at last pulling the scrunchie out of her hair. Her curls fell loose and free past her shoulders, and when she glanced at her hand, the way her fingers had lengthened into claws, she knew she had changed.

Molly gazed up into the sky and took a deep breath of night.

Clara, according to her own telling, had taken ages to figure it out. But for Molly, for whom all the world was a stage and who put on a character the moment she slid out of bed, this was no different. Turning from girl to monster to owl was as easy as flicking a switch or shifting between apps on her phone. She was practiced at putting on an identity and then putting on another. Slipping into feathers and wings and becoming an owl was little different.

The window to Anat's room wasn't hard to find, but rather than fly straight through, she landed on the fire escape a floor below so Anat wouldn't see her change. There, she put away her wings, and after throwing her hair back up into a messy bun, she was human again. Only then did she climb the wrought-iron stairs up a level and make her way through the window.

The dorm room was tidy but cramped. Half the room was covered in posters and playbills from Broadway shows (Anat's half), and half was a series of artistic renderings of the periodic table and a poster for something Anat said was called *Doctor Who*. Thankfully, her roommate, Emma, wasn't in at the moment, but even if she had been, nothing would have been able to pull Molly's attention from Anat.

She looked pale and a bit pinched, and her forehead shone with a thin sheen of sweat. She was already slight to begin with, but there was something about the bags beneath her eyes and the sharpness in her face. Had she been eating at all? When she got in her head and her work, she sometimes forgot. Yes, that had to be it. . . .

Anat approached the window but did not close it. Molly could feel Anat's heartbeat was off, a little too fast, and the rhythm strange. Almost like there were two heartbeats in the room. Was Anat's roommate hiding under the bed or something?

"Have you seen a doctor?" Molly asked, reaching out to hug her, but when she wrapped her arms around Anat, she did not return the gesture, instead just standing there, her arms motionless at her sides.

"You came," she said after a long moment. "Have you come to save me?"

"Save you from what?" said Molly, irritation returning.

She'd expected some kind of reaction, a biting remark. Instead, Anat acted like she hadn't heard Molly at all. She turned instead toward the window, pushing it upward, wider. "It's so hot in here, isn't it?"

"You probably need a doctor, Anat," she said. "I think you have a fever, or the flu, or . . . Anat?"

But Anat was clearly not listening to a word that Molly said. Instead, she had started to climb out the window and onto the fire escape. Ikh vil flien," she muttered. *I want to fly.* She continued to mutter in Yiddish, more to herself than to Molly, but loud enough that she could still hear. "I . . . want to fly. I think I can. It's so hot up here, isn't it?"

Molly inched toward the window. This wasn't right at all. Anat knowing the words to show tunes in Yiddish. Strange, but not impossible. But this . . . this wasn't Anat.

It wasn't Anat.

"Could you come down, please?" said Molly slowly, and then, when Anat did not so much as look at her, she repeated herself in Yiddish, her mouth suddenly dry. "Kenst arafkumen, bite?"

That got her attention. Anat's head turned. Her eyes had gone wide, her pupils just large enough to be wrong. Her face was twisted into a look Molly had never seen on her, the kind of terror Molly knew and had only ever felt once, on the day her heart stopped beating. It was the terror of someone dying.

"Ikh ken nisht!" she shouted. *I can't!* She swatted at Molly when she reached out to try and grab her arm. "I'm burning! I'm burning!"

"Du bist nisht!" *You are not!* Molly tried again to pull her girlfriend, who was not her girlfriend, off of the fire escape, but not only did Anat avoid her grasp, she inched closer still to the edge, grasping the rail like she intended to climb up onto it. Molly thought she heard something creak, and she did not trust that the flimsy-looking ironwork would be able to hold them both. Worse still, if Anat *did* jump, she had no idea how she could possibly catch her—her owl form, while strong, would be of no help. "You are

100

not burning. Now come back inside!"

Anat looked at Molly, her face half in shadow, and when at last she spoke, Molly was almost startled to hear English once more. "Help me."

There once was a girl who wore many faces.

She learned them from her mother, the faces a girl needed to survive without a man to protect her.

There was a face for asking for favors and a face for refusing them. A face to hide, to disappear. A tilt of her head, a bit of makeup, and she could be older, wiser than her years.

A face to invite attention.

The girl loved that face, and she hated it. Attention was as much a gift as it was a curse. It was a blade that could be turned on her at any moment. But on an island such as this, full to the brim with people, a girl who could not invite attention would surely be lost, swept away in the sea of people or crushed beneath the weight of the work of surviving.

She wore the face when she turned fourteen and left school for work. That face got her a job in the first factory she tried, stitching shirtwaists. That face got her attention she despised, lingering glances from hungry men, from judging and jealous girls.

That face got her attention from Lena.

Lena believed in girls with the same certainty that young yeshiva students believe in God. She believed that if all the Jewish and Italian girls on the floor agreed to unionize, they could demand better, that they would transform not only the way girls worked but the way they lived in this city. She believed that this girl, who talked endlessly of the Yiddish shows she'd seen with her mother at the Grand, could be a star if she tried. She believed there was nothing that girls could not do, could not become. She believed that the future belonged to girls like them, girls who burned bright.

And the girl believed in Lena. She believed that there was some strange magic in Lena's voice, because when she spoke, the girl's insides burned like nothing she'd ever known. She believed Lena enough to abandon her work to audition. And when she earned her first role, Lena was the first person she told, racing to her battered tenement in the waning daylight. And when, in the dim stairwell, they kissed, the girl believed that this was what the poets and playwrights meant when they wrote of love.

After all, it was a new century, and this was what it meant to live on the stage in a great city on an island where anything was possible, a place that was forever building and building atop wild and reckless and foolish dreams. And of all dreams, this was surely the most ordinary. To love and be loved, damn those who would stand in their way. It was the oldest kind of story.

And they were so careful, besides, even as the girl longed to abandon restraint. She wanted to announce their love in *Forverts*, the *New York Times*. She wanted to shout it from the tallest building in Manhattan.

But she didn't. Instead they found many dark stairwells and locked doors.

She had been so careful.

And under all the lights, the girl knew she had triumphed before the curtains fell. She felt it in her bones. The show had been unlike anything else that she had done before. She had known from the moment she had first stepped into the role that it was the part she had been born to play, the part that would make her. She had felt it in every rehearsal, in the quiet moments she practiced with Lena.

103

And it was certain when she'd stepped out onstage. In each scene she had the audience in her hands, their reactions hers to shape. Never had she been so in control. Of a role, of her performance, of a crowd, of the applause . . .

The rest of the cast was planning on going out for dinner to celebrate and had rushed out quickly after the curtain came down. But the makeup and costume she had worn for her part was more than any other member of the cast. It took time to remove.

While the hallways backstage fell gradually quiet and the last few members of the cast tried unsuccessfully to urge her out, she took off the heavy makeup, the deep shadows and gray-green streaks of greasepaint she'd used to appear as though she'd emerged onstage straight from the sea. All the while, she continued to glance at the clock.

"I thought you were still here!"

Standing in the doorway of the dressing room was the stagehand. The thorn in her side. His arms stretched across the doorframe like a rung on a ladder. Like a fence. Like a net.

Truly, she did not know a person more incapable of reading a situation, more incapable of taking a hint, than this stagehand. No matter how hard she tried, she could not seem to make him understand that she was not interested, that she would never be interested. These were things that ordinarily could go without saying, that everyone else understood without paying it much mind.

"I was just leaving," she said stiffly, pulling on her coat and tossing her scarf about her neck.

"What a coincidence," he said. "I was just going, too. We can walk over together."

The actress took her hat from the hook by the door and stood before the stagehand, tapping her foot impatiently. "That won't be necessary," she said. "It's five minutes away. I can manage myself."

"Come on, Molly," said the stagehand. "Let me take you. I promise I'll make it worth your while."

The actress shuddered. She could think of few things less appealing than what she assumed the stagehand had in mind.

"I would rather not," she said. She'd rather just about anyone else accompany her. It was not just that she didn't like men. She didn't like this man, specifically. He was forever trailing her shadow during rehearsals, leaving her gifts in her dressing room, notes that she promptly dumped without opening.

"I'm a much better time than that factory girl you've been so keen on."

The actress's heart stopped. "What are you talking about?" It could be nothing. She had brought Lena by weeks ago, introduced her as a friend, and no one questioned her.

"I saw the two of you when she came for the dress rehearsal," he said. "You did it right there in the dressing room . . . where anyone passing by might catch a glimpse."

The actress was not used to fighting. But deflecting she could do very well. By the time she had realized that she might prefer women to men, she'd become quite accomplished. "It's rude to snoop!"

"It wasn't right, what you two were doing," said the stagehand. "The law says so, God says so . . . and I'm sure Mr. Katz would think so, too, if he found out."

Everything inside the actress turned cold. She didn't have to guess what would happen if their director found out. There were plenty of directors who would turn a blind eye to her, actors who knew better than to throw rocks in glass houses, who had affairs and passions of their own they kept discreet. Such was life on the stage. But Mr. Katz had been scandalized when he had been introduced to the fiancé of a girl in the company, only to learn later that he was Catholic. What would happen to her?

"He's not going to find out," she growled. "Because I'll tell him that you've been harassing me, spying on me in my dressing room. Who is he going to believe? The star of his show or some Peeping Tom who turns the lights on and off?"

The stagehand swallowed, his smile wavering. Would Mr. Katz really believe her? She could not say. But there was power in confidence. A lifetime on the stage had taught her that.

"How dare you?" His knuckles turned white where he gripped the door, his mouth twisting in anger. "Zoyneh, think that you can throw yourself at me, only to make threats—"

"Me?" said the actress with a mirthless laugh. "You really are meshuggeh. Now, if you'll excuse me . . ." Bracing herself, the actress pushed him aside, with enough surprise and force that he momentarily let go of the doorframe, and she passed through.

But she'd barely taken two steps before he grabbed her arm. "Meshuggeh?" he snarled. "On the contrary, I've never seen things so clear."

He tried to yank the actress close to him. The actress was not a particularly skilled fighter but had seen plenty of men in the wild who had trouble understanding the word *no*, and kicked his crotch as hard as she could.

He let out a yelp of pain and let go of her arm. And so, the actress ran.

She ran toward the stairwell, stumbling and cursing her heeled shoes. Behind her, she heard footsteps, and her heart began to race. Why was he chasing her? He might not have been the first man to pursue her affections, but he was certainly the first to pursue her like this, chasing her down the hall like he was on a hunt.

The actress was near the bottom of the stairs when she missed a step. For a sickening moment there was weightlessness. Then she landed hard on the cement floor and heard something inside her crack. Ignoring the sudden, agonizing pain in her knee, she pushed herself to her feet. But the footsteps were growing louder, and her heartbeat was in her ears, and the slightest pressure made her entire leg burn white-hot in agony, a pain so great that she barely felt the stagehand grab her, barely felt the knife slide between her ribs.

The actress put her hand to her chest, just above where the knife was now lodged. When she tried to draw a breath, her lungs burned like nothing she'd ever known, and her good knee, the one she had not smashed, felt suddenly strange and weak.

"What have you done?" she gasped, struggling to save the little air left in her lungs.

He continued to stare at her, wide-eyed, before at last seeming to realize. He let go of the blade and murmured something that might have been an apology, as if a small part of him still yet believed she might come to love him.

The actress turned and pushed through the door. The ground tilted dangerously beneath her; she stumbled out into the alleyway as the stagehand continued to call her name. *Molly, Molly . . .*

The night was bone-chilling cold, too cold for February. Worse than the cold, however, was a numbness that had set in about her waist, a loss of feeling that frightened her more than anything had in her life.

She ran out onto the sidewalk, but it was after midnight, and the broad avenue was mostly empty. The few stragglers still out on the street had other things to mind than a girl stumbling and struggling to remain on her feet.

She tripped forward, and the ground swooped wildly beneath her. Like the Staten Island Ferry. No, like that ride she'd taken once at Coney Island, no . . .

No . . .

She fell again, and her knee screamed in protest, and she screamed, too, though she was barely aware of the sound she made, she was so cold. . . .

"Help me!"

The ground swayed, and she was no longer standing. Why hadn't she worn a heavier coat? It was so cold. . . .

It didn't make sense. Not the cold or the ground swaying, like she was in the bottom of the Ferris wheel, rocking back and forth to some distant music and the light of the moon. It didn't make sense. If he loved her, why would he do this? If he wanted her, why would he . . .

"Help me!"

She couldn't tell if she was shouting. She couldn't breathe, and her head had started to spin along with the ground. She touched the handle of the knife, still in her chest. She couldn't pull it out. Pulling it out would be too much agony to bear. It would kill her.

But she couldn't breathe, and that would kill her, too.

"Help . . ." But this time she was certain that no sound passed

108

through her lips. She tried to force more air into her lungs, but the attempt just sent a shock of pain through her, and when she coughed, she tasted blood.

She hadn't realized she was no longer alone, that someone had half pulled her up off the pavement, but she couldn't have told ground from sky, even if she'd tried, until there was a whisper in her ear.

"I'm here, I'm here. Don't be afraid," said the voice, soft and feminine. She thought of Lena, wondered if it might be her, when she saw the dark hair tumble into view. "I'm going to help you, but first I'm going to pull out the knife. Stay very still."

Lena. Surely Lena had come for her, would know the thing to do to make the spinning stop, the pain inside her, the terrifying cold. The actress was so far gone that she barely felt it when the knife came out.

There was a small moment of relief, a little rush of air, another breath. But the cold was descending, too, so fast that she did not think she'd get another breath and was glad that Lena was holding her so close.

"Don't be afraid," said the voice, the breath by her ear. The actress glanced at the speaker, hoping for one more glimpse of Lena's face.

But when she did, she saw that it was not Lena, not at all. It was a face that she did not recognize, though she was certain that it must have been ha'malach ha'moves, the angel of death, who had come for her. With her blank eyes and gray, drowned face, she was a monster not unlike the one the actress had just played for a packed house, the best performance of her career, the performance that made her, her last . . .

But that was just a mask, a face Molly wore. Perhaps that was what this was: a mask. Real monsters concealed their knives. Real monsters wore innocent looks of longing. Real monsters put the knife in; they didn't take it out.

So when she felt the bite, the teeth sink into her neck, she was not afraid.

12

CLARA

Clara stepped out onto the window ledge. She couldn't be in the theater when she was this angry. It was a bitter night, the kind of cold that cut right through her skin. She looked down once, to be sure there was no one standing below who might see, before letting herself fall forward and shifting into her feathers and wings.

For a moment, Clara just let the wind carry her. It had been too long since she'd flown like this, without an immediate destination in mind, flying just to watch Second Avenue run beneath her like a creek of light in the dark.

This made being an Estrie worth it. It was worth the hunger to have wings, the only thing she'd ever wanted, even when her heart still beat. It was the greatest gift Devorah had given her. She could live another hundred years, and still she would not come close to paying it back.

When she hit Fourteenth Street, she turned, cutting past the darkened Trader Joe's and flying straight toward Union Square. At this hour it was blessedly quiet. Most of the shops that bordered the square were shuttered, the autumn Greenmarket packed up hours ago, leaving no more than a towering pile of compost and scattered remnants of produce. Most of the chess players had left. She fluttered straight for the clusters of shade trees past the subway entrance and settled into the leaves.

This was what she needed, somewhere quiet where she could still hear the city racing around her.

Clara had been in Manhattan since the 1880s, but she'd never *lived* here, truly. She'd arrived as she was now, an Estrie. All appetite and ambition, no pulse. A monster in the shape of a girl who had wanted so badly to fly she'd nearly tried it without the benefit of wings.

Even now, glancing at the towering glass luxury apartments, the glowing LED lights of the Metronome, the clock keeping time down to the hundredths of a second, she remembered how she'd have given anything to go *anywhere*. She remembered when Vilna was the biggest city she'd ever seen, how buildings with more than three stories had been enough to impress her. Her world had grown so much bigger since then, it was almost laughable now.

Here with Devorah, they'd built the sort of life she had dreamed of. No, it was better than what she'd dreamed of. When she could still sleep, she had dreamed that she would fly thanks to a husband. Instead, she got a sister. This was much better. No boy, no matter how sweet and earnest, no matter how good he smelled, could give her what her sister had.

The tree swayed in the breeze, and she shifted closer to the trunk. A squirrel farther down noticed her and froze in his tracks. As if she'd eat *squirrel*. Even as an owl, she had standards.

She'd built something. A theater. A nest. The thing she'd

wanted, the thing she dreamed of, belonged to her and was better than anything she could have fathomed. Her heart had stopped, and she had her wings, and she couldn't sleep. She didn't *need* to keep dreaming.

She couldn't.

Could she?

The squirrel, perhaps sensing that she wasn't going to hunt him, carefully crept up the trunk of the tree. Clara thought about ignoring him, until his tail whacked her beak. She hissed, the sound sending the squirrel straight out of his skin as he shot up the rest of the way, to the very top of the tree.

No. Desire had not just killed Molly and her once. It had killed Devorah the second and final time. *That* was what it did to people. It made fools of them all. It sent brilliant women into burning buildings. It had the power to destroy them in a way that time no longer could. Soon enough, Molly would see that Clara was right.

When she returned to the theater, she felt better. Invigorated. Her head was clear. She would not let Boaz keep clouding her vision. Whatever drew her to him, the way his scent gnawed at her insides, that was animal. It wasn't real, and she'd be best off ignoring it. Because she was *not* an animal, and she would not blindly chase her hungers. . . .

She readjusted her hair, pinning it back into place and switching out her blouse for one freshly ironed, and strode into her office just in time for Boaz to arrive with his cash box. "Hey there."

"Good evening," she said, smoothing a few flyaway strands back behind her ears. A part of her was always afraid for the day that she'd have simply forgotten to put it up, that she'd have to deal with explaining to him her monster face for the few seconds before he forgot. "Finished for the night, then?"

He nodded, handing her the cash box. He was about to sit in the seat across from her, before stopping. "Sorry, let me get the door . . . for . . . um . . . privacy."

"There's really no . . ." she began.

He froze, his hand on the knob. "Wait, yes, you're right, open is more appropriate."

Realizing how Boaz had taken it, Clara shook her head. "No, no, don't worry about that."

"So I should close it?" .

"Only if you want to," she said. He struggled for a moment with what to do, swinging the door back and forth and inadvertently wafting his scent straight at Clara before at last settling on closing the door, then plopped into the seat.

Now the entire office filled with his scent. If anything, it was worse now that she had kissed him, that she had tasted a bit of his blood. She set the box down, fighting the way her face twisted, and immediately opened the window behind her desk. She realized she might have given something away, when she turned around and saw Boaz sniffing one of his pits. "Sorry, it's . . . just stuffy in here," she said.

"Do you want me to open the door, then?"

"Enough with the door!" she said, struggling to hide her exasperation. She took a deep breath and reminded herself to smile. He wasn't in trouble tonight, yet.

But that didn't seem to put him at ease in the slightest. "I think we need to talk?" he said at last.

"About what?"

"You know . . ." he said.

"I do not know what you are talking about, Boaz Harari." She fed the bills into her cash counter, refusing to look up. When that finished, she turned to the change.

"The kiss!" he said exasperatedly. "That definitely happened, right? Or did I imagine it?"

"There's nothing to talk about," she said, watching the change fall through the machine. The count was perfect. Because of course it was. Boaz had many faults, but he was actually quite good at his job, once he arrived. If he weren't so *late* all the time. "I'm very sorry about that. I was not myself. A moment's indiscretion. It will not happen again."

"No, I'm sorry!" he said. "I shouldn't have . . . Things have been *super* weird on my end, and I haven't been getting a ton of sleep, so, like, I way overstepped."

"No, I did." At last, she chanced a look at him. He did look tired, the shadows beneath his eyes darker than usual. Not that this was something she spent a lot of time noticing. Not at all. Nor was she going to ask him why he wasn't sleeping. Because she wasn't interested. Not . . . interested . . . at all. "It was my fault. And it won't happen again."

"Yeah. Definitely," he said, standing up. She could still see where his lip had split, even if it had mostly healed. At her probing gaze, he lifted a hand to his lip, brushed a thumb against it, and Clara flinched so hard she almost shattered the chair. He glanced up at her, his eyes soft. "You . . . sure you're not mad at me?"

She shook her head. "It's forgotten."

"Forgotten," he repeated.

Clara watched him leave, wishing that it were that easy.

13

BOAZ

Boaz was halfway down the stairs of the theater when he practically tripped into Molly and Anat.

"Why are you even still here?" Molly huffed as Boaz grasped at the railing, trying to regain his balance. "Don't you have somewhere better to be?"

"I'm *leaving*," said Boaz. It didn't take a genius to see that something was wrong. Molly's messy bun was sitting loosely on top of her head, and she was clutching Anat in . . . a bear hug? Anat looked like she was half trying to fight Molly off, but badly, sobbing in strangled gasps.

Evil. He thought of the warning from the ghost. What was Molly trying to do to Anat? This did not look good, and if what the ghost said was true . . .

"Is . . . everything okay here?"

"Does everything look okay?" said Molly, pulling Anat closer to her. "Now, if you will excuse us."

She tried to pass him, but Boaz, the warning still ringing in his ears, blocked her. "You're not going to hurt Anat, are you? Because if you are . . ."

Molly stopped, and for a moment, Boaz thought he saw something . . . different in Molly. She looked the same as ever, but the way she looked at him was unfamiliar, something sharp and dangerous in her eyes. "You'll do what? Fight me?" She snorted. "Please. I've seen more intimidating street pigeons. Now get out of my way."

"You didn't answer my question," said Boaz, his heart hammering.

But before he could say any more, Anat spoke up. Or rather, she shouted, so loud that his ears rang. "*Ikh vil nisht brenen!*"

"Since when do you speak Yiddish?" he asked Anat, whose face was half obscured by her hair.

"She doesn't," said Molly shortly.

"Well, she just did," said Boaz. "And I think Anat can speak for . . ."

But the rest of what he hoped to say died in his throat. Anat turned her gaze upward, and through her curtain of hair, Boaz could see that her eyes were nearly all black and fixed on his chest, her mouth agape. He knew that look, he realized. Intimately. He took one cautious step back along the stairs, just before she shrieked and lunged straight for him.

Boaz fell back, hard. Anat had him pinned, driving one of her knees into his chest as she clawed at his shirt, his neck. Boaz struggled to grab the railing, attempting to kick her off him without hurting her. She did not extend the same courtesy to him and was clearly trying very hard to hurt him. She'd ripped his T-shirt before at last Molly was able to yank her back, and he scrambled back on his feet.

"Yeah, so you're still going to fight me?" said Molly, clutching the half-feral Anat.

"She's possessed," said Boaz. Part of him knew he should just leave and let Molly get on with . . . well, however she was planning on handling this. But if Anat was possessed, there was no way Molly would be able to fix it.

"That's what I was trying to tell you," said Molly impatiently.

"No it wasn't," he said. "Do you even know how to fix a possession? It'll kill her if you don't do anything about it—"

"And *you* know how to fix it?"

"Yes, actually!"

"What is going on out here?"

Boaz turned. Clara was waiting at the top of the stairs, her arms tightly folded across her chest. She glared at the both of them, her eyes dipping down briefly to where Boaz's freshly ripped tee did a poor job of being a shirt. "Why are the two of you screaming at each other? And, Boaz, you should go home already. I need to . . . *Molly, why do you . . .*"

Clara put her head in her hands, and Boaz realized that if he didn't say anything now, Anat might never get the help she needed.

"I might know how to help Anat," said Boaz, trying to keep his voice measured. "I . . . I've done it before. If we could just get off the stairs."

Clara and Molly looked at him, and then at each other. Boaz swallowed. He was not lying, technically. He *had* successfully sent a few ghosts to Olam Ha-Ba, the World to Come. The shawarma ghost this morning, for one.

Well, that was the only time. But he knew Hila could do it. She'd talked about it. Sometimes there was an easy fix. The dead lingered for a reason. Figure out the reason and put it right, and they usually moved on. Usually.

Sometimes.

And that was, he ventured to guess, far more than Molly or Clara had ever managed.

"Up here," said Clara at last, pointing toward the door across from her office.

The four of them made their way up, Molly pulling up a still-restless Anat, who was struggling with an overwhelming desire to tear into Boaz. Clara, meanwhile, was struggling with an over-whelming desire to say *something* to her sister. Boaz would have laughed if he hadn't been still more than a little terrified.

Clara pushed open the door and switched on the light. It was a large storage room, with most of the available floor space taken up by the haphazard rows of chairs, some of them theater seats, and others that Boaz realized must have been old props, all covered in various levels of dust. On one side there were a few cracked full-length mirrors, and on the other, curling and faded, was an old-looking backdrop, a section of what appeared to be a village marketplace.

Boaz tried to take a deep breath and ended up coughing.

"Sorry," Clara began, "I've been meaning to take care of this room for ages—"

"No, no, it's . . . fine," said Boaz, smothering another cough in the crook of his elbow. They found an extra theater seat that didn't appear too dusty or irreparably broken and dragged it from the corner just in time for Molly to forcefully deposit Anat in it. Boaz stood back in the doorway as Clara and Molly argued about tying Anat. Molly gave in the second time Anat attempted to maul Boaz.

Clara found a ball of thick twine, the same that had been used to bind the rolled-up backdrops and sections of carpet that had been propped against one wall. "What *did* you do?" said Molly as she helped Clara wrap a cord across Anat's chest, repurposed from one of the rolls of spare carpet bundled up in the corner. When they finished, Anat seemed to give up fighting them both and sat motionless in the seat, though her gaze was still fixed on Boaz. "She was fine until she saw you."

"Really? She was totally fine?" said Boaz irritably. Why was it always *his* fault?

"Well, she did try to jump off a sixth-floor fire escape and is suddenly fluent in Yiddish, but other than that—"

"See, not my fault!" said Boaz. "When did she start doing that?"

"She was acting rather strange at the party we went to, but it's worse today—"

"*A party?*" said Clara. "You went to *a party* with her? Do my rules just mean nothing to you?"

"Oh my god, not now," said Molly as Clara strode toward the door, and Boaz wondered what Clara had against parties. Molly rounded on Boaz. "So how are you planning on fixing her?"

"Um, well, to get rid of a ghost, you have to figure out what it wants," he said, hoping that he sounded like he knew what he was talking about. Aunt Hila once said that the secret to *her* success was confidence. That while her powers were genuine, it was her confidence that sold the performance to her audience, not the honesty. He tried to remember what his aunt would say at the start of her big auditorium shows; he'd seen enough of them to at least do the monologue. "A ghost is a hunger, one so strong it outlives the body."

"You just got that from *Hila and the Haunted*," said Molly, folding her arms across her chest. "I watch late-night reality television, too, you know."

Well, at least he could drop the pretense. "I know that," he said. "She's my aunt. She's the real deal, and it runs in the family."

"She's . . ." Molly looked at Boaz, her brow furrowed. "No way! I *love* Hila Harari. She's my favorite. You know, Bravo marathons her episodes every Wednesday. I watch them all religiously."

"Do you sleep?" Boaz muttered. Ordinarily, he avoided all talk of the Bravo show like the plague. Going to a small private school and being related to a moderately famous television medium meant that half of his class was morbidly fascinated with the possibility of getting to meet his aunt, and the other half thought he and his family were all a bunch of freaks. There was no in between. "Those run until four in the morning!"

"Wait, what do you mean it *runs in the family*?" said Molly. "You mean to tell us that *you* are a medium? *You?*"

"What's so unbelievable about that?" said Boaz defensively.

Molly snorted. "I just don't think I've ever met someone so completely oblivious," she said.

"Oblivious to what?" said Boaz, heat creeping into his face. He glanced at Clara, hoping that she'd say something, but her expression was suddenly quite hard to read. She was looking at him . . . like, *really* looking at him. As though she'd only just noticed that he existed. He shifted uneasily. Maybe she wanted to forget the kiss, but he certainly couldn't, no matter what he had said to her. How did she seriously expect him to forget?

"Exactly," said Molly.

"Oh, don't be mean!" said Clara, surprising Boaz. Clara defending Boaz in anything that he did had to be a first.

"So anyway," said Boaz, rolling up his sleeves. He took a few, trepidatious steps toward Anat, hoping he still looked like he knew what he was doing. "We have to ask her what she wants."

"She only understands Yiddish at the moment," said Molly shortly. She had moved closer to Anat, and Boaz realized she was trying to protect her from him.

"Fine, then you ask her," said Boaz. "Ask her what she wants."

"Vos vilstu, teyere?" said Molly, crouching down beside the chair.

Anat turned to look at Molly, brow furrowed. "Ikh vil nisht brenen," she said.

"She says that she doesn't want to burn," said Molly, stroking her girlfriend's arm.

"Well, we're not going to burn her, so that's a start," said Boaz, trying not to let his frustration show. He could feel his father's ring dangling around his neck and wondered whether he should try to put it on, whether it would do anything. *Probably just make everything worse.* He didn't want to make the ghost stronger or louder; he wanted her to go away. "Can you tell her we're not going to burn her?"

"I've already told her that, *several* times, the entire way over here, actually," said Molly. "If that banished dybbukim, then this wouldn't be a problem."

"Well, tell her again!" Boaz needed to think. If Aunt Hila were here, she'd know how to solve this. But the problem of their work having no rule book was that . . . there was no rule book. He didn't know what he was supposed to do to fix this, except the one thing he couldn't do: admit to Aunt Hila what he had done.

Molly glared at him before turning back to her girlfriend. "Mir veln nisht dir farbrenen," she said soothingly, continuing to stroke her arm.

Boaz slid the ring on, rummaging through his pocket. "Do either of you have a . . . er . . . candle or something?"

Molly gaped at him. "A candle. You want to light *a candle* in here? In a room filled with very dry, flammable things?"

He turned to Clara, who shook her head. "No candle. Not in here. Or anywhere on this floor, for that matter."

"Fine," he said. He thought of the shawarma ghost outside. That one had disappeared without him lighting a candle. It had also taken a sandwich with it, but . . . well, it had been harmless otherwise. Surely, whatever had invaded Anat couldn't be much worse.

He raised his hands, but Anat glared daggers at him before turning back to Molly. "Ir kenen nisht tsutroyen im," she said, her voice low. "Zi zugt az du kenst im nisht getroyen . . ."

"What's she saying?" said Boaz, but Molly did not look at him instead continuing to look at Anat with alarm.

"'She says don't trust him,'" said Clara. She moved so quietly, he might not have realized that she was inches from him if she hadn't spoken.

"What, me?" said Boaz, affronted. "Why doesn't she trust me? I—"

"'She says don't trust him,'" Clara repeated, her own expression still difficult to read. "You asked what she said. 'She says—'"

"I get it, don't trust him." Boaz sighed. He could feel Clara's gaze still on him, but he wouldn't return it. This was embarrassing, and he was kidding himself. He couldn't charm the dead. He'd barely avoided disaster with the damn shawarma; God knew what would happen if he messed this up.

"Well, do you know why that might be?" said Clara. "Would she have a good reason not to trust you?"

"I have no idea why Anat wouldn't—"

"I don't mean Anat," said Clara, sounding exasperated. "'She says don't trust him.' That's what Anat said. Any idea who she might be talking about?"

It was then that Boaz understood what the look was that Clara was giving him. She was searching him, looking for a reason to agree with the ghosts, a reason not to trust him.

And he decided that he would not give her one. "No."

"She has to have a reason for saying that." Clara stood inches from him, close enough that he could smell her perfume, something a bit old-fashioned with rose water.

"No, she doesn't," said Boaz. "Ghosts are human hungers, and humans don't have to be right." Ghosts wanted impossible things all the time. Those were the ones hardest to get rid of. Like the girl on the N platform, or Anthony Janszoon van Salee. Some hungers were delusional, but that didn't make them any less real.

But he was saved from having to continue the argument when Molly cut in. "Are you calling your aunt or not?" she asked irritably.

"He is *not* calling his aunt," said Clara. "It is late, and the last thing we need is more people here to witness your girlfriend having a supernatural breakdown—"

"*Excuse me?*" Molly's hand drifted toward her scrunchie, until coming to rest instead on the doorframe. She was gripping it so hard that Boaz could see her knuckles go white. "It could kill her—"

"I could kill you, dragging us into a mess with dybbukim."

"Um . . . guys?" said Boaz. The air between the sisters was practically vibrating with tension. He wouldn't have dared interrupt, except that when he glanced past Clara's shoulder back into the prop room, he noticed a rather significant problem. "Where is Anat?"

"What do you mean? She's right . . ." Molly glanced back over her shoulder and let out a yelp. She darted back toward the chair, which now sat empty, the cord that had bound Anat still wrapped loosely around the arms. Boaz remained in the doorway while the sisters searched the prop room, but it was a fruitless exercise. Anat and the ghost that gripped her had both vanished into thin air.

14

CLARA

This was why there were rules.

"You didn't have to come," said Molly stiffly, pulling the thin leather jacket tightly around her shoulders as they stood at the door of Gehinnom. Clara had warned her when they left to wear something sensible, but like every warning she ever gave her sister, it had been ignored. Instead, she was wearing a perfectly unseasonable silver slip, teetering heels, no tights. "I told you I can handle this myself."

"Clearly you can't," said Clara. Her sister had lost control of the situation the moment she'd fallen for a college freshman. Worse, in that same moment, *Clara* had lost control of the situation. What would Devorah have said about this?

"You just want to kill her." They both ducked out of the way as the doors briefly opened and two boys with claws for feet tripped over themselves, laughing loudly as they barreled out onto the sidewalk. Clara scrunched her nose. She had no patience for the sheydim, certainly not ones that made drunk humans seem like positively delightful company.

"If you have another plan, I'd love to hear it," said Clara. She could think of ten things she'd rather be doing than this. She hated Gehinnom and sheydim on a Shabbos night. She'd rather vacuum popcorn off her theater floors than deal with them. She'd rather *eat* the vacuumed popcorn.

From a quick scan of the room, Clara caught sight of more sheydim, their birdlike feet on full display, and creatures shuffling through the crowd, some she couldn't identify. Molly suddenly elbowed her sister, pointing to the far corner. "I've never seen one this close—"

"Can you try not staring?" Clara muttered, resisting the urge to do so herself. The Ophanim, with their many eyes and the thin outline of fire around them, were celestial beings who rarely bothered with such pedestrian things as nightclubs and concert halls. Clara had seen one once in London, not long before she crossed the Atlantic and arrived in New York. They weren't the sort of thing one forgot.

"Why not? They are definitely staring," she said. "What do you think would happen if I went over? Do you think they'd go all 'be not afraid' or something?"

"I think they probably get that all the time, and if you did, they'd just set you on fire," said Clara. "But by all means, be my guest."

They found Ashmodai in his office. Though they had gone the exact way that Clara had when she had paid rent, the office could not have looked more different. Instead of the black polished walls, a kind of observation deck greeted them, like something tourists paid far too much money for up by the Empire State Building. The floor was the same as ever, black marble, but around them were windows looking out on a swirling night sky, the lights of Manhattan beneath them. Ashmodai was standing with his back to them, staring out at the city below. "I suppose this hardly impresses the two of you. Bird's-eye views being commonplace for you both."

"We don't mean to keep you," began Clara. This was higher than she ever flew, dizzyingly high, but it didn't scare her. There was no height that did.

Ashmodai turned to look at them. He wore a different face today, an older gentleman with dark hair and a neatly clipped beard. "Oh, I always have time for the Sender sisters," he said. "Come. . . . Perhaps you'll fly with me?"

Molly scowled, but before she could say anything that would jeopardize the entire visit, Clara cut in. "We're here to ask for your help."

Ashmodai laughed. "It is useless, anyway. I cannot leave. A cage is a cage, no matter the heights to which it might climb." Below them, the lights of Manhattan blinked brighter than stars. It might have been a prison to Ashmodai, but to her the view alone was the stuff of dreams. "Might I ask, how are things with your girlfriend, Miss Sender? It must be going well, to worry your sister so . . ."

Clara froze. She'd never told Molly what she had discussed with Ashmodai when she had come to pay rent, and from the smirk that played across Ashmodai's face, he knew that, too. She could practically feel the indignation radiating off of Molly, but she said nothing. Instead, Clara said, "She has disappeared, actually, and we thought you might know where."

"You have mistaken me for a higher power," said Ashmodai lazily, turning back toward the glass windows. "I don't do missing mortals. For that you'll have to pray or, you know, call the authorities."

"But that's just it," said Molly. "Whatever happened to her isn't something the police can handle. She vanished into thin air while possessed by someone who might have been my ex-girlfriend."

"Was she a sheyd?" said Ashmodai, still not looking at either of them. Clara glanced down, into the mirrorlike floor, and this time saw her owl face reflected back to her, wide eyes and a sharp beak, tufts of feathers where her French braids were fastened. It made her all the more desperate to leave; heights always made her crave her wings. "Did she have the feet?"

"No," said Clara. "She had a dybbuk inside her."

"Not my purview," he said. "If she had the feet, on the other hand—"

"You don't have the feet," said Molly. "We don't, not really, and you still speak with us."

"One, I have the decency to wear socks," said Ashmodai. "Two, I do not possess dominion over you. To you, my darling Senders, I provide advice purely on a take-it-or-leave-it basis."

"But dybbukim don't make girls disappear into thin air," said Clara. "Something else happened to her. She was more than just possessed."

She told him how Anat had vanished before they'd been able to make any headway with the dybbuk, save the warning. *She says don't trust him.* Not just *Don't trust him* but *She says don't trust him.* Possessed-Anat hadn't said, never got around to saying before she disappeared, who "she" was, and Clara wouldn't dare entertain her theories. Theory. She could think of only one woman who would reach out to her from beyond the grave, and the mere thought of it was too much. That kind of longing was too heavy to let in; it would crush her.

For a fleeting moment, Ashmodai appeared to genuinely be considering her.

But just a moment.

"Still, she is no sheyd."

"Do you have any idea who might be behind it?" Clara pressed, her frustration growing. "Does it sound like anything familiar?"

Ashmodai sighed, and for a moment, Clara noticed the observation deck grow lighter. The stars, which ordinarily could not be seen from even this height in the city, were fully visible. Ashmodai retreated to the window, a silhouette against the glass. "Dybbukim, they are no ordinary occurrence, yes? The dead are meant for the World to Come. But there are places where the space between worlds is thin, people who can cross too easily, who disrupt the fabric of things."

The light changed again, and Clara realized why: the cityscape below them had vanished. While the stars steadily brightened above them, there was simply nothing below but a thick and endless darkness. Clara ignored the unease in her stomach, instead looking toward Molly. But while Ashmodai's lecture meant nothing to Clara, it clearly did to Molly, because after a moment she spoke up.

"Boaz?" she snorted. "So he *is* responsible?"

"It takes little to rend the seams," he said. "But you said the dybbuk did not trust the boy, yes? If I were you, I would maybe ask why."

"You told me I should get closer to him!" said Clara indignantly. "The last time I was here, you said as much."

"Did I?" said Ashmodai.

"You did!" said Clara. "You told me we shouldn't stay away from mortals, that I—"

"Well, it would be easier to find out why the dybbuk didn't trust the boy if you did, now wouldn't it?"

Clara strode toward Ashmodai. She hated this, the riddles, the illusions. She wanted a straight answer, because she was certain he knew it. He *knew* why they ought not to trust Boaz, and he had no business not telling her.

But as she got closer to Ashmodai's shadow, she realized it was just that, a shadow. By the time she reached the glass, it had melted away entirely, leaving her and Molly alone.

15

MOLLY

They flew home from Gehinnom, and in the minutes it took to land back on the windowsill, Clara seemed ready to simply forget the entire incident. "You know, maybe this is a sign."

"Of *what*?" Molly abandoned pretending to breathe. It was useless; she was too panicked to find the rhythm of it.

"That we have rules for a reason!" she said indignantly. "There's a reason we don't get involved with mortal humans. Look at the mess they've made of things—"

"The mess *Boaz* made of things," Molly said through gritted teeth. She pulled her hair up in the first scrunchie she could find. "You heard Ashmodai. This is all his fault."

"That's not what he said!" said Clara.

"That is exactly what he said," she said, even though she knew it was little use. Boaz had long ago reduced her sister's good sense and reason to cottage cheese. Molly would have to take matters into her own hands.

Molly's phone had died in Gehinnom. When she finally was

able to recharge it in the early hours of the morning, something had clearly gone wrong. All her texts with Anat were gone, and the couple of photos she'd taken with Anat at her urging were gone, too.

When she went through her contacts to try dialing Anat again, she found that her number was completely gone. It had been so long since she'd been forced to memorize a phone number, and she realized with dismay she did not know Anat's number by heart.

That evening, Clara had asked her to help with the projection rooms, which, in the age of digital film, meant turning on a movie, double-checking that the projector was properly aligned, and then making sure that the room didn't spontaneously combust. When she had nothing better to do, she usually read in the booth or else worked on scripts for *The Second Avenue Spiel*. Tonight, she just made sure the film was set for the eight o'clock entry in the Winona Ryder retrospective before carefully ducking out. She took care to avoid passing by Clara's office in the process and headed straight to Boaz.

"We need to talk," she said. At the sight of her, Boaz looked positively panicked.

"Look, I'm sorry, I don't know what happened, but I swear I had nothing to do with it," he muttered before handing a customer the receipt. "The ring—it's supposed to let me see things. It's not supposed to make people disappear, and I didn't even . . ."

But Molly didn't believe him. She couldn't say what it was exactly. Maybe it was the old instinct, the one Clara had drilled into her, and one on which they could absolutely agree. Because while they differed on love, Molly was very ready to believe that no boy, certainly not one running around with a magic ring, could be trusted. "You're going to fix this, and you're going to fix it *now*."

"I don't know how."

But Molly had already summoned one of the bubbes to take over his desk, and ignoring Boaz's insistence that he could be of no help, she pulled him back up to the storage room, shutting the door behind her.

"Well, this is the last place we saw her," she said. Perhaps it was just her imagination, or all the dusty furniture, but she thought the air in here felt heavy and stale. "There has to be something in here that we missed. Come on, show me what you were going to do with the ring."

"What if that just makes things worse?" said Boaz uncertainly.

"So you mean it does have something to do with it—"

"I don't know!" he said. Molly stared him down, until at last he yanked at the chain around his neck and pulled out the ring. "All I've ever seen my aunt do with it is call the dead. I'm not responsible for everything weird happening here."

That was technically true. But Molly wasn't about to give him that. "We'll see about that. Come on." Boaz slid the ring on. "Do you feel anything now? Is she in the room?"

"That's not how this works!" he said defensively. "And no, I don't see her. I can see the dead without this thing." He turned toward the old, cracked mirrors, taking a deep breath. "Are you sure I can't light a candle in here? My aunt—"

"*No*," said Molly. What was with this boy and candles? Between the overcrowding of furniture, and the archive she and Clara had in the other room, the entire theater would go up like a tinderbox if he tried.

Boaz sighed, lifting his hands. "Could you give me a bit of

space? And stay out of the mirror if you can."

"What do you mean?" she said.

"Just stay out of the reflection!" he said. "My aunt . . ."

She took a few steps away from him, wishing that she had his aunt there, who apparently was the only Harari who had any clue what they were doing. Once she'd given him a bit of space, he turned back to the mirror. Still, she snuck a glance from the corner of her eye to watch what he was doing. He stared past the triangle he'd formed with his hands, let his gaze slide out of focus before closing his hands into fists.

At once, Boaz's eyes rolled back, with only the whites visible, and the fluorescents began to flicker. The air grew heavy like it was about to storm; the shadows that formed seemed, to Molly, off. They didn't match the light and were far too long for the furniture that cast them. And she swore some of them were moving. "Boaz?"

He didn't answer her, and she wondered whether he could even hear her. Was this even what was supposed to happen? What if he was in trouble? She knew he had told her to stay back, to not look into the mirror—

But then she heard it, a voice calling her name.

Molly. Meyn Molly.

That voice. It was . . . Anat? The voice was hers, but the Yiddish . . . It was so familiar, clinging to her like the scent of smoke.

She approached Boaz, trying to find the source of the sound, wondering whether the ghost who had found Anat had possessed him now, too. But when she heard it again, she turned without a second thought in the direction of the sound, looking straight into the mirror.

For a moment, she thought she might be flying. She was weight-less, the ground beneath her vanishing. She glided through open air as easily as if she had slipped into her wings. This feeling was famil-iar, it was freedom, it was . . .

No, not flying, *falling*. She couldn't tell up from down, and unlike flying, no amount of arm waving would keep her from crashing hard on the ground. When she looked around, Molly was certain of one thing: She wasn't in the Grand Dame any longer.

She was outside, on a narrow path cutting through what looked to be a sleepy market village. Crooked clapboard houses stood on either side of her, weak light glowing down from their windows, their roofs piled with snow.

There was quite a bit of snow, in fact. Mounds of it lined both sides of the path. It topped the thickly wooded forest that stood off in the distance. Molly was certain she had never been here before, but she couldn't shake the feeling that her bones knew this place, even if she did not.

"Molly!"

She turned. Boaz was trudging toward her through the snow, his eyes wide with alarm. "What are you doing here? You didn't look into the mirror, did you?"

"What is this place?" she said.

Boaz shook his head. "I don't know. I've never done this before."

"You've never . . ." The urge to throttle Boaz was suddenly very strong. "Why didn't you tell me?"

"I was trying—"

But then she heard it again. *Molly, meyn Molly.*

"Do you hear that?" she said to Boaz.

"We need to get out of here," he said. "I don't like this—"

"But don't you hear it?"

"Yes, and that's why we need to get out."

And then it hit her. This place, the sleepy, snow-covered village. Familiar and yet . . .

"Tsvishn Veltn," she said. "This place, it's the village, the backdrop . . ." She was about to say, *In the play I was in*, catching the admission just before it slipped past her tongue. "It's the backdrop in the room, an old set piece from *Di Shturem*. . . ."

Molly, meyn Molly.

Lomir flien. Ikh vil nisht brenen.

A shape approached them from the distance. It was slender and moved so easily that she thought it must be Anat. Anat, who always moved like a dancer. It strode easily over the snow, probably on account of the snowshoes it was wearing.

Molly began walking in the direction of the noise, her feet catching in the snow. It wasn't as cold as she expected. In fact, it wasn't cold at all, though it was hard to move through. Within a few steps, she found herself waist deep, trying to force her legs to move forward, practically swimming.

The shadow drew closer, until she realized, sluggishly, that the shape wasn't Anat, but that of a man, and that what she had thought were snowshoes were not snowshoes at all, but large taloned feet—

A hand caught her by the wrist, yanking her backward hard. Boaz, with a surprising amount of strength, tried pulling her back onto the path.

"No," she cried, unsure of who she was screaming at. "Let me go!"

For a moment, Boaz did, but it was only to raise his hands and rip at the air. . . .

And Molly landed hard on her knees. Not in the snow, but on dusty, familiar carpet, Boaz beside her, panting as he yanked the ring off his finger. "Next time, we light a candle," he muttered. "That thing could have followed us back. If it got any closer . . ."

That thing was a sheyd. That much had been clear. She wasn't afraid of sheydim. Sheydim she could deal with. But saying as much would have prompted far more questions from Boaz than she was ready to answer, not with Anat in trouble.

"But what about Anat?" she said, watching him string the ring onto the chain and fasten it around his neck. "I *heard* her. And if she's in trouble, we need to do something."

"I don't know what I heard," he said, rising to his feet. He looked pale enough to be a ghost himself, and his legs were shaking slightly as he made his way to the door. "I don't know what I did, and I don't know how to find her or how to help her, and I'm not going back there until we do."

Molly watched him go, unable to decide whether he knew more than he was letting on or was just a coward. But she'd recognized that voice; she knew she had. And if that was where Anat had gone, Molly would bring her back, no matter what it took.

16

CLARA

Clara found Molly in their apartment, her scrunchie ripped from her hair. Her curls fell in a thick curtain down to her chest, the thin veneer of life and color vanishing from her face, her eyes. Her hands had turned to claws, and when she slammed her hand on the table, a piece chipped off.

Clara stayed in the doorway, unsure of just how much of the monster her sister had unleashed. Molly wasn't one to lie around with her hair down, not when there wasn't a neck to bite.

She looked up, her blank eyes meeting Clara's. "We have a problem," she said, her voice a strained sort of whisper.

"Put your hair up. I can't talk to you like this."

"I can't think with it up," she said. "There's something wrong with Boaz."

"I mean . . . you're going to have to be more specific," said Clara. She remained in the doorway, folding her arms across her chest.

Molly told her about what happened in the storage room,

about how, for a moment, they had gone *into* the backdrop from *Di Shturem*, the one Molly had gone to great lengths to salvage when the old Grand Theatre had at last closed. Molly stood and began pacing the room. "Anat is there, I'm sure of it. I *heard* her."

"You heard someone speaking Yiddish," said Clara. "You don't *know* if it was her."

"I think I know what my own girlfriend sounds like," she said. With a cry of frustration, she shoved one of her full-to-bursting clothes racks roughly against the wall, but Clara was unmoved.

"You said it yourself—you saw a sheyd," she said. "If it was, then we should talk to Ashmodai."

"Really? Ashmodai again? Because he was such a help the last time." Molly yanked at her hair. "I don't want to talk to Ashmodai. I want that ring," she said.

"I don't trust it," said Clara. "This place isn't Gehinnom. There shouldn't be sheydim in the storage closets."

But Molly was on the warpath and would not be stopped so easily. She tore through their apartment in a rage, pushing aside the salvaged set pieces they'd turned into furniture and pacing wildly, as though she was looking for something to tear apart. "And I don't trust Boaz with that ring. Either he doesn't know what he's doing with it or he does, and Anat is in danger because of him."

"Now, I don't think that's fair," began Clara, "and who's to say you'd be any better at working it . . ." She trailed off at the look on Molly's face.

"You just trust him because you like him."

"I don't like him," said Clara, much too quickly.

"Of course you like him! I've known you for over a hundred

years—I can tell," she said. "He's the little yeshiva bochur you always wanted, your little nerd with skinny legs. Even if you haven't had him yet, I know you want—"

"*Enough.*" Clara at last yanked out the pins in her hair. A jolt ran through her, and her senses buzzed, like she was standing against the auditorium speakers. "I *don't want him*, understand? I don't want him, and I have no idea what happened to your girlfriend. Just because I thought she was a bad idea does not mean I want her dead or that I'd have the power to make her disappear—"

"But what if he does?" said Molly. She held the back of the kitchen table so hard that Clara could hear it cracking in her grip. "What do we really know about him?"

"I know enough," said Clara. He was a box office attendant. She knew he'd gone to that fancy private school and that he lived in Brooklyn, because he never stopped complaining about it. She knew he loved *The Mummy* and that he spoke Hebrew. She now knew he spoke to the dead, that his aunt was famous for it. She knew that he was infuriating for . . . reasons. That was more than enough.

"Do you really?" said Molly. "Do you know what he's even doing working here? What he wants from this place? He already knows so much, and—"

"And Anat didn't?" said Clara. "You told her *everything*. I've told him nothing of consequence. He doesn't know what we are, and he doesn't know how long we've been here, none of it. I'm not the one putting everything we've built in danger."

"I told her because I trusted her!" shouted Molly. She strode toward the window, throwing it open so roughly it rattled. "*She* was someone I could trust."

"And look what good that did you!" said Clara. "You should have been more careful! You being reckless has put us both in danger."

Molly stepped back, as if Clara had struck her. "I have been careful my whole life, and it has *never* kept me safe." Her sister's entire demeanor stiffened, and Clara realized too late that she had crossed a boundary she ought not to have crossed. "Are you going to help me find her, or am I going to have to do it myself?"

Before Clara could say more, her sister burst into her owl form, diving out the window and soaring out of sight on a gust of wind.

Clara thought about going after her, but there was still work to do. She had a theater to run, and Molly had always been like this. Dramatic to the point of distraction. Nothing was easy with Molly, not from the moment Devorah brought her home. They'd spent years arguing about why she couldn't take any more acting roles, years arguing about why she could only drink from other Jews, years arguing about vigilante justice and starting a flock and everything else.

Clara approached the window. Twilight wasn't far off, and gold light struck the trees. The air smelled cold and hard, and she could practically taste exhaust and grit, the perfect late afternoon punctured by incessant car horns and an ambulance siren. She slammed the window shut. She needed to think.

But without the horns, she could hear her sister's voice echoing loud and clear in her brain.

You just trust him because you like him.

She knew he loved film. And that he was always late.

What *did* she really know about him? The thought of him, it was like a sudden itch that, now that she had scratched at it, she could not stop scratching and scratching . . .

She sighed, twisting her hair back into place, shoving herself back into her presentable form. This was her theater, and she was a *vampire,* damn it; she knew better than to let the wrong one in.

17

BOAZ

The last hours of Boaz's shift passed like sludge. He couldn't focus and couldn't get out of there fast enough. Even though he had made it back into the world of the living, he couldn't shake the feeling that something was still trailing his heels as he left. It wasn't an unfamiliar sensation for him, as someone who knew well enough how a ghost could cling, but this was different.

Where had he gone? Was that seriously what happened to Hila when she wore the ring? She'd never talked about villages and bird-footed shadows. Was he really that incompetent when it came to using the ring? That not only could he not call forward a ghost or find Anat, but he called something else, something with *taloned feet*? Because things could never be an ordinary disaster for him. It always had to be catastrophic.

And the feeling only got worse once he got home and opened up his laptop.

Boaz, as a rule, did not dream up ghosts where there were none. The ones he saw every day were enough. He needed to imagine, for his own sanity, that sometimes a creak in the floor was just the weather, that a groaning in the pipes was just old plumbing, and that shadows were shadows, nothing more.

But sitting in bed with his laptop, well after he had turned out the lights and intended to sleep, the normal excuses escaped him.

He did not know what to expect when he had started googling the Grand Dame. He knew the theater had once been a Yiddish stage, because it was the whole charm, the old stage details and the Magen David in the ceiling were what made it different from any other indie cinema downtown. It was cool, but as he had explained to more than his fair share of disappointed ghosts in the city, his Yiddish was confined to the stuff that found its way into Hebrew and whatever else he got via osmosis after a lifetime of being a Jew in a Jewish day school in New York City. It wasn't his thing or his family's history. He couldn't speak it, definitely couldn't read it, and hadn't, admittedly, done much digging on the particulars of the theater's history with it at all.

He hadn't caught the name of the man who had tried to tell him that the Senders were evil, but he remembered what Molly had called the backdrop: Tsvishn Veltn. He wasn't sure *what* he'd get when he typed "Tsvishn Veltn, Yiddish theater" into Google, but he certainly did not anticipate getting a result on the first page.

It was an article from YIVO on scandals of the Yiddish theater, a recap of some lecture that had been given years ago on the biggest dramas to hit the Yiddish stage. He scrolled through paragraphs about rivalries, infidelity, and then . . .

One would be remiss to neglect the greatest unsolved mystery to strike the Yiddish stage, the fate of Molly Lewis. A rising starlet who, despite her years, had already nabbed a series of covetable roles beside the titans of the stage vanished without a trace after the opening night of Di Shturem: The Yiddish Tempest. *Reviews of the performance in* Forverts *devoted paragraphs to the particularly inspired casting of Lewis as the monster Chenya, trapped in Tsvishn Veltn, Between Worlds. It was a role that, had she not vanished, may have launched a storied career to rival the greats. Her confidence, theatricality, and the ease with which she inhabited both male and female characters had drawn comparisons to the great Sarah Bernhardt herself. Though authorities had been alerted and a thorough investigation was launched, apart from a dark stain on the pavement feet from the Grand Theatre and scattered reports of sightings through the city years later, no trace of Lewis was ever found.*

Beneath the paragraph were a pair of photographs. The first a scan of the poster for *Di Shturem*. Beside that, there was a portrait of Lewis.

It took only one glance at the photo for Boaz to realize that he knew the answer to the disappearance of Molly Lewis. Because he had seen that face before. He'd seen her Sunday through Thursday for the last six months.

The resemblance was too uncanny. She looked a touch younger in the picture, which the article said was dated 1909, about the same time she had joined the Hebrew Actors' Union, but it was the same face. The *exact* same face.

Boaz thought of the memes he'd seen claiming that some actor was actually a time traveler, their doppelgänger found in a vintage photograph. Those usually ranged from eye-roll inducing to mildly convincing, at least in the sense that some people simply had that kind of face, and that despite the infinite variety of humanity, sometimes people just looked deeply alike.

Boaz tried looking for additional photos, or any other information that might explain the disappearance of Molly Lewis . . . or the Molly Sender that he saw every day at work. But the couple of mentions he found were quotes linking back to the YIVO piece and gave him no new information. He tried without success to get into archive editions of *Forverts*, but seeing as he had no Yiddish and limited ability to access any kind of database, he quickly exhausted his search.

Add it to the things he didn't understand. First his father appearing in the mirror, then Clara kissing him—or maybe just Clara in general—and now this. His head spun relentlessly when he made a short-lived attempt at sleeping, so he eventually gave up and returned to restlessly googling until the sun rose at last.

He stood long enough under the shower, trying to wake up, that eventually his mom had to pound on the door. "Boaz! Did you fall asleep in there? Are you okay?"

I wish.

When he finished, he changed into fresh . . . or, well, the least wrinkled clothing from the pile on his floor that still smelled acceptable and brought his laptop to the kitchen table, moving between his now endless tabs of Yiddish theater archives and supernatural portals.

His mother glanced up. "What did I tell you about laptops at the kitchen table?"

"It's homework," he muttered, rubbing stubborn sleep out of his eyes.

"You graduated months ago," she said with a sigh.

"Are you sure about that?"

"Boaz!" she said sharply, rubbing her temples before taking a glass from the cabinet and pouring herself some hot water from the kettle, followed with a generous scoop of instant coffee. "Anyway, Ms. Rabinyan would never have let me forget it if you hadn't."

His mom had taken a bigger role at his grandparents' catering company in the last few years, and had been trying relentlessly to get Boaz to work there instead, not understanding why he insisted on commuting all the way into Manhattan to work for strangers when he could instead make his grandparents happy answering endless phone inquiries from stressed brides about the status of their kosher certification and what dishes on their menu were free of nightshades. "Are you working today?"

"Day off," he muttered, swallowing a too-large sip of the coffee and scalding his tongue.

"Then what is this? You usually sleep in," she said, eyeing him suspiciously.

"Researching," he said, before adding the thing he knew would shut the conversation down. "Ghost stuff."

She huffed. "Is this for Hila, then?"

Boaz shook his head. "No, it's just . . . research . . . something I noticed at work."

Boaz learned long ago that the less he involved his mom in matters of the dead, the better. She didn't like it in the slightest. When he was little and started asking her about the men he saw on the subway who weren't really there, the sweet grandmothers in synagogue who were years gone, he had legitimately frightened her. When he was old enough to ask Hila, she said his father had been good at keeping those kinds of observations to himself, and that for the sake of his mother's frankly fragile nerves, he ought to do the same.

"You know you could put that effort into applying to college," his mother said, draining her cup and grabbing a banana from the bowl on the counter to stow in her tote.

"What does that have to do with anything?" he asked, louder than he intended.

"I am just saying—"

"It's not my fault!" he said, his voice rising. "I didn't *decide* to see dead people."

"We're all dealing with things, darling," she said. "But you're *letting* yourself get distracted, and wasting all your potential in the process."

The back of Boaz's neck went hot, and before he could stop himself, he said the thing he knew would end the conversation. "That was Dad's problem, wasn't it?"

He knew the moment he said it that it had worked. The moment he brought up his dad, he saw his mother shut down. She heard the words, to be sure, and she even furrowed her brow, but she would say nothing more about it. She *never* said anything more about it. It was the easiest way to sever the threads of the conversation.

She shook her head. "Don't spend the whole day on the computer," she muttered, before heading out the door.

18

MOLLY

Lomir flien. Ikh vil nisht brenen.

Let's fly. I don't want to burn. The voice she'd heard in Tsvishn Veltn had lodged itself in Molly's brain and drowned out everything else. It had to mean something. She'd heard Anat say that before, from the fire escape. She'd also told Boaz she didn't want to burn right before she disappeared. If she couldn't reach Anat in the theater, maybe her dorm room would be a way to her. Or at least give her a fresh lead.

When she reached the dorm building, she half expected there to be some evidence of chaos. Anat had been gone long enough for someone to notice she was missing. Surely one of that gaggle of karaoke-loving girls had reported her disappearance, or someone in that immersive theater class of hers, or a professor. Molly figured there would be caution tape, police detectives, signs, anxious students. She could imagine the scene so vividly. But nothing could have prepared her for what she would find instead.

Nothing. Not so much as a missing poster. No tape, no

detectives. Molly could see the lights glowing from Anat's window, but the blinds were drawn. Despite her efforts to peer through, she couldn't make out more than the cracks of light. When a student leaning out their window to smoke spotted her, she took to the shadows a few blocks down and shifted back into her human form.

She would have to use the front door.

The only bit of security was the usual bored guard that she'd slid past plenty of times. Molly waited casually by the door until a gaggle of girls sufficiently large came through. Molly tried to slip in with them through the door, but she got maybe five steps before the man at the security desk called out to her and demanded she sign in.

"Your friends not waiting for you?" he said gruffly as the gaggle continued on without her.

"Oh, I know where they're going," said Molly, carefully arranging her face into happy innocence. It was, in many instances, the most powerful mask she owned, more powerful than her true face. Even more powerful than her ability to inspire pure terror was her ability to disarm powerful men with a smile.

She signed her own name on the form and confidently listed herself as a guest of Anat Shalev, and her room number.

She was already turning away from the security desk when the guard called out to her.

"Wait just a minute!" he said. "I have to confirm that's a resident here. I don't recognize the name."

"Really?" said Molly.

After a moment of keying the name into the computer, he shook his head. "There's no . . . er . . . Anat Shalev in this building," he said.

"What do you mean? Did you spell it right?" Molly leaned over

151

the desk to try and get a glimpse of the computer.

"I spelled it just the way you wrote it, miss," he said. "And I don't have any record of anyone ever living here with that name. Now, unless you can text one of your friends to come down and sign you in, I'm going to have to ask you to leave—"

"But there has to be some mistake—I know she lives here. I was in her room two days ago. If you just let me go up, I'll get her, and we can sort this out." Molly made her way to the elevator, but the guard rose to his feet.

"Look here, miss, if you don't leave now—"

The door opened, and she pushed through the group of boys that spilled out and slammed her hand on the Door Close button just before the guard could stop her.

Molly's head spun. Had she forgotten something? Did she have the building wrong? She was certain that was impossible, but she was also certain that her girlfriend lived here, that she had come here not two days ago to speak with her, and now . . .

The door rattled open on the sixth floor, and Molly raced down the hall, stopping for a moment when her eyes caught the bulletin board, where club announcements and sign-up sheets and RA announcements were stacked on top of each other, competing for attention. On top was a large flyer announcing the show dates for *Kaddish: The Immersive Experience*.

Molly tore it down from the board, eyeing it quickly before folding it up and shoving it into her pocket. Maybe if this was a bust, she could try Anat's classmates; maybe they'd have leads on where she might be able to find Anat.

She stopped in front of the door that she remembered. Each door had names tacked on the front in careful calligraphy done by the RA. But where she knew it had once read *Anat* and *Emma*, it now read just . . . *Emma*.

Molly banged on the door. When it opened, Molly recognized Emma, Anat's roommate, the girl with the periodic table and *Doctor Who* posters. Same light brown hair and clear-rimmed glasses from Anat's Instagram.

When she saw Molly, she furrowed her brow.

"Excuse me?" she said. "Are you in my bio-chem lab?"

"It's Molly, Anat's girlfriend," she said quickly, Anat's name catching in her throat. "Do you . . ."

"Who?"

The word landed like a punch to Molly's face. She could accept the security guard was clueless, but Emma *knew* Anat. They shared a room. Molly *knew* they shared a room.

Didn't they?

"Your roommate," said Molly, her voice rising with panic.

But Emma just shook her head. "I don't know what you're talking about. Maybe you got me confused with some other Emma?"

"No, I haven't!" said Molly. What sort of sick game was this? It didn't make sense. Emma began to close the door, so Molly jammed her foot in to stop it.

"Then where is Anat?" Molly yelled, her last grasp on her patience slipping away. "She's here! Why can't you tell me where?"

People were staring again, and not in a good way. Like stepping out onto a stage without remembering her costume, or her lines, or a stitch of makeup. Like finding out she was the only person not in on the joke.

At that moment, she heard the bang of a door behind her. The security guard, now joined with backup, glanced down the hallway, before catching sight of her. "You there!"

Molly froze. She could shift here. Tear apart the building until someone told her something useful about where she might find Anat. Her hands twitched toward her scrunchie, but one look at the bewildered Emma was enough to convince her against it. They would forget, but she wouldn't.

"Sorry, sorry," said Molly, turning away from the girl and toward the security guard. She dialed her voice to its sweetest octave, her face to its most innocent, girlish mask. That alone was usually enough to deescalate the situation, and it did not fail her now. The security guard did nothing but nod at her curtly as she passed him by on the stairs. "I'm leaving now! So sorry for the confusion."

It would have been no use, fighting the girl. Molly knew what lying sounded like: a racing heart, missed beats of speech, an averted gaze. This girl just looked confused. No one knew what she was talking about, who she was talking about.

Anat wasn't just gone. It was as though she had never been there at all.

19

BOAZ

When he woke up Shabbat morning, Boaz realized that he had less than fifteen minutes to make himself presentable *and* get to shul at a time that was acceptably late. Too early was for the elderly and their ghosts, and too late was too late.

Aunt Hila never went to shul. Ever. She could be coerced into attending a Bar Mitzvah ceremony, but otherwise her Shabbat was a big dinner. In Israel, Aunt Hila was the sort who had much preferred spending her Fridays in the company of people she liked and her Saturdays at the beach.

But being active, upstanding members of the congregation mattered to his mother's family. More to the point, it mattered to Daniel's family, and Boaz needed to catch him before he went back uptown. He wasn't about to wait until sunset to do it.

He made it while people were still trickling in. He found Daniel in his usual seat beside his father and younger brother; when their eyes met, he waved Boaz over enthusiastically. Boaz slid in next to his friend, still adjusting his tallit and trying to keep the prayer shawl from slipping down his shoulders.

"Don't you miss this?" he muttered, grinning. "Don't tell me this isn't more fun than Shabbat in the Heights?"

"What will it take to get you to come uptown for a change?" Daniel asked. "It's actually a lot of fun, you know. Maybe you'll even like it."

"Doubtful," said Boaz. "I don't do upstate."

"Washington Heights is not *upstate*."

"Which is exactly what someone who lives in Washington Heights would say," he said, prompting an irritated shush from Mr. Sayegh. "I heard you can see Greenland from your dorm—is it true?"

Boaz still hadn't gotten used to not seeing Daniel every day. For the entirety of his educational career, Daniel had been there, a constant. He knew every major and minor detail in Boaz's life, from his particularly harrowing ghost encounters to his latest film obsession. He was the only person in their entire year who hadn't ditched him once they got wind of what he could do. He was the one person who he could tell, apart from Hila, about the things he saw.

And maybe an hour and a half each way on the subway wasn't technically Canada, or even Albany, but it wasn't around the corner. It wasn't at his lunch table, or at the library, or on a carpool home. Texting, FaceTime, it wasn't remotely the same.

They made it through the morning musaf exchanging meaningful glances and occasionally muttering what amounted to plans to hang out after, and it might have been an otherwise dull Shabbat morning had it not been for Allan Gindi.

Allan Gindi had died weeks ago from a bad bout of pneumonia. Boaz had noticed him lurking in the very back row of the sanctuary when he had arrived but had made a conscious effort to ignore him. When he'd glanced back and found that Allan had moved up a few rows, he ignored that, too. He might have made it all the way to the Torah reading without having to think about him, but at last he felt a cold breeze of a whisper by his ear.

"Boaz, can I have a word?"

Boaz tried to focus on Rabbi Pardo, trying to pretend that he couldn't hear him. "Boaz, can you hear me? Boaz?"

"Not here," breathed Boaz before they launched into the amidah prayer. Which was *supposed* to be silent, a basic fact that, even in death, Mr. Gindi decided to ignore.

"Of course not *in here*," he said. "I would never interrupt the silent amidah."

"You are *right now*."

In life Allan Gindi was always inserting himself into things that categorically weren't his business. He wasn't a member of the shul's chevra kadisha, the burial society, but he was the first to ask them for details about crime scenes or to offer *his* opinion on the deceased, as if it mattered. It was how he had wound up adding himself to the number of Gravesend Jews who knew that Aunt Hila wasn't just a good actress when it came to her chats with the dead and Boaz wasn't just the fucked-up day school kid with a habit of squandering potential.

Which was, apparently, why he was showing up to ruin Boaz's morning.

"This is important."

Boaz turned briefly, scowling, and realized a second too late that to everyone else it might appear that he was grimacing at the pair of elderly men in the row behind him. Boaz quickly turned back around, hoping no one had noticed.

Daniel, who was sitting next to him, did. "Everything cool?" he muttered under his breath.

Boaz nodded, but Mr. Gindi was making so much noise behind him that he couldn't focus. The moment the amidah ended, he muttered, "I'll be back in a sec," left his siddur on his chair, and slipped out of the hall toward the restrooms.

He didn't need to check if Allan Gindi knew to follow him, because the moment the door to the sanctuary closed, the man raised his voice to full volume. "Really sorry to bother you, but this is important."

"Why are you still here, anyway? Did a piece of you get left behind? Did the chevra forget something?"

Mr. Gindi coughed, shaking his head. "You should remind Itzik Sutton that a shomer must watch the body *at all times* between death and burial," he said, chuckling. "He stepped out to take a phone call at the morgue, and I decided that . . . Well, if I moved on, what would you all do without me?"

"Mr. Gindi, what is it?"

"Not out here," said Allan, glancing down the hall. "Come, come, we're not interested in humiliating you."

"Who is 'we'?" said Boaz, following his gaze. A gaggle of girls who looked like they were still in middle school were gossiping loudly by the doors, and when they saw him looking, a couple of them tried to wave and get his attention. Why couldn't everyone just ignore him? Boaz would like nothing more than to be left alone; it would have been a lovely change of pace from his current circumstances.

"Ah, just some of the old crowd. They wanted a word with you."

Boaz stopped, folding his arms. "Is this about joining the chevra? Because I've already told them a thousand times that even if I wanted to do it, which I don't, Rabbi Pardo *absolutely* doesn't want me there."

"It's not about the burial society, boy," said Allan, leading him down the hall and into an empty classroom. "Though, for the record, it is a mitzvah, and think of the gossip, all those post-deathbed confessions—"

"Make it quick," said Boaz the moment the door closed.

The classroom was filled with ghosts, each flickering in and out of sight. Boaz recognized them at once. The old crowd was about a dozen men and women, who, for some strange and infuriating reason, would not move on. Ever. Some of them Boaz had known forever, like Rabbi Maimon, who he had met the first time he came for the children's classes and had been in the shul since its founding. Others, like Allan Gindi, were new additions, people he had known in life.

"Fine, then. What's this about? My aunt?"

"I wasn't going to say anything, you see," said Allan, "but then you came in with that ring—"

"How'd you know about the ring?" said Boaz. It was still tucked into his shirt. The idea of Allan Gindi or any of the ghosts being able to see through his clothes was too terrible to contemplate. *That* would be the fact that would put him over the edge.

"It radiates energy," said Allan. "It's in the air. From the moment you walked into the shul, I could sense it. I've never felt something like this since dying."

Boaz checked his watch. If he didn't go back soon, people would start to notice . . . or, well, Daniel would. "What is it that you wanted to tell me?"

"Just that what I've heard, asking around, is that you should get rid of that ring at once," he said. "It's dangerous in the best of hands, and, well—"

"It's no good," said old Rabbi Maimon. "Brings nothing but trouble."

"Nothing I can't handle," Boaz said, not ready to mention the strange encounter he'd had with the shawarma ghost in the Village or whatever had happened in the storage room with Molly. He still didn't understand for certain *what* had happened then. "And given the way you've all decided to bombard me . . . on *Shabbat*, no less . . ."

"We all feel it," said Frieda Cohen, a fussy woman who had, more than once, snuck her cat with her into services when she was alive. "But it is not a mere amulet. It is an ancient object and best handed to the appropriate stewards—"

"Who? My aunt?"

None of the ghosts spoke for a moment. That Boaz had been able to get *silence* from this crowd, however brief, was a small miracle. Except that he also realized, slowly, what that meant. "You don't mean my aunt?"

"We . . . don't like how she uses the ring, either," said Rabbi Maimon at last.

"Why not?" said Boaz.

"Party tricks," said Frieda Cohen. The other ghosts made noises of agreement. "And the consequences, if that ring fell into the wrong hands . . ."

"But we could protect it, you see," said Rabbi Maimon.

Frieda Cohen nodded vigorously. "Yes, yes. We could protect it."

"You can trust us," said Allan. "We've only ever had your best interests at heart, now. Haven't we?"

They all murmured in agreement, and Boaz had to bite back the urge to laugh. A bunch of dead busybodies who knew nothing about him and what he could handle, what he handled every day without complaint. "Um, first off, this is a family heirloom. Second of all, no. Third of all, you all seriously think I would just hand it over to you because you asked nicely?" Boaz turned toward the door. "Yeah, that's not going to happen, sorry."

But when he reached for the door, Frieda Cohen beat him to it, blocking his way out. She was now inches from his face, suddenly solid and barely flickering.

"We thought we'd start by asking nicely."

They all had risen to their feet, standing in a semicircle around him. Allan Gindi piped up. "I told them you wouldn't agree. But they didn't believe me."

"You're a fine young man," said Rabbi Maimon. "But this is much bigger than you."

Boaz reached for the chain around his neck, but they drew closer, bringing with them an icy wave of air. The chill rising off of them caught in his chest and made the hairs on the back of his neck stand on end.

"I wouldn't do that if I were you," said Allan. He reached up to grasp Boaz's arm, but his hand, to Boaz's horror, did not pass through his arm like smoke and vapors the way it was supposed to have done. Instead, it rested there, ice-cold as anything, but solid. "Now, give us the ring, before we get . . . not so nice."

Boaz swallowed, his mind drawing a blank. How was he supposed to fight off all of them? Could he, if they were solid? And what was this sudden interest in the ring?

At that moment, the door behind him swung open and Boaz fell backward into someone who, he realized almost at once, was Daniel.

Daniel stared down at him, and then up, his eyes scanning the room. "What . . . the actual—"

Boaz scrambled to his feet, and grabbed Daniel. "Get out of here now!"

Boaz ran, properly ran, narrowly avoiding mowing down the gaggle of girls as he went. He had let go of Daniel but heard his footsteps behind him. Would they be able to outrun the dead board of the shul, if it came to it? Boaz had no idea whether they could be followed and for how far. Not when ghosts were going solid, and crossing boundaries they were not supposed to be able to cross. He had no idea what they might be capable of.

"Boaz!" They had made it outside, down the wheelchair ramp, and out onto the sidewalk. Daniel looked at him, his eyes still wide. "What *was that*?"

"Sorry, it was the ghosts, I can explain—"

"Those weren't ghosts," said Daniel, shaking his head. "I could *see them*, dude."

"You could . . . what?"

"Allan Gindi, Frieda Cohen . . . and was that Rabbi Maimon? Because he looks very little like his portrait out in the front lobby, let me tell you."

That . . . wasn't supposed to happen, had never happened. Daniel wasn't supposed to see ghosts. Daniel never had. Not when ghosts trailed them on the subway or on class field trips. Daniel had no idea how many dead people lurked at the Eighty-Sixth Street subway station. "I . . . don't know what happened," said Boaz. "They've been doing that lately, getting more solid."

"You mean to tell me this has happened before?" said Daniel. "When were you going to tell me?"

"You're uptown now. I didn't have the chance."

"*It's just Washington Heights*," said Daniel. "Dude, I thought you knew you could tell me when your weird stuff gets *weird*."

"I don't think that's what's happening here, but if I get wind of that, you'll be the *first* to know." Boaz glanced back at the shul, and even though no army of the living dead burst through the doors, he wanted to put as much distance between that building and the ring as possible. He started walking fast, Daniel trailing after him.

"Anything else you haven't told me?" Daniel asked, clumsily folding up his tallit as he went and slinging it over his arm. "You have my undivided attention now, I can assure you."

"Um . . . I think the girls who run the theater are dead?" Boaz said. He wasn't sure where would be a good place to go and have this conversation. Certainly not back to his apartment. His mom already thought the job was a bad idea. If she found any of this out, she'd probably keep him from ever going back.

"What do you mean . . . you *think* they're dead?" said Daniel, suddenly sounding unsettlingly like Aunt Hila. He caught Boaz by the shoulder, and for a moment they stopped, just before the intersection that would have put him on Avenue U. "Are they, or are they not?"

"Well, that's where it gets complicated," said Boaz.

"I know you're the expert here on dead things," began Daniel, "but last time I checked, that is the definition of *not* complicated. Either someone is dead or they're not dead. And you were the one who made me watch *The Mummy* so many times that I would have thought you learned by now to leave the dead alone," said Daniel.

Boaz groaned. "They're undead, okay?"

"Great, exactly what *The Mummy* warned you about. What kind of undead?"

A knot in Boaz's chest unwound. This was why they were friends. It wasn't because Daniel shared his taste in movies (he did not). It wasn't that they didn't argue (they did, a lot). It was that no matter how weird things got, Daniel was the only person who would believe him without question. Daniel never thought he was too weird. He had seen all the skeletons in the closet, and never flinched once.

"I . . . have no idea," he said, before telling him about what the ghost had told him outside the theater, about the YIVO page he found. "They're not ghosts. Ghosts can't run a theater."

"Isn't *that* the plot of a movie, though?" asked Daniel. "That is *definitely* the plot of something you forced me to watch."

"The Phantom in *Phantom of the Opera* isn't actually dead, just a creep who lives in the basement."

Daniel snorted. "You know what I think? I think the best thing you could do is quit. Get a job at an AMC. Or another indie theater, if you want to be snobby. But they don't pay you enough to care."

"You sound like Hila or my mom," grumbled Boaz. Daniel had a point. Of course he had a point. It didn't matter that he kind of loved his job, that he was actually pretty good at it, all things considered. There were other theaters, probably some that weren't run by the dead.

But Molly was obsessed with the ring. Everyone wanted the ring, apparently. He could work at some soulless multiplex, and it wouldn't change the fact that if they wanted it, they'd keep coming for him.

"I don't want to quit," he said at last. "I just need to know what I'm dealing with."

Daniel didn't say anything at first. He just stood there, and Boaz wondered whether he'd finally gone too far, if he had at last reached a skeleton that even Daniel couldn't handle, if this was the day he noped out.

Instead, he said, his voice low: "In that case, I think I've got an idea."

There was once a young king who had been set an impossible task.

The king needed to build a great temple for his people, a place in which the ark and sacred covenant made between his people and the Most Holy, Blessed Be He, would be honored.

But it was no ordinary task, for this was to be no ordinary sanctuary. No part of the temple could be built by or with that which had spilled blood. His father, a great warrior in his own right, had not been able build such a temple, for his hands had spilled too much. So, the task had fallen to the young king, who had not yet seen war and had not taken the life of any man.

It was not long before the young king encountered a problem. For it was not enough to assemble builders who had only lived in times of peace and had yet to take up a sword. The very tools that were to be used, clubs and blades and hammers, had or could easily have been used to draw blood and would not do for the task at hand. But how was he to build a great temple without them?

The problem vexed the king endlessly. He slept little, working deep into the night and tossing the problem over in his mind even as he lay in bed. He spent long hours with his advisors and his builders. He called the greatest minds from all twelve tribes of his people to hear how they thought this problem might be solved.

But none could come up with answers. After countless hours, countless plans attempted and abandoned, the task had been deemed impossible.

But the young king did not believe in impossible. Such a concept should not exist among his people, who had survived in exile, in slavery, in the wilderness, who had crossed the sea on foot and vanquished foes far greater and more numerous than they.

But this task would need more help than that which a mortal man could provide. So the young king sought the advice of the Prince of Demons.

It was known among the Sages that when the Prince of Demons came to this world, he favored a water cistern atop a summit not far from the gates of the city. It was known, too, that he would not walk in daylight. That he could be met only in shadow, on the border between worlds. If the Prince of Demons was to be found, he would be found there, and he would not appear before dusk.

So the king traveled to the mountain at the first light of day, bringing with him a donkey laden with caskets of wine and a retinue of men, soldiers he trusted with his life and his secrets. Upon reaching the cistern and finding it unattended, he worked quickly, draining the shallow pool of its crystal-clear water and replacing it with the heavy, fragrant wine of his court.

Then he and his men lay in wait. He waited three days and three nights in which the moon shrank in the night sky.

On the fourth night, it was Rosh Chodesh, a new moon, when the night sky is at its darkest, lit by naught but the light of stars. So dark it was that no one, not even the Prince of Demons, would see the king waiting for him in the shadows, or that the cistern was filled with wine.

The king took care not to stir when he heard the footsteps

167

coming from the deepest depths of the cave. He did not dare breathe as he watched the prince dip his hands in the cistern and take a sip of the wine.

The plan worked. The prince, delighted by the first sip of expensive wine and the great fortune by which his cistern had been filled with it, continued to drink until the pool was entirely drained, and, his senses clouded, he sank at once into a heavy sleep.

Once he was certain that the prince lay sleeping, the young king got to work, binding the prince's hands in bonds inscribed with the names of the Most Holy, Blessed Be He, so that he would be powerless once he woke. He then waited for the sun to rise again.

At last, the Prince of Demons began to struggle out of slumber. He took one look at the branch of sunlight creeping in from the mouth of the cave and shrank from it. He made to stand, to move farther into the shadows, but when he noticed the bindings and the king sitting across from him, he was enraged. "How dare you bind me? Do you know who it is you have dared touch?"

"I would come out to this place for no one but the Prince of Demons," said the young king. "I know to whom I speak."

The prince snarled. "You have no idea, boy. You, who have barely been weaned from your mother's breast, who calls himself a king with hands as soft as those of a babe. I have seen a thousand lifetimes come and go, a hundred kings rise and fall. Your own life will be but a blink and breath in mine."

The young king expected this and did not let his apprehension show. "I have come to you because I need your help. I need you to show me the stones by which I might build the temple, those that might be cut and honed without tools and yet stand as a monument still."

The Prince of Demons barked a laugh. "And now the boy king wants favors? What makes you think I can help you, or that I will?"

"Help me, and I will release you," he said.

"That is not an offer, but a threat," said the prince. "I do not take kindly to those. No. If you want my help, you must offer me that which only a king could give."

"You want money?" asked the young king. Surely the Prince of Demons had no need for gold or coin, though if that was all the demon asked for, then he would gladly give it.

But the Prince of Demons only laughed. "I have coin enough. No, surely you can offer more than that."

The young king sighed. Still, he would not give up so easily. There had to be something that only he could give, and he was so desperate for the stones. "I will give you power, then," said the young king. "Influence."

"I am already a prince," said the demon. "I have a kingdom of my own."

"But not in this world," said the young king. "In this world, I am king, and you will have the power that I give you."

The young king watched as the Prince of Demons considered his offer. What arrogance, thought the Prince of Demons. Surely a king would know that the Most Holy, Blessed Be He, and He alone, could bestow power, and that a demon was a greater creation than any mortal man.

The prince eyed the ring on the young king's hand. It bore his seal, a six-pointed star. He had heard much of this young king and the great power he possessed over that which was his dominion, and his alone.

And the prince knew so long as the young king wore that ring, whatever power he claimed to grant would be meaningless.

But a young king could not hope to understand the will of demons.

"Prove it. Allow me to carry your ring," said the prince.

The young king scoffed. "The ring is royal property, not that of demons."

"Am I not royal, too, Your Highness?" asked the prince. "But even if I wished it, even if I trusted your words, I would still need the ring. For my dominion is Gehinnom, between your world and the World to Come. Just as you need the ring to walk in my kingdom, to speak to me as an equal, so would I need to possess it if I am to guide you in your world and lead you to the stones. If I do not hold it and your favor, I cannot take you, unable as I am to walk in sunlight."

The young king removed the ring from his finger and clutched it in his palm. He did not trust the Prince of Demons. He was young, but he was no fool. He knew the cunning of shadows and the beings that walked in them.

But he did not see another way. And he was still king, with men to command and a kingdom to rule, and the demon prince was still his captive.

So the young king held out the ring. "You may hold it while we walk. But you will remain in chains."

And so this way, bound and chained with the ring on his finger, the demon prince led the young king for miles. They traveled endlessly, it seemed, stopping only when it became too dark to see, and starting again at first light. Days became weeks, until at last they ran out of food and water and were in barren lands where no amount of foraging might satiate their appetites.

"Do you mean for us to die?" asked the king, staring out around him at the vast stretches of unforgiving desert. There was little shade here for miles, and the air was heavy with heat and salt.

"We are not far now from where the stones lie. Why, they are simply up those cliffs, and through the caverns. But if I am to guide you there, I cannot do so in chains."

"If I free you, what will stop you from fleeing to the edge of the wilderness?"

"How little faith you have in me," said the Prince of Demons lazily, twirling the signet ring. "I will not walk with you like this. We walk as equals, or not at all."

The king, desperate and without any more time to linger, knew he could not afford to refuse the prince's demands. But he was not such a fool as to think that he could simply free the prince from his bonds and not suffer consequences.

"Fine, then," he said at last. "I will remove the bindings, but I will bind one of your arms to me. You may lead me. We will walk as equals, bound to one another. But this way, you cannot escape without taking me with you."

The Prince of Demons paused a moment, then nodded, concealing the smile that threatened to play upon his lips. He had rather been hoping the king would suggest just that.

Bound as he was to his foe, the king followed the Prince of Demons into the mouth, the darkness of the caverns, until the light vanished, and he had to feel his way forward with his feet. The king could see nothing ahead of him, and almost at once regretted not bringing fire with him into the cave.

"We should turn back," said the king at last to the prince. "I cannot walk like this."

"Well, it is lucky for you that I can," said the Prince of Demons silkily. "And we are so close, Your Highness. Trust that I will lead you." When the king hesitated, he added, "Unless His Highness is afraid of the dark?"

The young king, determined then to betray no sign of weakness before the Prince of Demons, gritted his teeth and walked on. He was the king, after all. He was not afraid of the dark.

They walked for what seemed like miles more, before at last they stopped. "Here are the stones that you seek," said the Prince of Demons. "Come. Together we may lift the first and bring it back to your men, so that they might see it by the light, and return with us here to mine the rest."

"I still cannot see a thing," said the king. It was not just that he could not see. He had never been amid such darkness. It was as if the darkness was a solid thing, pressed against his eyes and his mouth, as though he would be smothered by it. "How do I know you are not lying to me?"

"I would never lie to you," said the Prince of Demons. When the young king scoffed, the prince added, "Shall I light a flame?"

"How?" said the young king. "It is too damp here, and there is no wood."

"Have you forgotten who I am?" asked the prince.

After a moment, the caverns filled with bright, dazzling light.

Around them, the king could now see the stones. It was just as the Prince of Demons had promised. The entire cave was full of a pale, smooth stone, giant boulders that when he touched them proved soft as silk. They were the finest stones he had ever seen and would undoubtedly be perfect for the temple.

The king turned to the demon prince, who held his hand aloft to cast the rays around them. But when he looked at the prince, he was no longer the Prince of Demons. Instead, he saw what could have been his own reflection, his own face staring back at him.

A king and a prince entered the cave, but two kings emerged.

"He has stolen from me! He has stolen from me!" shouted one king, spitting with rage. "He is an imposter who wears my face!"

All the king's men could see, clear as anything, that one was an imposter, that one must have been the demon prince in disguise. It was easy enough to determine. One carried the royal seal, the heavy blank ring like no other. The other, for all his ranting and raving, did not.

So above the ravings and protests of the distraught Prince of Demons, the king's men removed the bonds from the king and wrapped them twice round the imposter. When still he continued to shout, he was gagged, for none wished to hear any more of his poisoned tongue, and set about removing the stones from the depths of the cave. When they emerged many hours later with the first of their haul, the imposter was gone, nowhere to be found.

Of what happened next, the Sages disagree. Some say the king eventually took back his ring with force. Some say with cunning. Some say that the king returned to his palace, and a crowd demanded that the king show his feet, for one could always tell demons by their bird feet, even when they wore the faces of men. Some say that the king enlisted the services of the great Shamir, a worm who could cut stone, and with this worm completed his work. Still others say that the king did no such thing, that he lived in exile, a broken man whose past was but an ever-diminishing dream, a life to which he could never return, that a king forced to the shadows cannot escape them, and that a demon allowed to walk in sunlight will not be returned to the dark.

20

CLARA

Clara had a gift, a purpose. That gift meant Clara could get whatever information she required from just about any man . . . in theory.

And she needed information from Boaz. At least so that she could tell Molly she tried, that the boy simply had *issues* and an old family ring but no answers.

She waited until eleven, when the last show of the evening was over. Boaz was scheduled to help close, but there were no more tickets to sell, and in the event that things took a turn, she wanted to make sure that no one saw them.

Molly was out, which was probably for the best, because Molly took stubborn to an art form and could not be convinced to trust Boaz. The best Clara could hope for was to keep her sister far away from him and handle things herself.

When she made her way down, the lobby was empty except for Boaz, who was swiveling in endless circles on his stool. He abruptly stopped when she got close and gave her a small wave.

"You're going to break the stool doing that, you know," she said by way of greeting.

"But I haven't yet," he said, holding her eyes a moment too long. Finally, he cleared his throat, fixing his gaze on his knees. "What brings you down here? I thought you wanted me to close."

"I do," she said. "But I've . . . resolved the numbers for last week already, and I just thought . . . You know, I wanted to check on how you were doing, especially given . . ."

She wasn't sure of how to put "since I told you to forget us kissing and Anat's girlfriend disappeared off the face of the earth" without setting off alarms, and the whole point was to put him at ease. She needed him to relax so that he'd open up and tell her what was going on.

"Look, I'm really sorry, really . . ."

"It's okay," she began, but Boaz shook his head. His heart was racing as well, and she thought of what Molly had told her, that she was certain Boaz was lying to her. But she also knew that they both had this effect on people. Whether or not a human knew *what* they were, an instinct inside them knew to be on alert, to be just a little afraid.

And, deep down, Clara rather liked that. Usually.

"Look, I know you tried."

"I really did," he said, swallowing hard. "I really thought that guy was bad news. I mean, he was way too excited about that French movie. . . ."

Nope. Nope. That was not the conversation Clara wanted to have right now. She had already made up her mind not to talk about it, and that boy was not going to convince her otherwise. "I mean with Anat; Molly told me what happened," she said, trying to redirect the conversation as quickly as she could. "She's really worried,

176

and the whole thing is so strange. If you knew anything about what happened, you would tell us, right?"

"What?" Boaz started spinning again, and she could see a flush rise up his neck, even if he didn't admit that was not what he had been about to discuss. "Yeah, of course," he said.

For a while, neither of them spoke. He kept swiveling in his chair, looking at her as if he was waiting for her to say something more, but the only thing she wanted to ask was the very thing she couldn't. *Can I trust you? I can trust you, right?* Because it wouldn't matter the kind of answer he gave. She had learned from Devorah that there was no way to build trust on words and promises alone.

At last he spoke. "Hey, um, you wouldn't mind actually letting me cash out now? It's getting late and I should really . . ."

"Yes, yeah, no problem!" she said, too cheerful. She didn't want him to leave. She hadn't decided whether she could trust him yet, but surely she would if he could just stay here a bit longer. And the idea that he didn't want to stay stung, though she couldn't quite put her finger on why. "You can head out if you want. I'll take care of the register."

"Really?" Boaz threw his jacket on with a bit too much cere-mony. She stood up, too, not sure why until she was on her feet, only that when he went toward the door, she was in his way, and that when she tried to move out of the way, he moved with her, like they were caught in a dance. His heart rate was still up. Maybe he wasn't afraid of her, but if that was the case, he really ought to get that checked out. "Great, thanks! I'll . . . see you tomorrow, yeah?"

"A gute nakht," she said, watching him spend a great deal of time fussing with the zipper of his coat before hurrying out the door.

She was just about to remove the cash box and head upstairs when she heard the shout.

She knew it was Boaz at once. It could be no one else. She bolted through the doors and stepped out into the night. He had gotten about ten feet from the entrance.

Boaz was doubled over, clutching his stomach, while an assailant with a sweatshirt hood pulled low over his face lobbed punches at him. To his credit, Boaz attempted to throw a punch back, but it didn't seem to do very much. Apparently, he could only land a punch on someone drunk on her Estrie charms.

The assailant yanked off Boaz's backpack, and he crumpled to the ground.

Clara didn't think. She *really* didn't think.

She pulled the pins out of her hair.

"Leave him alone." Clara lowered her voice to its most animal growl, spitting the words out from between her now sharp teeth.

The assailant stopped at once, staring at her. Even with his hood pulled low, she still caught that flicker of fear, the way his breath hitched when he saw her. Like a groom pulling back a veil and finding no bride beneath. A wave of pure satisfaction ran through her. "Give it back," she said, holding out her hand.

The assailant who had taken Boaz's backpack dropped it, turned, and ran. For a moment, she thought of running after him, but then the smell hit her.

Blood.

A lot of it.

Her head spun with the smell. She hadn't forgotten it, the taste she had the other night, and that was nothing compared to this. Salt and metal and something that was *him*, precisely Boaz Harari and

178

no one else. Something clawed in her stomach, roaring with hunger for it.

"Boaz!" She hurried toward him as he reached for his backpack, groaning. "Boaz, are you all right?"

He tried pushing himself to his feet but wobbled so dangerously that she swooped to his side to catch him. One look at the stain spreading down the front of his shirt from his face was enough to see that his nose had been broken. For a moment, she thought she might lose it right there and bite him. She had forgotten how hungry she was until she was presented a meal like this, dripping.

"I'm . . . fine," he muttered, snapping her brain back into place. He didn't *sound* fine. His voice sounded thick, muffled, and when she looked at him, she remembered that her hair was still down, and therefore what he was looking at.

There was bruising around one of his eyes, but he was definitely staring at her, and if it weren't for his heart, she wouldn't have known what to make of the expression. His heart was hammering *loud* in his chest, louder than she'd heard it in the theater. If he hadn't been afraid before, now it was absolutely certain.

"Come on, I've got a first aid kit in the theater," she said, doing her best to ignore her roaring hunger. "I know it's . . . Well. But there's nothing to be afraid of; I won't hurt you."

A lie. Of course he ought to be afraid. It had been a ridiculous thing to say. She couldn't promise him that. Quite the opposite.

But apparently Boaz had gefilte fish for a brain, because in spite of everything, he looked at her with the same expression he had that day in the box office. His eyes were glassy, unfocused, and, if she was not mistaken, he almost *smiled*. "I know."

21

BOAZ

This was, without question, the worst idea Boaz had ever had.

No, it was the worst idea *Daniel* had ever had. He had not been the one who had suggested getting Boaz's face smashed up in the name of drawing out a monster. That had, 100 percent, been Daniel's idea. *It's like the time I saw sharks with my family in the Bahamas.*

You what?

Sharks! Yeah, they're smart. They don't usually come up to a ship and announce their presence, not unless you throw fish blood and guts in the water first . . .

Boaz still hadn't quite gotten over the mental image of Daniel on a ship in the Bahamas looking for sharks, but that was beside the point. His thought, that a fight and a bit of blood would draw out the Sender sisters if they were in fact monsters, had . . . worked.

It had also ruined his face.

Clara pulled him back inside the theater, depositing him on a bench outside theater one. No, the monster, which by day he knew as Clara, deposited him there. This wasn't Clara, not the one he knew, the girl who was a brilliant business owner and too uptight and looked like she'd walked straight out of an old silent film.

Instead, she was . . . He didn't even know how to describe it. Like something he would have dreamed up from beneath his bed, with blank white eyes and gray skin and rows of razor-sharp teeth. Her dark hair, now out of its usual buns or braids, was longer than he'd thought it would be, to her waist. This wasn't the ghosts, the dead who to his eye at least looked human. No, this was something else entirely. He kept searching for a comparison, dully trying to remember a movie that could speak to it. He thought of *The Ring*, one of the first horror movies he'd seen when he decided that watching more of them would make seeing the dead bearable, and how he'd had nightmares for weeks about it, about girls like *that* climbing into his room. . . .

"I'm getting the first aid kit," she muttered, avoiding his gaze. "And water. Do you need water? I'll get you water."

Boaz's face had begun to throb in earnest, and he could only kind of breathe out of his nose. When he got home, he was *absolutely* going to have a word with Daniel. His nose had been one of the few things he didn't entirely hate about his face.

When Clara returned, her hair had been pulled back again into a loose ponytail, and her face returned to normal. Gone was the blank-eyed monster. Her cheeks had shifted from gray to a delicate olive, her eyes to their dark brown. Her hands, which had become long and clawlike, had shrunk to their usual, ordinary shape. Even her hair seemed shorter, and when she spoke, her teeth were no longer sharpened to a point.

Like nothing had happened.

She handed him the largest of the concession stand cups, filled to the brim with tap water. "Sorry about that," she said lightly.

Boaz tried not to look too interested, but it was difficult not to.

"I'm sorry you had to see that," she said, still avoiding his gaze, as she returned to the first aid kit, the lid of which she suddenly struggled to take off.

"Do you want me to try?" Boaz offered after a moment, reaching out. Watching her lose her battle with the box was almost as frustrating as the throbbing on his face.

"What? No, I've got it." She yanked, wrenching the lid off with such force that it snapped in two. "There, see? Now, what do we have in here . . ."

She rummaged through, handing Boaz antibacterial wipes, a tiny bottle of peroxide, Band-Aids, and a few packets of ibuprofen that had an expiration date of two years prior. "I think I need a new one. . . . We just, you know, don't have many accidents here, usually. . . ."

She stopped, gnawing on her lip, and after a long pause, inched a few steps away from him. "You really are a bleeder, aren't you? Do you want me to get you some paper towels?"

"It's fine," Boaz began, but she had already darted off. She returned with fistfuls of paper towels from the bathroom, half of which she'd soaked in cold water. "Here, you should be the one to clean yourself up. . . . Do you need a mirror?"

"No, it's fine," he said, taking the giant wad of paper towels and trying delicately to wipe away some of the blood from around his mouth and chin and neck. Then he held a dry one to his nose, pinching and tipping his head back.

"I'd help, it's just . . . better if I don't."

"It's fine," he said again, sounding like a Muppet with a head cold. "It's not a big deal." He would need a mirror to assess the entirety of the situation with his nose, but he was afraid that if he said as much, she'd go and rip one off the bathroom wall.

Clara watched him like a hawk, still keeping a solid five feet between them as he finally let go of his nose and then tried wiping the blood from the collar of his shirt. After a moment of indecision, he popped one of the expired ibuprofen.

"Not that one!" said Clara, a second too late. "That one slows down clotting—you're just going to keep bleeding all over yourself."

"It's really not that bad," he said.

"Yes, it is!" she said. "Trust me, you have no idea what you smell like right now. It's—" She stopped suddenly, eyes wide with embarrassment.

"What are you?" he asked, figuring that the most direct question would be best.

She continued to chew on her lip, arms folded tightly across her chest. He expected her to tell him off, or to pretend things were normal, when obviously they weren't.

Instead, after a moment, she simply said, "An Estrie. Ever heard of it?"

He racked his brain but came up with nothing. When he shook his head, his whole face throbbed.

"Well, it comes from the French word for owl," she began.

Logically, Boaz knew it probably wasn't a good idea to argue with Clara. There was still the very real possibility that she could kill him. But he'd actually gotten excellent grades in French. It was one of his better subjects at Arbel Academy, and he was very proud of it. "No it doesn't," he said. "*Owl* is *chouette*. Or *hibou*, if it's male."

She looked surprised. "Fine, *Old* French, maybe Latin or

something," she said, flustered. "And since when do you speak French?"

"Je sais ce que j'ai appris à l'Arbel," he said. "It's good if you're into film history. And my grandparents used to make me practice with them."

"Of course you know French," she muttered in a tone he didn't quite understand. What was *that* supposed to mean? What about him knowing French was obvious? "An Estrie is a night owl. In our tradition, she is a woman who can become one, who, like a vampire, feeds on blood to survive."

He looked down at the damp paper towels, now a delicate shade of pink, and the stubborn stains down his shirt front. "Um . . . sorry about this."

"Why are you apologizing?" she said irritably. "You didn't ask to get hit in the face."

He basically did. If she found out that his mugging had been staged, she would definitely kill him. And now he knew that she certainly had the teeth and claws and will to do it. He swallowed. "Why have I never heard of Estries?"

"*Sefer Hasidim*," she said. "Have you read it? We're all over that. Someone must not have been careful. Judah of Regensburg and Elazar Rokeach seemed to more or less know . . ."

"No, I have not," he said. "Need I remind you, I don't know deep-cut Ashkenazi stuff; it's not my thing. Like, I barely understand kugel. Is it a dessert or a side dish? Is it noodles or is it cheesecake?"

"You're asking the wrong person. The last time I ate a kugel, Russia was ruled by a Romanov."

At this, he laughed, which made her laugh. It was a nervous laugh, but a laugh all the same, and it made her eyes light up.

"When . . . When you said you'd seen *The Lightning Raider*—"

"What?"

"That Boris Karloff film, the one that's lost," he said.

"That's what you care about?" she said. "I just . . . I just told you I'm a *vampire*, and you're asking me about . . . Of course you're asking me about Boris Karloff," she finished, in the same tone she'd said *Of course you know French.*

"Did you see it when it came out?" he asked.

She paused, and he saw that she understood what he was asking. "Yes," she said curtly.

"That came out in 1919," he said, swallowing thickly, the taste of blood coating his throat. How could he have been so dense? He hadn't needed to get his nose broken. She basically told him that she was . . . that she was . . .

"I know."

"Can I ask . . . how old you are?"

"I was eighteen when I was turned," she said curtly. "In a village of no consequence, in what I now think is Lithuania." She shrugged. "I left and didn't look back."

"But you're a little older than that?" he said, suddenly worried that he was being rude.

"A little, yes."

For a moment there was silence, and then, because there were a hundred places he didn't want the line of questions to go: "Did you see Theda Bara's *Cleopatra*?"

And she laughed again, so hard that he began to, even though it kind of hurt, because it was so absurd. He was talking to a girl who was well over a hundred years old, who was some kind of Jewish vampire, and he was still chiefly worried that he'd been impolite, that he'd somehow hurt her feelings.

"I *met* Theda Bara in her prime, for your information, and she was a riot, and the movie was fabulous. It's a shame about the fire."

"And did you see—"

"Oh, come here," she said. She headed toward the stairs, waving at him to follow. For a moment, Boaz paused. Following a vampire deeper into an empty theater while he was still covered in his own blood seemed like a spectacular way to ensure he wouldn't see morning. But if she was going to kill him, she'd have already done it . . . right? Besides, she was making a point to keep out of arm's reach of him, and he was dying to hear more about Theda Bara.

He followed her to the second floor, past her office and the projection rooms, to another room he had never entered that was always kept locked. Clara pulled keys from the pocket of her skirt. "Molly and I had loved cinemas for years, even before we had the opportunity to move into the Grand Dame. We knew the theaters in the city better than anyone, probably. We saw everything. It's like dreaming, watching movies. Seeing as we can't sleep anymore, this is the next best thing."

"Oh." He tried to come up with something intelligent to say, but words failed him. Clara was *definitely* a monster. And she was *definitely* the coolest girl he'd ever met. Trying to reconcile both just made the throbbing in his forehead worse. "That's . . . rough. I love sleeping."

The room was a few degrees cooler than the hallway outside, Boaz could feel it the moment she pushed the door open. She flicked on the light.

For a moment, Boaz didn't know what he was looking at. There were rows and rows of metal shelves in this room, each filled with

186

thin, gleaming boxes. In the far corner was a long workbench with a lamp and a number of fat binders stacked up beside it.

"We started collecting," she said. "Films that cinemas were trashing. If a theater shut down, we raided the basements. And occasionally, if we liked a film enough when we saw it, we'd have a . . . er . . . word with the projectionist about it."

Boaz had no doubt the "word" involved teeth and those blank eyes. "They're film reels?"

"We have storage elsewhere, but we've been keeping the rare, nitrate stuff in here. Got to handle it carefully so it doesn't burn the whole place down now. This stuff is just as bad as gunpowder. You so much as *think* about fire enough, and it ignites. That's why we didn't want you lighting candles up here. I'd say about a third of our collection is 'lost' films, but we still need to confirm—"

Boaz turned to look at her, eyes wide. "You have lost films?"

"Well, we definitely have a full reel of *Cleopatra*," she said. "And the rest of Theda Bara's filmography—Molly had a massive crush on her. And the sound version of the 1925 *Phantom of the Opera*. We've even got some Cantonese films, courtesy of an old contact of Molly's from the opera in Chinatown, the complete collection of Esther Eng's work, some rare Fei Mu. We keep trying to figure out the logistics of putting together a showcase."

"You seriously mean to tell me," said Boaz slowly, "that you've been *sitting on* an extensive collection of rare and lost films and haven't told anyone?"

"Well, we've got to be smart about it," said Clara rather defensively, folding her arms across her chest. "The long-term plan *is* to digitize them properly, but we can't just release our giant collection of films without inviting questions, now, can we? If we did, people would want to interview us. The interviews would get posted online. People would want to take a closer look at the theater. And we'd have to come up with some convoluted story to explain how two eighteen-year-olds just happen to have Hitchcock's *The Mountain Eagle*—"

"*You have* The Mountain *freaking* Eagle?" Boaz, who had been very proud of himself up until now for how chill he'd been at the sight of Clara's face and getting his nose broken by his best friend, was officially about to freak out. The Senders were sitting on *the single most sought after lost film* of all time. He'd walked past the room filled with all his lost movie fantasies for the last six months and had no idea. "I . . . I have so many questions."

But before he could ask them, his phone began to buzz so loudly in his pocket that she clearly heard it.

"You should get going," she said, sounding almost . . . sad? Her gaze lingering on him. "And get that."

"It's probably spam," he said, even though a glance was enough to tell that it was Daniel, presumably trying to see if he'd been eaten yet. He silenced it and shoved it into his pocket. "But I probably should go, I guess. We can discuss this more tomorrow. Unless, like, that would be weird. We can also just agree not to talk about it, if you'd rather."

She sighed. "Oh, don't worry, we won't talk about it. You won't remember tonight."

"Are you . . . quite sure of that?" The memory of her real face was something he was certain he'd never forget. He wasn't scared easily, but that had frankly been the stuff of nightmares.

She was still watching him closely, like she was studying him. The back of Boaz's neck prickled; he'd never been looked at like that by a girl, certainly not one who could eat him if she wanted. "Men never remember the encounters they have with Molly and me. Not really. By the time you get home, you won't be sure what you saw, and by tomorrow . . . maybe you'll remember I helped you. You won't remember my real face."

"Well, if I do still remember——"

"Which you won't," she said quickly, and for a moment she almost seemed angry with him for it. But maybe he was just imagining things. "Men never remember."

"But if I *do*," he said, "you have to promise to tell me about Theda Bara. And let me watch *The Mountain Eagle*."

"Fine, but you won't," she said, her voice cracking. "Gute nakht."

"You too."

Boaz waited until he reached Union Square before daring to pick up the phone.

"Dude, where are you?" shouted Daniel by way of greeting. "I've been trying to call you for ages. I thought you were dead."

"You broke my nose!" said Boaz, wincing. "If I have to see a doctor, you're paying for it. The health insurance my mom and I have is total shit——"

"Well, was it worth it, at least?" he asked.

Boaz stopped. *Men never remember.* Clara's words still clung stubbornly to him as he asked, "What do you mean, was it worth it?"

"I mean, did she change or not? Did you get the proof you needed?"

You won't remember my real face. Was it true? He closed his eyes. He was certain that he still remembered, that he could draw it if asked. In fact, he was certain that he'd never forget. How does someone forget something like *that*? The sight of her, eyes empty and teeth bared, was burned in his brain. Half of him wished he'd forget so that he could continue to see just the Clara he knew and nothing else. "Yeah, I got proof."

"Really?" said Daniel, sounding surprised. "Wow, I wish I could have seen it."

But you did. "I got to go, I'm still at Union Square," said Boaz quickly. "We'll talk tomorrow."

But Boaz didn't go underground right away. Instead, he stood by the stairs, wavering. How was this supposed to work? Was it a distance thing? Would descending into the labyrinth of the Union Square subway station be enough? Because he still remembered. Or was it time? Had not enough time passed? How much would be enough? Should he write it down? Try drawing her face?

He opened the notes app on his phone, preparing to type out some sort of message to remind himself, but couldn't bring himself to do it.

He thought of Clara laughing, and how beautiful she'd been when she laughed. The way her eyes crinkled, the way she'd said, *Of course you know French.* That was the Clara he knew, the Clara that made his stomach flip, that he wanted to know better.

In fact, there'd be nothing better, if he could forget the rest. He closed the app and descended the steps. Forgetting would be the best thing, he thought. If he could forget, they could go back to being what they were. Which was good. Maybe they could never be more, but they'd have *that*. Her face alight with laughter and movies. Yes, forgetting the monster between them would be best, the *right* thing.

Boaz struggled to stay awake as the N jerked its way back to

Gravesend. But every time he closed his eyes, he saw her: eyes blank, teeth bared, hair long.

Men never remember the encounters they have with Molly and me.

Daniel didn't remember. He'd forgotten almost as soon as he had fled the scene, no memory of how she'd come at him with the face of a monster, how she'd become that monster right before their eyes.

Men never remember . . .

He waited the whole walk home from the station. Surely, any minute now, the fog would descend. He'd forget and be all the happier for it.

Men never remember . . .

He crept into the house and could tell from the murmur of the television and the fact that she said nothing when the door opened that his mother was comfortably asleep on the couch. Which was for the best. He didn't want to have to explain his face to her. He wanted to forget.

He crawled into bed, sliding so effortlessly into sleep that when morning came, it caught him by surprise. He woke with his face throbbing, still wearing the same bloodied clothes from the night before.

And even by the light of day, he still remembered.

22

MOLLY

The visit to Anat's dorm building hadn't been a complete loss. According to the poster she had taken, there was still one week left to buy tickets for *Kaddish: The Immersive Experience*. It was better than nothing.

So she arrived early the next day in the lobby of the Tisch School of the Arts, where she found two girls selling tickets from a table just by the door marked with an elaborately hand-illustrated poster advertising the event. Molly recognized them from the Minetta Lane party at once, the two girls who had dragged Anat and her into karaoke.

"Hey, what's this?" said Molly, trying to make the question not sound like an accusation, even if it was, a bit. Anat had always said the show was her idea. But if Anat was gone, and if no one seemed to remember her, then how could it happen?

"Our final project," said one of the girls, handing her a flyer. "Experimental Theater 101. You want to come?"

She waited. She couldn't bear to say Anat's name aloud, but

surely they hadn't forgotten *her*. Molly was still here, after all. And she wasn't going anywhere. She thought she saw a flicker of recognition in one girl's expression, but it was fleeting, gone as quickly as it appeared.

"Could I have a ticket?"

The ticket called for "your best midcentury look," which wasn't a problem for Molly. She'd pulled the dress she'd worn at a memorable night at Edie Kerouac-Parker's, a sleeveless black dress that skimmed her knees, and even went through the trouble of setting her hair in rollers and pinning it the way she had for years. Finished with an ungodly amount of hairspray, her mask felt firmly fixed in place. In life she had always put her faith in the power of a dress and perfect smile, and in death it was still her armor of choice.

The event was in a town house that she guessed the university owned. When Molly arrived, a sizable crowd had already gathered outside, trailing up the front steps in various interpretations of the midcentury dress code. A few people had gotten it right, in black turtlenecks and thrifted finds that cut a convincing impression of what people were wearing the night she decided that actually beatniks were the Worst. But sprinkled throughout were a few Party City hippies, poodle skirts, and others who had simply not bothered to try at all, wearing whatever they would have for a typical night out.

Molly climbed the stairs and slid inside, handing her ticket to a girl at the door, and was promptly handed a black mask that she tried to refuse. The girl pushed it into her hand anyway. "You need to wear it. It's how you can tell who is in the production and who isn't."

Molly took the mask reluctantly, sliding it on before stepping into the first room, a parlor crammed with people. A Ray Charles record crackled in the corner, and at the center of the room in an old armchair was a boy without a black mask in a white T-shirt and suspenders and thick-rimmed glasses, hunched over a siddur and muttering what Molly recognized as the mourner's Kaddish. She winced. Estries were not vampires; religious symbols had no effect on them, and synagogues remained the most surefire way to find a Clara-approved meal. But she didn't like the prayer. She hadn't liked it when she was alive, and she liked it even less after she died. What kind of mourning prayer made no mention of the dead? It made her feel forgotten.

After a few more people entered, the door to the foyer closed, and the little bit of murmuring from the black-mask wearers died down. The lights of the parlor room dimmed, and the boy began saying the Kaddish louder, at full volume, once more before snapping the siddur shut. He turned to the crowd that had gathered.

"Thank you for coming, thank you for coming," he said, his voice carrying. "I know Naomi would have been touched to see you all here to honor her memory. Please remember that this is a shiva. You are free to wander the apartment as you wish, but do not address the mourners directly unless you are spoken to first." He sat back down in the armchair, turning the siddur in his hands but not opening it. When he spoke again, it was lower, and Molly recognized at once the opening lines of the poem. "'Strange now to think of you, gone without corsets and eyes, while I walk on the sunny pavement of Greenwich Village.'"

A second door opened into another dimly lit room, and "mourners"—actors without masks who Molly assumed were Anat's classmates—filed in, a few carrying tiny plates with rugelach, others wailing perhaps too theatrically into handkerchiefs. Each mourner, after a moment of lingering among those with black masks, would tap a couple on the shoulder or gesture for them to follow, drawing some of the crowd out and through the next room.

Molly went on her own. The next room was dark and quiet, save the faint sound of a horse galloping in the background. She remembered the poem saying something about horses, maybe Emily Dickinson's? She couldn't quite remember, and her attention was drawn instead to the small scene on the other side of the room, where a Charlie Chaplin silent film was being projected against the wall with an ancient-looking projector, older even than the ones Clara still preferred in their theater, and two girls were sitting in front of it, transfixed, even as she lingered in the back and as some of the other guests filed through, following mourners onward into the hallway. She had to admit it was clever: *Nor your memory of your mother, 1915 tears in silent movies weeks and weeks forgetting, aggrieve watching Marie Dressler address humanity, Chaplin dance in youth, / or Boris Godunov . . .*

One of the girls at last turned to look at Molly, beckoning her forward and moving aside, making space for her between the two of them in front of the film. Part of her wondered whether she should just keep moving. She'd seen this movie, in theaters, no less. But the girls seemed insistent, and she supposed this was the point.

The moment she sat, the two girls turned back to the movie. The horse clopping sound seemed loud, louder than the faint classical music that she supposed had been paired with the film. She watched, waiting for something to happen, but the two girls just remained where they were, pretending they were completely transfixed by the movie in front of them.

Molly didn't really get it. At last she decided she'd had enough and would move on to the next room. But when she attempted to stand, one of the girls caught her by the wrist.

Molly tried to yank her arm away, but the girl held fast, and when the girl turned to look at Molly again, it was no longer the stranger, but Anat. Her eyes lit up with recognition.

"You made it!" Anat crowed. "I knew you'd find me!"

Molly froze. It was Anat. Anat *here*, her hair tucked back behind her ears, her eyes the light, interesting hazel. When she spoke, her voice was not the strangled, too-perfect Yiddish, but her own: "I didn't think you'd come."

"But . . . But how did you . . . What about that girl?" Molly didn't understand. Anat, *here*. Anat, who had vanished from memory, *here*.

"You haven't forgotten me." Anat inched forward until she was pressed up against Molly's chest, and Molly was struck by how cold her girlfriend was. Molly didn't have a pulse and knew she ran colder than most, but it was like a block of ice had crawled up against her.

Molly wanted it to be her; she wanted it badly enough that she let herself believe. She pulled Anat in closer, her whole body shuddering with the chill. "Of course I came."

"I told you not to trust him," Anat said at last, her voice low and quick. "You and your sister can't trust him. He'll destroy everything. He's all masks and lies."

"What do you mean?" said Molly. "Is this about Boaz? What has he done to you?"

"You need to get the ring back," she said. "Can't you feel it? The lines between Here and After are thinning, thinning. It's that ring. You must—"

Anat suddenly gasped, staring past Molly at something behind her.

Molly turned as well. Projected on the wall in thin, shaking light was a face she had not seen in so long that the sight of it struck her like a train at full speed.

Lena. The way she remembered her, the way she appeared when they first kissed, hair pulled back in an effortless braid, her searching eyes staring straight through Molly's core.

Molly knew the words she wanted to say, but they died in her throat. Because Lena was *there* in light on the wall, and it sounded like her, and it had been so long since she'd heard that voice, the voice that she would have given just about anything to hear again.

"You're not here," choked Molly. "Lena, you're . . . You're not . . ."

Because while Anat was missing, Lena was dead. That hope, that Lena would one day stand before her like this, had been long ago buried.

"Oh, really?" Lena asked, her face ghostly on the wall. When she spoke, something about her voice sounded distant and tinny. "What makes you say that?"

"Because you cannot *be here*," Molly repeated. It was the closest she could come to saying it aloud.

"Neither should you," she said, laughing in a way that didn't sound at all like the Lena she knew.

"You died in that fire."

The face on the wall grinned, beautiful and terrible and too wide for the words she spoke. "You died, too, remember?"

Molly shook her head, but Lena continued, "You bled out on Second Avenue mere weeks before the fire. Leo Goldfaber stabbed you. . . . You really disappointed him," she said, laughing a little. "That night, your heart stopped beating, and it never started back up, and I outlived you."

"I'm not dead!" Molly began to struggle to her feet, only for Anat to grab her arm and yank her back to the floor.

"And it was remarkable you lived at all," said Lena. "Your mother always said, meyn nis meydl, my miracle girl. You both should have died the night you were born, and she should have died in Kiev beside her betrothed, but for a little luck. . . . Too much luck, really. None of you should be here at all—"

"Stop it!" Molly's voice was hoarse, but it was louder this time. Because it wasn't Lena, couldn't be her, even if she sounded like her, even if what she said was true, it couldn't. Just like the hands on her wrist couldn't be Anat.

And then, they suddenly weren't Anat's hands—just two strangers, one on either side of her, playing their parts, watching a horse projected onto a wall.

Molly turned about the room, looking frantically for Anat. But Anat was gone. Molly ran toward the door, but when she opened it, all she could hear was Lena.

"If you still walk, why shouldn't I?" Lena's voice was just above a whisper.

"Stop pretending to be her!"

Another voice cut through: "Someone call security!"

Molly had thrown herself on the ground, holding her hands over her ears. She couldn't keep listening to Lena, to the things she was saying. It wasn't true, she didn't die that day, because she was still here, she was still here . . .

"Maybe she needs help?"

Molly didn't recognize the voice; she didn't recognize any of the voices. She chanced opening her eyes.

The lights had come on in the room, but Ray Charles was still playing through the speakers. She was surrounded by people, all dressed like they were attending a funeral in the 1950s . . . hers.

Not hers.

She recognized the boy who had said Kaddish. She was still at the immersive play, and they were all staring at her. One girl, one of the ones who had been watching the film, had a cell phone pressed to her ear.

"I'm fine," said Molly quickly. "I'm . . . sorry, I didn't mean . . . I'm fine."

"An ambulance will come by in a second," said the Kaddish boy, almost sympathetically. "It happens. I told them the flickering lights were a seizure risk. Don't worry. Help is on the way—"

"No, I don't need it!" said Molly, forcing herself to her feet. She pushed herself through the small crowd of actors and patrons. Ripping her black mask off, she ran out of the town house before any of them could grab her, not stopping until she was in the cold night once more, slipping on the perilous stone steps down from the front door.

She wanted so badly to loosen her hair then and there, but there were too many people. Throngs of them gazing at her like she was standing up onstage. *No*, like she was a freak on display in an old Coney Island sideshow, as though they could see straight through her pin curls and vintage dress to the monster beneath, the monster that was suddenly desperately hungry and gasping for air like she was unable to breathe.

She needed to feed. Yes, that would stop it. She needed a breath and pulse to calm her, something alive she could match, so she could fix her mask and keep pretending. . . .

She scrambled away from the town house when she spotted him, a young man who would be perfect for her purposes. His hair was slicked back, and he was dressed like he intended to go to the show, in a vintage-cut, slightly rumpled suit, his suspenders exposed. He was alone. And most importantly, when she met his eyes, she could tell at once he was interested, that he wanted her close.

"Going to the show?" she called, her voice high-pitched and strange. She was surprised she could speak at all; her breathing was all out of rhythm. Nevertheless, she smiled and batted her lashes. It was too easy.

"Maybe," said the young man. "Maybe not. I think I'm already running late."

"Or you're just in time," said Molly. Ordinarily, she would banter. Ordinarily, she would figure out if he was a Jew. Ordinarily, she cared about the rules. But she was hungry, and she didn't feel like talking. "The play wasn't very good, but I can give you a better show."

"Well, if you insist," he said.

She took his hand and led him toward the end of the block, just far enough from the curious eyes of students. When they had fallen out of sight, she pushed him against a lamppost.

He went in harder than she had expected, and for a moment, she stumbled before catching her balance. Usually, men were soft by the time she got them out here. But this time she was in a hurry. His mouth was on hers, and she tried to reach up to undo her hair, tried listening for his breathing the way she had done with Anat. If she could find her way back to breathing, she'd stop panicking. She'd be able to think clearly and forget what had happened in that house.

She yanked out a fistful of hairpins. She didn't have the patience for this. She shook her hair free, still stiff with hairspray, and promptly let her teeth sink into his neck.

But she'd barely drunk a sip before she realized something was wrong.

There was a way blood was supposed to taste, warm and salty and thick, a taste she couldn't quite place and the only thing that would satiate her craving. Like a thick broth, the kind of food that was supposed to make one well.

But this? It was *cold*. Ice-cold, and bitter, and viscous, like she'd taken a swig of gasoline. She gagged, trying to spit it out, but she knew she must have swallowed some, because she could feel it coat her throat all the way down.

"What the *actual fuck*," she shrieked, trying to push him away from her, retching. It was worse than when she'd tried food. Food tasted like ash. Gross, but not *this* . . . cold and slimy and *alive*. "What is wrong with you?"

"What, didn't your mommy ever tell you not to eat whatever old thing you find on the street?" he asked, laughing. He kicked off his shoes, revealing bird talons where his feet ought to have been. A *sheyd*.

She snarled. She didn't know the last time she'd felt so raw, so animal. They weren't supposed to drink from sheydim. It wasn't even one of Clara's rules; it was just *wrong*, a boundary that was not supposed to be crossed. It was like marrying a corpse. They were not supposed to try and sate their hungers with demons and the dead. They already lived along the razor's edge of this world. It did not take much to slip. Stray too far into the World to Come, and there would be no coming back.

Molly wanted to tear him apart for fooling her, for taking the rising panic in her chest and making it worse, but he was already backing into the street, vanishing before her eyes even as she tried to follow him.

"Why did you trick me?" she shrieked after him.

"Ashmodai sent me," he said, smirking. "I was asked to deliver a message to your sister and her little pet boy."

"What's the message?" she spat. An icy cold was spreading in the pit of her stomach.

He made a grand gesture with his arms, as if presenting the main course of a decadent meal. "You are," said the sheyd, just before he slid entirely into shadow. His mocking, wide smile lingered, and Molly shuddered at the chill that crept down her spine.

23

CLARA

Of course he spoke French.

Clara could not stop thinking about Boaz Harari through the night. Of course he spoke French, and of course the only thing he could think to ask her, when it became clear she was over a hundred years old, was what long-lost films she'd seen. Of course.

No one who got a proper look at her face stuck around. Boaz should have, by all accounts, run out of the theater screaming.

To be sure, he'd been frightened. She could hear that much, the way his heart kept racing, faster even than when he was getting mugged. It was clear who he thought would kill him, and it wasn't the stranger beating his face in.

But he hadn't run.

Nor did he flinch when she brought him inside, even though he got a full view of her, with the lights on and everything. *He'd asked her if she'd seen* The Lightning Raider *in theaters.*

No romance.

Her own rule dropped in on her thoughts like a brick, squashing her fantasies. It was impossible. It did not matter that Boaz wasn't afraid of her face. It did not matter that he wanted to talk lost films to her. They could not happen. *Ever.* It was her own rule, and the rules existed for a good reason.

It was nights like these that Clara Sender wished for sleep. She needed a break, but there was nowhere else to go. After restlessly starting and stopping concession inventories and making a few phone calls about delays in film deliveries, she did the only thing left to her and decided to watch a movie.

It was half the reason Molly and she wanted a theater in the first place. It was true what she told Boaz: movies were like dreaming. When there was nothing left to do, when she needed to rest, to let herself empty, to go somewhere else for a few hours in the dark, there were movie theaters, which were cheap and cool and open late. Live theater was too . . . alive. Too present. There were too many people and pulses, and when she needed a break, she could not stop hearing them all.

Besides, it was a Tuesday morning. There was hardly anyone there, and that new Scandi noir would be playing to an empty audience if someone didn't go and sit inside.

She poked her head into auditorium one. The theater was empty, not great for business but exactly what she was hoping for. She picked a seat in the center of the balcony and closed her eyes as the lights came down. Finally, she was alone. . . .

And she was, until halfway into the previews, when she heard a heartbeat behind her and recognized the smell at once. It made her feel featherlight for just a moment, like she could have taken to the air even without her wings.

Boaz. She turned, scowling, as he dropped into a seat two rows behind her. "What are you doing here? Your shift doesn't start for hours."

"I . . . hadn't seen this one yet?" he said, keeping his voice low even though they were the only two people there and neither of them were paying attention to the previews, the meticulously edited advertisement for the cult horror retrospective Molly had been plotting, complete with some dreadful clips from a movie called *Troll 2*. "I try to see everything that comes through, and I can't watch it during my shift."

He looked rough. Even by the light of the previews, she could see it, the dark bruises that had bloomed along the bridge of his nose and under his eyes. He appeared about as exhausted as she felt.

She sighed. She had wanted to be alone, but storming out now would be petty, and the next film wasn't starting for another hour, down in auditorium three. And she needed the break.

"Fine. It's fine," she said. "Just . . . be quiet."

"I know how to behave in a movie theater, actually," he said.

Of course he did. Clara turned back to the screen. One other person wasn't so bad. And wasn't this a good thing? It meant that he must have forgotten. They'd gone back to being what they were. Everything had been put right. The wall between them had returned.

The movie was dreadfully dull, but she didn't care. She closed her eyes and let low-muttered Swedish wash over her, glad at least this was a language that she hadn't yet learned. If it were up to her, they wouldn't have acquired it, but it had won all these awards on the film festival circuit, and its absence would have been noticed.

She didn't even realize the movie had ended until she heard a pointed throat-clearing behind her. She startled and noticed the credits were almost to the end.

"Were you sleeping?" Boaz asked, throwing his backpack on. "I thought—"

"No," she said defensively. "I was trying not to think. What were you thinking?"

"That I wouldn't have blamed you," said Boaz. "That was dreadful. Seriously. It's like my aunt always says, if it has won lots of awards at festivals, it's either awful or life-changing, there's no in between."

"Right."

He clearly wanted to say something to her. Instead of bolting, he kept shifting uneasily, fidgeting with the straps of his backpack.

"What is it?"

He glanced toward the door. "I just thought you should know . . . I remember."

"What do you mean, you remember?" she snapped.

"I mean, the things you said I would forget last night . . . I haven't."

"That's impossible," she said. Surely, he was mistaken. Of course he would remember some things. He'd remember the conversation they had before, and maybe what they spoke of in the end. He'd remember the fight, certainly with his face bruised the way it was. But that she was an Estrie? Her face, that was a detail that was supposed to slip into the cracks of time and vanish as quickly as it had come. That's how they survived. They were there and they were not, the details always forgotten.

"Trust me," he said. The door of the theater opened, and one of the bubbes, armed with the broom, poked her head in. Boaz lowered his voice. "I remember *everything.*"

"Why are you telling me this?" she said.

"Because I thought you should know," he said. "Because . . . if you think people forget and they don't, you might be in danger."

"Do you want me to come back later, Clara dear?" asked the bubbe as Boaz at last bolted down the aisle and out the door.

"It's fine," she said, still staring after Boaz, his words loud in her brain. *Trust me.*

If what he said was true, and she was pretty sure it was, then she did not trust him at all.

Clara made her way back up to their apartments, only to find Molly leaning against the wall, surrounded by clumps of feathers.

She'd never seen her sister look this way. Though her hair had been piled up, her skin still appeared lightly gray and sickly, her features human but gaunt. There were feathers tangled in her hair . . . a *lot* of them, piled on the floor beside her and, Clara realized with a sickening lurch, actively sprouting from the back of her neck.

"What happened?" Clara grabbed the first bread she could get her hands on, the half a loaf of challah sitting on the counter, and a well of salt before rushing to her sister's side. It was the only thing she could think to do, the only kind of medicine that existed for them, save a willing neck.

Molly had made a strange, almost strangled noise, and the frantic way she had shoveled down the leftover challah told her enough. When Molly spoke, she revealed her teeth were still sharp. "We have to talk."

"Of course," said Clara quickly.

"No, *really*," she said, her voice raw. "I need you to believe me just this once and not argue with me."

Molly told her what happened at that *Kaddish* play, about the ghosts and the sheyd that had appeared. When Molly admitted to biting one, Clara bit back a retort. Biting a sheyd *wasn't done*. She ought to have known better. "I don't know what that sheyd was going on about, but he said it was a message from Ashmodai, for you and Boaz."

"What? Molly—"

"Why can't you believe me just this once?" Molly shouted, her voice cracking.

"I do!" said Clara. "I swear I do. But what does Boaz have to do with sheydim?"

"I don't know, I'm just telling you what the sheyd told me," Molly said, still gasping as she sank into the couch.

"Are you okay?" said Clara. It felt absurd the moment she asked it. She was *sprouting feathers*; of course she wasn't okay. Sheydim were creatures of shadow, not truly of this world and unable to walk in sunlight. To bite one, to stray too far into their world, would leave them stranded in shadow, too.

"What if it can't . . . What if we can't fix it or find her or . . ." said Molly. "I can't lose someone else."

Clara shook her head. No, Clara couldn't either. She could not bear losing her sister. "I won't let it happen."

24

BOAZ

Boaz considered ditching Daniel no less than ten times between his house and Williamsburg. This early morning stop on his way into Manhattan seemed like a truly terrible idea, even by Daniel's standards. And in light of recent events, Boaz was all the more certain that Clara would in fact literally murder him if he showed up late.

Daniel had turned finding an expert on Estries into something of a personal project. After a call with Rabbi Pardo and a crowd-source of several of his YU WhatsApp groups, someone told him of a chevra kadisha, a burial society, he could try. That burial society told him, numerous times, to stop asking about monsters and perhaps seek professional help. So instead, after consulting about a dozen sketchy websites, a monster fan wiki, and a chatroom that looked like it had emerged straight from the depths of 2004, he apparently found someone in Williamsburg willing to talk to them about Estries.

"Oh, good, you made it!" said Daniel when Boaz met him along Bedford Avenue. "And your nose is looking better!"

"Yeah, right," grumbled Boaz. He could breathe out of it, which, according to WebMD, meant that it wasn't broken *that* badly, but it had a way of throbbing and looked bad enough that his mom had tried to get him to go to an emergency room.

"Is this really necessary?"

"You said your boss is an Estrie," said Daniel matter-of-factly. "We know nothing about Estries, and this guy apparently knows everything, so yes."

"Does it matter, though?"

Daniel looked at Boaz like he had sprouted six heads. "I don't get you sometimes."

"I'm just saying . . ." said Boaz, but *he* didn't know what he was saying, exactly. He had told Daniel about what he'd seen. And what he had seen did scare him. The Sender sisters were monsters, blood-drinking monsters. He was supposed to be afraid of them. And yet . . .

They reached a run-down brick home at the end of the street, which was completely indistinguishable from the houses on either side, save that there were at least three cats weaving between the fences and the trash cans.

"You sure this is the place?" Boaz asked.

"This is the address he gave me." Daniel shrugged and then double-checked his phone. "Shall we?"

Boaz sighed loudly before Daniel rang the buzzer, and after a minute of waiting and a great deal of unlocking, the door opened, just a crack. "Who are you?" The man who poked his head out was younger than Boaz had expected. He looked college age, *maybe* grad school. When Daniel had mentioned going to Williamsburg to find one Rafi Edelman, he had assumed they were meeting with some disaffected Hasid. But the guy who greeted them at the door, still in flannel pajama pants, a beanie, and a bit of beard that looked decidedly like an artifact of laziness rather than religious obligation, was definitely not.

"I'm not interested in buying anything," he mumbled.

"Hi! Rafi Edelman? I'm Daniel Sayegh? Me and my friend Boaz here had some questions about Estries."

Edelman gave Daniel a withering look, and Boaz decided he suddenly liked him a lot more. He waited a long moment before at last removing the chain locking the door and opening it just wide enough for the two of them to enter.

The ground-floor apartment was dark, the curtains on the few windows drawn shut. The place reeked of pot smoke and . . . cat piss? At least, Boaz hoped it was cat piss. The carpet was worn down, completely threadbare in places, and standing by a shoe rack, Boaz found himself being watched by a large, deeply unsettling golem poster and a black light Tree of Life Kabbalah poster that Boaz was certain came from one of those occult stores that hawk "Jewish" magic next to Aleister Crowley texts and crystals. He shot Daniel a murderous look that his friend carefully avoided.

"This way," muttered Edelman.

They were led into a large bedroom. The curtains were drawn. On the far end was a bed piled high with laundry and a fairly extensive desk and computer setup, complete with three monitors that were providing the brightest lights in the room. Edelman directed them to a long, squashy sofa.

"Sit," said Rafi Edelman before turning to a large bookcase, positively bursting with books, that dominated one wall.

They both sat gingerly. In front of them, there was a coffee table filled with books, and an ashtray piled with butts sat in the center, still smoking slightly.

Beside Boaz, Daniel tried shifting some of the open books away without knocking off one of the several dirty coffee mugs. Rafi settled in the chair across from them, tenting his fingertips and staring at the both of them, eyes wide. "Well?"

Daniel cleared his throat loudly. "Boaz can explain. I think, he has . . . er . . . more experience with the women in question."

"More than one?" Rafi said. "So you're saying it's a nest of them?"

"I . . . I wouldn't call it *that*," said Boaz uneasily, trying not to look too alarmed as he watched a roach emerge from one of the mugs.

"Well, that's the term," he said. "Rav Elazar of Worms says as much, that they traditionally live in nests made from the hair of young virgins cut the night before their wedding. . . ."

"Um, that sounds gross. I don't—" Boaz was about to argue, but Daniel stepped on his foot. "They run a movie theater. I'm their box office attendant. And who the heck is Rav Elazar of Worms? I don't think that's a person."

"Fascinating," said Rafi in a tone that sounded oddly condescending, but maybe Boaz was imagining it. "How do you know, then? That they're Estries?"

"Um, well, they told me?" said Boaz awkwardly. "Plus, I saw one transform. . . . She let down her hair and, well, she turned into a monster—"

"That's impossible," Rafi said. He reached over to one of the books sitting open on the desk and began to riffle through the pages. Even in the dim, purple-tinged light, Boaz could see the back cover photo of an aging man in an ill-fitting suit, who he presumed to be the author. "This one here, Dr. Abraham Abrams, in the *definitive* book on Jewish women monsters, says himself that the Estrie does not reveal her form to men under any circumstances."

"What does a guy in a three-piece suit named Abraham Abrams know about women monsters?" snorted Boaz. From the look on Edelman's face, he realized this was the wrong question.

"You guys should leave." Edelman snapped the book shut. He put up his rather large, socked feet on the filthy coffee table. "I could tell the moment you walked through the door you guys weren't serious."

Daniel spoke up. "Don't mind my friend. He's got a lousy sense of humor; he didn't mean anything by it—"

"Excuse me? I have a fantastic sense of humor, and I absolutely meant what I said. Why should I believe that guy or you know anything about Estries?" said Boaz, incredulous. "I know what I saw."

Edelman leaned back in his chair. "Well, that's just it, isn't it?" He rummaged under one of the open texts, until he pulled out a red onion. Boaz watched as he unpeeled the outermost layer before taking a bite like it was an apple. "You shouldn't have seen anything. All the sources agree that no one walks away from an encounter remembering their face. Whatever you saw wasn't an Estrie."

"I remember. He doesn't," he said, pointing to Daniel.

"What do you mean, I don't?" said Daniel. "I didn't see."

"Yes, you did," said Boaz, before turning back to Rafi. "He doesn't remember. I don't know why, but—"

"Boaz sees dead people," said Daniel. "His family is cursed or something."

Boaz glared at him, but this seemed to satisfy Edelman.

"Zee'shin Veltoon," he said, without further explanation.

"What the fuck are you saying?"

"It's Yiddish," said Rafi smugly.

"No it isn't!" said Boaz.

"Boaz, what do you know about Yiddish?" said Daniel.

"*Tsvishn Veltn*, is that what you're saying?" said Boaz, over Daniel's objections. He couldn't believe that he was lecturing someone on their Yiddish, but he supposed there was a first time for everything. "I've been there."

"It's not a place."

"Well, I've been, and I saw them change, and I remember it, and if you don't believe me, you can go back to hawking your nonsense monster hunting kits on Etsy." Boaz stood up. "I have to go to work—I don't have time for this."

"Boaz . . ." began Daniel, but Boaz ignored his friend. Daniel might have had some objectively terrible ideas in the past, but this was another level. He should have known this was a bad idea, as if they were going to get anything useful off of some weirdo they found deep in the darkest bowels of the internet. He could hear Daniel stand up reluctantly behind him, and Boaz was halfway to the door when Edelman suddenly burst out laughing.

"Sit back down," said Edelman. His voice had changed, turned deeper and more commanding. "Your friend is right. You wouldn't know a joke if it bit you in the ass."

Boaz turned. His face had gone hot. "That was a joke?"

Edelman grinned. "A test. I needed to know how much bullshit you'd swallowed before you got here. You wouldn't believe the messages I get in my DMs, asking for magic spells and pet golems. It's brisk business, peddling nonsense to children who fancy themselves

witches. If this impressed you, I would have given you a compli-
mentary salt packet and sent you on your way."

Boaz froze. He didn't know what to make of this. He hated
being embarrassed by anyone who wasn't Clara. But more than that,
he couldn't shake the feeling that something was *wrong* about all of
this. How could this be a trick? The dirty coffee cups, the bed that
looked like it hadn't been slept in, that *smell* . . .

But Daniel was already lowering himself back onto the couch,
and an itch of curiosity overcame him. "Why should I believe you?"

"Because no one else will believe *you*," Edelman said. "And no
one else will be able to help you with what comes next." He cleared
his throat. "As it so happens, I have heard things about that theater.
You are sure they are Estries?" he said to Boaz.

"I saw it. I'm sure."

Edelman leaned forward, taking another large bite of the onion.
"Then you must bury them."

"What?" Boaz had been so distracted by Edelman's snack pref-
erences that he was certain he must have heard him wrong. "Did
you actually say . . ."

Edelman held up a hand. "Fire or the grave. To kill an Estrie,
you must either burn it or bury it in the ground, packing its mouth
full of earth. You *must* do this, or it will keep feeding on the men of
the community. They will kill with impunity."

"I don't think you understand," said Boaz. "I don't . . . They're
very nice, mostly. I mean, one of them hates my guts, but it's . . .
complicated. They're just, like, regular girls."

"They're not girls," said Edelman. "They're monsters."

"What, did Abraham Abrams tell you that?"

"It's not like they'd admit it to you, though, right?" said Daniel uneasily. "They kept being Estries secret from you for so long. What else might they be hiding?"

"If they were serial killers, I think *someone* would have noticed by now. Their theater is in the middle of the East Village; it's not a secret!"

Edelman shook his head. "It does not matter. An Estrie survives on blood. They have lived in Manhattan for a long time. They have killed, and they will keep killing. You think it is an accident, that they do what we are accused of? That for hundreds of years, Christians have accused us of draining Christian blood, of using it for wine, for matzah?"

"I *know*, I get it," said Boaz.

"Then you understand why we cannot have Estries roaming around the city, feeding on the vulnerable. Can you even begin to imagine the consequences if such a thing were discovered? If the very monsters they feared walked among us?" Edelman took another bite of the raw onion. "You see the dead?"

Boaz nodded, watching the ashes that dotted the free space on the table.

"Then you know. The dead who linger among us, they are not happy to be here. The dead wish to move on to Olam Ha-Ba. It is misery for them to remain. An Estrie is dead. They have already died once. Their hearts no longer beat; blood does not run through their veins. They grow no older, cannot taste food, save blood and bread. They remain because they died suffering, because, like the spirits you see, they died hungry for that which was denied to them in life. They are hungry, and like a dybbuk, they want satisfaction. . . . They *want* to rest at last," he said. "I have done it before. It is not easy, but it is necessary. And beautiful, even."

"You have?" Boaz swallowed hard. Was this another joke? Was Edelman really full of shit? Because if he wasn't, then that meant . . . That he just admitted to . . .

"I can assure you, it is a kindness. You do them and us both a great service by putting one back in the ground where it belongs."

Boaz bit his lip. He could tell Daniel was into it, that *this* was exactly what he'd been hoping to find. But if he wasn't mistaken, then Edelman was *dangerous*, and they were talking about burying Clara and Molly alive.

CLARA

Boaz was closing the theater that night, and when Clara padded down the stairs, she found him busy explaining their hours to a caller.

"No, I said *eleven*," he said. "The Grand Dame opens tomorrow at *eleven*, not . . . Ma'am, it's almost midnight. You'll have to wait for tomorrow's showings. . . ."

She snatched the phone out of his hand and hung it up, losing patience. Her sister was in trouble, and this was the kind of box office nonsense that could wait. She'd been watching Molly before this, waiting for her to turn back to normal, to go back to grating on her nerves and breaking her rules with impunity. But in the last few hours of the shift, feathers had begun sprouting across Molly's shoulders, and she'd begged Clara three times to go to Ashmodai for answers.

There was only so long that Clara could say no. Because Molly was right. If Ashmodai wanted to talk with her so badly, he would give her answers about everything—Boaz included.

"Hey, I'm heading out to do an errand," she said to Boaz. "And I thought you might like to come with me."

Boaz looked at her, his eyes narrowing, and huffed out a sigh. Clara fought to keep her thoughts straight. Her sister was in trouble, and her sister would always come first. No boy, even one who smelled like fresh coffee and sugar, would change that. "Why would I come with you?"

"Because it will be interesting," she said. "I'm not going to eat you," she added, though saying it aloud, she suspected, didn't do much to inspire confidence.

"As enticing as you make that sound," he said, "my shift doesn't end for another half hour."

"I'll pay you through midnight," she said. Of course today was the day he decided to pick up a couple of brain cells? Where was the Boaz that was ready to punch out a guest to defend her? "And overtime," she added. "Plus, you'll get to meet the Prince of Demons. Won't that be fun?"

Boaz laughed, until horror crept up onto his face. "Wait, you're not kidding, are you?"

"Why would I joke about a thing like that?" she said. "Come on. There's no one else coming."

"Is everything all right?" he asked her when they started out. "You seem . . . tense. . . ."

"Me, tense?" She laughed in a way that even Clara realized sounded *really* tense. She sighed. "I don't like visiting Ashmodai," she said. "I don't do it when I can avoid it."

"And you can't avoid it now because . . ."

Clara avoided his gaze. *Because Molly thinks you're the problem.* "Molly is sick. I don't know what happened, but Ashmodai is probably the only person who can help her."

He seemed to accept her explanation and said nothing else about it as they kept walking. They had just reached the Bowery when Boaz suddenly asked, "You really mean to tell me that Ashmodai lives in the East Village?"

Clara shrugged. "I don't think the club is *literally* in the Village, just a door."

"Ashmodai has a nightclub?" he snorted. "A nightclub with a door in the Village, but the *club* isn't in the Village."

"Um . . . yes?" she said. "There are other doors to Gehinnom, I think. They open up all the time, dark spaces in the city that we can step through. Lots of doors, but they all lead to the same place, Gehinnom, and Ashmodai can't leave. The closest one used to be in the Kmart in Astor Place, but then they closed that down . . . which, thank goodness. Some places are just too cursed."

"Wait, are we going to a club or *Gehinnom*?" Boaz stopped. "Like is this a nightclub or is this literal Jewish purgatory?"

"I thought you said you trusted me?" she said, reaching over to squeeze his arm. It was so warm, and thrilling to have his pulse for even a moment in her hand, a thrill even better when he didn't so much as flinch at her touch.

"It's not that I don't trust you," he said. "I just didn't think your evening plans included . . . you know, dying."

"No one's dying tonight," she said lightly, hoping that it was true. Maybe she'd go to Ashmodai and find out that Molly had the whole situation entirely wrong. It was perfectly in the realm of possibility. Molly got things wrong all the time. And Boaz . . . What could Boaz possibly have to do with an errant sheyd on the NYU campus? "I won't *leave* you in Gehinnom."

"You better not," he said.

Clara didn't truly feel the November cold, but his touch sent a delicious wave of heat straight to her core. For a brief moment, she thought about abandoning the mission altogether. Maybe they could come up with another way to help Molly. . . .

No, they needed to talk to Ashmodai.

"So he doesn't live in the Village technically. It's just, you know, a doorway?"

"You really seem to be struggling with this."

"It's more the *idea* that he's just . . . chilling in the Village, you know?" said Boaz. "Like, of all the places in the world the Prince of Demons would be hanging out . . ."

"Are you trying to say that there are other places in the world you'd rather be at this moment?" she said, stopping. It was absurd. She'd lived well over a hundred fifty years and had never been more confident that there was no single other place on the planet that she'd rather be than Manhattan.

"*No, of course not*," said Boaz, without a trace of sincerity. "You're right, there's nowhere on earth I'd rather be than running toward the Prince of Demons on a freaking *cold* November night on—*That was a rat, I stepped on a rat!*" Boaz made a noise that she'd never heard from him, or from any mortal man. She looked over to see that Boaz had turned white as a sheet, and she glimpsed the small movement of a rat disappearing into a nearby pile of garbage bags. "Yeah," he added, his voice weak, "nowhere else on earth I'd rather be."

"It was just a rat," she said, gesturing for him to start following again. "I thought you were from Brooklyn?"

"You try stepping on a rat the size of a golden retriever!" he said loudly, now giving a wide berth to the garbage bags. Clara supposed she shouldn't have found it funny. Everything he said was completely reasonable, and yet she suddenly found that she'd started laughing and that she couldn't stop, leaning on his shoulder for balance.

"It wasn't *that* big," she said. "Don't tell me you're a Brooklyn boy afraid of rats."

"There are objectively more rats in Manhattan!" he said defensively. "And they are way more entitled, I might add. Manhattan rats expect you to give them the right of way."

"Come on, let's go meet the prince, shall we?" she said, and was delighted when, after a moment's decision, he reached and took her hand.

She had worried that they'd run into problems with the door. After all, humans weren't supposed to see it. But something was wrong with Boaz, and if he could remember her face and see ghosts, it only seemed logical he'd be able to find his way into Gehinnom. "You can see it, right?"

"A very black door," he said. "Yeah, why wouldn't I be able to?"

"Because your heart is still beating," she said.

He mouthed wordlessly before the door opened and a figure burst out, a demon that Clara did not know by name. He paused, looking between them both, before grinning at Boaz. "Oh, Clara, you brought dinner."

Boaz, for his part, didn't blanch half as much as when he'd stepped on the rat. In fact, like the sight of her own face, the existence of monsters seemed to be something that barely surprised him.

"Leave him alone," Clara said smoothly, not taking her eyes off Boaz. "We've got business with Ashmodai."

"No matter," he said. "Then I'd have to wait *so long* for a dairy dessert." The demon laughed as he vanished into the night.

Clara held the door open and gestured for him to follow her in, still carefully watching his face. "You seem calm," she remarked.

"Well, after you told me that you're a Jewish vampire, there isn't much left that's surprising, is there?" he retorted as the door closed behind them and the floor and stairs came alight with the false silver stars.

"Says the person who had a heart attack over a rat," she said.

"That's different."

But Clara didn't think it was, and as she led him down into the club, she hoped she wasn't making a mistake, bringing him here. She wanted an explanation from Ashmodai; the goal wasn't to get Boaz offed tonight. But the boy seemed determined to do just that without her help. It was late enough that the club was full. The music was at full volume, and she was not ten steps in before she realized that she had lost track of Boaz.

"Damn it, where are you?" She muttered a few choice curses under her breath in Yiddish before craning her neck and seeing Boaz . . . pinned against the far wall.

She marched across the floor, yanking a few pins from her hair. As she got closer, she could see it was a snake. Not *the* Snake, of course. *The* Snake had better things to do than drown his failures in alcohol and endless jazz. But he had kin, snakes like him with arms and legs and a habit of getting inside human heads.

"Get off him. He's with me!" she shouted over the music, trying to push the snake away, scales and all, from Boaz.

The snake, who was not *the* Snake, turned to Clara, his yellow eyes unblinking. Clara grabbed Boaz's arm and yanked him toward her. "No need to get sssssso defensssssive," he hissed. "We were only chatting. It'sssss not every day one meetsssss a young man whose reputation precedes him."

"Yeah . . . chatting," said Boaz, straightening out his jacket. Clara didn't let go of him as she pulled him around the edge of the dance floor. "That wasn't . . . *the* Snake, was it?"

She shook her head. "I've met him, you know. *The* Snake. Much more charming."

"Yeah, I mean, if that one was in charge of the Tree of Knowledge, we'd never have gotten out of Eden," he said. Then his brows knit together, and after a moment, he shouted over the music, "What did he mean by my reputation? You haven't been talking about me when you come here, have you?"

"You really think I just come here on my precious little time off to tell snakes all about you?" she asked. "They're all trying to mess with you because you've got a heartbeat. Don't take it seriously."

"You don't need to keep clutching my arm, you know. I won't run off."

"What?" Clara remembered the viselike grip she had on his arm. She instantly let go. "Oh, sorry. But stay close?" When no one tried approaching her, she made her way to the bar to ask about an audience with Ashmodai. The bartender looked ready to wave the both of them through, but paused, narrowing his eyes at Boaz. "And him?"

"Yes, and him," said Clara, more than a little exasperated. "It's important. Please? It won't take long."

He pointed to the door behind the bar. "You know what to look for. If he wants to talk, he'll talk."

They walked through what seemed like endless hallways, before Clara reached the familiar door and knocked.

"Let me do the talking, okay?" She waited for him to nod in

agreement before pushing open the door.

Ashmodai was behind his desk when the door opened. Books were spread out along the entire length, which took her by surprise. She had never really considered the possibility that the Prince of Demons read, and despite the evidence, she still doubted.

"Oh, you've brought company!" Ashmodai rose up from an impossibly high-backed chair beside the fire. "Did you come to show off your little bashert? I am so glad. It's not good for you to be alone, little bird."

"Oh, he's not . . ." Clara began, at the same time that Boaz began to say much the same thing. Ashmodai folded his arms across his chest. "I don't live alone; I have my sister."

"Well, who am I to judge? Of course, of course," said the prince, reaching out to shake Boaz's hand. "Welcome to Gehinnom. I do hope you find the club to your liking."

"About that," Boaz said. Clara watched the color drain from his face. "This isn't . . . Is this *really* . . . ?"

Ashmodai let out a deep laugh. "Why? Where did you imagine the wicked dead go before Olam Ha-Ba? Did you think the music would be worse? That there wouldn't be alcohol? Did you seriously think that I'd be able to keep the doors open without it?" When Boaz remained speechless, his mouth just slightly agape, Ashmodai at last shook his head. "This is just a place between for those to pass through. You're only as dead as you feel." With another grin at Boaz, the prince turned his gaze to Clara. "So why did you come here, my little bird?"

You sent me a message, and I received it loud and clear. Clara bit her tongue, choosing her words carefully. She couldn't have Boaz think she'd dragged him into a trap. "I need to know what's wrong with my sister," she said. "I think you know, just like I think you know what happened to her girlfriend."

"And you brought *him* here because . . ." Ashmodai trailed off, watching Boaz, his bright eyes catching the light from the hearth and glinting in the dark. A small smirk played at the corner of his mouth. At first she thought he might be laughing at her, realizing that she did have a type, because Boaz's wasn't unlike a lot of the faces she'd been paying with. Until she remembered, with a jolt, that Ashmodai had seen Boaz's face before, because it hadn't been too long ago that she'd paid her rent with his face.

"He's agreed to help me," she said shortly. "And he's so far the only person we've found who still remembers Molly's girlfriend and has a pulse. . . ."

"He is, what you may call, tsvishn veltn, bein olamot . . . between worlds," he said. "Like you and myself. We all come to it in our own way. Now, run along, dear, the adults have something to discuss." He waved his hand at Boaz, and the door to the office opened.

"Um, I'll stay here, actually," said Boaz, without sufficient conviction.

"First door on the left will get you to the club. You can wait at the bar. Whatever you want, it's on the house," he said. "While this is all very gallant of you, I can assure you that your girlfriend will be fine."

A flush rose up on Boaz's neck, and he suddenly struggled for words. "She's . . . I'm not . . . We're—"

"*Run along now,*" said Ashmodai. "Before I . . . lose my patience."

She did not like the idea of Boaz wandering Gehinnom alone one bit, but she couldn't leave the club without talking to Ashmodai, either. She owed it to Molly. "It's fine, Boaz. This won't take long." Clara sighed. "I am sure *His Highness* won't have any useful advice—he never does."

Boaz backed awkwardly out of the room, and Clara watched him go. The door closed, and when she turned back, Ashmodai was standing much closer to her than she had anticipated, within arm's reach. It took a century of training not to flinch.

"So what's the message, then? According to Molly, the sheyd she drank from was there to send a message from you," said Clara, struggling to conceal a snarl. "What do you want?"

The smile on Ashmodai's face grew. "It's not what I *want* so much as what must be done. I merely wanted you and your sister to know that you ought to kill that little pet of yours while you still have the chance."

That was not what she was expecting, not from Ashmodai. "You were the one who told me to get close to him!" she said. "I did what you said. I let him in."

"Exactly. You got him to expose his pretty little neck to you, enough that you know all his little secrets, including that ring he wears around it."

"So it is the ring?" A sudden, burning anger rose up in Clara. "Is that what this is about? I don't care about his damn ring. He doesn't even know how to use the thing."

"Don't tell me you cannot feel it." Ashmodai's eyes flashed, and Clara thought the facade of humanity wavered, that she could almost see the demon that lay beneath. "That pull, that tug in your chest. It is to the ring he wears around his neck. It calls to all of us who are not of this world because, like us, it does not belong to this world, either. It will call and call until at last it is returned to its kin and kind. It is an old relic, and it belongs with old relics like us. And it's getting stronger."

Clara said nothing, but it made some sense. Of course she felt a pull toward Boaz. Even Molly had seen it, had thrown it in her face when they had argued, her *little yeshiva bochur*. It made more sense that it was something else. She couldn't possibly feel things for someone who was always late, who was afraid of her and yet thick enough to keep showing up to work when he should have been running in the opposite direction.

"You need to call off the sheydim," she said firmly. "And you need to help Molly. Biting that sheyd made her sick."

"Oh, your sister will be fine, soon enough," he said with a wave of his hand. "And the sheydim only have your best interests at heart," he added when Clara rolled her eyes. "They are trying to *help you* . . . in their way. If you don't take that ring back from the boy, they might get to it first, and maybe they should." His eerily perfect face, for once, grew serious. "Someone has to stop that boy. The fate of our world depends on it."

"You need to keep them away from Molly and me." Clara swallowed hard, Molly's voice echoing in her brain. *I can't lose someone else.* Clara couldn't either. Above all else, she could not lose her sister. "I don't care what it takes."

Ashmodai approached her. "Then take care of him."

26

BOAZ

Coming here had been a bad idea. He should have fought her harder, he should have come up with a better excuse. Now he looked like a proper fool in front of Clara. He might as well have shown up with a giant sign around his neck that said "Eat Me, I'm Clueless."

He waited for Clara by the bar, as instructed, and wondered whether he should just run. It wasn't just that this was all profoundly embarrassing, though that was certainly part of it.

It was the way everyone kept looking at him. The snake, the sheydim, even Ashmodai. Everyone looked at him like they were sizing him up, like they were hoping to take a bite. Ashmodai in particular . . . He couldn't say what it was exactly, but when he left that office, he couldn't shake the feeling that Ashmodai somehow had already gotten his jaws into him, like he had left a piece of himself behind.

It was a small bit of relief when she emerged from Ashmodai's office at last. "All good?" he said, his voice coming out too high-pitched.

"Can we sit down somewhere and talk?" said Clara.

Boaz stood and moved toward her, but Clara was already striding toward the door. She eyed him suspiciously, and Boaz's heart hammered in his chest. He wondered suddenly if she could hear it. "Fine."

Twenty minutes later, they were back on Second Avenue at B&H Dairy, the only decent kosher place between Gehinnom and the theater. Boaz didn't think they were ordinarily open this late, but when they reached the awning, they found the lights still on. He had insisted that he wasn't hungry, and that he ate vegetarian at non-kosher places, but she would not be swayed.

The narrow diner was empty at this hour, save a pair of cooks. He was hit at once with the smell of coffee and frying potatoes, and in spite of everything, especially the close encounters with footed snakes and sheydim, his stomach growled. After all the effort of trying not to become their next victim, he had worked up an appetite.

Clara clearly heard. "Oh, don't worry about me," she said in a fake-deep voice meant to mock him. "I'm not hungry." They were seated at a small table in the back of the restaurant, and the glare he threw at her only made her laugh. "You should probably know by now that it's useless to lie to me. I can tell when you are."

"You want to bet?" he muttered, in spite of his better judgment. She glowered at him then, and for a second, he wasn't sure if what he was seeing was simply Clara, inches from absolutely losing it with him, or a monster. "Come on, like you've told me everything about you."

When a bored-looking waiter came to them, Boaz ordered coffee and a couple of fried eggs and hash browns, and Clara ordered toast. He assumed it was just for appearance's sake and was surprised when the food did come that she promptly began emptying the salt-shaker over the slices and biting into one.

"You can eat that?"

"One cannot live on blood alone," she said between bites. "Although it's not nearly as satisfying."

Boaz stirred a generous heap of sugar into his coffee before taking a sip. "That's . . . kinda funny, actually."

"Kinda funny," she scoffed.

"I didn't mean . . . I don't think *you're* funny."

"Good, you shouldn't," she said evenly.

"Of course not. You're terrifying," he said, taking a bite of egg.

"Oh, now you're making fun of me."

"I'm not!" said Boaz. He was, a little. But she made it so easy for him. "What I meant was, it's *interesting*, given what gentiles historically think we do with blood, that you also eat bread. You're, like . . ." He took a large bite of hash brown to avoid having to say more, because judging from the look on her face, it hadn't been the right thing to say at all.

"I'm like what?"

"Nothing," he said, swallowing too much coffee and scalding his throat. "Lost my train of thought."

"You're lying," she said.

"You're, like, that Jew gentiles warned about," he said quickly, as if that would end the conversation faster. He didn't even have to meet her eyes to know that it wasn't going to be the end.

"I've never *killed a child*," she said, her voice low and deadly enough to leave little doubt that she had certainly killed *someone*. She was just discerning. Which, given how mad he had made her on multiple occasions, wasn't particularly comforting.

"Oh, well, not all blood libels are about kids," he said quickly. "In the Damascus Affair, it was a monk."

"I would never," she said. "Nor would Molly."

"Oh, I wasn't suggesting you personally were, like, doing a murder in nineteenth-century Damascus," he started, even though he knew that was exactly what it sounded like. Despite himself, he tried a bad joke: "Were you?"

Clara didn't laugh. "No."

"Good," he said, forcing himself to take a bite of food. "That'd be super awkward. I mean, if you believe the stories my aunt tells." He swallowed. "It's just, that whole thing—and what they did to my family because they thought they killed some monk to use his blood to make matzah—she thinks that's why we're all cursed. She's got a bunch of theories. You know how it is. It's like how all our holidays are some version of 'they tried to kill us, we won, let's eat.' There's, like, ten different potential historical traumas that have messed us up enough that we can still talk to dead people, I guess." He let out an awkward laugh. "I still think it all comes back to the ring."

A group of girls entered the diner, taking the stools at the counter. They were wearing long dresses, and from the way their hair was pinned, he might have thought they were ghosts, except that the cook on the other side clearly saw them and took their orders before disappearing into the back. Boaz even tilted his head to check for a flicker, but they remained perfectly solid.

Clara took a bite of her bread, and for a moment, Boaz thought he saw Clara's real age, a flash of something much older just beneath her surface. "Where *did* they even get that ring?" she asked. "What do you know about it?"

Boaz shrugged, taking a deep breath to remain calm. He didn't want to test her lie detector powers. "It's been in our family forever. Like I said, Hila's got theories. They change according to her mood."

For a moment, neither of them spoke. He just ate his eggs and tried not to stare at Clara's hands while she tore the bread into tiny pieces. She had fingers like a pianist, he decided, delicate and perfect. He remembered what they had looked like when she took her hair down, what she really looked like underneath, but somehow that didn't seem to matter as much sitting here with her.

Boaz glanced at the girls at the counter and realized that two were looking right at them. He leaned toward her. "Do you think the girls at the counter are listening to us?"

"What?" Clara spun to look at them a moment before turning back around, her brows drawn.

"They're weird, right?" he insisted, lowering his voice to a whisper. Something about them was really freaking him out. He kept tilting his head. They didn't shift out of sight, and they were definitely sitting on the stools. But something about them still seemed *off*, something that he couldn't quite place. And where had the cook gone? It was only then that he realized how quiet the diner was, that the staff had disappeared and never reemerged.

They turned to look at him again, all three girls, all in perfect time, and when they met Boaz's gaze, Boaz knew at once that he didn't like it.

"Hey, Clara?" he said carefully, slowly pushing back in his chair. "We should get going."

The chair made a long, painful squeak as it skidded across the tile. Something was *very* wrong indeed. One of them had a fork clutched in her hand, and another a knife, and they were all looking at them with a hunger that made the hairs on the back of Boaz's neck stand on end.

"I think you're right," Clara said, keeping her eyes fixed on the girls as she, too, tried to slowly extricate herself from her chair. Her hand drifted up to the clip that held her bun in place. And then, in a low but clear voice, she said, "Boaz, they don't have heartbeats."

27

MOLLY

The last time Molly had been this tired, she still had a pulse.

The bread that Clara had attempted to ply her with had done little good. She'd scarcely tasted it, even when she'd taken it with half the salt cellar. On the contrary, it only worsened the sticky heaviness in her stomach.

Molly had drawn the shades shut, and for a while remained where she had settled on the fainting couch, hoping that it would pass, that she simply needed to shake the sheyd blood from her system. But rather than resolve itself, the aching worsened, her limbs weak and her head pounding. She closed her eyes, even using a pillow to cover her ears in an attempt to block out the sounds from the street below, which had only grown louder, and louder . . .

And then she heard the horses.

At first, Molly thought she was imagining it, the clomping and clatter mixed in with the ordinary traffic of Second Avenue. But she continued to hear it, louder and clearer as the minutes passed, until at last she worked up the strength to reach the window and push back the curtains.

The light was like a knife into her skull, but those were horses that she was hearing.

Moving between and among the regular car traffic of Second Avenue was something Molly had thought she'd never see again, something she had not seen in well over a hundred years: horse-drawn omnibuses crowding the avenue.

She blinked hard, expecting them to disappear, for them to be a delusion brought on by her first sickness in nearly a hundred years. But the horses only came into sharper focus, along with an unusual number of people on the sidewalks below.

Molly slid open the window, still waiting for reality to kick in and make the delusion fade, but even from here she could see that the crowds along the sidewalk were nothing like she'd ordinarily expect. Among the regulars, who appeared to know very well what century it was, there were others who did not, women in long trailing dresses, cinched waists, and hats balanced on carefully pinned hair.

It didn't make sense. Surely, there had to be some explanation. She hadn't even swallowed much of the sheyd blood. Nor did her reflection in the window make sense, the blank eyes staring back at her. Her hair was up, wasn't it? Molly forced the window open wider, her hands not yet claws, but still a ghastly gray that she associated with her monstrous form. Without even ripping out her scrunchie, she slid into her owl form and took to the sky.

For a moment she thought she had it, the air catching beneath her wings the way it ought.

But it was fleeting, and the world began to spin around her, and she couldn't say whether it was in her head or if she herself was actually spinning, though by the time she crash-landed on the sidewalk, she realized it was probably a bit of both. She shifted haphazardly back into a girl, her throat suddenly parched. She tried clearing her throat, but it was more than dry; the scratchiness was choking her. She coughed until she gagged, until feathers came up.

This isn't happening. Molly wiped the feathers from her hands as the ground beneath her tilted dangerously. *This isn't happening, this isn't happening . . .*

She turned back toward the theater and started walking down a few blocks. The sidewalks were still busy, and she was certain someone would notice a gray and monstrous girl hacking up feathers and stumbling along. But no one so much as glanced in her direction, not even out of fear.

When she reached the Chase Bank at Second and Tenth, the blue lights glowing, she looked down at the stars of the Yiddish Walk of Fame, her legacy, carved into literal concrete, installed when the Chase Bank was a deli, when people still thought it worth remembering what Second Avenue had been, the talent that had passed through, the way modern American theater had been born *here*. The usual stars were there. Ida Kaminska, Fyvush Finkel, and . . .

Hers was gone.

She paced up the whole length of stars, as if she had somehow forgotten where hers was, even though she had seen it thousands of times. She even wondered if it had been ripped up, if some vandals had taken it. But there were no signs of destruction, no signs that someone had run off with it. It was just . . . gone.

28

CLARA

Clara let down her hair, but Boaz didn't move. "Boaz?"

Clara had barely paid the girls any mind when they came in, and now she understood why. Their presence made too little noise. With the sounds of cooking gone, there was nothing to disguise the fact that none of them had heartbeats.

"Boaz?" Her voice rose. The girls climbed up onto the stools, until they loomed over them both. Now that they were standing, their skirts were high enough that Clara could see their clawed feet. The restaurant was too narrow; it would be impossible to make it to the exit without crossing into their reach. There had to be a second exit somewhere. "*Boaz . . .*"

She glanced toward Boaz, who'd grabbed the dustpan and broom behind him and shouted, "Clara, watch out!"

She turned, swinging her arms as she did so, and caught the girl straight in the chest, throwing her backward. The girl shrieked, an unearthly noise that raised the hairs at the nape of Clara's neck. Then she clambered up, but before she was even on her clawed feet, one of the others flew toward them. *Flew*, the way she leapt up too high and too fast toward Boaz. Clara blocked her, stumbling and smacking her own head against the chair in the process. But before the girl could get a grip on her, there was a whoosh of air and a shriek as the girl was knocked aside. Again, Clara tried to straighten up and saw Boaz standing just behind her, wielding the broom like a bat. He whacked the girl a second time, giving Clara a chance to steady herself. The girls came forward again, and Clara didn't think. She bared her claws, thrashing and digging wherever they happened to land. Boaz, meanwhile, wielded the broom with surprising efficacy. It was absurd, but it bought them the space and time for her to try and think through an escape.

Boaz grabbed her wrist and nodded toward the counter. Seeing the kitchen door, she understood. She leapt on top of it, and Boaz followed, almost managing to vault over it. For a moment, he was caught, suspended over the top, and Clara looked back in horror as one of girls, her hands along his thigh like claws, yanked him backward.

The yelp from Boaz was enough. She shrieked and dove back over the counter, clawing at the girl. She would make her let go of Boaz. She would make her . . .

One minute, she had the monstrous girl by the shoulders, pulling at her just as she pulled at Boaz, but with her claws, with the total strength of a hundred years of being a predator. The next, something smashed down hard on her back.

A shock rattled her bones, like she'd been struck by lightning. Her knees buckled, and her vision swam, and she wondered for a moment if this was dying, whether she'd been cleaved in two.

Then came the wave of pain, such as she had never felt since her first death, the kind of pain that could rip a mind in half.

Her insides still rattled, and stunned, she barely registered that she was being half carried, half pulled. Where were they taking her? She didn't have the energy to snarl in protest, and only at the sound of a metal door slamming shut behind her did she realize it was Boaz, his soft, warm hands around her, his big eyes checking her face.

Clara shook her head, the world in half-hazy focus. Beyond simply being beaten, she was numb, unsure of what in her still worked. From where he deposited her on the floor in something of a heap, she watched him take the broom and use it to block the door, holding it back against the rattling barrage of girls throwing themselves against the glass, trying to ram it off its hinges.

They were in the back kitchen of the restaurant.

"Clara . . . Clara?" Boaz called. She forced herself to focus, to make herself move. "We need to get out of here. You'll have to move. I don't think I can carry you fast enough."

She tried lifting her arms, and it was then she felt the trouble, a searing in her left shoulder. She tried again, and she cried out in pain, something she almost never did.

Beyond the door, the pounding continued.

"I can't," she choked out, her voice small. "I think they broke something."

"You can break bones?" Boaz asked. "But I thought—"

"I'm not invincible; I just don't age," she gritted out, allowing herself to sink back onto the tile. Her head swam. "I can't turn like this." She broke off to pant, the pain making her feel short of breath. "There's . . . There's no way I can fly. You should just go."

Boaz shook his head. "I'm not leaving you here."

There was a tremendous thud against the door, and the broom bent a little. "Leave," she said, making her voice as sharp as it would go. "I will be fine."

"No." He stared at her, and she decided that Molly was absolutely right. Totally her type. His warm brown eyes wide with concern, trying to decide something, though she wasn't quite sure what, until something in him seemed to snap into place, and he made up his mind. He began to pull off his hoodie. The banging on the door stopped. From the sound of it, they were tearing through the restaurant, but she didn't know how much time they would have. "Will blood heal you faster?"

She nodded, before realizing what he was asking her, and before realizing that the motion made the world swim around her. "Boaz . . ."

"Tell me how it works," he said quickly. "Like, if you bite me, will I turn into one?"

She shook her head once. "Men don't turn . . . I think? I don't know," she said. "I bite men all the time, and they're fine. They don't even remember. If I don't drain them completely, then they're fine."

"You sure?" he said. "Because if you kill me, I'm haunting the theater forever, and I promise to be an asshole ghost. I'm going to mess with the bathroom lights *endlessly*—"

"You don't have to do this, Boaz, really. You should run."

"The box office is the best job I've ever had," he muttered, though when his eyes met hers, he looked ready to say something else. He was so close to her, and she saw the flicker of something in his eyes that she hadn't seen before. Not when he'd been punched in the face, not when he'd seen her hair down. That flicker of fear, the thing that he had tried so hard to hide.

He began to roll up his sleeve, but she shook her head. "Neck is easier."

"Right," he said, now avoiding her gaze. She heard his heart, loud and a little frantic, and saw how hard he was trying not to look afraid. She thought of how hard he had worked to not be afraid, and how it wasn't even her face that did it, but this. His face was inches from hers. He undid one of the buttons of his collared shirt and looked down at the floor. "Right, yeah, go on."

This wasn't usually how things happened. The men she bit she accosted at parties, weddings, at the theater. She knew nothing of them, and they nothing of her. They wouldn't remember.

Boaz, though, he knew everything; he remembered. He knew enough to be afraid of her and yet was still offering up his neck. Like he *trusted* her.

She reached up with her good hand and brushed it along his neck, over a chain he wore around it. She thought of what Ashmodai had said, but his voice was so far away here, and there would be time to worry about the ring. Under her fingers, Boaz shivered. She smelled soap and sweat and the lingering scent of something else that she couldn't quite name. Her lips were nearly on his neck when he suddenly flinched. "Oh, come on . . ."

"Is this where you tell me you don't bite?" he muttered, a slight note of fear in his voice. "Because, like, that is categorically not true."

"I'll be gentle," she said, leaning forward and pressing her lips to his neck. She remained there for a moment before at last letting her sharp teeth sink into his flesh.

She expected him to flinch again, or try to pull away, but he stayed where he was, perfectly still. No, that wasn't true. His heart was beating loud, hard, even if he was holding his breath. He was all pulse and movement, warm and so overwhelmingly alive in her grasp. The moment his blood passed her lips, feeling burned back into her limbs, like she'd been dropped into a hot bath after being caught out in the cold. It made her head feel light and present. She couldn't remember the last time she'd felt so alive.

Her arm and shoulder began to prickle, like they had fallen asleep, and she tried to drink slowly. But still Boaz didn't pull away, even when she let her hand rest on his shoulder, even when she chanced touching the curls at the nape of his neck. Part of her knew she could keep going forever. She was so *hungry*, and she didn't think she'd ever felt this way drinking someone, not in this lifetime.

The moment she was sure that she could move her shoulder again, she pulled away. The place where she'd pierced his neck was red but had sealed shut behind her, leaving little more than a mark, a touch of light bruising.

"You okay?" she asked softly. He was breathing heavily, as if he'd been running again, and for a moment, she was worried that she'd taken too much, that she had made him sick. She met his gaze and was certain that he looked a bit pale, that the faint greenish tinge from his still-healing nose was more pronounced, that she'd done something to hurt him.

But after a moment, he let out a small nervous laugh. "I'm fine."

The door rattled again, and the broom splintered. She realized that her hand was still on the back of his neck, and she only reluctantly took it back. Now they did need to get out of here.

"Come on," she said, rising to her feet. She felt incredible, the best she'd ever felt, like she could shoot straight into the air, like she'd been made new. Had drinking blood always felt like this?

Or was it something to do with Boaz? Boaz, between two worlds. Boaz, who tried so hard not to be afraid of her and her face. "Now we can get out of here, come on."

Boaz followed suit, pushing himself to his feet. But the moment he did so, Clara realized her mistake. Boaz's eyes glazed, the color vanishing from his face as he collapsed back onto the ground.

BOAZ

When Boaz came to, the first thing he noticed was how cold he was.

"Oh, good, so I didn't kill you."

He forced himself upright, ignoring the dizziness that remained. It didn't take long for him to figure out why it was so cold, why a persistent wind cut through his jacket and smacked him across the face. They were on a rooftop, somewhere still in the Village, he figured, by all the low-slung brick buildings around them.

"How did we get up here?" Boaz asked cautiously, looking over at Clara. She was sitting inches from him, her hair now back in its usual twist. She had a small Duane Reade bag in her hand and at once began rummaging through it.

"Unlike you, I can carry someone," she said. She handed him a sleeve of Nutter Butters.

"Um, thank you?"

"Eat some," she said. "Before you try sitting up again."

"I'm not really hungry?"

"Eat it, or I'll make you," she said, her voice just serious enough that he was rather afraid she meant it. He ripped open the box and took one out.

"How'd you know I liked these?"

"You keep a stash in that file cabinet in the box office," she said. "I noticed. Told you not to keep food in there. It'll draw your best friends, the rats."

"You were going through my things?" he asked, though in truth he was more flattered than anything else. He never considered that she had noticed or would bother to remember his packaged cookie of choice.

He polished one off in two bites, and then sat up a little further, glad that the dizzy spell was already ebbing. "What else is there?"

She pushed a plastic canister into his hands, and squinting into the dark, he saw they were iron supplements. "That way you can't blame me for making you anemic."

"Um, thanks?" he said. He tucked the canister into his sweatshirt.

"You're not going to take one?"

"I can't take pills dry," he said, before eating another Nutter Butter so she wouldn't force him to take iron supplements in front of her. "Are you feeling better?"

"Much," she said. "Thank you. That was . . ." For a moment, their eyes met again, and Boaz felt something low in his stomach clench. None of it made sense. He had just let her, a monster, *bite his neck*. To fix a broken shoulder. It was absurd and impossible, and he couldn't shake the feeling that he rather wanted her to do it again.

He should have been properly scared. This wasn't one of his movies, something he could turn on and off. There was no screen between them. *She drank his blood.*

And yet . . .

"Do you pass out easily when you give blood?" she asked accusatorially.

"I don't usually give it from my jugular vein," he said. He had in fact passed out when he'd given blood for the first time, at a blood drive at Arbel he'd signed up for because it had been an excused absence from gym that week. Like he was going to tell her that. He rubbed the spot where she'd bit. It was a bit tender, like a fresh bruise. "Why'd you come up here?"

"I like having the high ground." She glanced up at the night sky. "And at least from up here, we'd see those sheydim coming."

"You . . . If you turned into an owl, how did I—"

"*That's* what you're worried about?" She laughed again, and his stomach did a complete backflip. Yes, for that smile he would definitely let her bite him again. She pointed to a metal door opposite them. "How on earth would I have gotten you up here as an owl? I carried you up the stairs. It's the theater."

"Oh." Boaz chanced standing up and was pleased that he didn't pass out again. That would have been embarrassing. "You know, it all looks very different up here."

"I am aware," she said tersely, but then she continued to look at him, as if she regretted it. When she spoke again, her tone had softened. "Thank you, really. It was very . . . gallant."

"Well, I wasn't going to be the one to get us out of there, now, was I?"

"I seem to recall that you were showing an impressive amount of skill with the broom," she said.

He stared back at her. She was practically glowing, a laugh in her eyes and playing on her lips that made his insides grow hot. He'd never thought about her lips this much, but now they were all he could think about. Were they always that perfect? He thought of what Edelman had tried to tell him, that the dead who remained on this earth suffered greatly. They wanted, more than anything, a chance to move on. The dead were miserable. They suffered when they remained above ground. . . .

But lit by moonlight and the light emanating from the bustle of Second Avenue below them, he wasn't sure what to make of it. She was smiling. That wasn't how the ghosts who accosted him looked at him. They made it clear they were longing for help. Clara, though . . . If that was longing, it was for something else.

"So, am I just staying up here the whole night?" he said at last. "My mom might start to wonder."

Clara folded her arms, glancing down at the street below. "I haven't seen them since," she said. "I don't know where they went, but I don't think they followed us here."

"Who were they, you think?" said Boaz. He ran his fingers through his hair. "You've never met them before? Never saw them at the demon nightclub, or . . ."

Clara shook her head. "I don't forget faces." But Boaz thought there was something she wasn't saying. Frankly, it didn't feel fair, that she could hear all the little signs of him lying, and the only thing he was left with was a feeling.

"You . . . sure?" he said. "Not to be argumentative, but you've been in the city a *long* time."

"A hundred and fifty years," she said quietly.

"Yeah, um, see?" he said, trying not to sound shaken by the small reminder that she only looked eighteen. That, actually, she had been born well before his great-grandparents. He knew this . . . and yet, that didn't quite capture it. She *wasn't* his great-grandparents, who had died long before he was born and lived only in a handful of grainy pictures and some stories from Aunt Hila. She wasn't even like his grandparents. His mother's parents, who lived down the street from them, were sharp and a little intimidating, but still frail. Even compared to five years ago, ten years ago. No, Clara wasn't like that. She wasn't fading or aging. She was eighteen, just someone who had been that way for a long time.

"Well, that's New York City for you," Boaz said. "Doesn't matter how long you've lived here. There's always some scary shit you haven't seen yet."

And when she met his eyes, he wondered whether she could see what he wanted. She never said anything about being able to read his mind, and he didn't think she could. . . . Otherwise, she would know about the conversation he had had with Daniel, with Edelman. She would have known everything before; there would already not be any secrets between them.

But he couldn't help but feel like she could tell, because she held his gaze a little too long. She was so beautiful in that light. Surely, she knew . . .

"I should get back," he said again. "My mom will get weird if I'm not," he added quickly.

Clara looked surprised but nodded. "Yeah, of course," she murmured, the moment vanishing as quickly as it had come.

There once was a young man who could speak to the dead.

It was an old family curse. Some said it was a scar left behind by the Damascus Affair, the blood libel that had driven his Harari ancestors from the city for good. So great had the torture been for information he did not have that even though he lived, that Harari and each of his descendants did so with one foot in the grave always.

Some said the curse was older. That the family had in fact spoken to ghosts since the days of the Temple, when their ancestor believed he had bested the Prince of Demons, only to find that no one escapes such a test unscathed.

Eli Harari couldn't have cared less who had cursed him, what sorry ancestor had been responsible for this fate. What was past was past, and he had far too much else to worry about.

His in-laws, for one. When he had followed Adina to Brooklyn, he'd promised her, promised her parents, that he would find a job before they got married, that he could get a green card on his own, that he wasn't using their daughter as a key to America.

That hadn't happened. Excellent guitar, passable English, and charm had served him well enough in Tel Aviv. His regular gig at a café in Florentin and some bartending had been enough to get him a cramped studio apartment and an American fiancée who made him feel alive, plenty enough for him.

But Adina wanted to be near her parents, and Eli wanted to be as far from his own ghosts as possible. So they came to Brooklyn, chose this life instead.

But this life didn't come cheap.

The Dahans had Expectations. Adina's father had come to America as a refugee, and, within a few years, had become one of the top kosher caterers in Gravesend. He reminded Eli at least once a shift, regaling him with stories about how he had triumphed in America with no income and no English and no safety net to speak of save this community, while Eli arranged platters of hors d'oeuvres and tilted beneath trays of baklava. Their daughter was supposed to have a husband who could buy her a summer house at the Jersey Shore and send her children to Jewish schools. Cater waiters couldn't afford shore houses. Cater waiters employed by their in-laws could barely afford rent.

Then of course there was the baby.

Boaz wasn't going to be like every other Harari. He wasn't going to eke out an existence living in the shadow of death. That had been the whole point of Brooklyn. He was going to have two parents who cared and grandparents who doted on him and spend summers in a house on the shore. He'd go to university right out of high school and study whatever he wanted and be happy. Properly happy. They would live well, and they would break the Harari curse once and for all.

And for several months, he really thought he had made progress. Between work and Boaz, he was busier than he'd ever been, so consumed with making this life work that he had scarcely said two words to the dead and had almost forgotten Her.

Until she'd appeared on the television.

It had taken months of inviting a third cousin of Adina's who did electronic repairs, a friend of a friend from his kindergarten days in Bat Yam, and two different questionable cable boxes, but he'd finally managed to get Israeli television live on their one set in the living room. The Dahans had scoffed when he'd mentioned it, said he'd have an easier time dropping his accent if he stuck to American programming. But he had no intention of dropping his accent, and he was never not practicing his English. What he needed when he was up late was something that sounded like home.

Boaz had been fussing, and it had been Eli's turn to get up and feed him. He didn't mind, really. He'd always been a night owl, and they were both happier when Adina got something almost like a full night of sleep. Eli had taken him to the living room, flicking on the television and keeping the volume low enough not to disturb Adina, and before long, Boaz was quiet, trying to grab the heavy ring Eli always wore around his neck, the one thing his own father had left him other than disappointment and unanswered questions.

He'd landed on a morning talk show, because it was already daytime in Israel. The two familiar hosts were in an animated discussion about Eurovision, and he might have turned it off if not for the girl he saw sitting beside them.

It was her.

He blinked hard, sitting upright so fast that he had to clutch Boaz tight to keep him from sliding onto the floor. He shook his head, like jumbling his thoughts would make them fall clearer, let him see that he was mistaken.

But the girl was still there, looking just the same as he remembered her. For years he'd been desperate to see her, to have one final conversation with her, the girl who he had once thought he would marry. The girl who had known all his secrets, the girl who had taken a piece of him to her grave. The girl who had died and left him and never once looked back, that no amount of searching with the ring could ever find.

His insides went numb. This couldn't be. He had already tried to reach her, tried a thousand different times, even wearing his father's cursed ring as he grasped, futilely, into the dark. Sometimes the dead went beyond even his reach. Or maybe she just didn't want to talk to him.

He knew he was supposed to move on. That Hararis always died at the hands of their own ghosts. He had a wife now, and a son, and too much to lose. He hadn't put on the blasted ring in months, hadn't so much as looked in the direction of a ghost. Why now?

Eli thought about turning off the television, going back to bed. Had he not done just that a thousand times? He knew how to turn his back on the dead. He'd survived this long walking away. But instead, he sat there frozen as Boaz squirmed against his chest, tugging at the ring, and the girl turned away from the conversation on-screen to stare directly into the camera.

Directly at him.

She stood up from her chair and began to approach the camera, and Eli snapped to his senses, hurrying Boaz back to his crib.

He would end this, he decided. He would confront her. She'd had plenty of chances to come back to him. He had lost too many nights and shed too many tears for her. Now was not the time. He had buried her, and she would need to stay dead. He needed to go on living.

When he returned to the living room, his stomach dropped. The two hosts were gone, their prattling with them. It was just her now, filling the screen, her hair loose and tumbling past her shoulders in perfect waves; her warm eyes, focused directly on him, flickered with television static.

"Eli, my love," she said, like she was greeting him on the phone.

This was impossible. This wasn't how ghosts came to him. He didn't like any of this.

The remote was sitting right there on the coffee table, beside Boaz's empty bottle. He could shut it off, end it. He had to—

"What are you doing here?" he asked, his voice barely more than a whisper. He couldn't wake up Adina. How could he possibly explain?

"I missed you, Eli," she said. Her voice was just the same as he remembered it, soft and sweet. "I never forgot you."

"Neither did I," he said, swallowing hard. His mind was racing. For years, he had longed for just this. For one more conversation with her, one last chance to end things. But something about this felt wrong. The time for her to come back had long ago passed.

"Yes, you did," she said, her face falling. When she spoke again, her voice was too low, crackling in the speakers. "You found someone else. You left me behind."

"I had to keep living," he whispered. He reached for the remote, but her voice stopped him.

"I thought you loved me."

She reached up and pressed her hands on the other side of the screen, as if it were not a screen at all but a window. She tested it, as if any moment she'd simply push right through. If this was no ordinary ghost, he did not know what she might do, what she *could* do. He felt the front of his shirt for the ring. His father's ring drew ghosts and demons close—and could send them away. He wasn't very good at it, but he'd made it work before, forcing back that

254

which was not of this world. He did not know what she intended, and he did not want to find out.

"You thought you could bury me," she said.

But when he felt the front of his shirt, he realized the ring was gone. He thought of Boaz, clutching and tugging at it. What if he still had it? He glanced back at the room for a second, then to the floor, searching the carpet, before she spoke again. "Oh, do give me your ring, Eli," she said, giggling. A chill ran down his back. "I'd love to try it on."

Suddenly, she whacked her fist against the glass, and a crack stretched along the entirety of the screen like a spiderweb, the colors distorting, bands of deep red stretching across the image. At last he grabbed the remote and jammed his thumb on the power button, but nothing happened. Nor did anything happen when he tried to change the channel.

She whacked again. For a moment the image went dark, except for a small hole that had opened in the center of the screen. A hand emerged, reaching and grasping into his living room. "Prove it, Eli! Prove that you still love me. Let me try it on."

Prove it. Prove that he could walk away from the things buried. Prove that things would be different this time. That he would break the curse. That they would live well. That his son would not walk as he did, waist deep in his own grave.

This was all wrong. Whatever this was, whatever demon wore her face, it wasn't her. It wasn't a ghost. It wasn't anything he'd ever seen in his twenty-seven years.

But if there was one thing he did know, it was that he couldn't let it into their living room. He couldn't let it get ahold of the ring.

And there was absolutely no way he was letting it get anywhere near his family.

He didn't need to think. He threw himself forward, hoping to smash the screen, and instead fell straight through. *Whatever it takes*, he thought. This life didn't come cheap. And if his life was the price, so be it.

30

BOAZ

Boaz knew there was a problem the moment he smelled it.

Coffee.

Not just any coffee. Coffee on the stovetop, with just a hint of hawaij, from the smell of it.

This was bad. His mom made instant coffee; she couldn't be bothered with any other method and never went through the fuss of spicing it. Never.

That meant Aunt Hila was the one making it, and that couldn't be good.

Boaz yanked himself out of bed as quickly as he could. It was already late, after eleven, and sunlight streamed through his bedroom window, half blinding him as he quickly threw on an old pair of sweatpants. He glanced into the mirror to confirm that, as he suspected, he looked like death. Even more than usual. The total lack of sleep, the fight for his life against monsters who wanted to kill monsters, passing out, having Clara *drink blood out of his neck* . . .

He looked at his neck, the memory of last night burning

through the fog of everything else. If he thought of it, he could still conjure the feeling of her teeth in his neck, the feeling of her hands in his hair, lips on his skin, the way his stomach had flipped. He half expected it all to have just been some weird dream, a hallucination conjured up by his own stress and panic and the stubborn crush that he continued to harbor for Clara Sender, even though he knew she wouldn't, couldn't.

But it was there. Faint, but visible, a small bite mark on his neck. He threw on a ratty old sweatshirt from the bottom of the pile on his desk chair, making sure the hood was high enough to hide the mark, and at the last second remembered to rip the necklace and the ring off, stashing them in the drawer in his desk before drifting out into the kitchen.

"Hello, Boazi, boker tov," said Aunt Hila with too much brightness. He was in massive trouble. "You're just in time. I bought bourekas, and they are still warm."

"Doda Hila, eizo hafta'a." But before Boaz could finish asking what the occasion was for coffee and bourekas, he realized that what he should have been asking was why Aunt Hila was still using English, a question that was answered when he saw that they were not alone. Rather, the little kitchen table was crowded, with both his mother and Daniel occupying two of the usually empty chairs.

"I don't remember planning brunch," said Boaz, switching back to English. "What's the occasion?"

It had to be bad. Daniel wasn't looking at him, instead staring into his cup of coffee like it was the single most interesting book he'd ever read. His mother, meanwhile, looked livid. Her mouth was pressed into a thin line, and she said nothing.

"Sit," said Aunt Hila. It wasn't a request. He was in deep, deep shit. He kept looking at Daniel for an explanation, but he was still interested in his coffee. At last, Boaz yanked back a chair and sat in front of one of the empty plates. Aunt Hila handed him a cup of coffee.

"It's . . . not my birthday, is it?" said Boaz, yanking up the collar of his sweatshirt and hoping Aunt Hila didn't notice the motion. He didn't know why he said it. From the looks on all their faces, either they had found his dad's body, or . . .

"Daniel texted us last night with a very interesting story," said Hila, sitting directly across from Boaz, pouring herself a glass of orange juice. "So, I thought we'd all have a little discussion about it."

"You did *what*?" said Boaz, rounding on Daniel, who still wouldn't look at him. "What did you tell them?"

"Let me explain, then you tell me if I've got it right," said Aunt Hila, her voice deadly even. This was when she was at her most terrifying, when her voice was just a *touch* too calm. "Daniel here says that you went to meet a strange man you found online—"

"That *Daniel* found online, to be clear," Boaz interjected.

"Because you thought it very likely that the girls at your work were *vampires*." She took a sip of her orange juice, and if it hadn't already been far, far too late, he would have stomped on Daniel's foot under the table. "He agreed, and then confirmed that for *everyone's* safety, you had to kill the vampires, yes?"

"No, that's—"

"What part isn't true?" said Aunt Hila. "Is everything I said true, or no?"

"Yes, but—"

"Now, Daniel texted us, very worried because he said that not

259

only did he suspect we hadn't been told about the *vampires that you work with*, but that you might have some . . . doubts, that you might have some . . . *confusing feelings* about the whole matter."

Daniel was supremely lucky, Boaz thought, because if his mother and Aunt Hila hadn't been there, he would have actually strangled him.

Boaz had never really gotten *a talk*. Nothing like the bulk of his friends and kids he knew at Arbel got. His mother couldn't be bothered; talking about relationships sometimes set her off. Aunt Hila bought him a box of condoms and told him that she would make him regret being born if he ever hurt a girl or guy, which she always added, no matter how many times Boaz insisted that he was straight. Not hurting anyone had been easy because through high school the entire sum of his romantic life had been a date with a cousin of a cousin of Daniel's, who admitted that she had only agreed to go on the date to make her actual crush jealous.

This was not how he wanted to have a proper talk with his mom and Aunt Hila. "I . . . am not confused," he said indignantly, his face beginning to warm. He was certain that he was turning red and that it wasn't helping his case at all, because Aunt Hila's eyes narrowed.

"You know that the vampire girl is not alive?" she said.

"I . . ."

"Yes or no?"

Boaz took a long drink of his coffee to avoid speaking. The one consolation was that Daniel looked miserable, like he wanted to vanish just as much as Boaz wanted to, which was absurd because he had 1) caused this and 2) was not currently being grilled about his "confusing feelings" about vampires.

"I know," Boaz finally said.

"You know you cannot chase after a girl who is not alive?"

Boaz spat out his coffee. "What? I—"

"Your father chased a girl who wasn't alive," she said, a deadly waver in her voice. "A girl we went to school with, who died suddenly a week before he graduated. It did not matter what I told him, what anyone told him—he could not let her be dead. Eli could *never* let her go, and you know where he is now?" She threw her arms up. "Ein li mosheg, I have no idea, and nor does *anyone else*. It is worse than him being dead."

"Doda Hila," Boaz began. He turned to Daniel, but his friend had his head in his hands, as if he were suddenly attempting to fight off a migraine. "I'm not chasing a dead girl."

But Aunt Hila's composure was rapidly vanishing, and she would not let Boaz off so easily. "So you're telling me Daniel is lying?"

"Boaz, you know there's weird shit going on!" Daniel interrupted, still rubbing his temples. He didn't look so different from Boaz's mother, who, at the mention of his father, appeared to also be fighting her usual headache. "You were the one who said the ghosts were connected to your bosses—"

"So, what, you're just going to ambush me?" He had no appetite for the bourekas. He didn't know what possessed Aunt Hila to think that he'd eat while being berated for being too much like his father. He wasn't like him. He wasn't *anything* like him. "Now, if you'll excuse me—"

"Oh, no," said Aunt Hila. "You aren't going anywhere until you promise me—"

"What? That I'm not Dad? That I'm not dating a vampire?"

"Yes!" said Aunt Hila.

"Why don't any of you think I can take care of myself?"

"Don't pretend to *me* that you're any good at it," said Aunt Hila, her face turning red. "That won't work on any of us, but *especially* me."

"Boaz," said Daniel, his voice suddenly small. This was *all* his fault. This terrible excuse of an intervention was his doing. "I've already confirmed things with Rabbi Pardo. He didn't want to get involved—"

"Because it's not his business!" Boaz burst out.

"He said that if Edelman is an expert, he should handle it, and I agree. I don't expect you to help, but if you're not going to, you have to promise to stay out of the way."

For a moment, there was quiet. Even Aunt Hila paused. Everyone was looking at him, as if he were six and throwing a temper tantrum, or like he was a time bomb, about to erupt any second. And that *was* how they saw him. A kid who couldn't take care of himself, who had been ticking away toward self-destruction for years, who couldn't tell the difference between the living and the dead, who was no better than his father.

"What, so you're going to have some guy who we know *nothing* about except that he gives off major serial killer vibes go and storm the Grand Dame?" he said. "Maybe light the whole place on fire? That sounds like a fantastic idea."

"Well, what do you suggest?" Daniel asked, his voice rising to match Boaz's. "This can't go on, you know that."

Boaz thought of Clara's hands in his hair, and her teeth in his neck, that momentary thrill of fear, followed by . . . trust? He knew it wasn't logical, knew that.

"I'll help," he said, hoping he sounded convinced. "Okay?

You're not going to be able to do it without me anyway. You don't know the theater, or the sisters." When he stood up again, he heard his aunt Hila start to say something, but he preempted it. "I promise, and I'm *not* my father," he said, before storming away from the table and back to his bedroom.

Boaz was trapped. He couldn't leave while Daniel and Aunt Hila were still there, but he hated sitting there, in his tiny, sun-drenched room. Everything about him was still rank from the night before, and more than that, he was boiling. How dare they all gang up on him like that? He *could* take care of himself, whatever they said. . . .

Eventually, he heard Daniel mumble goodbyes and hurry out the apartment. He thought Aunt Hila would follow him out, but instead there came a knock on his door.

"Boazi? Open up."

Boaz unfolded himself from his desk chair and opened the door. There was no use keeping the door closed on Aunt Hila. For starters, it didn't have a lock.

"Look, I'm still here," he grumbled. "Haven't run off with any vampires yet."

Aunt Hila's mouth was as tight as his mother's had been. She was already wearing her coat and looked ready to leave. He relaxed, accidentally dropping his hood. In an instant, Aunt Hila's hand shot forward to his collar. She pulled it back, and Boaz could practically feel her gaze on the bite mark Clara had left behind.

Aunt Hila held the fistful of his sweatshirt so tightly that her hand shook. When she at last looked at him, she was as angry as he'd ever seen her. Angrier than the times he'd come by her apartment drunk, or the time she had to confront the Arbel administration on the meaning of avodah zara. He swallowed hard, thinking that she'd shout at him. But the low, dangerous words she spoke instead were somehow worse. "You stop this *now.*"

"I . . . I promise," Boaz stammered. There was nothing else he *could* say, no way he could explain what happened last night on the roof of the Grand Dame. A monster in the shape of a girl had sunk her teeth into his neck. He had *let* her. She had killed before, and could again, and he would have let her. He wanted her to bite him again. "Really, I promise."

He wasn't sure if Aunt Hila believed him, but there was only so long she could stand there, clutching him like she was afraid of him escaping from between her fingers. Only when his mother called out and asked if she wanted to stay for lunch did she at last let go and leave. When she had gone, and his mother had retreated back into her own room, only then did it fully sink in what he had just promised he'd do.

31

CLARA

When the knock came on the door, Clara jumped.

She shouldn't have jumped. She had *asked* him to come here, because she had made up her mind.

Then take care of him.

She had to drain him. It was as simple as that. When she came down from the roof after Boaz had gone home last night, she'd found their apartment empty, the window thrown open with far too many feathers littering the windowsill, and no Molly.

She'd gone searching, only to find her sister, barely more than a shell of herself, by the Chase Bank a few blocks away, her star gone from the faded Yiddish Walk of Fame. The vanished star still seemed to bother Molly more than the fact that she was barely conscious and far too feathery and needed to be carried back to the theater. The panic Clara had been able to outrun in the diner had grabbed hold of her with a vengeance. She could survive death, but she was not sure what she would do without her sister.

"Come in!"

Clara had worn her hair in a low, loose braid for the occasion, and she could feel her true self close beneath her skin, prickling just under the surface. When Boaz shuffled in, she could hear his pulse, his breathing. Her senses were filled with him, and her stomach lurched with longing.

It wasn't real, though. Ashmodai said it was the ring. Which made far more sense than her attraction to Boaz ever did.

"You wanted to speak to me?" he said. Something about him seemed off, uneasy. Sweatier than normal. His heartbeat a little quick. But still he didn't run, wouldn't run from her. Even though he should. Even though she rather wished he would.

"You can close the door," she said. "I wanted to have this conversation . . . um, in private."

"Who are you expecting to barge in?"

"Just *sit!*" she said, exasperated. God, why did he have to make this so hard? Why wouldn't he *run?* Clara fidgeted with the bottom of her braid as Boaz sat down gingerly in the seat across from her. She should just do it. Yank out the braid, go in for the kill.

Her fingers twirled in her hair around the base of her braid. *Just undo it.* "So . . . um . . . I called you here because . . ."

Boaz fidgeted with the band of his watch. "This isn't about the free-ticket vouchers again, is it? I swear I triple-checked the accounting before I turned them in. The numbers should be good this time."

"What, no! It's not about the vouchers." This was the thing he was concerned about? Whether their voucher and gift card numbers were lined up? Had he forgotten the part where she'd bitten him the night before? Or the part where they'd fought off monsters? He was honestly, after all that, thinking about *vouchers?*

"Clara, do you . . ." He looked down at his shoes and ran a hand through his hair. "Do you want to go for a walk?"

"What?"

"Let's get out of here. Do you want to get bread? Now that I know you can eat it, like, that opens up so many possibilities, doesn't it? Do you want to get some?" He swallowed, and finally met her eyes. "I'm sorry. Never mind, that was too forward."

"No, not at all," she said. "Actually, let's go for a walk."

Relief passed over his face. A bit of prey granted a reprieve. Did he know what she was planning? She stood up and banished the thought as quickly as it had come. If he knew what was coming, he wouldn't have invited her out for a walk.

This was for the best. Killing in her office would have been a messy business. This was completely the wrong place to do it. Outside, she could find a quiet place in the park, a shadowy patch of sidewalk . . .

They went outside, and after some debate about where they could buy bread at this hour, they settled for the Westside Market, and their usual, adequate-if-unexciting bagged loaf of challah. Boaz gallantly offered to pay, and Clara tried ignoring the gnawing guilt in her chest. Taking a loaf of challah from the boy she was about to kill didn't feel right.

They set off toward Tompkins Square Park, taking turns at reaching into the bag and tearing off chunks of the bread. It was mild for a November night, the streets still busy and lively with people as they crossed onto Avenue A. Boards set out on the sidewalk advertised happy hours and prix fixe Thanksgiving meals, and everywhere there seemed to be couples laughing and chattering, spilling out of bars and restaurants and hurrying off to some unknown destination for the night. Clara drew as close as she dared to Boaz, trying not to wonder what it would be like to date him, what they could be if they tried pretending to be an ordinary couple.

She forced the thought from her mind. She couldn't let herself think that way. There would be no ordinary for them. There never would be. And before midnight, he would be dead.

"This whole bread thing is really convenient, you know," he said, taking a bite. "For you, I mean. It must be great. Beats having to, like, eat squirrels or something."

"Eww, why would I eat a squirrel? Those aren't kosher."

"Wait, so you're worried about whether squirrels are kosher when your diet mainly consists of *blood*."

"It's pikuach nefesh," said Clara indignantly. "Preservation of life matters above all else."

"But . . . aren't you already dead? Isn't it a bit late for that?"

She smacked him with her tote bag, and he laughed.

The park was mostly quiet at this hour. Clara continued confidently down the pathway through the gate. He held her back by the bag of bread they shared, reaching for her with his free hand when the bag threatened to rip.

"You sure you want to go in there?" he said. "Doesn't this park get nasty after dark?"

"Still afraid of stepping on another rat?"

"Yes, actually."

She waved him over, trying not to seem too eager. If he caught on to what she had planned, he'd probably run. Or try to attack *her*. And that would just make the whole affair messy. No, she owed it to herself and to Boaz to just get this over with as quickly and as painlessly as possible. "Come on! I'll make sure you don't have to worry about the rats."

"You promise?"

"Of course!" She wasn't lying to him, exactly. It was, categorically, not the rats that he needed to fear.

Clara found them a bench in a quiet, particularly unlit corner of the park and promptly sat, still eating the challah. After a moment, Boaz sat rather gingerly beside her.

Now he filled her senses. Warmth and boy and something like fresh coffee. His heartbeat was a fast and stuttering thrum. This was the moment to do it, while they were alone in the dark and he could trust her totally.

Boaz turned, and their eyes met. There seemed to be a question in them, one that she couldn't quite read. He breathed and leaned toward her until their lips met.

It was not what she meant to do, and yet it was *exactly* what she meant to do. The tension between them broke, and everything was Boaz. She put her hands in his thick curls. His heartbeat was louder in her ears. She was so hungry, and this was so good that now she wondered, for the first time since her heart stopped beating, whether she had misunderstood her appetite.

She couldn't remember the last time a boy made her feel like this, like her heart would start up again, the color would return to her cheeks, like she was still that girl in the shtetl perched up in the tree and ready to soar. The girl who had not learned that no man could make her fly.

"Let's go back to the theater," she said at last. Yes, that was a plan. She should probably still drain him. That was what she'd brought him out here to do. And it felt so good to have her mouth on him again. But her thoughts had become hopelessly tangled, and the only thing that she was certain of was that it would actually be easier to sort all of that out in private.

"We can't!" he said suddenly, his voice strained. He took her hand and held it fast, as if that would keep her from running off. "I mean, not yet? Let's just—"

"What, why not?" She could feel a few strands brushing the side of her face that must have come out from her braid. Her monster was so close to the surface, prickling and alive beneath her skin . . . her, the monster. She wanted it to go away, but she couldn't tell whose hunger was radiating through her, from her stomach to the base of her throat to the tips of her fingers. "Let's go back," she said, more firmly.

She longed to tear out her braid, to let her hair fall loose. Never in this life or her first could she remember feeling this way, like she was a paper-thin vessel for something so hungry *and* so alive that she could feel it pounding beneath her skin, as if the monster inside her, the monster that was always there, for the first time had a pulse.

She wanted Boaz so badly. *Boaz.* Lanky, movie-obsessed Boaz, who knew her secrets and trusted her still, who had offered up his neck willingly, and remembered it, and would still look her in the eye, would kiss her. Boaz, who himself walked between the worlds, one of the few people with a still-beating heart who might understand something of the life that she led.

Clara kept a firm grip on his hand as they made their way back to the theater. She thought of the boys she used to imagine, the ones that had once filled her dreams, the ones she believed could make her fly. How long she had been sustained on those dreams, handsome young men with curls and kind smiles who would love her without condition. It had taken dying once and finding her wings on her own, but she had found him. She had never forgotten that dream. It wasn't just her monster who wanted him. *She* wanted him, in a way that she had thought impossible. That part of her she thought had died that night on the windowsill was still with her, as alive as she'd ever been.

They got as far as the back door of the theater before she gave in just a little, pulled him toward her, and their lips met again. He kissed her hard, as if trying to prove to her that he was not afraid. *He was not afraid.* Not even with everything he already knew of her. He passed his hands gently over her hair, and everything inside her was electric.

If he wasn't afraid, she wouldn't be, either. Clara slid a hand under his shirt and felt for the warmth of his chest before he gently pulled away. "Let's . . . not go inside?"

Clara laughed. "What are you so afraid of?" She leaned in close to him, so that their lips nearly touched again. "I won't hurt you; I promise."

Clara was about to push through the door when Boaz stopped her hand. His heart was still racing, and she could feel it against her skin.

"You're not nervous, are you?" she asked, smiling.

"I . . . no, *no*, I'm not . . . not nervous," he said, like someone who was definitely nervous. "But let's leave, yeah? Let's go back to the park, or . . . I don't know, go to B&H Dairy again? Or Veselka, or anywhere else."

He kept his hand on the knob, his gaze suddenly down at his shoes. She didn't want to scare him, not any more than he clearly already was. So, this was what it took to scare Boaz Harari. His heart was pounding loud now. "Breathe, yeah? Your heart's going a mile a minute."

"Clara, we have to get out of here," he said quickly, trying to pull her back from the door. She leaned in again, trying to calm him, but he pushed her gently away. "I'm so sorry, this was a mistake, and I'll explain. But first, but we have to get out of here." His voice shook.

"Sorry? About what?"

"Clara, it's a trap."

The words were barely out of his mouth before she registered another heartbeat just on the other side of the door. She barely had time to notice it open behind her before a hard blow landed against the back of her head.

32

MOLLY

The announcement came with a knock outside the door.

"Dreysik minut tsu forhang!" *Thirty minutes to curtain!*

She had barely been able to stand when Clara found her, but now when she tried her feet, they obeyed her. They always would for a time check, because when it came to her work, Molly was nothing if not a professional.

She pulled herself to the mirror, an old impulse, and at first did not understand what she saw. Her eyes had not gone blank. She still had pupils and irises. But her skin was pinched and gray, and her hair hung lank, not her ordinary tousle of curls, but thin and lifeless, and not at all the way it usually appeared when she let down her hair. Her fingers were long but brittle and useless, and her teeth were her own.

Then she realized that she did know this costume, knew this mask.

Chenya. The monster that had been her own making, the part she had been born to play. The one that she became entirely.

"Du zehst shein oys." *You look beautiful.*

It was then Molly saw the other reflection, just behind her own. Lena. At least, it might have been Lena. It had her features, her soft brown hair and the familiar smile. But after *Kaddish: The Immersive Experience*, Molly knew better than to trust what her eyes wanted so badly to see. "Is it really you?"

Maybe-Lena did not answer her. Instead, she placed a hand on Molly's shoulder, a touch she *felt*, that sent a shiver down her back. "The show is going to start soon," she said, her breath on Molly's neck.

But when Molly turned, there was no one.

CLARA

Clara had entirely lost her sense of place.

The strike to the back of her head hadn't knocked her out but disoriented her enough that she'd been unable to stop the bag that had gone over her head.

She was in the trunk of a car—she could tell from the rumble of the engine, the rattling around her. She was bound in such a way she couldn't quite free herself from the rope, not with her hair still braided, and whatever had hit her left her skull too tender to try rubbing the braid out from this position, curled up in the trunk.

She could hear nothing, though, over the roar of the car, and Boaz's own words, which seemed to play on loop, echoing in her mind and making her angrier with each passing refrain.

Clara, it's a trap.

Clara, it's a trap.

This had been his *plan*. He had set a trap for her, and she had been fool enough to fall for it. Was this because she had bitten him? If her head hadn't been throbbing, she might have laughed. *Of course it was.* What kind of fool was she, to think that it would be any different? That he wouldn't have had a problem with her being a *monster.* One who needed—no, *wanted*—to drink his blood straight from his neck.

It was a long time before the car came to a stop. Clara heard the muffled sound of shouting, arguing, before at last the trunk opened, and the cool November night air flooded in.

"Let's just get this over with," said a young man's voice, one Clara did not recognize. She heard two heartbeats clearly, but before she had a chance to figure out anything more, she was yanked unceremoniously out of the car by two sets of hands. "Let him wait in the car if he's going to be weird about it."

"The bag," said the second voice, gruffer.

"Oh, right."

The bag was pulled off her head, but she barely had time to see the face looking down at her with some combination of fear and loathing before she was suddenly thrown, hard, on the ground.

The first thing she registered was the cold and the dirt around her, which was wet and smelled of moss and decay, as if it had only recently been turned. She was at the bottom of a hole, the high dirt walls around her were evidence of that. Above her the sky seemed far, far away, though she could see the faintest pinpricks of starlight. They had to be well out of the city, to see stars.

It was then she realized what this was. Even before the first shovel of earth fell.

This was a grave.

This was *her* grave.

"Hey!" she shouted. "Stop this! I *demand* you stop that now!"

After a moment, a head popped over the side of the hole, the young face she had caught a glimpse of before. He opened his mouth but was cut off by another man. "It is the same as the ghosts, and the dybbukim. They will fight you when you try to bury them, but you must not listen to them."

"You *will absolutely* listen to me!" shrieked Clara. Even more than fear, she was burning with rage. How dare he tell his accomplice to ignore her? Clara had been ignored before, but that had stopped when her heart did. Now she *would* be listened to. "Stop this right now, or I swear—" But before she could finish the thought, one of the men threw a shovelful of dirt directly at her face. "Stop that!" she said, louder, coughing and sputtering.

"You must work quickly. This is when she is both at her most vulnerable and her most dangerous."

"I will be dangerous if you don't let me go *now*!" said Clara, as loud as she possibly could, though as another shovelful of dirt landed on her, she realized it might not be enough and it wasn't true. Devorah had always said that it was one of two ways they could die. Either burial or fire. If these two succeeded, then . . .

"You are dangerous!" the younger man shouted, suddenly gaining his confidence. "Biting my best friend, enchanting him—"

"What are you talking about?" she asked. "I haven't enchanted him!"

"So he just *let* you bite him?"

"Yes, actually!"

"Don't listen to her, Daniel," said the other man.

She shrieked as she never had, thrashing at her bonds, trying to will herself into an owl. Never had she felt her monster so close, so raw and angry that it seemed remarkable that it hadn't simply torn through her flesh and attacked on its own accord. It wasn't just the fact of her burial, that this Daniel had dropped yet another shovelful of damp earth on her, and that even with her movement, she was finding it increasingly hard to keep the earth from covering her face or filling her mouth. It would not be long before he'd have her covered, and that would be it. She would not be able to get out. But the threat against Molly, that they knew of her *from Boaz*, that did it. The betrayal of it, the way he had grabbed at her heart, had drawn her out in a way no one ever had . . .

"BOAZ!" she bellowed, so loud that the name seemed to have claws carving at her own throat. "I want to speak to Boaz!"

"You *tried to kill him*. You would have drained him and discarded him like you did the rest," Daniel huffed.

She wanted to say that she never would have. That Boaz had come the closest anyone had, in this life or her first, to making her feel the way she had dreamed love might feel, like she might take flight without the need of feathers and wings.

But that was before he had so utterly betrayed her. "If I wanted to kill him, he would have been dead a long time ago!" she snarled, which was true, and yet, from the next shovelful that fell, did nothing to help her case.

She wanted to explain that she had tried so hard to avoid him. That she had wanted to fire him. That *he* had been the one to enchant her, that he had gotten inside her head despite her better judgment. That he had pretended to like her, that she had been fooled enough to trust him. She had been ready to throw away the rules that had kept her alive for a hundred and fifty years for him. *She* was the one who had been fooled.

Somewhere she thought she heard the faint sound of . . . Boaz?

Maybe? She shouted his name again and heard it: muffled shouting and a faint, faraway pounding.

"What did *you* do to Boaz?" she shouted at the boy instead.

"You've messed with him so badly," said Daniel, "that we had to tie him up. He was a danger to himself and to all of us—"

"You *what*?"

Suddenly, Clara heard a tremendous thud, and something, or someone, landed on the grass above. "Clara!"

She heard more arguing and the slam of a car door, and then Boaz appeared at the edge of the grave. "Clara! I'm sorry, I'll fix—"

"Boaz!" she shrieked, craning her neck upward, attempting to see him. "You get down here right now, or I swear I am cursing your entire bloodline twice over until Moshiach comes."

Boaz leaned over again, but before he could say anything more, the other, older man barreled toward him, knocking him to the ground and out of sight, though she could hear them fighting.

"Get off me!"

"Get back in the car!"

"Hey, dude, get your hands off of him!"

At last, Boaz peeked over the edge, looking down into the grave as he slid rope from his wrists. It was too dark to see more than his silhouette, his eyes, but she could tell his curls were a mess and a bruise was forming across his jaw. It did nothing to assuage her anger. After all, she was the one about to be buried alive.

"I'm sorry, Clara," he said at last, his voice hoarse. "Really, I am."

"You are going to be sorry if you don't get down here right now," she said. She tried to remember if she knew any curses, any kind of magic. Maybe she could simply scream something at him, and it would be enough. She thought again about ripping out his throat, and whether it was possible like this, two-thirds submerged in earth.

After an interminably long pause, he slid into the grave, landing on her foot. She hissed, and at once he muttered, "Sorry!"

"You betrayed me."

"I tried to warn you," he said, his voice wavering. He did not look her in the eye. "I tried to stop it—"

"Only after you set me up!"

"Boaz, come on," said Daniel. "She's dead, bro. We're supposed to bury our dead."

Daniel might as well have thrown a stone at her; it had the same effect. Of course she knew this. That was the gift Molly and she both lived with, the knowledge they had been given a second life when their first lives ended all those years ago. That girls were not supposed to keep walking the earth after their hearts stopped beating. But to hear him say that, that was worse. It was an admission. That he did not in fact see her, really see her. The living could love the memory, but they could not love a ghost.

"A girl has vanished, and no one else remembers her," she said, her voice stony. "I care that my sister's heart is broken. And burying me won't put any of that to rest."

Boaz at last looked her in the eye, and she could hardly bear it. Because it was the same Boaz. Same warm brown eyes she had trusted, filled with regret, as if she was supposed to feel bad. As if *he* had been the one who had been hurt.

"Come on, Boaz," said Daniel at last. "Get out of there. She's just trying to . . ."

Boaz knelt and began pushing dirt off of her. He was close

enough to Clara that they could have kissed. She could hear his heartbeat, smell him, and it made her ache the way nothing had in a long time, a strike of grief and longing and betrayal that cut so deep she swore she bled. Close enough that even in the dark she could see the glint of the chain around his neck. He reached for her hair, and though she knew what he was trying to do, she hissed at him all the same. "I'll do it myself."

He nodded silently and instead helped undo the rope around her wrists. He continued to stare down at her hands in lieu of meeting her eyes, as if he were worried that she'd try to strangle him. She thought about it. For a split second, she considered it, and how much temporary satisfaction it would give her.

Instead, she reached delicately up to his neck. His gaze was so intent on hers that he didn't notice as her fingers found the clasp. "Don't bother coming back to the theater," she said, her voice low and hoarse from all her shouting.

In an instant, Clara unwound her braid, already loosened from her attempts in the car. She did not bother to shake it out before transforming into an owl and shooting up toward the air, leaving Boaz and the grave behind, the ring on its chain dangling from her talons.

34

BOAZ

There was a long moment of dead, disbelieving silence.

Then the shouting started.

"What have you *done*, Boaz? Are you actually possessed?"

Boaz rose to his feet, trying in vain to wipe the dirt from his trouser legs and the sleeves of his sweatshirt. He was freezing cold and caked in grime and sure of absolutely nothing except that he had just made a series of horrible mistakes, each worse than the last.

Over Daniel's shouting, Edelman was coming to, having been knocked out by some combination of Boaz and Daniel.

Boaz jumped, pulling himself awkwardly out of the grave, before rounding on the both of them. It was so dark out here, save for the lights from the car and the one flashlight Daniel had brought along over Edelman's objections that they could not risk being seen at their work. The moon wasn't even out. "You were going to bury a girl alive, and *I* am the one possessed?"

"I was going to bury a *dead girl*," said Daniel. "She is dead. Dead people are supposed to go into the ground, or did you forget?"

"She's not dead!"

"She doesn't have a heartbeat!" shouted Daniel. He stalked toward Boaz, and for the first time ever, Boaz thought his friend might actually hit him. "She's over a hundred fifty years old and drinks blood! I thought you understood that just because you can talk to someone doesn't mean they're *not dead*."

"Your friend is right," said Edelman. Boaz turned. Edelman was sitting upright, his face unmarked, even though Boaz was certain that he'd seen Daniel land a punch square in the guy's face. He leaned forward and began, of all things, untying his shoes. "It used to be that a heartbeat meant something. But soon enough, it won't matter one way or the other."

"What's that supposed to mean?" snapped Boaz, but Edelman ignored him, instead kicking off his unlaced shoes and then peeling off his moldering socks, flinging them into the grave and revealing not feet but bird talons beneath, which he stretched and wiggled.

At last he turned to Boaz and Daniel, a smirk on his face. "I would have preferred it my way, but hers is just as good."

And before either of them could register what was before them, the sheyd turned and stalked away, after a moment disappearing into the shadows.

Neither of them spoke. Boaz, who had at least the benefit of witnessing errant sheydim before, recovered first. Daniel's mouth was still agape when Boaz rounded on him.

"What fucking website did you find *him* on?"

"That . . . That was a sheyd, wasn't it?" stammered Daniel, his gaze darting between the shadows where he disappeared and the pair of socks in the grave.

"Yeah, it was a sheyd!" Boaz groaned. "I told you something

was off about that guy—his apartment smelled like death."

"And you knew he was a sheyd?" said Daniel.

"I knew it was wrong!" said Boaz. "If you had just listened to me . . ."

Daniel's face went hard. Boaz wasn't sure he'd ever seen his friend like this. It was more than mad. It was as though he'd just shut down. "Anything else you want to tell me about, seeing as you apparently know everything? Am I a Ziz? Is my sister a unicorn? Maybe my dad is a leprechaun?"

"This isn't funny!"

"No duh, it's not!" said Daniel. "But apparently since graduation, you just pal around with monsters now, because seeing dead people wasn't messing you up enough as it was."

Boaz knew he was right. But it did not stop the angry throbbing in his brain, the thing burning inside him. "You have no idea what it's like!" he shouted, kicking the shovel away.

"You think I don't know what this does to you?" shouted Daniel. "I have known you longer than anyone—"

"Just because you like following me around—"

"That's what you think I'm doing? Following you around? Yeah, sorry I want to see my best friend. I must be a stalker." Daniel laughed bitterly. "Have you ever considered maybe, I don't know, trying a little harder not to fall off the face of the earth?"

"I'm not going to *fall off the face of the earth*. I'm not my dad."

"Sure, yeah," said Daniel. "Keep saying that over and over again, and maybe it will be true."

Boaz turned and stormed into the dark, his hands balled into fists. "And where do you think you're going?" Daniel called after him. "You can't walk back to the city from here. It'll take you two hours, and it's pitch-black."

Watch me. He'd walk back to Gravesend himself if that was what it took. He strode down the path, running through the options in his mind. A savage part of him wanted to do it, just to prove a point, even if that meant walking until morning. He could call a Lyft, but a glance at his phone was enough to tell him that it would cost him a day's salary. And who was going to willingly drive all the way out to a cemetery in the dead of night to pick up a boy caked in dirt and not ask questions?

Which was when he remembered that Aunt Hila owned a car.

It took him three tries to get Aunt Hila enough information to pick him up. Once he told his aunt what had happened, she had raced down in record time, her deep red, battered Cadillac roaring up to the gates of the cemetery with its brights on and coming perilously close to running over him in the process.

The car was thick with the smell of Hila's perfume. A hamsa with a few dangling tassels swung wildly on the rearview mirror. She waited a minute, as if she expected him to say something, but he was still simmering, and after he simply buckled his seat belt in silence, she began to drive.

Until they got onto the expressway, the only sound between them was the endless playlist of Sarit Hadad music from her Spotify. He'd heard them all a thousand times, and he quickly stopped listening, each running into the last.

Boaz played with the sleeve of his hoodie, trying to pick off the dirt clods that still clung to it. He wasn't sure he wanted to talk about it now, that he *ever* wanted to talk about it. Harari men made for unreliable partners, but this was next level. Even his father hadn't gone and tried to bury anyone alive.

"You couldn't do it?" Aunt Hila asked.

Boaz shook his head. She tried to reach over to pat him on the shoulder, but he shifted away, folding his arms across his chest and staring resolutely out the window.

"I can't do this."

Aunt Hila made a clucking noise as she switched lanes without looking and set off a few furious horns behind her. "No use being upset; it's done. We'll figure things out in the morning?"

"It's not just her," he said. He wasn't sure he could even say Clara's name at this point. The look of betrayal from her was burned into his brain. He might not have buried her, but he'd ruined what they had all the same. "I can't do any of it. I'm not good at the dead and I'm not good at the living and I wasn't good at school, and I can't—"

"You have many talents, Boazi. Don't talk like that."

"It's true! You know it's true!"

Hila exited the expressway back into Brooklyn, and Boaz remembered why he never let his aunt drive him anywhere. His stomach lurched. He couldn't even remember the last time he'd eaten. He rolled the window down just enough to let a bit of air into the car.

What was his aunt even talking about, having many talents? A talent for fucking things up, maybe. He ruined everything he touched, whether it was a job, this job, the best he'd ever had, or school, or relationships. He was just as bad as his dad. Worse, even, because he couldn't just disappear into the night quietly. He had to torch his oldest friendship as well, burn that to the ground along with everything else.

"I'm worse than Dad. At least Dad could play the guitar."

"And look what good it did him," grumbled Hila.

"And I am pretty sure I just ruined things with the only person who can stand me that's not you."

"Give it time, and apologize," she said. "Daniel will forgive you. That boy has put up with much worse from you."

"Gee, thanks."

For a brief moment, Boaz entertained the idea that Hila had a point. That there would be a tomorrow, that come morning, he would try and fix things, do a bit of groveling to Daniel and a *lot* of groveling to Clara.

But the moment was very brief.

Because when Boaz reached for the chain around his neck, the ring, he realized it wasn't there.

"Um . . . Doda Hila?"

35

MOLLY

When Molly stepped out into the hall, the floor swayed slightly, the dark suddenly too thick, as if the lights had been dimmed. Had she dimmed them? Her knees threatened to buckle as she reached the stairs and made a last-ditch attempt to stay upright. Beside her, she saw the shadows and the shimmering echo of stagehands and wardrobe attendants and actors hurrying past her, laughing and chattering in Yiddish. A few seemed to notice her, sliding past and acknowledging her with a nod and smile she could not return.

The lobby of the Grand Dame was empty, and she glanced at the clock above the coffee station, but no matter how hard she squinted, she couldn't read the time. It took too long to realize she could not, because the hands were gone and the clock face sat bare.

She needed Clara, but Clara was . . . Where was Clara? The scratching returned to her throat, and despite her best efforts to keep them down, she coughed up more feathers, fistfuls of them. When she steadied herself against the counter of the coffee bar, she noticed the trail of feathers she'd left in her wake.

The only sound in the theater, from what she could tell, came from auditorium four. Was there a movie on? She tried to listen for an audience, for some neck she could bite into—she didn't care whose anymore. She just needed the burning to stop. She couldn't hear anyone, no breathing or heartbeats, but it was hard to hear much of anything; it was like someone had stuffed cotton in her ears. Even the sounds of the movie seemed far away.

She crossed the carpeted lobby, her head swimming, and pushed her way inside.

The theater was empty, but there was a movie on the screen, an old black-and-white. The scene was a table in a fancy Chinese restaurant. Molly racked her brain, trying to remember what was playing, whether she had seen this movie and why it looked so familiar, when Lena stepped out into the shot.

Lena's hair was wound in a careless braid, her hands resting delicately on the back of a chair, as if she intended to sit. The light was low from the rows of paper lanterns, and waiters drifted through the scene, carrying trays laden with food. Molly remembered every detail of this moment. November 1910, the week before opening night. Her girlfriend was waiting for her. She knew this scene better than any movie; it was burned into her brain like no movie ever could be.

Molly took a few cautious steps deeper into the auditorium, still struggling to stand. She watched Lena turn until her gaze caught something just off camera. Molly held her breath, unsure of what would happen next, unsure how any of this was happening, except that it was the only thing that, even for a moment, made her forget her thirst.

But it was more than a memory, *better* than one, because soon another figure appeared beside Lena: Anat, styled as she'd been for one of the *Second Avenue Spiel* videos they had done together. Her hair pinned in place and wearing a dark, beaded dress, she looked right at home among the crowd in the party—no, in the movie, in the memory. . . .

Molly walked farther down the aisle, waiting for one of them to speak to her. They were deep in conversation and seemed familiar with one another, their words mostly subsumed by the music playing in the background.

Anat and Lena, thirty feet tall on the silver screen. In the best place, the best moment, the one she would have gladly lived inside of forever if invited. Watching the screen, she could hardly remember the thirst that had brought her here, the trouble that Clara was managing, the clock without hands. . . . She wanted only to watch the movie, to let everything vanish.

No sooner had she thought this than Lena and Anat ceased their conversation and turned to look directly at the camera.

Molly was already not breathing, but the look was enough to steal away even the possibility of breath. There they were, her past and her present, taken from her and yet *right there* on the screen, staring down the camera directly, as though they were staring straight at her.

They *were* staring straight at her.

At last, Lena spoke. "Minka? Is that you?"

Molly nodded. None of this was possible.

"I knew you'd make it!" said Anat, and the sound of her voice was enough to at last sweep the ground away from Molly entirely. She could have been floating or flying. She didn't care. She didn't care if any of it was real—it was better than anything that was.

Anat's face turned teasing. "Are you coming or not?"

Molly tried to open her mouth and say something, but the dryness in her throat prevented her from making a sound. She didn't need to, though. All she had to do was listen. Molly forced herself forward, making her way through the heavy air. She stood before the screen, certain she could practically smell the restaurant, the heavy perfumes of a room full of divas and ingénues. There was nowhere else she wanted to be more.

"Come on!" said Lena, her voice like music.

Molly wanted to go. She put her hand against the screen. The need, the want, practically made her heart beat in her chest, so she was barely surprised when her hand passed straight through.

36

BOAZ

Aunt Hila raced back toward Gravesend, Boaz gripping the car door for dear life, replaying the scene over and over again in his mind. He could not remember the moment that Clara took the ring from him. He'd been too . . . what? Distracted by how close he was to her and how much she hated him, how deeply he had failed her, even after he had gained her trust. Boaz tried to force the thought from his mind, of Clara's hands on his chest, his heart pounding as she found him in the dark. But it was no use. He could still see her, hurt and burning with rage, half buried in dirt.

"Are we going up?" gasped Boaz when Hila yanked the car roughly into her parking spot. His heart was in his throat, and he reminded himself never to ask for a ride from her ever again.

"What? No, who would I talk to? We don't have the ring." She grabbed her bag from under her seat and raced out of the car, leaving Boaz to trail in her wake. "We'll have to find someone the ordinary way."

He was unsure of where he was going and frankly afraid to ask. Usually, when Aunt Hila got mad, she gave him an earful. He didn't know anyone who could eviscerate someone with words quite like Aunt Hila.

So when she was at a loss for words, the way she was now, that scared him. Now he rather wished that she would yell at him.

Boaz followed her until they reached Gravesend Park. By day the park was busy, the network of playgrounds in constant use and usually with someone out on the baseball field. But at this hour, it was mostly empty. "What are we doing?"

"What do you think we're doing?" said Hila, at last coming to a stop at one of the newer playground spaces and rummaging through her bag. "We are finding the ring."

"Maybe we should go back to the theater, then?" said Boaz. "Knowing Clara, she went straight back to the theater."

Hila scoffed. "Your girlfriend could have gone anywhere in the entire city. She could be in *New Jersey*. She's not going to make herself that easy to find."

"But I don't think she's running from me," he said. "And the theater, and the sheyd . . ."

Hila at last extracted from her bag a thick, heavy-looking candle, which, after furtively glancing about the park, she placed at the base of the plastic tree trunk. "Hold it steady, will you?" she said. "Lighter?"

Boaz handed her his, and she set it on the wick. "Is this even going to work? Without the ring."

Hila shrugged. "Someone will show up. They always do."

After a moment, Boaz thought he could feel the air ripple

about him. There had to be more than one ghost near them, from the sheer tension in the air, the prickle on the back of his neck and the sense of being watched.

The darkness around them thickened, and from the periphery of his gaze, Boaz saw ghosts approach, first a few stray figures and then more, gathering like moths around the light Hila held, flickering along with the flame.

Then the light from the candle steadied. The air crackled as a figure stepped slowly into view.

The figure wore a heavy hooded cloak that obscured its face. It stopped just beside Aunt Hila, and only then did it pull back the hood. . . .

Anthony Janszoon van Salee.

"I see you're looking for someone to talk to!" he said jovially. "If I might be of assistance—"

"Can you get Lady Moody?" Hila asked, exasperation written all over her face. "I need someone compe—I mean, someone who can help us."

"Oh, allow me!" he said. "I am nothing if not a great help to the weary searchers among us. What is it that I can do for you?"

"I want Lady Moody," she repeated. "I need someone who can tell me what is going on, and where we can get our family ring back—"

"Oh, I can certainly help you with that!" His eyes sparkled. He looked, in Boaz's estimation, happier than he had ever seen him.

"By getting Lady Moody—"

"No, no, that is entirely unnecessary!" the ghost insisted. "I know well enough what has been going on."

"You know about the ring?" Boaz asked. "That the ring was taken by my boss, I think? Her name is Clara Sender, and, like, I think I know where to find her, and . . . Well, she's really mad at me, but I don't think she'd *do* anything particularly bad with it."

Anthony grinned. "At last, I will finally get what is mine."

Hila rolled her eyes. "This has nothing to do with your claim on Wall Street or Coney Island or whatever. Now if you could *please*—"

"Oh, but it does." His mustache quivered, as if it had taken all his restraint to not burst out with the news. "Don't you see? It is all connected. I had a need, you see. A single desire. I would have thought you two, of all people, would understand that desire does not die, even when our bodies do."

Hila shot Boaz a glare, as if the fact that Anthony's inability to rest was his personal fault and responsibility. "I may have lived but for one petty and meager lifetime, but for over three hundred years since, I have desired one thing, that what is rightfully mine to be returned to me at last."

"Dude, I get it. The Dutch West India Company fucked you over, but . . ."

Now it was Anthony's turn to glare at him, and Boaz's stomach dropped. It wasn't Anthony's usual expression, the easygoing indignation. He couldn't say what it was exactly, just that the energy that radiated from him seemed . . . different somehow? More purposeful, more threatening, more solid.

"There have been whispers for weeks, a murmur that grows louder with each passing day. Surely you have felt it?" At Boaz's blank stare, he said, "My dear Hararis, you cannot seriously think you could do what you do, mangle the borders between worlds, without leaving holes? That you could ignore, belittle, and pass us by?"

"We've never ignored you, Anthony," said Hila testily. "But we cannot give you what you want. You've been dead for hundreds of years, now—"

"And yet still you speak with us," he said. "You take and take. You tempt us by tearing holes, creating gaps between this world and that to come. Did you seriously think you could do such a thing and that we would simply sleep?"

"Yes," said Hila. "Because you are *dead*."

"Not for much longer," said Anthony. "The demon prince, he understands. He listens to us. He has not forgotten us because we're gone."

"Ashmodai?" Now it was Aunt Hila's turn to be skeptical. "You seriously mean to tell me . . ."

Boaz looked at Anthony, and even in the dark, he realized that he *could* see a difference. It wasn't just his presence, and his anger. Though he flickered still in the light, he did flicker less than a ghost ought. He was more solid than any ghost Boaz had seen, more solid even than the shul's dead board.

"Ashmodai has no power over you," Hila said haughtily. "Only the ring—"

"Clara wouldn't give it to him, though, would she?" Boaz interrupted.

"I do not know this girl of whom you speak," Anthony said slowly. "But if she is like us, if she must walk in shadow because her heart has stopped beating, then she has everything to gain from placing her trust in the Prince of Demons." Anthony reached toward Aunt Hila and the candle. Boaz watched as, to his and Aunt Hila's shock, Anthony took the candle from her. "I do not have any designs to harm you, or any of the living. I cannot say the same for the rest who walk amongst you."

It was then that Boaz got a proper look, less obscured by the shadows, at what now surrounded them. He could no longer see the playground equipment and realized for the first time that the swirling dark that he'd thought to be nothing but shadow was in fact inhabited. Full figures, not the mere whisper of them, clamored about from all sides, a full, solid dark, only growing when the dead inside it began to take shape—and move in, tightening around them.

It wasn't how Aunt Hila's readings ever went, and it only took a glance at Aunt Hila to know that she felt it, too. She cleared her throat uneasily. "Thank you so much for your help, Anthony. Now, if you would just . . . give me the candle back, we will go and . . . take care of things."

Aunt Hila reached for the candle, but Anthony held fast to it. Around them, Boaz saw the dead shift with the movement of the light, lurching toward it.

"Anthony," said Aunt Hila, her voice growing louder. "Give me back the candle."

"And why would I do that?" he asked, contempt rising in his voice. "Why would I condemn me and mine to remain in the dark, unseen? I have been dead for too long, Miss Harari. I grow weary of it."

Aunt Hila tried again without success to swipe the candle from his hands. "Anthony—"

"Do not test me," he said, his voice suddenly dangerous.

Aunt Hila's eyes widened. This was *definitely* not how readings should go. Ordinarily, the ghosts did not want to linger. They obeyed Hila. They did not make threats.

Boaz looked frantically to his aunt. She was the one who knew how to handle things. He'd made the shawarma ghost vanish, but nothing like this, and frankly he had no idea what they were supposed to do. If they had just gone to the theater, then they would have a lead. Or Clara would have murdered him.

But given their current circumstances, they might very well end up murdered anyway.

Aunt Hila was staring at Anthony and the candle. Boaz thought her gaze fixed, but she glanced his way for a brief moment, before he noticed the flicking motion she was making with her thumb. Boaz wondered whether something was happening to her, until she spoke. "Anthony, you can't mean that. You know as well as I, the dead wish to rest, they—"

"*Do not tell me what I want!*" boomed Anthony, so loud that the very ground beneath them vibrated. "*Witch*, truly, your arrogance knows no bounds to think that so! I want my land! I want my life back! I want justice against all who betrayed me, mocked me, and condemned me to live in shadow."

Aunt Hila glanced at Boaz again and watched the movement of her thumb. It was only then that it hit him. *The lighter.*

Boaz put his hand in his pocket, just as his aunt began to say, "You're right, Anthony. I misunderstood you. I will not make that mistake again. Now, I believe we are done here."

And after glancing for an instant at Boaz to make sure he had the lighter in his grasp, Aunt Hila leaned forward and blew the candle out, and the shadows rushed in.

CLARA

The city seemed suddenly vast and sprawling, and Clara had never felt more lost. She might have been spat out somewhere on the other side of the world.

She flew hard against the wind, Boaz's ring clutched in her talons, trying to shake the memory of his throat under her hand, of the cold of the grave, but he was so loud in her mind that he was no more possible to outrun than the moon. Did it matter that he had freed her? Part of her wanted it to, she knew that. The part of her that ached for him past reason, who ached for the boy that had made her laugh, that had known her real face and still offered up his own neck.

That had been a lie. A fantasy that she had let herself believe in because she was a fool.

And part of her still wanted to believe it anyway. Because she was so hungry, and in spite of everything, she was still the foolish girl, waving in the tree branches and imagining her dress might be wings, doomed every time to fall into the same traps.

She flew straight to the theater. She wanted to bathe. To disappear into an empty theater and be left alone, and there was nowhere else she could do that than in the Grand Dame. She couldn't shake the feeling of the dark closing in around her, the weight of dirt on her limbs, the feeling of the ground threatening to swallow her whole.

She flew hard and fast, refusing to stop until at last she soared through the open window of her apartments. The lights were still on, but Molly was gone, again, the door wide open and a trail of feathers leading out into the hall.

She pocketed the ring but hadn't even had the chance to pull up her hair before she sensed something was wrong.

The theater should have been empty by this hour. It was well after midnight. And while she didn't put it past Molly to not have closed things up, being concerned as she was about Anat, there was no way the theater should sound this *full*.

She could hear it, the patter of footsteps, many running restlessly along the floors beneath her.

Clara tied her hair back loosely and ran down the hall and the stairs into the lobby.

And at once she pulled the elastic out of her hair. There was music playing, perhaps a swing band. The song was and was not familiar, an old song on an old record player, turning slightly too slow. She followed the music, conscious of how heavy the air seemed to sit, how there was a kind of damp that clung to her skin still, though that could very well have been from the grave.

The lobby was as busy as she'd ever seen it. She'd never had a crowd like this, even at her most successful film festivals. There were clusters of people everywhere, waiting by the coffee station, the concession stand, milling outside the door to auditorium one, a steady hum of chatter just above the music, which ought to have been perfectly ordinary. It ought to have been thrilling, the kind of crowd she dreamed about, the kind that meant the lights would never go out in the Grand Dame.

Except that she could not hear a single heartbeat.

She wandered farther in, expecting an explanation, wondering if something had happened to her in the ground that had caused her to lose her footing in this world, why everything seemed to move just too slow, until at last she saw the bird feet on a group of boys at the back of the popcorn line. They were sheydim. The crowd that had turned out here in the Grand Dame, the crowd that had filled it to capacity, were demons. All of them.

Clara reached the center of the lobby before a few of the sheydim at last noticed her. The first was a group by the coffee station, who, upon seeing her, burst into rowdy applause that swept the lobby like a wave, cheering and hooting so that for a brief moment, they almost hid the absence of sounds of real life.

The lights of the lobby briefly lowered and brightened. A cue that the show was soon to start. There was a show about to start? They never did this for a movie. Who was even running things? When she'd left Molly last, she had been in trouble. Clara felt inside her pocket for the ring. It was ice-cold against her palm.

The ghosts and sheydim abandoned their positions and began to mill into the theater, flashing her grins and murmuring congratulations, though she couldn't understand what they were even congratulating her *for*. She tried to stop someone, to ask for an explanation—how had they all managed to take over her theater, for starters?—but no one seemed interested in talking to her. Instead she followed the crowd toward auditorium one, her indignation overwhelmed by confusion.

Clara poked her head into the doorway of auditorium one. She'd never seen so many sheydim anywhere in one place, young and old and all in between. Not even in Gehinnom had she seen so many. If it weren't for the fact that it was her theater they had overrun, she might have even been impressed.

The room was lit the way it would be for an event. The screen was dark, but a spotlight illuminated center stage. She did not have to wonder long, though, because a voice announced, too clear to be their own aging sound system, "Thank you all for coming. Please unwrap any loud candy and silence your cell phones. The show will begin momentarily. . . ."

Clara backed away from the door, standing helplessly in the main hall. What was any of this? Part of her wanted to run, to turn out of the theater and fly somewhere far away. Another, even madder part wanted to go back to Boaz, to demand a proper explanation. Yes, that would be it. She'd give him back the ring and then run him out of the city, warn him that if he ever so much as thought about setting foot in Manhattan again, she would finally do what she should have done from the start and drain him dry, then use his blasted ring to call back his ghost to shout at him some more. Her life had been so much better, so much easier, before he had waltzed into it, before he'd gone and set fire to the success and stability that she had carved into the world for herself.

But more than anything, she needed to know what all of these demons were doing in her theater.

Clara had taken a few cautious steps toward the door, unsure of whether she ought to make a scene or just blend in, when something careened straight into her, knocking her to the floor.

"Oh, shit, sorry—"

The sound of his voice was enough to send anger rising in her throat.

"What are *you* doing here?" Clara snarled, staring up into Boaz's sweaty, familiar face. The same tousled curls that spilled onto his forehead, the same warm eyes. When he offered her a hand to help her up, she refused it, instead struggling to her feet herself.

"I couldn't . . . I couldn't leave things the way I did," he said. "I can never apologize enough for what happened. I wish I had done more to stop it—"

"Oh, you have done more than enough," she said. It hurt to see him, to stand so close to him with the dirt of her intended grave still caked under her fingernails. This boy was supposed to have been different. She was supposed to have been different, smarter, too clever to once more court death at the hands of a man. "*Leave.* Before I do what I should have done weeks ago."

"Look, I know you hate me," he said quickly. "And I know that there's no possible way I can ever win back your trust. But *please* just give me back the ring."

"Why should I?" she said stiffly, her hand automatically drifting to its weight in her pocket. She clutched the ring tight, afraid that if she removed it, he would take it from her.

"Why? Look at this," he said, gesturing to the packed auditorium. "This is Ashmodai's doing. If you give him the ring, there's no line between the living and the dead and demons. Is this really what you want? It would break everything about this world."

Clara craned her neck to look into the theater. She had never seen anything like it, this many sheydim walking openly outside of Gehinnom, making no effort to disguise their feet or their true natures.

"Maybe it needs to be broken," she said quietly.

"You don't believe that," said Boaz, holding out his hand. "I know you."

"No you don't!" She turned, surprised by how close he was standing to her, so close that she could have very well kissed him. "You don't know anything about me. You wrote me off for dead. You were ready to bury me. You would bury all of them, too. I'm just another ghost to you."

Boaz looked her dead in the eye. "You are not like them. You are not a ghost, and you cannot be buried." He reached for her hand, and when he took it in his, she did not pull it away. "Please, let us fix this. I want to make it right."

No, she still wanted to sink her teeth in his neck again, to reverse time, to make things right between them. She wanted it more than she had ever wanted anything, for things to be put right, to finally have a boy she hungered for, who hungered for her, too.

She pulled out the chain and handed the ring to Boaz. When she did, an incredible weight eased from her shoulders.

Boaz took the ring. For a moment, he stared down at his palm, wonder brightening his face, as if he could not believe it had been returned to him while he still had a pulse.

Except, Clara realized slowly, he did not. She had not been paying attention, had not noticed that no one, not even the boy before her, had a heartbeat.

"My wonderful, clever little bird," he said, his face shifting, a shadow sweeping across what had been Boaz, revealing the favored red hair and glinting eyes of the Prince of Demons. He smirked before yanking away the chain and sliding the ring onto one of his fingers. "You did so well. *Now* the work begins."

There were once three Estries taking in the morning in Washington Square Park. Dressed in their best, they appeared to be no more than three young, very pretty women who had eaten well the night before and were enjoying the cool, bright sunshine before determining from whence they might find their next meal.

But this is not a story about the monsters.

This is a story of a fire.

It was not the first of its kind. Nor would it be the last.

Some would say that it was a single ember from a lit cigarette. Some would say one of the machines, badly in need of grease, cast the first spark on the dried threads and cotton. For the Triangle Shirtwaist Factory was nothing if not thousands upon thousands of unlit wicks waiting for flame.

What was certain, though, was that the doors were kept locked. To keep the girls working, to keep them inside.

The eldest Estrie smelled it first. The city air was always thick with coal and dust and smoke, lower Manhattan worse than all, but this was different. This was not the smell of the burning that ran a city, the burning of a ceaseless engine kept running by backbreaking work, an engine unlike anything else in the world. This was not coal or wood that burned.

She said nothing to her sisters, but instead quickened her pace, running in the direction of the acrid scent. She had found the building, just off the square, and saw the smoke beginning to leak from the windows, and then, following it, the shrieking.

It was said that three things made an Estrie. The first was a hunger, a desire beyond that which ordinary food could fill. The eldest Estrie had never met a girl of her people who did not possess such hunger, though she knew so many who lived with it, a hunger that went unanswered in the name of work, and children, and survival. But such a hunger lived in them still, whether it was met or not, and it was that hunger that could make a girl's heart beat even when all else failed and her veins ran dry. Immigrant girls, the girls who worked in the Triangle Shirtwaist Factory, were the hungriest of all.

The second was a desire for flight. The girls were restless things. They longed to soar. They longed for something to get them off the ground.

The third was a cry for help into the dark.

The sisters ran hard, shoving past the crowd that began to gather, until they caught up with the eldest monster as the girls in the uppermost floors struggled to open the windows and leaned out, coughing and gasping for air, shrieking and staring down at the gathering crowd of people below, shouting in English, in Yiddish, in Italian, that the doors were locked from the outside, that they could not descend the stairs.

The youngest reached for the pins in her hair, her hands shaking with panic. Even in all the shouting and confusion, and the bells of useless fire brigades, she could have sworn she heard her love's heartbeat, could have sworn she heard her call out from inside.

She had changed weeks before, but this form was natural to her, easier than any other mask and face and costume that she had ever put on. She could save her love yet, she was sure of it. What was the point of such a gift, such powers, if not to use them in this moment?

But the eldest stopped her. She had already rolled up her sleeves. "Let me. You stay back."

"It's too dangerous!" said the middle sister to the eldest, even though she knew it was no use. The fire did not matter. What mattered were the girls, teetering on the edges of the windowsills, staring down at the ground below, smoke at their backs. What mattered was the look on the youngest's face, stricken with a fear so great it was as though she herself were in that building. What mattered was that even the tallest ladder in the possession of the fire brigade was not tall enough to come anywhere close to the windows at which the girls stood, calling for help, for something that might let them live, let them fly.

The eldest pulled the pins from her hair, shaking out the thick, chestnut waves that fell to her waist. All eyes were fixed on the girls in the windows, so none saw the monster standing among them in the crowd, eyes now blank and hands twisted into claws.

"But the fire—"

It was then that the first girl jumped.

The Estrie watched the girl fall, arms outstretched, the longing for wings so clear on her face. She watched the girl fall and fall until she hit the ground with a crack that turned the Estrie's stomach, that made everything inside her at once deathly cold and alight with rage. She had lived through much, had seen countless things, the desperation of girls, the cruelty of the world, but never had she simply stood by to watch a girl try to fly and fall to the earth instead.

She ran toward the door, over the protests of her sisters, over a few calls of men in the crowd, the few who tore their gaze briefly away from the girls and were baffled that a young woman would run toward the fire. It did not matter that fire and earth were the two things that she and her sisters could not withstand, would not overcome. It did not matter that the windows billowed thick dark smoke, and that she could see from the door and every available window bright red flame, tables and equipment and countless threads alight. She could not watch girls fall, not when she might give them wings, not when she could.

38

MOLLY

Molly could not remember a time she had been this happy ever in her life. She wasn't hungry or thirsty. On the contrary, she was *fantastic*, weightless and completely content. The light of the restaurant was low, the hum of conversation steady all around the packed dining room, just the way she remembered from the night, the best night.

No, better, because Anat was here. Not vanished from memory, a ghost in a play, but *here*. In the best place, the safe place. Molly didn't want to ask the questions tugging at her sleeves and tapping her on her shoulder. Why should she? This was perfect, a place that she would be more than happy to live inside forever. She had wanted to be an actress; why not live in film? Especially this one. . . .

"I'm so glad you made it," said Lena in her light and familiar Yiddish. Molly thought she could detect a note of worry in her voice, which was absurd. Of course she'd make it, she would never forget. . . .

"Well, you know how it is with rehearsals," said Molly, the words slipping out so easily she scarcely noticed them. Rehearsals. Yes. Molly had been so busy preparing for *Di Shturem*, she had not had any time for her girlfriend. All her waking hours it seemed were spent in the theater. That was why tonight had to be perfect. She didn't want Lena to think that she had forgotten her. That was why she was here tonight. Probably.

She was wearing the dress she'd worn that night, one of her favorites, and she realized her hair was down. For a moment, her stomach flickered with a panic she didn't quite understand, but when she caught a glimpse of her face in the reflection of the wine-glass, it was hers. Human. Because of course it would be.

"Did you try the duck?" Molly asked, handing a plate to Anat. "It's the best here, I've never had anything like it."

But Anat wouldn't take the plate. Instead, she shook her head and pushed it aside. "Molly, can we leave? Do you know how to get out of here? I've tried, but once I came through, I couldn't seem to . . ." Anat paused, grabbing at the front of her own dress and wincing.

This wasn't at all how the scene was supposed to go. Molly laughed, shifted uneasily in her seat. "What are you talking about? What's the hurry?" said Molly. "This is nice, isn't it? I always thought the two of you would get along." Molly looked desperately to Lena. "I've wanted to talk to you so badly. . . ."

"Minka," Lena whispered as she pulled away from her, Molly's skin still burning from her touch. The way Lena said it, Molly might as well have unbuttoned her blouse and stripped her bare there in the restaurant. "Both of you should go."

"Why not after dinner? I've waited so long to see you," said Molly, taking a large bite of duck. Yes, there was a quiet, persistent thrumming somewhere close, a constant thud she couldn't quite name, but that didn't matter. What mattered was how happy she had been here, how happy she was *now*, in this moment. Here, no one had to be dead, and gone, and buried in the past. Here, she was herself. The self that she was supposed to be, no monster beneath her skin.

"Neither of you have the time to waste," said Lena, her voice more urgent.

"But, Lena, you haven't gotten the chance yet to meet . . ." said Molly loudly, hoping that her old girlfriend would change the topic of conversation. Why couldn't she stay here longer, and on her own terms? Didn't Lena realize that they weren't finished, that they never got to finish? They had been a perfect movie until Leo Goldfaber and a fire had taken a knife to the film.

"We are very well acquainted," said Lena, her voice firm, just the way she had sounded in life, when Molly needed someone to gently tug her back to earth.

"You are? Oh, yes, I suppose . . ." She turned between her two girlfriends, her two favorite people, wishing they'd both just stop looking so alarmed. Why were they so eager to leave? This was Mon Lay Won, Chinatown's Delmonico; she'd spent a small fortune on this meal, this night, this . . .

She looked down at the table, at the meal laid out before them. There was a slice of duck, a bowl of soup in front of her, but now that she gave them a proper look, something about them didn't appear quite as appetizing as she had remembered. She poked the piece of duck, which a second before she was certain had been piping hot, and found that it was ice-cold. She didn't understand how she hadn't noticed that or that the duck on the plate that she'd handed to Anat had no weight, or that the scene around them was lit not by the lanterns or chandelier above them, not really, but the tungsten light set up around and above them. The color was sapped from the scene, the entire room cast in grayscale, and a trail of words had drifted past them along the floor, translating the things she uttered into English.

Set. It was a set. A detailed, elegant re-creation of Mon Lay Won, but a re-creation nonetheless. She had stepped not into the past, or even a memory, but into a film. Perhaps they were not so different. The warm, happy haze Molly had enjoyed at once evaporated, and her head cleared. This was a set, and Lena was gone, and Anat was missing and in trouble.

"I tried to warn you," said Lena. "We tried to warn you and your sister. This is no place for the living. And out there is no place for the dead."

"What are you talking about? And who is *we*?"

Lena gestured at the tables around them. Molly hadn't even noticed when they had fallen silent, but they had. Around each table sat young women and girls, not dressed for a night out on the town, but like they had just come from work . . . with neatly pressed shirts and simple but pristine skirts. Most looked like teenagers; no one looked much older than Molly did.

And though she didn't know the girls exactly, she did. The girls who had wanted to fly, who had been so in need of wings, the girls Devorah had tried and failed to save.

314

"The Grand Dame is a mirror, and therefore it is also a door. Not all who come through, who move between the worlds, mean you harm. Not all hungers are malign, but it does not matter. None of us should walk there; the cracks in the living world are already beginning to show."

Molly didn't like this, she didn't like any of it, the way Lena spoke. *What did you mean you tried to warn . . .*" But even as she said this she remembered the graffiti on the door that Boaz had tried so helpfully to wash away.

Di Grand Dame muzn brenen.

The Grand Dame must burn.

"Ashmodai would tear the door from its hinges, let every manner of sheyd into the sunlight, and bury the living in shadow," Lena said. "The only way to close the door for good is with fire. Fire will redraw the line and reset the threshold."

"No." Molly stood up and turned away from Lena. "No, no, *no.*"

"It's the only way to set things right."

"You can't ask me to do that!" she said. "*You*, most of all, should understand why I can't."

She looked at Lena, whose eyes were flashing. "You think I don't understand fire?" she said, her voice rising. "You think *any of us* don't understand the cost of burning?" Molly could feel the eyes of the girls on her. Half of her boiled with rage against them, against Lena for even daring to ask the terrible thing they expected from her. The other part simply ached. "Fire is the source of our suffering *and* how we honor memory, and time, and the spaces most sacred to us. Fire is destruction, and it is life, the World That Is and the World to Come."

The low thrumming. That was the sound she was hearing,

the low background noise. What she'd thought must be music, or the crowd around them, was Anat's heartbeat, just like it had been the night on the fire escape. Dangerously, impossibly fast. When she noticed it at last, it was all Molly could hear, a heart that at any moment could break beyond repair. "This is not a place for the living. And what dies in shadow vanishes without a trace," said Lena.

Anat shifted, clutching at her chest and looking toward Molly for a solution. She had gone pale, and Molly knew she couldn't keep second-guessing. She stood and, taking Anat by the hand, stumbled toward the door. Surely, if they had come through so easily, leaving shouldn't be . . .

But beyond the tables, where the entrance to the restaurant ought to have been, there was scaffolding, and beyond that, heavy darkness, shadows even Molly knew better than to touch. Where Doyers Street ought to have been, there was nothing but ominous shadow that Molly was not about to test with her or her girl-friend's life. She slammed the door shut and turned back to Lena.

"How do we get out of here?" asked Molly. "Is there a door? There's got to be . . . How did I get in here? I was just in the Grand Dame—"

"Promise me you'll burn it," said Lena instead. *"Promise me."*

"I promise I'll think about it," said Molly quickly. Anat lost her footing beside her, and Molly swooped down to catch her and lifted her up into her arms.

"There's no time. If Ashmodai gets his way," said Lena, "there will be nowhere left for the living, there will be no way to measure the cost."

Molly held her girlfriend close to her chest. She knew, deep down, what she needed to do. She knew Lena, the *real Lena*, would not lie to her. She could feel Anat's heart against her, could see how glassy her eyes had become, how there could be no remaining here much longer. She would do anything if it meant saving Anat. But still it tore something inside her to speak the words. "I promise."

"The camera," said Lena at last.

"The . . ." Molly fought a sudden, bizarre urge to laugh. *The camera*, of course. That was how to break the fourth wall, wasn't it? The way that any actor could, with a look, destroy the artifice, the pretense of reality on film.

Molly searched the ceiling, forcing herself to look past the familiar paper lanterns, past the suggestion of a ceiling. She could see lights, and even the edges of the walls, the hints of scaffolding—

"Stop avoiding it," said Lena. "*Minka*, you know where it is."

Maybe she did. Maybe that wasn't the hard part. Maybe, even though she knew she had to, she didn't really want to leave Lena behind. Even as she told Molly to leave, the very sound of Lena was enough to make her want to stay.

But Anat's heartbeat was in her ears. Too fast, too hard, the kind of beating that could break a girl in its desperation to keep going.

She would not be the one to let it stop.

Forcing herself to focus on that sound, Molly turned, and at last she saw it, the big, old-fashioned camera balanced on its stand. She focused beyond it, on the empty auditorium and the bright, blinding glare of the projector. Squeezing Anat as tightly as she could, she stared straight into the lens and charged forward.

317

39

BOAZ

For an instant, they still had the light from the street and buildings, for the city rarely turned entirely black.

Then the shadows descended. Boaz heard a shriek that he thought might be his aunt Hila, or something else, or maybe both. The tug on his shirt he had felt before became a yank, and he stumbled backward, struggling to keep on his feet and to get the faulty lighter to ignite. He kept flicking at the spark-wheel, pressing so hard he could feel it cutting into his thumb. After one great tug from behind, he fell backward at last and barely registered the damp of the grass beneath him, so immense was the weight of the ghosts, the dark, and a sense that a heavy kind of cold would soon overtake him, that it was creeping inside him, gripping his chest and flooding his lungs.

At last, when he spun the wheel, the light caught.

At once, whatever shade had gripped his shoulders and limbs receded, just enough that he could clamber back onto his knees and shakily force himself to his feet. The flame on the lighter was smaller than that of the candle, and the spirits stayed closer, giving him less of a berth. But they let go of him, which was all he needed.

"Doda Hila?" he shouted, trying to crane his neck over the wall of shadow and figures surrounding him, faces fixed on the flame. "Doda Hila!"

He listened, but apart from the distant sound of a siren and the quiet moan of what he thought was wind in the trees, he could not hear her. He tried to steady his breath, but even in spite of the light, he felt the ground sway beneath him again. If something happened to his aunt, if *she* was gone, he wouldn't be able to bear it. Nothing else he'd do next would matter; the battle would already be lost.

Boaz looked about him. The figures, lit by the flame, were barely more than outlines and shadows, more skeletal than anything. Boaz swallowed. He could not *leave* without Hila.

The flame flickered dangerously. He wasn't sure how much time he had left before it went out, but he didn't think it was long.

"I'll come back for you," said Boaz at last, aloud in case Aunt Hila was there and might hear him. "I'm just . . . I'm going to find the ring and get that back. That will fix it."

One of the ghosts tried reaching slowly for the lighter, attracted and repelled at once, but he kept it out of their grasp. Gritting his teeth, he did the only thing he could think to do, and holding the flame out before him, pushed his way forward.

Boaz had expected the spirits to attack him again, but the flame seemed enough to keep them back, so long as he did not allow any of them a chance to take it. He pressed forward, ignoring the chill that cut straight through his clothes and into his chest. He did not look any in the eye.

It felt like an eternity before he finally broke free of the ghosts and found his way back to the road, and even then, he could not shake the feeling that he was being followed, as if a ghost remained close, watching his back. The shadows hung thick over the park like a fog. Even the few people still out at this hour could sense it, hurrying past and making a point to keep closer to the road.

Keeping the lighter lit, Boaz ran. He ran as fast as his legs would allow toward the subway, vaulting himself over the turnstiles and practically diving into the train car to make it on before the doors closed. Only then, under the bright fluorescents, did he let the lighter go out, clutching it like a security blanket.

The train was busier than he expected it to be at this hour, almost all the seats filled, and only when he chanced a glance at the figure by the door, a woman wearing a dress with a bustle big enough to block the entire entrance, and she momentarily flickered out of sight, did he confirm his suspicions. Nearly everyone in the train car was a ghost, and their apparent lack of interest in Boaz seemed to be more a function of the fact that *they* thought he could not see them. He kept his eyes on the ground and did not dare so much as to make way for the ghosts passing around him as he waited to reach his stop.

He'd try the theater first, he decided. Even if he couldn't find Clara, perhaps he'd find Molly. If he could convince Molly to help him reason with Clara, surely he could convince *her* that allowing Ashmodai to tear into the fabric of this world would not end well for any of them.

When he reached the theater, his lungs and legs burning from the cold and the effort, he knew something was wrong. Not a single light shone in the entire cinema, and the darkness that had settled on the eaves and window ledges seemed denser than the night. The true sign that something was wrong, however, was not the darkness, but that the front doors remained open, despite the fact that there was no one at the box office window. Clara would *never* allow that. Which meant either that she wasn't there or that she was in trouble.

Boaz pushed his way inside. The lobby appeared abandoned, but it was impossible to see much of anything in the complete dark. After a few cautious steps inside, he tried the lighter again, his heart thrumming in a way that had little to do with his running and everything to do with the eerie quiet. But even after getting it to spark, it seemed a sad and inconsequential attempt against the dim light and thick air.

It was then that he heard the voice coming from auditorium one.

Ashmodai, his voice as smooth and clear as ever.

With the ring, Boaz might have believed he stood a chance. But without, he wasn't that much of a fool, to think he could take on the Prince of Demons. Not without a plan. A plan, he needed a plan, and he needed the ring, and he needed to get out of the middle of the lobby. . . .

He ran upstairs, breathing hard as he made it to the second floor. He needed a proper view of what he was up against, of what was even going on. He darted toward the projection room, relieved when the door swung open easily.

The room was cramped but empty, save for the neat stack of reels and the projector, which was currently humming through a large reel. Boaz crept up to the porthole, where he could see the apparently full seats. On the stage was Ashmodai, standing at the ready, like he was about to give a lecture. When Boaz looked down, he saw what appeared to be the top of Clara's head in the center aisle, but he couldn't say for certain. The mere possibility of it being her sent a fresh wave of guilt through him. How had he let the burial get that far?

"What are you doing here?" Molly burst through the door, half carrying a wan and gaunt Anat, who was struggling to stay upright. In the other hand, she held what Boaz recognized as a storage box for the silver nitrate film from the Grand Dame's archive room. Anat let go of Molly briefly, settling with her back against the doorframe, while Molly began to busy herself with the fastenings of the case. The shock of seeing her there, alive if obviously not well, jolted him.

"Did you do this, too?" Molly bit out.

"Why is everything always my fault?"

"Because it usually is," said Molly. "You should get out of here, unless you want to go up with the rest of the theater."

"What . . . You're not . . ." Boaz looked at Molly, and then at the film reel, a title of a movie even he did not recognize. Molly's hands trembled, and for a moment she hesitated, unwilling or unable to touch it, before at last reaching in and roughly unspooling the film. "Have you actually lost your mind?"

"If you haven't noticed," she said evenly, "the theater is currently a wide-open door to Gehinnom. Actual Gehinnom, not the nightclub," she said. "The only way to close it is with fire, so if you don't mind—"

"So what, you're just going to start a fire here in the projection room?" Boaz's head spun. "That seems like a perfect way to get us all killed and fix nothing. Especially when the things down there in the auditorium are either already dead or were never alive to begin with."

Molly kicked the film reel, and for a moment Boaz wondered whether she'd try to bite him. "And," he continued, "I don't think closing a door will do much good if they're already *out here*. They'll just stay, and once they get the ring—"

"Why would they get your ring?" said Molly, her voice rising.

"Ask Clara!" Boaz struggled not to shout.

Molly pulled at her hair, her hand drifting toward the scrunchies securing it loosely. She glanced through the porthole. Whatever she saw, it clearly shook her, even worse than trying to pull out the reel of silver nitrate film.

She turned back to him. "We need to get them out of the theater," she said.

"And where, out into the world?"

"On the other side of the door!" she said, thrusting a hand toward the screen, to the scene there that still played, too real to be anything but. "Then we burn it down."

40

CLARA

Clara's head spun. This was worse than rage. No, she'd been a fool, once again, in the name of a boy. She had half a mind to turn and fly out of the theater and never look back. Her skin crawled when she looked at the Prince of Demons, a reminder of how easy it had been to trick her.

"Come now, there is no need to look so distraught," said Ashmodai, holding a hand lazily out to her. She realized belatedly that he intended for her to take it. "You will see. I meant what I said to you the other day. This is the beginning of a new era, a new chance for those like us to step from the shadows and into the light."

"You tricked me!"

He shook his head. "My poor, hungry little bird, soon you will be freed from your baser appetites."

Ashmodai had stepped up onto the stage, leaving her baffled and confused in the aisle. When he spoke, his voice resonated as if he were using a microphone. "Today is a day for joy and celebration."

Clara looked frantically around her. The room was packed with demons, and she thought she saw the slightest shimmer of ghosts in the back, all hanging on Ashmodai's every word. "Too long we have lived under the tyranny of the living, banished from this world and all that it offers. A world that is as much our right as it is theirs. No longer."

The cheers and applause that erupted from the audience were greater than anything she'd ever heard before in the Grand Dame. The ground beneath her shook with it as many jumped to their feet in an enthusiastic standing ovation. Ashmodai grinned, strutting across the stage, the light of a single spotlight following him.

There was a tap on her shoulder, and when she turned, Boaz . . . Or at least it looked like Boaz. Clara no longer trusted her eyes. She was about to tell him off when he shook his head and instead pointed up.

Across the top of the ceiling, there were the remains of what had once been the catwalk of the theater. They had left it intact for lighting, and it wasn't worth the trouble to remove it, but when she glanced upward, she now saw the shadow of a figure creeping across toward the stage and screen, a silhouette she recognized at once as Molly.

Clara felt a wave of relief wash over her.

But only for a moment.

"What's *he* doing here?" a particularly wizened sheyd sitting nearby shouted, as only just now did he even think to turn away from the scene unfolding on the stage. He sniffed. "He's so mortal, I can smell him rotting from over here."

"Speak for yourself!" Boaz snapped back, which was proba-bly the absolute worst way to handle the situation. She should have expected as much.

Clara turned, intending to shove him out of the theater, but it was too late. Other sheydim began to turn, wearing expressions from amusement to disgust at the sight of Boaz, standing there . . . so . . . *alive*.

"*Boaz, you need to . . .*"

But before she'd finished admonishing him, several sheydim leapt into the aisle and reached for him. Clara bared her claws, but she couldn't get a scratch on any of them. The two of them were quickly overwhelmed, and the sheydim grabbed hold of Boaz and dragged him unceremoniously onto the stage.

"Oh, we have company!" said Ashmodai brightly. If he was annoyed by Boaz's interruption, he didn't show it. "I was wondering how long it would take you to arrive. You and your kin are deeply predictable. Absolute fools when it comes to the things they want."

The sheydim deposited Boaz at his feet before hurrying back to their seats, as if they were afraid of missing any moment of the show about to unfold.

Boaz lunged toward Ashmodai, and Clara ran down the aisle, intending to stop him. He was a lying fool and had broken her heart, but as much as she hated to admit it, it would break again if Ashmodai just incinerated him on the spot.

Ashmodai stepped easily out of the way. With a lazy wave of his hand, ropes appeared around Boaz's hands and legs, and he fell. Ashmodai was now laughing, a sound that gripped Clara with its chill.

Boaz struggled against the bonds, but it did little use. The air itself in this space was no good. Even Clara could feel it pressing on her chest. And, as always, he'd clearly run all the way to the theater, sweaty and exhausted. What did he even expect would happen? He had no chance of taking on one sheyd, who did not tire and could not die, never mind an entire *theater* full of them.

"It is only by pure luck that your kin have avoided returning this to me for as long as you have," said Ashmodai, holding up the ring. "Your father was particularly easy. He barely needed any persuasion to wander so willingly into my grasp—human hearts are pathetically predictable."

"You're lying!" Boaz spat, and for a wild moment, Clara thought he might actually manage to break free; she'd never seen him so mad.

"Quiet, you, or next time I'll bind your wrists with your tongue," said Ashmodai, his voice dangerously calm.

Clara glanced up again frantically toward the rafters, looking again for Molly. But she saw no sign of her sister, and wondered now whether she had imagined it.

Ashmodai, meanwhile, had turned his attention back to his audience. "How fitting that you should bear witness to this, the end of the reign of tyranny of mortal men over the World to Come." He turned back to Clara. "Clara, darling, do you mind telling the crowd why we have gathered here today?"

Clara's hands balled into fists. "Well, it wasn't because you were invited."

He laughed. "Now, now. Remember, this place is mine to do with as I wish," he said. "This little cinema that you have so lovingly maintained is uniquely suited to our purposes here today," he said, before pointing up toward the back of the house. "A cinema with a history, with many lives layered on top of one another. The old projectors that you have so lovingly maintained work because they possess mirrors. And as you well know, every mirror is not just a mirror, but a door."

With a wave of his hand, the projector clicked on in the back. Clara could hear the familiar whir as the light momentarily filled the stage area before the MGM logo and lion began to flicker on the screen.

Boaz had been inching away, as if he intended to run, and Clara silently cursed him. Truly, even by his ordinary standards, what he was doing was useless; there was no escaping Ashmodai's notice, and there was no getting off that stage.

Ashmodai glanced at him, and tsked as if Boaz were a poorly behaved puppy. "No, you can't leave so soon. I thought you'd help me in the demonstration. Now, on your feet."

Boaz jerkily rose to his feet, and after a moment's thought, Ashmodai conjured a rope between them, tethering them together by the wrists, with only a yard of slack. "Can't have you wandering off, now, can we?"

With a wave of his hand, he conjured a thick candle and placed it in Boaz's hands.

"Leave him alone!" shouted Clara. She still wasn't sure whether she could ever forgive him, exactly, but she couldn't stand to see him hurt. "You have the ring—just let him go."

But Ashmodai laughed. "Let him go where, little bird? Nowhere will be safe for him, not after what happens next."

Ashmodai turned, his arms raised and his fingers splayed, as he stared directly up at the camera.

Boaz looked toward her, and then did something that she did not expect.

He *winked*.

"Maybe I wasn't trying to escape," he said, turning to Ashmodai, his voice low.

Suddenly, ribbons descended from the ceiling toward the stage. At first, Clara didn't understand what she was seeing or where they were coming from, until she noticed the first empty spool land with a thud. Three more followed, leaving a small tangle of film reel, nitrate film reel, just before Boaz and Ashmodai.

With that, Boaz dropped the candle onto the film reels and lurched backward, sending the ring flying into the air as he plummeted through the screen, taking the Prince of Demons with him.

41

BOAZ

Despite what Molly had told him, Boaz had half expected to hit brick when he fell back through the screen. When instead he simply kept falling, it was like missing a step on a staircase—or a whole flight. His stomach swooped, and he momentarily lost his sense of direction, before finding it by landing hard on his back.

He'd done it. He actually had managed to fool Ashmodai. The triumph of it was pure electricity in his veins. He'd shown *him* "pathetically predictable." It wasn't just the Prince of Demons who could turn someone's deepest and most desperate wanting into a trap.

But when Boaz caught his breath, he noticed two things.

One, the rope bonds had slackened, and Ashmodai was gone. He thought he'd seen Ashmodai come through the screen with him. But he'd also expected Ashmodai to smite him on the spot, whatever smiting entailed, once he realized what Boaz had done.

Two, he probably should have waited until *after* the MGM lion had faded before falling through.

The lion craned its neck through a hole maybe a foot over his head. Boaz had never been this close to a lion, but he was quite sure this one was many times the size of a real one. The big cat looked down, eyeing Boaz with a look first of confusion and then contempt, before letting out an iconic and ear-shattering *roar*.

Boaz scrambled backward, his head rattling. The lion was still watching him, eyeing him like he was some broken-legged zebra. At least, though, it seemed confined to its little porthole, unable to do more than crane its neck and stare him down as Boaz drew himself uneasily to his feet.

Boaz stood motionless, trying to decide whether turning and running or standing there making eye contact would piss the beast off more. The brief foray into the Book of Daniel aside, day school had given him absolutely no practical advice on how to survive being trapped in the company of a giant lion, nor did his stint at Jewish summer camp, unless he counted an entirely unmemorable lecture about bears—

"*Boaz Harari!*"

His heart sank the moment he heard that voice. *Clara*. She wasn't supposed to be here. She was supposed to have stayed out of this, to have found Molly and run straight for the door.

He turned, and when she stalked toward him, he realized with a start that though her hair was down, her face was just her face. The face he was used to, the human one she wore in the theater. But before he had a chance to say a word, she shouted, "What is *wrong with you?*"

"Clara—"

"First, you have the indecency to charm me," she yelled. "Then, you try to *bury me alive*, and then you go and get yourself *literally entangled* with the Prince of Demons and jump into a damn movie screen—"

"Clara, maybe not now—"

"Are you trying to get yourself killed or me killed?" she yelled. "Which is it? Because if you wanted to die *so badly*, I would be more than happy to help you along and save us both the trouble—"

"Well, you're going to have to compete for the privilege of eviscerating me with the *giant lion*."

"Giant lion? What are you even—" Clara paused, her eyes only then sliding toward the oversize lion, who returned the look with a snarl. "Oh. That giant lion."

"Clara," said Boaz, swallowing hard and not breaking eye contact with the lion. He thought, absurdly, of Hila's cat, Mishmish, how he had *never* met a cat who liked him.

The beast, meanwhile, decided that it had had enough of just watching the two of them and proceeded to ease itself through the hole and slink through onto the floor. No, it hadn't been a trick; that lion was *massive*, much larger than anything that existed outside the world of film. "You don't know how to fight a—"

"Distract it," said Clara, panicked. Boaz reached into his pocket and pulled out the only item in it, the lighter. Did cats like fire? Did this count? He held it out, and before he could think of anything better, flicked it on.

Boaz saw the lion's eyes train on the small light in his hand, in the way that a cat gravitated toward anything small and shiny. It took a step forward.

"That's not distracting it!" she said, exasperated. "You've just made us that much more interesting." He glanced behind him, where even mad, even feet away from a grisly death at the hands of

332

the MGM lion, Clara was beautiful enough to momentarily stop his heart.

"Well, then, what do you suggest?"

Clara reached into his hand and yanked the lighter out. She wound up her arm and threw the lighter, sending it soaring over the lion's head and into the shadows beyond them.

It worked. The lion turned and ambled into the dark in search of it. But it was little comfort, and Boaz was certain that as soon as the lion realized they were a much more appetizing prospect than a flimsy lighter, it'd be back. Only when Clara seized his arm and pulled did he remember that he ought to run.

"We are not finished talking about what you did!" Clara said, irritated, as they plowed through heavy dark. Boaz couldn't see a thing in front of him; the only reason he knew what direction to run was that she held tight to his arm, pulling him along.

"Well, did you have a better idea?" he said defensively.

Boaz wasn't sure how long they ran, or whether they had managed to put any real distance between them and the lion. But before them the dark seemed to ease, enough that he could see the shiny floor and unsettling reflections that reminded him at once of the hallways of Gehinnom. He took care not to look down.

Then he heard the music.

The tune was instantly familiar. A tinny orchestra striking up a tune so familiar it was practically a cliché. Clara had stopped running, and when she turned to him, she furrowed her brow, and the two of them spoke at the same time. He squinted at the light that had appeared up ahead, a towering wall of hieroglyphics on which the familiar opening credits wavered unsteadily.

"*Swan Lake?*"

"*The Mummy*."

Clara scoffed. "Seriously?"

"Yes, seriously," said Boaz. There was almost nothing in his life he could say he was sure of, except for this. "*The Mummy*, the original 1932 one from Universal, opens with *Swan Lake*. I told Molly to find something I'd recognize. Am I that—"

But before he could finish, they plunged back into darkness as the credits vanished. His stomach flew up into his throat, and Boaz fell upward, shooting through the air like he had suddenly become weightless, like he was being sucked through a giant vacuum, before landing hard again moments later on a dark surface.

He heard the familiar puttering of an old propeller, recognizing for an instant the Universal logo above him, the giant globe being encircled by a small airplane. It was still *The Mummy,* he was sure of it. He wondered vaguely if Molly had tried to rewind the film as his head spun and he fought off the urge to be sick.

Worse still, he'd managed to lose Clara, and was once again alone in a film.

Now that the Universal globe had faded, a scene was growing around him. He must have seen the movie a thousand times, so he recognized this brief establishing shot before the credits. He stood on sand, between a sphinx and closely set pyramids, the words "Carl Laemmle Presents Boris Karloff In" hovering before them. Ordinarily, the words should have vanished and the landscape spun to reveal a pyramid bearing the film's title, but Boris Karloff's name did not leave the screen, and he wondered whether Molly had hit pause.

At first glance, it seemed real enough. He might have believed he was standing in the midst of actual ruins, but the longer he looked, the more he realized the proportions were all wrong. The pyramids were not tall enough, the sphinx a fraction of what he imagined its true height to be, and the scene beyond them too flat to be real. As he walked, he could feel beneath the thin layer of sand a hard, smooth floor.

"Boaz?"

Clara came running toward him. She was wearing the long dark jacket and small hat he would have recognized a mile away as being straight from the wardrobe of Helen Grosvenor, the love interest of the 1932 film. Relief washed over him, but it was dampened almost immediately when he noticed his family's onyx ring on a chain around her neck. "Where did you get that?" he asked automatically. The last time he'd seen that ring, it had been on Ashmodai's hand. If the ring was here, then the Prince of Demons couldn't be far behind.

"I found it," she said. "Just now, when the scene changed; it had gone flying when you fell. It must have fallen through with you two—"

"Well, that's one thing sorted," he said, his voice unsteady. "We just have to find my aunt and get out of here before Ashmodai finds us."

And they didn't have to wait long. Boaz was still getting his bearings and fighting the nausea from the brief rewind when he heard hurried footsteps and saw Hila running toward them.

His aunt was here, rendered in black-and-white and *mad*, but here nonetheless. She wasn't wearing what he had seen her in last, but he wasn't either. He was wearing trousers and suspenders and a mussed-up collared shirt that looked like it needed ironing, and she had ended up in something similar, like the two of them had just emerged from an early twentieth-century dig.

"Do you have anything to do with this?" she growled by way of greeting. "Because if you do, I can assure you you're going to be so grounded. *So grounded*, you won't set foot in Manhattan again until you're seventy. But I found your girlfriend. We just need the ring, and I can—"

"We have the ring," said Boaz uneasily as he pointed to Clara. "What do you mean you found my girlfriend?"

But the answer was already running to join them, from the same shadows that Hila had emerged from. It was . . . also Clara, in an identical hat and coat to the Clara beside him.

Boaz turned to the Clara with the ring, hoping for an explanation. But she was momentarily stunned into silence, her brow furrowed. Meanwhile, when the other Clara got close, she glared at Boaz, livid. "What have you *done*?"

Boaz backed away from both, his gaze shifting restlessly between the two identical versions of the girl he'd willingly given his neck to, the girl he had betrayed and nearly had buried. They both looked equally eager to throttle him.

"Boaz, we need to get out of here," said the Clara with the ring, finding her voice and reaching for his arm. Her touch was cool and familiar. . . . Or was it? He wasn't sure what was worse, that she was the Prince of Demons or that she was Clara and that he did not believe her.

"Boaz, get away from her," said the other Clara, the one Hila had found. "That's not me."

"Well, obviously," said the Clara beside him indignantly. "Boaz, you know Ashmodai can change his face—that's how he got the ring in the first place—"

"And he's doing it again," said both Claras simultaneously.

Boaz ran his hands through his hair, his heart racing as he looked desperately between the two Claras. His sluggish thoughts went to Edelman and his bird-taloned feet. Did Ashmodai have the taloned feet? He didn't remember them at Gehinnom. But then again, what did he know of demons? Would Clara care if he asked? He didn't want to; he had already ruined things with her once this night, maybe beyond repair, by mistaking her for a monster. . . .

Then he realized that there was a very simple way to find out, even more certain than feet. *Pathetically predictable.*

"Clara, can you give Hila the ring?" he asked, wincing at the look that played across her face. Maybe he had miscalculated. Or maybe that wasn't Clara. All he was certain of was that the real Ashmodai, if he held the ring, would never let go of it willingly.

"What, so you can bury me again?" she said, her voice icy.

"So we can get out of here," he said. "You don't need to trust me again. But if you want things to be put right, you'll give that thing to Hila *now.*"

And he knew, as she removed the chain and handed the ring to a bewildered Hila, that he had his answer. But before he could say more, he felt something sharp press against his neck.

"I had rather hoped you'd fall for that one," said the other Clara, who was clearly not Clara. Her voice dropped, returning to the familiar voice Ashmodai had used in the theater.

Boaz swallowed. *Try to remain calm.* But his heart was pounding wildly, despite his best efforts. He could already feel his pulse quickening, a nervous energy he couldn't stop. Molly had warned him this would happen. If Ashmodai's knife didn't end him, then his own heart would—inside the movie, in this halfway point between worlds, this was no place for the living. "Last time I checked, you were the one who fell for *my* trap."

"I have had enough of your games." His grip tightened on Boaz's shoulder. "I have had enough of your heartbeat. I've had enough of your impudence. I've had enough of chasing you and your kin seeking what is rightfully mine."

Hila made toward Ashmodai, as if she intended to tackle him, but he held fast to Boaz, a knife still pointed squarely at his neck. "Now, my dear Miss Harari, please return it to me, and I'll let the both of you have a running start—"

"Don't hurt him!" Clara yelped, her eyes widening with panic. She'd taken an urgent step toward Boaz. At the look on her face, something inside Boaz's chest ached. It wouldn't have come to this if he hadn't ruined everything. They might have been something good.

But they could never be, if he was to fix it. "Hila, you have the ring. Go with Clara and—" He broke off as Ashmodai snarled and the sharp edge of the knife bit still deeper into that space under his throat, where his pulse beat so hard he could not swallow.

Hila made a furious noise, shaking her head as if he had only forgotten to purchase the right brand of paper towels, and was already shifting slowly toward Ashmodai.

"*Clara*," he said, avoiding Hila's gaze. "You can explain to Hila. You know what's at stake. He can't get the ring back. It's okay, just leave me. . . . I've always loved this movie. I'll be fine."

Ashmodai pressed the knifepoint harder against his neck, and Boaz shuddered, all but certain he had broken skin. "Enough of that, now. Miss Harari, the ring?"

Boaz looked desperately at Clara. *Please go*, he mouthed. Before he lost his nerve. Before his heart burst on the spot. If this was how he was going down, then it was. If it meant the living world kept going, that the borders between worlds would be set right, that *she* could keep working whatever magic it was that could make a darkened theater come alive, could stop hearts with a glance, then so be it.

Hila was holding the ring out in her palm when Clara suddenly spoke. "Boaz, do you know what the Sages used to say could expose sheydim?"

Boaz didn't say anything, certain that if he did, Ashmodai would actually disconnect his head from the rest of his neck once and for all. Clara, perhaps sensing this, acted as though he had answered. "Cats. Well, specifically rubbing the ashes of a cat's . . . You know, it's not important. It was a terrible idea, bad enough that it could have been one of yours. But they were onto something. Cats are very perceptive, much more than humans. Do you like cats, Boaz?"

His eyes met Clara's, which were flashing with a warning . . . or was it a laugh? Was *she* laughing at him, with a knife at his neck? Or was it something else?

Did she actually have a plan?

He trusted she did. Enough that he managed to squeak, "No?"

"In that case, *get out of the way.*"

And with that, Clara yanked the ring from Hila's hands and tossed it in Ashmodai's direction, a little too wide, so that he had to reach for it, letting go of Boaz in the process. Boaz slid to the floor, struggling to regain his footing, at the same time that he heard a rumbling that might have passed for thunder. *The lion.*

Boaz swung around wildly, searching for the direction of the sound. It seemed to come from everywhere, to make the floor vibrate. He braced himself to be struck, but Clara, the real Clara, grabbed hold of him and pulled him toward her.

"Ashmodai, es iz shoyn tsu lang."

A commanding woman's voice spoke. It was not half as loud as the lion's roar, and yet Boaz swore the floor vibrated all the same, that he could practically feel the words in his core. Boaz knew it was in Yiddish, but the subtitles that wavered on the floor translated. *It has been too long.*

The lion pinned Ashmodai firmly to the ground as a woman emerged from the shadows, from the very edges of the set, where, if Boaz squinted, he thought he could see the riggings of a sound-stage. The dress she wore was not from *The Mummy*, but rather a long gown, more suited to a ball than an expedition. Her light hair was pinned up elegantly, and though she was not particularly tall, she had a presence that matched that of the lion's. *Regal* was the first word that came to mind. *No*, he realized slowly. *A Grand Dame.*

He looked to Clara, and it was clear at once she knew this woman. No, more than knew her. Her face had lit up with admiration and with longing.

"Treacherous witch," Ashmodai spat. The woman ignored him. She stepped beside the lion, stroking it as though it were her pet, before reaching down and plucking the ring from Ashmodai's now immobilized grasp, keeping him pinned while the woman strode over to Clara and gave her the ring.

Her hand lingered on Clara's. Boaz could see Clara struggling for words, but the woman merely smiled before turning back to the Prince of Demons. She pulled from her carefully styled hair a long, thick ribbon upon which Boaz caught Hebrew embroidery, the letters too small to make out the words. As she knelt to bind him, Ashmodai howled, "What, do you enjoy this cage? You would condemn us to shadow, together forever?"

When she spoke again, he thought at once of Clara, a presence that commanded attention and respect. They were, he thought, of one kind.

"Why should I fear shadow? It is no cage. It is where my girls have always found me, and they never forget who answers them in the darkest places with wings and shows them how to fly." She turned to Clara. "Show them how to fly."

For a moment, Clara's glance flickered to Boaz. As if she really thought she needed *his* permission to use the ring. The thought was laughable. Clara didn't need him to fly. And she hardly needed him to bend the worlds to her will. She had already bent his, and he wouldn't have it any other way. He shook his head. "You've got this."

42

MOLLY

Molly unspooled another film reel, leaving a trail up the aisle. Right by the door to auditorium two, Anat kept watch, the both of them trying to ignore the blaring fire alarms and the creep of smoke uncurling from the hall as fire spread through the theater. Amid the flames, the sheydim had mostly fled, some straight through the screen of auditorium one as soon as it began to burn. Anat had shoved the projector out of its booth, hoping that it would be enough to smash the glass before racing here to try and bring Boaz and Molly's sister back.

"They should hurry up," said Anat, glancing anxiously at the screen in front of them and then out into the hall. "Should I—"

"*No*," said Molly. If anyone was going back in there, she was. If she had to drag Clara out of there kicking and screaming, so be it; she was not going to lose her sister because that ticket-taking himbo could not tell the difference between her beloved sister and the Prince of Demons. "The only place you're going is out of here."

"You know I'm not . . . not leaving . . ." Anat struggled to get the words out, the smoke from auditorium one now a steadily worsening haze. The sprinkler system kicked in overhead, providing only limited relief, soaking the both of them but doing little to disperse the smoke. Silver nitrate burned *hot* and fast, and even now her eyes itched furiously, and she could taste a chemical soot on her tongue. Molly, who did not need to breathe, had stopped to save her throat and keep her head clear. But Anat couldn't do that. Anat kept breathing the poisoned air.

But not for much longer, not with the smoke the way it was. Anat's heart rate had returned to normal, but she still didn't look well at all. She'd begun hacking and struggled to stop. The sight of it was all it took for Molly to make up her mind. She bent down and scooped Anat up, ignoring whatever protests she managed in her coughing fit. Trying to keep low for Anat, she ran, clutching her girlfriend close. The heat in the theater was now impossible to ignore and the smell too familiar. She would not let someone else she loved burn.

She got as far as the Chase Bank before leaving Anat in front on the faded stars of the Yiddish Walk of Fame. The sirens had begun drawing onlookers, and Molly could hear the distant wail of a fire engine.

"I'll be right back," she said, as if saying it would be enough to make it true, before bolting inside.

Flames had made their way into the lobby, catching on the thick carpet, on the restored wallpapers, the posters. Everything she and Clara had so carefully curated over nearly seventy years was aflame, already beyond rescuing.

But not her sister. Not yet. The fire had yet to reach auditorium two, though it was getting close, but the projector was still running, the movie playing, and when she watched the projection on the screen through the haze, her eyes locked on Devorah.

For an instant, there was no screen between them, no doorway, no past or present. Just an ache in her chest for the woman who had given her, had given them, wings.

Then came the rip.

Clara tore through the screen, emerging with Boaz and his aunt Hila in tow. Molly raced over to help her sister, whose arms were filled with Boaz, who she held as though terrified he might slip from her grasp. She knew that fear well. When they had all come through, Molly thought her sister was waving at Devorah, until she saw the ring on her finger. With that single motion, the rip knit back together, and the screen at last went dark.

"*This* was your plan?" gasped Clara, moving up the aisle, shifting under the weight of Boaz. Something in the walls groaned. Boaz wheezed, and Clara began moving toward the door. She looked past the point of panicked, to defeated. "We'll never get the Grand Dame back!"

Molly struggled to hold a brave face at the grief on her sister's face and felt her own twist to match. It was true. They could not undo fire. That was the point. There was no coming back from such a death, no path of return. This would no longer be a gate for demons, but it would no longer be their beloved cinema. This was a death, in the same way that Molly Lewis had bled out on the sidewalk, her career and accomplishments and her loves all but forgotten.

And yet . . . Molly Sender had *flown*.

In her restless hunger, she had not died. She had been found and rescued from the dark. And that actress who had bled out was with her still. Molly Lewis had not truly died, but became a dream, a memory.

And dreams did not burn.

"She's one of us," said Molly. "We won't let her die."

At this, a piece of the ceiling collapsed, forcing them to move. Clara dragged Boaz and Hila toward the lobby. Molly shifted into her wings and roughly knocked the projector to the ground. She barely heard the shatter.

Molly refused to look back at the crumbling auditorium around them and joined the others. This theater deserved to be remembered as she had lived. Together, they raced toward the lobby doors, not stopping until they hit clear air. The Grand Dame would follow them. She was their dream and their sister. They would give her wings.

Epilogue

CLARA

It was nine o'clock in the evening, and Clara Sender was already, once again, considering the relative merits of murder.

The festival had been Boaz's idea: "Mummy Dearest," a retrospective on mummy monster films, based on a project he had done in school, with a slate of Q&As and special guests, a few cult favorite actors who were local to New York City, and a couple of media studies professors who were happy to volunteer their time to help restore a city institution like the Grand Dame Cinema following the massive, unexpected fire that had gutted it.

Their film collection was gone, save a few pieces that Molly had managed to digitize. In the weeks that followed, Molly had uploaded those clips online, and the resulting interest and ad revenue was what first convinced her that they might one day be able to rebuild.

Clara still had her doubts about fundraisers. Fundraisers required advertising and publicity. They required asking favors of people, which she did not like to do. It meant acknowledging that they needed help.

It had taken no small amount of her Estrie charm and Boaz's film expertise to wear down the patience of at least four different East Village independent cinemas, who, while competitors, were united in their shared antipathy toward AMC and their weakness for Boaz's infectious enthusiasm and flattery.

She sympathized. She, too, was doomed forever to fall for it.

"Where *were you*?" she whispered by way of greeting as he crept in five minutes before the end of the film, dropping into the seat just beside her. "You were supposed to be here at *seven*!"

"I know, I know," he said. "But there was a ghost in Gravesend, an old classmate, hit by a car, buried without his foot and *really* mad about it. He kept messing with the streetlights. . . ."

Clara was unmoved. "*Seven*. I had to give the opening remarks myself!"

"It was a paranormal emergency; surely you, of all people, would understand," he whispered, before she frantically shushed him. Boaz shrugged out of his sweatshirt, freeing the chain and ring around his neck after it was caught in the zipper. He had taken to wearing it like that whenever his aunt wasn't filming, which somehow had turned into Boaz deciding that ensuring every errant ghost found rest was his personal problem. It all would have been very noble if it didn't give him yet another excuse to treat the time as a suggestion. "I *swear* it won't happen again."

"I don't believe you," she whispered.

"Well, next time maybe you can join me," he said, leaning over to brush a kiss on her forehead, as if that would suddenly turn the clock back two hours. "Harari, Sender & Co.: Monster Hunters has a nice ring to it, I think."

"The name is Sender, Harari & Co. You know this."

"Quite right."

"Of course I am," she said, grinning in spite of herself.

They were interrupted by a smattering of applause. The credits began to roll, and he joined, leaping up to his feet when the lights rose and plucking up the microphone she had resting on her lap. He clicked it on.

"Now, everyone, please remain in your seats. We'll get this panel going shortly, and we have some pretty incredible guests," he began, before reciting the bios of the three speakers from memory, grinning wide. It was like a switch had been flicked on, his batteries replaced. He led the three speakers through an animated discussion about mummies and Orientalism, rattling off trivia like a human Wikipedia page and asking questions that delighted each speaker in turn with his knowledge of their work.

And there it was, the reason Clara's ordinary good sense had and would always be abandoned when it came to him. It was infuriatingly wonderful to watch him talk.

Clara made a point of looking distinctly unimpressed, waiting for him to finish chatting with their guests and for the audience to file out. Every time he caught her eye, he grinned sheepishly, clearly hoping that he could melt her resolve.

It wasn't going to work this time. It didn't matter how good he had looked up there, how expertly he had run the panel. They needed to have a proper conversation about the merits of a wristwatch.

As he trotted off stage, Clara could hear his heart pounding loudly in his chest, so hard she could practically see the pulse in his neck. "Molly and Anat should really talk with that NYU professor. She just came out with a book about biblical narratives onstage. There's a few chapters about Yiddish theater that probably overlap with the videos they've been doing."

"I'll . . . mention that to her," she said, even throwing in a somewhat strained smile. She was not going to pretend she understood whatever it was on social media that the two of them were attempting, and why it was at all appealing to the youth of today to watch brief, incomprehensible homemade videos, but Clara had made promises to be more . . . flexible.

Besides, it turned out that they also were incredibly effective fundraising tools. And if this was what it took to rebuild, and to make Molly happy, and she swore at length never to appear on camera, there were worse things. And Clara had lived long enough to know that sometimes she didn't need to understand.

"You've got the rest of the evening free?" Boaz asked, yanking on his jacket. "I want to stick around anyway. I heard there was something weird happening over by Hudson River Park . . . heard whisperings from a few ghosts that it *might* be a leviathan, though I will say the ghost who said that was, like . . . maybe a Viking? I say maybe because I didn't think Viking ghosts could speak English, but also, like, he really believed in sea monsters and he *looked* like a Viking, so you never really know—"

"Boaz Harari, you are not going to go chasing biblical sea monsters alone on a Tuesday night!" she said, marching over to him. This was hardly the laughing matter he seemed to think it was. She'd had to wait nearly one hundred and fifty years for a boy to love her the way he did. She wasn't about to let that boy get eaten, even despite all his efforts to make just that happen.

"Come with me, then?" he said. He reached for her hand. His grasp was so warm, the touch alone was enough to send a line of heat running straight to her core. "What better way to kick off Sender, Harari & Co. than by tracking down a sea monster?"

With their hands wound together, she could feel his heartbeat, so close it might have even been her own. She leaned in to kiss him, and it was almost like flying. "Let me get my coat."

AUTHOR'S NOTE

The Grand Dame Cinema is fictional, but if you find yourself in New York City's East Village, I would recommend stopping inside Village East by Angelica, located at 189 Second Avenue. The indie cinema has been known by many names, but began its life as the Yiddish Art Theatre, a project by Maurice Schwartz and Louis N. Jaffe, who designed the theater to be a permanent home for the Yiddish Art Theatre Company on the "Yiddish Rialto," a stretch of Second Avenue that by the 1920s became the center of American Yiddish theater. While this theater does not (I think) contain a secret collection of lost films, it does honor its roots as a Yiddish stage in its preservation of original detail, most notably in auditorium one.

While it is perhaps difficult to imagine today, at its peak in the early decades of the twentieth century, weekly attendance at New York City's Yiddish theaters equaled that of the English-language productions. Yiddish theater, like Broadway today, was a rich and diverse array of storytelling, and would transform not just Jewish cultural life, but American pop culture forever. The generation of actors, writers, and theater professionals whose first encounters with live theater were on Second Avenue would take that background with them and leave their mark on Broadway, Hollywood, and beyond.

While *Di Shturem* is not a real play, its conceit reflects a popular trend among Yiddish plays that reimagined the tropes and structures of beloved Shakespearean classics onto the lives and histories of its audience. The play's explicitly sapphic plot, meanwhile, draws inspiration from *Got Fun Nekome*, or *God of Vengeance*, which enjoyed wide commercial success in Europe and in 1922 became the first romantic same-sex kiss on a Broadway stage when it was translated into English (causing the production to be shut down and the actors arrested on charges of "indecency"). The play's tumultuous history is recounted in Paula Vogel's Tony-winning play *Indecent*. For a full and richly detailed account of the people and history of the Yiddish Rialto, I also recommend *New York's Yiddish Theater: From the Bowery to Broadway*, edited by Edna Nahshon. And if you'd like to see a professional Yiddish production today, you can check the website of the National Yiddish Theater Folksbiene, the oldest continuously operating Yiddish theater company in the world, for their latest offerings.

As much as possible, the places mentioned in this book are either real or greatly inspired by iconic spots in the Village. I highly recommend enjoying a bite at B&H Dairy, stopping for a moment in front of the Chase Bank to try to read the names etched into the stars on the Yiddish Walk of Fame, sharing a bagged challah on a sunny day in Tompkins Square Park, or attending a show at the Bowery Ballroom to find a piece of the Sender sisters' world. And while no one has (yet) attempted to stage Allen Ginsberg's "Kaddish" as an immersive theatrical production, similar shows from Punchdrunk's *Sleep No More* and others that emerge each season are some of the most exciting and unique theatrical work New York City has to offer.

New York City Jewish history is not, nor has it ever been, a single story. It can sometimes seem, in pop culture, that the great waves of refugees from the Pale of Settlement in the Russian Empire were the start of the American Jewry, but for that one would need to go back some two hundred years, at least, to the Sephardic Jews who arrived by way of colonial Brazil and the Caribbean, seeking both economic opportunity and freedom from persecution. Subsequent waves of immigration of Jews from all over the world have shaped the trajectory of Jewish life in New York and beyond. Brooklyn's Syrian Jewish community is as much a part of the New York Jewish story as the delis and Yiddish theaters on the Lower East Side, and both are but pieces of a wider tapestry of culture, language, history, and experience.

ACKNOWLEDGMENTS

This book is a love letter to family and all the forms that takes. So first and most importantly, a massive thank-you to mine. Mommy and Abba, my first and biggest supporters, for always believing I could do it. And my siblings, Oren and Liat, for making me a better person. And, of course, Toby Vishny. I love you all.

I feel lucky to be with a talented and passionate publishing team like this one. Sara Schonfeld, my editor extraordinaire, I knew you understood *Night Owls* from the moment we first spoke. Thank you for making this book's heart beat. Thank you to Jenna Stempel-Lobell, for your artistic vision; Zach Meyer, for the most breathtaking illustrations an author could hope for; Ana Deboo, for your patience with my echoes; and Mikayla Lawrence, Gweneth Morton, Kristen Eckhardt, Audrey Diestelkamp, David Koral, and everyone at HarperCollins whose efforts and enthusiasm have made this possible. And a very special thank-you to Evette Hakimian and Sarah Biskowitz for your thoughtful feedback and expertise.

I first met my agent, Linda Epstein, at the 2019 Jewish Symposium at the Highlights Foundation, when I had nothing but a manuscript that was not this book. Linda has stuck with me and championed my work through countless rewrites, rejections, crushing disappointment, emails (so many emails), phone calls, and a global pandemic. Thank you for being someone I could trust so completely with my heart, and for making this dream happen for me.

I've become the writer I am through the help of so many brilliant critique partners. Thank you to Meera Trehan, who first took my work seriously and helped me level up my craft. I'm so glad the Author Mentor Match program brought us together. My Monday night friends, Sam Farkas, Malavika McGrail, Shannon Spieler, and Sadhana Daruvuri, who have been with me through the highs and lows. Carina Finn Koeppicus, the first person to offer feedback and get excited for *Night Owls*. S. A. Simon, Felicia Grossman, and Julie Block, for your friendship, brilliance, and the space to vent.

I've benefited tremendously from organizations who believe in authors in all stages of their careers. Thank you to the Highlights Foundation for the space to connect and find my people, and for the gracious scholarship support from PJ Library. Thank you to the authors I met in those places who took me seriously and treated me like a peer, even without a book deal under my belt. Thank you especially to Melanie Fishbane, for our chats; Rena Rossner, for your wisdom and for introducing me to Estries; and Susan Kusel, for your advocacy on behalf of Jewish books.

Thank you to the Association of Jewish Libraries and to the friends I've made through it. Rebecca Levitan, Aviva Rosenberg, Talya Sokoll, I don't know where I'd be without our group chat. And a special thank-you to Rebecca for your time and feedback on this project.

I wouldn't be the writer I am without Hey Alma, who first paid me for my work and gave me a platform to hone my voice and explore the subjects I love. A special thank-you to Molly Tolsky, for your editorial eye and for your support of early-career Jewish writers.

Nor would I be the writer I am without friends and colleagues from all stages of my life. Aaron Deitsch, this book wouldn't exist without you or your ticket acquisition skills and passion for Movie-Pass. Thank you for everything; I really wish you were the one I had taken to *Hamilton*. Sarah Lesser and Hannah Nacheman, Estries to the core, I think of you whenever I eat a carb or have big Jewish feminist feelings in the East Village. The Butterfedlians, who taught me how to fall in love with the process, Rose Underhill and Kerry Ditson especially. And the colleagues past and present who think it's cool that I write, with a special thank-you to Angie Rho, Michelle Weiner, and Berni Vann for your enthusiastic encouragement, advice, and support.

And finally, to you, the reader, who took a chance on this book, thank you for spending time in these pages. I hope this book found you when and where you needed it.